Harry Bowling was born in Bermondsey, London, and left school at fourteen to supplement the family income as an office boy in a riverside provision merchant's. Called up for National Service in the 1950s, he has since been variously employed as lorry driver, milkman, meat cutter, carpenter and decorator, and community worker. He now writes full time. He is the author of fifteen bestselling novels, *The Chinese Lantern, The Glory and the Shame, Down Milldyke Way, One More for Saddler Street, That Summer in Eagle Street, Waggoner's Way, The Farrans of Fellmonger Street, Pedlar's Row, Back-street Child, The Girl from Cotton Lane, Gaslight in Page Street, Paragon Place, Ironmonger's Daughter, Tuppence to Tooley Street* and *Conner Street's War*. He is married and lives with his family, dividing his time between Lancashire and Deptford.

As Time
Goes By

Harry Bowling

headline

First published in 1998
by HEADLINE BOOK PUBLISHING

First published in paperback in 1998
by HEADLINE BOOK PUBLISHING

8

ISBN 0 7472 5882 1

Typeset by
Letterpart Limited, Reigate, Surrey

Printed and bound in Great Britain by
Clays Ltd, St Ives plc

HEADLINE BOOK PUBLISHING
A division of Hodder Headline PLC
338 Euston Road
London NW1 3BH

To Doctor Frank Rugman, consultant haematologist, Royal Preston Hospital, with gratitude and with the realization that, without his dedication and professionalism, this book may never have been written. And to his wife, Elizabeth, and their children, Edward and Peter.

Prologue

Albert Levy opened up his wireless shop at the stroke of nine on Monday morning and went straight into the back room, which served as a workshop, to put the kettle on. It was a ritual he had carried out almost without thinking for the past six years and he had always been eager to get another day of trading under way. Today however a dark shadow lay over him; his mind was troubled and his insides were churning. Less than twenty-four hours ago he had sat on the sofa in his living room along with his wife Gerda while the Prime Minister spoke to the nation over the radio. He had taken the news calmly but Gerda had broken down and sobbed quietly into her handkerchief. 'This will kill Abel. I know it will,' she had gulped. 'He's talked of nothing else for weeks now.'

Albert had tried to reassure her but he too feared for his old friend. Abel had said it many times and he was utterly convinced of it: if war was declared the country would be overrun within weeks.

As he poured the boiling water into the chipped china

1

teapot and covered it with a cosy, Albert glanced up at the clock on the wall. It was nearly ten minutes past the hour and Abel had still not made an appearance. Lately business had been brisk and there were at least half-a-dozen wire-lesses awaiting repair and several accumulators to be put on charge, which Abel was well aware of. Normally he would have been standing outside the shop chafing at the bit but, as Albert hardly needed to remind himself, today was no ordinary workday.

At nine thirty Albert Levy put the closed sign on the door and walked out into the bustling Old Kent Road. His old friend and employee lived ten minutes away, in Carter Lane, a small, insignificant backstreet in the riverside borough of Bermondsey, and as he hurried along Albert could not suppress the tension inside him. It was in the air, every-where, and it showed on people's faces as they passed by.

The international events of the past few days had been shocking, but had succeeded in drawing together two coun-tries as unlikely allies, and the shopkeeper took comfort in knowing that the country of his birth and England, his adopted country, had become united in their opposition to the Nazis. Albert Levy was Polish and had moved with his family to Germany at two years old when his father, a minor official in the Polish Diplomatic Corps, was posted to Frankfurt. He had been happy growing up in Germany and remained there with his mother in a small Jewish community in Wiesenbad after his father died in office. Proud of their roots the family decided to retain their Polish nationality, and Albert prospered in business, opening his first shop in Wiesenbad while still in his twenties.

As he made his way into Carter Lane to seek out his old

friend and employee, the shopkeeper thought how different it would have been for him and Gerda now, had his mother decided to become a German citizen all those years ago.

Abel lodged with Daisy and Bill Harris at number 12. He was a frail, private man in his mid-fifties, in the habit of keeping a discreet distance from his neighbours, not out of cussedness, but rather from a natural shyness and an inability to comprehend the language properly. The locals knew him as Mr Abel the Jew and that was about it. His full name was Abel Finkelstein and he had a six-digit number tattooed on the inside of his right forearm. Once a skilled technician at a large radio firm in Wiesenbad, Germany, Abel had enjoyed a good life until the Brownshirts began their campaign of terror. Arrested and convicted on trumped-up charges by a vindictive Gauleiter during the early days of the persecution, he was convicted and sent to a concentration camp in eastern Germany.

Albert Levy had been Abel's childhood friend and had left Germany for England with his wife Gerda at the first serious signs of German racial purification, before it became obvious that a mad canker was consuming a nation's soul. He had built up his wireless business and had managed to save enough to secure the release of his old friend with a large bribe before the loophole was finally closed.

Abel Finkelstein arrived to begin a new life in England in '37 as a refugee sponsored by Albert, but the scars of his internment remained with him, and when he listened to the Prime Minister's broadcast on Sunday morning he knew without a doubt that the nightmare was about to start again. It was just a matter of time.

'Good morning, Mrs Harris,' Albert said, doffing his

trilby. 'I'm calling to see if Abel's well. He hasn't come in this morning.'

Daisy Harris knew Albert Levy from his weekly visits to Abel, when the two men enjoyed a game of chess and a few glasses of wine, but today she looked troubled. 'I 'aven't 'eard 'im about this mornin' ter tell yer the trufe,' she replied. 'P'raps yer'd better go up. 'E was worried sick last night over the war startin'.'

Albert climbed the steep flight of stairs and knocked on Abel's bedroom door. Getting no answer he went in and saw his old friend lying on his back in the bed with his hands clasped at his throat. His eyes were closed tight and a film of froth had dried around his blue lips. On the chair at his bedside was a tablet bottle with the lid lying beside it, next to a half-empty bottle of brandy. Albert turned to Daisy as she stood behind him speechless, and he shook his head sadly. 'We'd better get the police,' he said. 'It looks like he's left us.'

The declaration of war had had an immediate impact on two of Carter Lane's residents. One was now past caring about anything this Monday morning, but the other was slowly and painfully coming to life in a police station cell. His head felt as if it would explode at any minute and he groaned in agony.

'Yer better pull yerself tergevver, Joe,' the duty policeman said grinning as he handed him a plate of streaky bacon, an over-fried egg and a slice of burnt toast on a tray. 'The beak'll chuck the book at yer if 'e sees yer like this.'

Joe Buckley eased his legs over the hard bed and sat forward, supporting his pulsating head in his huge hands. It was slowly coming back to him now and he winced. 'Is the dingo pressing charges?' he asked.

'I dunno, I've only just come on duty,' the officer told him.

Joe ate the food with some difficulty, but after using the toilet he began to feel a bit better. 'I hope I didn't give you any strife, mate,' he said to the policeman who came to escort him.

'Nah, yer came in like a good 'un,' the officer said with a smile. 'Mind you, yer language wasn't all that clever, considerin' we 'ad Farvver Feeney 'ere at the time.'

'What's he been up to?' Joe asked.

''E was visitin' a prisoner,' the policeman replied.

Joe noticed from the wall clock that it was ten o'clock as he was escorted up from the cells and taken along to the court, where he sat pensively on a hard bench alongside the officer and waited to be called.

'Joseph L. Buckley, you have been charged with drunk and disorderly conduct, assault, and damage to property at The Sun public house in Dockhead. How do you plead?'

Joe looked up at the elderly magistrate and gave him a sheepish grin. 'Guilty, your worshipful. Guilty as hell.'

Mr Durrant looked over his spectacles at the huge character before him and smothered a smile. 'Sir will do, and we can dispense with the expletives,' he said in a reedy voice.

Joe nodded dutifully. 'Guilty, sport. I mean guilty, sir.'

Durrant had the case file in front of him and he studied it for a few moments. 'I see here that you are Australian.'

Joe nodded with a brief smile.

'I understand that the aggrieved has decided not to press

charges and the publican has waived the claim for damages,' Durrant continued. 'I would say that you are a very fortunate man. You could have been in much more trouble than you are, but nevertheless the charge of being drunk and disorderly still stands. Throwing someone over a pub counter because they disagree with your point of view is not a proper way to carry on, and taking up police time by refusing to move from the pavement is deplorable. Do you realise you had to be carried into the police van?'

'I was dead beat, sport – sir,' Joe said quickly. 'I was stretched out ready to sleep when the blue boys came along.'

'Do you consider that sufficient justification to have said, according to Constable Perkins' report . . .' The magistrate turned the papers in front of him and frowned. ' "Chew on your boot, you Pommy shirtlifter. May your ears turn into arseholes and crap on your shoulders. Mate." ' He looked up and fixed the accused with an intent stare. 'Do you have anything to add to that before I pass sentence?'

Joe scowled inwardly. The bloody poofter didn't have to write that down, he fumed. Next time I'll just save my breath and conk him. 'If you don't mind, sir, there is something I'd like to say,' he replied, standing up straight and throwing his shoulders back.

'Go on, and be brief,' Durrant said peremptorily.

'I shouldn't be here in the first place,' he began, 'but things got a bit smelly back home, so I decided to move on.'

'So you chose England.'

'No, I went up to Queensland where I earned some good money as a jackaroo on a sheep station. It was fair yakka really, but I got the ants in me shoes again an' off I went.'

'To England?'

'No, Padang.'

'Padang?'

'Yeah. It's in Sumatra.'

Mr Durrant sighed in exasperation. 'I asked you to be brief, Mr Buckley,' he said in a tired voice.

'I will be, sir,' Joe answered, 'I just wanted to give you the drum, so to speak. You see I'm a marine engine mechanic by trade an' I thought if I went to Sumatra I could make a fresh start. A good mate o' mine was in the marine diesel business there, but when I arrived I found out that the bastard 'ad crocked it.'

'Watch your language, please, Mr Buckley.'

'Sorry, your worship. "Died", I meant to say.'

The magistrate pinched his temples and slowly drew in a deep breath. 'Go on, Mr Buckley,' he sighed.

'I suddenly got this idea o' seeing the old country,' Joe continued. 'I knew that things were starting to go down the pan over here, what with Adolf digging in dirtier than a shithouse rat, and I thought the Royal Navy could do with a good marine mechanic if the worst came to the worst, so I worked me passage on a ship bound for Southampton. I wanted to get in on this war but I wasn't too keen on going back to Oz and waiting to be drafted into the infantry.'

'So here you are,' Durrant said summarily. 'In the country five minutes and already you've caused criminal damage and assaulted a customer at a public house.'

'I couldn't stand by and listen to the crap this dill was coming out with,' Joe replied with conviction. 'He said we should've signed a pact with Hitler and let Poland get on with it. I told him he was talking cobblers and he chucked a punch at me. I just grabbed him, to restrain him, like.'

'And somehow he ends up being "restrained" over the bar counter,' Durrant said sarcastically.

'I was spitting blood, your worship,' Joe went on. 'Our two countries are mates, after all. We fought together in one world war and it looks like we're together in this one too, so I let him know the best way I could that you don't kowtow to the likes of Adolf Hitler.'

'Your sentiments are admirable,' the magistrate said, moving his spectacles up onto the bridge of his nose, 'but your methods leave a lot to be desired, and I have to treat your unruly behaviour with the due means at my disposal. Tell me, are you still intending to join the armed forces?'

'Soon as ever I can, judge,' Joe told him firmly, 'I'll be off like a bride's nightie.'

Durrant cleared his throat and looked very serious. 'Taking your patriotism into consideration, I fine you forty shillings or fourteen days,' he declared.

'That's a pity,' Joe said sighing. 'I'm pretty well cleaned out at the moment. I'll have to take the fourteen days.'

An hour later Aussie Joe Buckley was back at his lodgings in Carter Lane. His landlady Liz Kenny had been in court that morning and she had paid the fine. She also had a few words of advice for her erring lodger. 'Yer'd better control that temper o' yours in future, Joe,' she said sternly. 'You was lucky this time.'

The big Australian looked up at her as he sat at the parlour table, his wide blue eyes full of remorse. 'Yeah, you're right. I'll pay you back soon as I can, Liz,' he said. 'I hope your Bert doesn't lose 'is dummy over this.'

'You let me worry about Bert,' she told him. 'Now get cleaned up an' I'll fix yer somefing to eat.'

8

'You haven't got a drop o' the old grog handy by any chance, have you?' he asked.

Liz held back a smile as she nodded towards the sideboard. 'I dunno why I bovver,' she sighed.

Joe poured himself a tot of whisky. 'I hope Sadie Flynn doesn't get to hear about me little barney,' he said anxiously.

'Don't make me laugh,' Liz chuckled, slipping her hands into the arms of her clean apron. 'It'll be all round the street in no time.'

'Yeah, that's what I thought,' Joe replied with a pained look on his wide handsome face.

Chapter One

Carter Lane was a small backstreet of two-up, two-down houses that faced each other, with a corner shop and a public house called The Sun at the Old Kent Road end and a small factory at the other end. The turning linked Defoe Street with Munday Road, which ran alongside the railway. The factory was owned by the Solomon family and had been there as long as anyone could remember, producing leather goods and providing employment for some of the Carter Lane folk. The corner grocery shop was owned by Tom Jackman and his wife Sara, a genial couple in their late fifties.

At number 11 Carter Lane, Dolly Flynn was chopping vegetables into a large stew-pot on the scullery table. She was a buxom woman with grey hair which she had fixed hurriedly on the top of her head that morning. She was nearing her fiftieth birthday and was still attractive, with a wide, open face and piercing blue eyes which were watering as she sliced a large Spanish onion. Dolly felt like crying anyway, without the onion's pungent fumes. Her boys had been full of the war last night and she knew it wouldn't be long before they were in uniform. The eldest Frank had been going on about getting into the navy and Jim was set on the air force. Pat, the baby of the family, was an independent cuss and he had announced that if his brothers were for the air force and navy then he had no choice other than to go in the army.

'Surely they won't take all three of yer,' Dolly had said. 'They didn't in the last war.'

'Oh yes they did,' Mick had told her. 'The Sullivans 'ad four in uniform at one time.'

Dolly recalled how she had rounded on her husband and sons. 'You treat it like a Sunday-school outin', an' you should know better, Mick. You saw enough fightin' in the last one. This'll be a bloody sight worse, you mark my words.'

Mick had realised how upset she was and tried to make light of it, but even he could not hide the concern and worry in his grey eyes. The girls had had their pieces to say too, just for good measure. Sadie reckoned that all single women would be called up for war-work, and young Jennie had said she was going to see about joining the ARP.

A knock on the front door jerked Dolly back to the present and she smiled when she saw Liz Kenny standing on her doorstep. They were old friends and Liz could always be relied upon to cheer her up when she was feeling down. 'Come in, luv,' she urged her, 'I was just doin' the veg fer ternight.'

'Don't let me stop yer,' Liz replied. 'Carry on what yer doin' an' I'll make the tea.'

'Nah, you sit yerself down,' Dolly told her. 'I've almost finished anyway.'

Liz Kenny walked into the parlour and sat down in the

armchair with a deep sigh. Slightly built with dark hair and brown eyes, she presented a distinct contrast to her old friend, but they shared much, not least a lively sense of humour. Today though there was little gaiety in either woman's voice. 'Gawd knows what's gonna 'appen to us all now,' Dolly sighed when she came into the room. 'I still can't get it inter me 'ead that we've gone ter war.'

'Nor can I,' Liz said heavily. 'An' ter crown it all I bin up the court this mornin'.' She saw the enquiring look in her friend's eyes and smiled wryly. 'Big Joe got in some trouble last night at The Sun.'

'Yeah, Mick told me about it,' Dolly replied. 'From what 'e said, Cafferty got what 'e deserved. 'E's a loudmouth git at the best o' times. Mick can't stand 'im.'

''E seems to 'ave done a runner anyway,' Liz went on. ''E didn't press charges an' Charlie Anson didn't ask fer damages. But it still don't alter the fact that Joe was out of order doin' what 'e did.'

'Ter be fair, Liz, Big Joe ain't one ter take liberties,' Dolly remarked. 'Mick told me Cafferty punched 'im first, an' 'e ain't no light-weight.'

Liz shrugged her shoulders. 'Anyway, Joe got fined forty shillin's. 'E didn't 'ave a pot ter piss in an' they was gonna give 'im fourteen days, till I told 'em I'd pay the fine. Mind you 'e'll pay me back soon as 'e can. 'E was upset about it but I fink 'e was more concerned about your Sadie findin' out. Joe finks the world of 'er.'

'It's a pity she don't feel the same way about 'im,' Dolly replied. 'She could do a lot worse. I just can't understand 'er at times.'

'Is she still seein' that feller?' Liz asked.

'Yeah, but it's an on-an'-off fing,' Dolly told her. 'If you ask me the bloke's tryin' ter patch it up wiv 'is wife, from listenin' ter Sadie. Why she ever got in tow wiv 'im I'll never know. Gawd almighty, there's enough single fellers about. A gel don't need ter get 'iked up wiv a married man.'

Liz rubbed her aching calf muscle and settled back in the armchair while Dolly went out to see to the tea. 'What about young Jennie? Is she still keen on that feller at work?' she called out.

Dolly grinned despite herself. 'Nah, it's all off,' she answered.

A few minutes later she came back into the room with two mugs of tea. 'I don't fink I'll ever live ter see all my crowd married off,' she sighed. 'The boys are the same. They spend most o' their time up The Sun. Young Pat'll be the first one ter get spliced. 'Im an' that Ross gel seem ter be 'ittin' it off, so I s'pose I gotta be fankful fer small mercies.'

A knock at the door interrupted their conversation, and when Dolly finally came back into the parlour she looked shocked. 'That was Mrs Bromilow. Did you 'ear what she was sayin'?'

Liz shook her head. 'No, I never.'

'Apparently they took a body away from number 12 this mornin'. Mrs Bromilow finks it's their lodger.'

'Mr Abel?'

'Yeah.'

'Good Gawd. I didn't know 'e was ill,' Liz said quickly. 'Then again, p'raps 'e wasn't. It could 'ave bin an 'eart attack or a stroke.'

''E always looked a sick man ter me,' Dolly remarked. 'A very nice man though. 'E always nodded an' gave me a smile.' She sipped her tea. 'Did you know 'e was in prison in Germany?'

Liz shook her head. 'No, I never did.'

'Mrs 'Arris told me,' Dolly went on. 'Apparently 'e 'ad a number tattooed on 'is arm. Abel's guv'nor paid ter get 'im out an' bring 'im over 'ere by all accounts. Cost 'im quite a bit too.'

''E must be a good guv'nor,' Liz chuckled.

'It's that feller who owns the wireless shop in the Old Kent Road,' Dolly explained. 'That one next ter the greengrocer's by The Dun Cow.'

'Yeah, I know it,' Liz replied, 'though I've never bin in the shop.'

The two women sipped their tea in silence and then Dolly put her mug down on the table. 'Will your Bert 'ave ter go on war-work?' she asked.

'I shouldn't fink so,' Liz told her. ''E's gonna be needed 'ere if the air raids start. Bert knows the buildin' game inside out. 'E can do plasterin' an' joinery an' everyfing else. Besides, 'e's talkin' about goin' in the rescue squad. They're callin' fer volunteers ter do trainin'.'

'It's the same wiv Mick, 'im workin' fer the Council on the roads,' Dolly said. ''E's gonna be needed too.'

Liz put her cup down next to Dolly's. 'Well, I'd better be off. I gotta sort me washin' out.'

Dolly saw her to the door and then went back into the quiet room. Normally she enjoyed the lull in her busy day, but this morning it was different. The quietness set her thinking too much and she slipped on her coat to go out for some air.

Big Joe Buckley had recovered sufficiently from his drunken exploits at The Sun to visit the recruiting office in the Old Kent Road. When he arrived he found a crowd milling around the entrance and there seemed to be some heated discussions going on.

'It's a bloody disgrace,' one slim young man was saying. 'There's a bloody war started an' you can't sort fings out.'

'We can and will, if you'll just be patient,' the recruiting sergeant replied with a sigh. 'They're sending me some help and in the meantime I'll take your particulars, if you'll just form an orderly line.'

As Joe reached the unruly mob a man who looked to be in his fifties turned to him. 'Short staffed, would you believe?' he growled. 'In the last war they come round the street wiv the brass band an' we all marched off be'ind 'em. I was in France before I 'ad time ter spit. Four years I did. Saw it all frew. Lucky Bob they called me. I got trench foot an' dysentery though. Bloody painful that trench foot.'

'I should fink you've done your bit already, mate,' the slim man remarked to him.

'Yeah, an' I'm ready fer anuvver basinful,' the older man replied enthusiastically.

Joe smiled. 'I'm after goin' in the navy.'

'You sound like an Aussie,' the older man remarked.

''S right. Joe Buckley's the name. Anything's me game.'

'Yer'll 'ave ter go ter the navy office in East Street then.'

'East Street? Where's that, digger?'

'See that pie shop over there across the road?' the man said pointing.

'Yeah, I got it.'

'Well it's down the side o' there.'

Joe thanked him and set off, only to discover when he arrived that things were no more organised over there. The place was full of volunteers and a long disorderly queue curved round the room.

'Over an hour I've bin standin' 'ere an' the bloody queue ain't moved,' the man in front of him complained.

Joe stood patiently for a while and then decided to come back the next day. By then things might be more organised, he thought. He walked off, his mouth grown dry and his head still aching from the hectic night before. His pockets were empty and he desperately felt the need for a drink. He couldn't ask Liz Kenny for a sub. She had already paid his fine and it wouldn't be right. Maybe he should go into The Sun and apologise for the upset he'd caused last night. Charlie Anson might feel disposed to give him a drink on the house. Then again he might show him the door and tell him he wasn't welcome any more.

As he was about to turn into the backstreets Joe got an idea.

One of the very few possessions he had of any value was the fob-watch nestling in the breast pocket of his shirt. There was no chain with it but the watch itself had cost him quite a bit back in Sydney when he had money to spare. He might be able to get a few pounds on it and he could redeem it when things looked brighter.

The pawnbroker screwed his eye up round the lens and grunted. 'Yes, it's a nice piece but it's only gold-plated. I couldn't let you have more than two pounds, what with the war and all.'

'Can't you make it fifty shillings, mate?' Joe asked.

The pawnbroker took the glass from his eye and looked at

the fresh-faced young man across the counter. 'All right. I'll give you a ticket.'

Joe walked out of the shop feeling as though he'd parted with an old friend. The watch had gone everywhere with him and now he had two pounds ten shillings in his pocket that would soon evaporate.

He made his way back to Carter Lane and gingerly pushed open the door of the public bar.

'Cor blimey! Look who's shown up,' Danny Crossley said grinning.

Joe smiled sheepishly at Charlie Anson as he walked to the counter. 'Wotcher, sport. Am I still welcome?'

Charlie looked at him severely. 'You cost me a nice few bob last night,' he growled. 'It's a good job the mirror wasn't smashed. It's a figured antique.'

'I'm very sorry, Chas, but you saw what happened,' Joe said holding out his hands. 'That one-pot screamer was out of his stroller, going on like that.'

The landlord looked a little confused. 'Well, that's as it may be, but yer can't go chuckin' customers over me counter every time yer fall out wiv 'em,' he said firmly. ''Ow'd yer get on in court?'

'Forty shillings,' Joe told him with a shudder.

'You should fink yerself lucky,' Charlie replied. 'They could 'ave sent yer down.'

'It won't happen again, mate,' Joe assured him. 'Now let me shout you a drink.'

The elderly Danny Crossley ambled over and gave the Australian a toothless grin. 'I gotta tell yer,' he said with a wink, 'me an' the regulars were pleased yer sorted that Cafferty geezer out. 'E caused trouble 'ere the ovver night wiv 'is poxy rebel songs. Shorty Beaumont was gonna give 'im what for an' I 'ad ter stop 'im. Yer know what Shorty's like when 'is dander's up.'

Joe smiled as he laid a ten-shilling note down on the counter. Danny Crossley's friend was seventy if he was a day and he coughed noisily every time he lit up his Nosegay-packed clay pipe. 'Yeah, I know,' he said, and turned to Charlie Anson. 'Give Danny a drink too, Chas.'

The Sun at lunchtime was usually busy, but today it seemed as though very few people were in the mood for drinking and Danny remarked on how quiet it was. 'The bloody place feels like a morgue. I should fink they've all gone ter join up. I only wish I was a few years younger. I'd be there.'

'I've just tried to sign up,' Joe told him. 'I've gotta go back tomorrow.'

'What yer put down for, son?' Danny asked.

'The Royal Navy.'

'Good fer you. Yer'll look the part in that uniform,' the old man chuckled. 'Yer'll 'ave all the young women after yer. I just wish I was young enough ter go.'

The door opened and Shorty Beaumont walked purposefully in. 'Bloody 'ell!' he said, holding on to the bar as he fought to get his breath back. 'I was sayin' ter me ole dutch last night, you reminded me o' the Iron Duke the way yer bounced that no-good git over the counter.'

'The Iron Duke?' Joe queried.

'Yeah, the wrestler. The Iron Duke's the British 'eavy-weight champion,' Shorty informed him. ''E chucks 'em out the ring every time.'

The landlord leaned on the counter. 'I understand there's a

19

few schools round 'ere sendin' the kids away ter the country,' he said, apropos of nothing. 'Just as well too. They should evacuate all the kids before it gets really nasty – an' it will, mark my words. We'll be in fer a right ole pastin' before long. Yer've only gotta look at what's 'appened in Spain wiv the German airforce. Besides, they'll be after sortin' out the docks an' wharves, an' the factories round 'ere'll be on their list too, yer can bet yer life.'

''Ere, that reminds me,' Shorty piped in. 'I just come past that shelter in Munday Road an' I saw a couple o' geezers stickin' up a wooden stand outside. I stood there watchin' 'em fer a while an' then I 'ad to ask 'em what they was doin'. Apparently they was puttin' up a poison gas warnin'. There's a flat board wiv paint on it an' when it comes inter contact wiv gas it changes colour. So that's 'ow yer know.'

'That's bloody stupid,' Danny Crossley remarked scornfully. 'I was in the trenches in the last lot when they dropped gas shells on us. I can just picture our ole sergeant major sniffin' the air an' sayin', "It smells like gas. 'Ang on lads, I'll just take a look at the board ter check." '

Their merriment died abruptly when another elderly customer walked in and announced that the German navy had sunk a freighter in the North Atlantic. 'It come over the wireless just as I was comin' out,' he said wide-eyed.

Joe finished his drink and refused the landlord's offer of one on the house. Somehow he felt that he couldn't stomach it and he made his excuses to leave. The two pounds nestling in his pocket would repay Liz Kenny and then it was the navy or bust.

On the first full day of the war the Flynn family gathered

round the table for their evening meal of beef stew laced with dumplings. Dolly sat at one end and glanced lovingly from one to another as they chatted together. Mick her husband sat at the head of the table facing her, his shirtsleeves folded back over his brawny arms and his thick dark hair combed back from his forehead. To his left Frank sat mopping up gravy with a thick hunk of dry bread. At twenty-six he was the eldest of the brood, dark, stocky and broad-shouldered like his father, with brown eyes and a physique kept well toned by his job as a drayman at the local brewery. To Frank's left was Sadie who was a year younger. She had fair hair that was cut short and set in soft waves around her ears, and her pale blue eyes seemed preoccupied as she cut into a dumpling. Jennie, who sat the other side of Frank, was a pretty redhead with large hazel eyes, a small nose and expressive lips. Facing her was Jim who was eating like a starving man, and Dolly had to smile to herself. Food was a passion with him and her beef stew was his favourite. Jim was dark like Mick and Frank, though he had deep blue eyes which sometimes looked almost violet. He too worked at the brewery as a drayman, and was as muscular and broad-shouldered as his brother. Patrick, coming up to nineteen and the youngest of the clan, sat at the corner of the table wedged between Dolly and Jennie. He was sandy-haired with grey eyes like his mother, of a slighter build than his two older brothers, and he was a carpenter by trade.

'There's some more stew left if anyone wants any,' Dolly told them.

Everyone shook their head contentedly, with the exception of Jim, who gave his mother a crafty smile. 'I fink I could just about manage some more,' he said, looking round for a reaction.

'I dunno where 'e puts it,' Mick remarked shaking his head.

Jim smiled. 'I'm tryin' ter put a bit o' weight on,' he replied.

Dolly ladled the steaming stew onto Jim's plate and added a dumpling. 'I fink I'll let you do the washin' up,' she joked.

'Yeah, I'll do it,' the young man answered, reaching out for another slice of bread. 'I ain't above 'ouse'old chores like those two,' he said grinning at his brothers.

Dolly sat down again and tried to appear relaxed, but it was not easy. Here before her was her family, the ones she loved more than life itself, and hanging over their heads was the war. Soon there would be spaces at the table with the boys away, fighting for their country. They seemed eager to go and Dolly had to concede that their sentiments were noble, if foolhardy. But she knew that sooner or later they would all be called up anyway and there was nothing she could do about it.

'That was a bit special,' Jim said, sighing as he rubbed his midriff.

Sadie pushed her chair back. 'You put yer feet up, Mum. Me an' Jennie'll wash up.'

Mick stood up and belched loudly. 'I'll put the news on,' he said.

Dolly watched while her two daughters cleared the table, then ignoring their suggestion that she relax she went out into the backyard. The sky above was clear and tinged with orange as the sun sank slowly into the west. This night, with the whole family sitting round the table together, was something she wanted desperately to imprint on her mind. A moment in time she would be able to call up in the uncertain days ahead. What the future held for them all was something Dolly tried not to think about, but the thoughts came regardless, and her heart was breaking.

Chapter Two

By Wednesday Joe Buckley had managed to volunteer for the Royal Navy and he went back to his lodgings around midday feeling pleased with himself. He had also managed to waylay the works foreman at the site where he had done some casual trench-digging work and he had finally got his money. At that moment he was free of debt, and if his call-up came soon he would stay that way.

'You look like the cat that's ate the canary,' Liz remarked as he sat down at the scullery table.

'Yeah, I just got meself all fixed up, Liz,' he told her with a wide smile.

'You signed on?'

'Too true I did.'

'I'm gonna miss yer, Joe,' she said. 'Bert will too.'

'I'll be lobbing in when I get some leave, don't worry about that,' he replied.

Liz Kenny sat down at the table facing him and clasped her hands on the well-scrubbed surface. 'What time d'yer make it?' she asked, her eyes narrowing slightly.

Joe glanced over at the battered alarm clock on the dresser. 'Is that bloody contraption jiggered again?' he replied. 'It's about ten after twelve.'

Liz stood up and reached for the clock. 'I fergot ter wind it last night,' she told him, moving the hands round the dial. 'Give us the exact time, could yer,' she said, staring at him.

The big man tapped the breast pocket of his grey cotton shirt and grinned evasively. 'Strewth, I ain't got me watch.'

'You pawned it, didn't yer?' Liz said knowingly.

Joe shrugged. 'I needed the money, girl,' he replied.

'There was no need ter pay me back so soon,' she chided him. 'I told yer I could wait.'

'Aw it's no hardship,' he assured her. 'I got paid up for the work at the site so I've got a few quid, and I'm gonna ask Sadie Flynn out for a drink as soon as I see her.'

'I fink yer wastin' yer time, Joe,' she warned him. 'Yer know she's seein' a bloke. Apparently 'e's married, so Dolly Flynn told me.'

'Well, I'm not chucking the towel in yet,' Joe said firmly.

'I wish yer luck,' Liz sighed.

Frank and Jim Flynn had finished early that afternoon and they sat together in the brewery canteen discussing their plans.

'I've bin givin' it some thought,' Frank said sipping his mug of tea. 'I've decided it's gonna be the army fer me.'

'You've changed yer mind quick,' Jim said frowning. 'Why's that?'

'I wanna get in soon, Jim,' his brother told him. 'Vic Moseley was tellin' me 'e volunteered fer the navy two weeks ago an' 'e's still waitin'. 'E was tellin' me they're pickin' men wiv trades that's suitable, like engineers an' electricians.'

Jim put down his empty mug. 'Are yer goin' down the recruitin' office terday?'

'Yeah.'

'Come on then, let's go.'

Frank gave his younger brother a questioning look. 'You're goin' in the RAF ain't yer?'

Jim grinned at him. 'Nah, I've changed me mind. We'll join up tergevver. Yer gonna need somebody ter look after yer, yer dozy big git.'

'You saucy little sod,' Frank said slapping his brother round the head playfully. 'You show a bit o' respect. Well come on then, let's get goin'.'

Albert Levy walked into the small workshop and sat down heavily on the high stool, staring down sadly at the tiny solder balls and bits of coloured wire that were strewn over the wooden worktop. A wireless chassis stood apart from its Bakelite casing ready for inspection, and to one side was a box of assorted valves. Abel was gone for ever and Albert found it very hard to come to terms with the fact that he was dead.

'Why, old friend?' he mumbled aloud. 'You were safe here in London. The Nazis'll never reach here. You should have known that. Didn't I tell you? Every time we spoke about those things I tried to reassure you. Was I talking to myself? It seems I must have been. And what about me? Did you give me a thought when you poured that brandy down your throat and swallowed those tablets? Who do I play chess with now? Gerda can't play, as well you knew. You were good, Abel. Very good. I was getting your measure though. Soon I would have beaten you. I nearly did the last

27

time we played. It's all right, I collected the chess box and board as you instructed. But you left me feeling guilty, old friend. I should have listened more than I did, not given up till I was sure that I'd put your mind at rest. I should have insisted you stayed with me and Gerda, instead of letting you go into lodgings, even though I knew it was what you wanted. At least I'll always be thankful I was able to get you out of that camp. It was the one thing I took real pleasure in being able to do. Well anyway, you're at peace now and I know that wherever you are you'll think of me kindly. We'll talk some more, old friend. Now I've got to see the young man who's going to take your place. According to his references, he seems skilled enough, but he won't come up to your standard. You were the best, Abel.'

Albert Levy walked out of the room and glanced round at the smart wirelesses and the two new press-button sets that were on display. Abel had mastery of them all and it wouldn't have taken him long to get the measure of those push-button ones too, he thought. Later he would have to go through his old friend's personal effects that were still in the workroom cupboard. Abel had been a hoarder and it was going to be a painful experience.

The leather-goods factory on the corner of Carter Lane seemed to have been there for ever and the older locals thought that it hadn't changed much since old Abraham Solomon drove up every morning in his horse-drawn trap. Now the firm was run by Abraham's two grandsons Martin and Joseph, and on Wednesday morning the two of them assembled the workforce in the main workshop to give them the news.

'I reckon we're goin' on war-work,' one of the stitchers remarked.

'I reckon it's about that shelter they were finkin' o' puttin' in down the basement,' her workmate said.

Sadie Flynn worked in the accounts office, and as she hurried down from the first floor to join the rest of the workers she feared the worst. Rumours had been flying round, and when she saw Joseph Solomon standing at the side of the room talking to Leonard Parker the works manager she knew it was a serious matter.

'Good afternoon, everyone,' Joseph began his address. 'I have some important news to give you. From next month we will be working solely on Government contracts. Our luxury range of leather goods will be suspended for the duration of the war, and as from next month we will be producing leather flying suits and gloves, as well as various other items of equipment for military, naval and airforce use. Now obviously you will be unfamiliar with the new methods of manufacture, so I want you to know that ample training and guidance will be available, which brings me to the most important point of all. As you will be aware, this area of London is vulnerable to air attack, given its position with regard to the docks and wharves, so in the light of that, and because of our important contribution to the war effort, it has been decided to move our operations to Bedfordshire.'

A mumble of voices grew in volume and Joseph Solomon raised his hands. 'It is unfortunate that this step has to be taken, but rest assured that all of you who decide to move with us will be found accommodation locally, with the advantage of being near enough to London to come home for the weekends. Now the company does understand that for some of you this move will be out of the question, for family reasons, so we will be talking to every one of you personally in the next few days. We have to move fast on this because of the training programme which will begin in two weeks' time. At the end of next week those wishing to leave may do so with two weeks' wages in lieu. Our factory in Bedford is being prepared and we hope to make the move by the end of the month. Now if there are any questions Mr Parker will be able to deal with them, which only leaves me to say good luck to you all whatever you decide to do.'

Sadie went back to the office and sat down to think. She had been happy at the firm and she had made some good friends, but the thought of being away from her family during the week did not appeal to her. It wouldn't be so bad at the moment, but what if air raids started? She would be worried sick if she were not around. Then there was Len Regan to think of. She would only be able to see him at weekends and he wouldn't be too pleased about that, to say the least.

'What are you gonna do, Sadie?' one of the girls asked her.

'I really don't know,' she said frowning.

'I'm gonna move wiv the firm,' the girl told her. 'My bloke'll be goin' in the forces soon an' I'll be alone 'ere anyway. I might just as well get away from London in case the bombin' does start.'

A few minutes later Audrey Smith the office manager walked into the room and sat down heavily at her desk. 'I've just left a sorry sight,' she said, sighing sadly. 'Some of the girls are crying and poor old Mrs Chambers is inconsolable. She's been here for donkey's years.'

Sadie tried to concentrate on her work but found it almost impossible. She was meeting Len Regan at lunchtime, the first time for a whole week after his extended business trip to Brighton, and she was looking forward to seeing him again.

'I've heard that Martin Solomon's going in the army soon,' Audrey told her colleagues. 'I always felt he was more approachable than Joseph.'

'Yeah, he's very nice,' one of the girls remarked. 'He could take me out any time.'

'If we stay in London we'll end up being recruited for war-work,' another girl groaned. 'There's been a lot in the papers and on the wireless about recruiting single girls for essential work. We could be sent anywhere.'

Midday could not come quickly enough for Sadie, and when she finally stepped out into the warm sunshine excitement was rising inside her. Len had arranged to meet her at Giuseppi's Restaurant in the Old Kent Road, one of his usual haunts, and Mario Giuseppi would have made sure Len's regular table was available.

As expected she saw him sitting by the window and he looked immaculate in his light-grey suit and pale-blue shirt. His thick dark wavy hair was brushed back from his forehead and partly covered his ears, his slim silver tie was knotted tightly and the peaks of his shirt collar were held together with a thin gold tie-pin. He smiled at her, showing his even white teeth, and Sadie felt a familiar thrill as she slipped into the seat facing him. A few of the customers were looking at them together. Len was well known in the area and his position as business manager and right-hand man to Johnnie Macaulay gave him respect. Mario tended to fawn over him and there were always nods of recognition wherever he went, but he rode the attention calmly and with good humour.

'You look good, Sadie,' he said smiling. 'Are you eating?'

Mario was there at her side with his notebook, pencil poised. 'Would the lady like something to drink first?' he asked.

Sadie shook her head. 'Er, just water, please,' she replied.

Mario was soon back with a jug of iced water and he filled the two tumblers. 'I can recommend the meat pie and veg,' he said encouragingly. 'Or maybe an Italian dish. The spaghetti's very . . .'

'I'll 'ave the meat pie,' Sadie decided.

'That'll suit me fine too,' Len said smiling at the owner, and as Mario hurried off he leaned forward over the table. 'The poor geezer's worried sick. Apparently there's bin some threats made against 'im. Someone dropped a letter frew the door this mornin' sayin' the place was gonna be torched. It's all this talk about Italy comin' inter the war. It's a shame. Mario was born over 'ere. 'E's as English as you or me.'

'Is there anyfing you can do about it?' Sadie asked as she sipped her cold water.

Len shrugged his broad shoulders. 'The word'll go out that if this restaurant gets done a few known troublemakers'll answer for it,' he told her. 'That'll ensure that the small mobs keep their 'ot-'eads in order. At least it should work that way, but yer never know. It could be someone independent, some-one wiv a grudge, or a nutter. Anyway, let's not get too tied up wiv Mario's problems right now.'

'Tell me about Brighton,' Sadie said brightly.

'It went off very well,' Len replied. 'We've got control o' the Blue Max night club an' Johnnie's bid fer the big 'ouse facin' the promenade was accepted.'

'What's 'e want that for?' Sadie enquired innocently.

'You shouldn't ask,' Len said with a sly smile.

'Let me guess. It'll be turned into a brothel.'

'A top-notch one, not some seedy establishment.'

'I shouldn't be knowin' these fings,' Sadie said, her face suddenly becoming serious. 'You won't be involved in settin' it up, will yer, Len?'

'Nah, of course not,' he chuckled. 'Chance'd be a fine fing. No, I'll get a suitable person ter recruit the right gels an' run the place, an' I'll organise a bit o' back-up in case o' trouble, an' that's me finished.'

'I've missed yer, Len,' she said in a low voice as Mario came over carrying a laden tray.

'I've missed you too, kid,' he replied with a saucy wink.

They tucked into a delicious meal, chatting casually, and Sadie told him of her firm's plans to move away from London. 'Obviously I won't be goin' wiv 'em,' she said, 'but I'll need ter get a job locally that's involved in war-work, or I might end up in some munitions factory 'undreds o' miles away.'

Len pushed his plate back and sighed contentedly. 'Mario was right. That pie was first rate,' he remarked, then reached for his cigarette case. 'I shouldn't worry about lookin' fer anuvver job just yet. I might be able ter come up wiv somefing.'

'There's no way I'm gonna work in that Brighton establishment,' she said wide-eyed and smiling.

'No seriously, leave it ter me,' he told her. 'I'll see what I can do.'

'Len Regan can fix it,' she mocked. ''E can fix anyfing.'

'That's what Johnnie Macaulay pays me for,' he grinned.

''Ow did yer get involved in the first place?' she asked. 'You were gonna tell me, remember?'

'Not 'ere,' he said quietly. 'Let's get some air.'

They walked out into the bright daylight and the tension was evident everywhere. Serious-faced people passed by, many already carrying their gas masks over their shoulders. Sandbags were being placed outside the Council rent office and in every building windows were being strengthened with brown paper strips. The tops of red pillar-boxes were now all painted in a yellowish gas-detector paint and high above in the clear blue sky silver barrage balloons floated like huge toy elephants.

'Johnnie an' me grew up round 'ere,' Len said as they walked into a small Council park in Defoe Street. 'We were good pals. We did Borstal tergevver an' then Johnnie got two years fer ware'ouse breakin'. I was able ter take care o' fings for 'im while 'e was away an' 'e never fergot.'

They sat down on a wooden bench facing a row of swings where children were playing noisily and Len smiled. 'Me an' Johnnie used ter play on them, would yer believe? It seems a lifetime ago now, an' I s'pose it is. We went our own ways after we grew up, as usually 'appens, an' Johnnie got involved as a minder wiv the Logans. 'E built up a reputation an' went from strength ter strength. People were beginnin' ter sit up an' take notice.'

'An' what about you?' Sadie asked.

'I went inter business cartin' machinery up an' down the

country an' fings were lookin' good,' Len remarked, his face becoming more serious. 'I 'ad three lorries an' plenty o' work, an' then it all fell apart. It was soon after I got married when the trouble started. Ann was very ambitious an' she encouraged me ter go in wiv 'er farvver who 'ad a transport company workin' out of Essex. They 'ad a big contract fer movin' sand an' gravel an' fer a while fings got better an' better. I sold my lorries an' the machinery contract an' bought four tipper lorries. The money I 'ad left I sank inter the gravel business. We 'ad plans ter make the company the biggest around, but it wasn't ter be.'

'What went wrong?' Sadie asked, intrigued.

'Ann's farvver was a compulsive gambler,' Len said contemptuously. 'Unknown ter me an' the rest o' the directors 'e started filchin' money from the company. That was the beginnin'. Then Ann started 'avin' an affair. I s'pose it was partly my fault. I was obsessed wiv buildin' up the business an' I left 'er alone fer too long. Anyway one night I came 'ome an' caught 'em tergevver. I went over the top an' beat the geezer up pretty badly. I was sent down fer two years an' it would 'ave bin fer longer if I 'adn't 'ad a good barrister. It cost me a fortune but after all, two years was better than seven, an' that's what I was starin' at. When I got out the business was failin' fast. Ann's farvver did a runner wiv a lot o' cash an' there were creditors under every stone. So that was it. I cut my losses an' pulled out, wiv less than two 'undred smackers.'

'Let me guess,' Sadie cut in. 'It was then that yer met up wiv Johnnie Macaulay again.'

'Yeah, but not in the way yer fink,' he told her. 'I moved back ter Bermon'sey an' went inter business wiv an ole pal

o' mine, Joey Spain. We rented one o' those arches in Druid
Street an' got a contract ter make wooden crates fer the local
brewery. We was doin' very nicely, but what we didn't know
was, we were steppin' on Johnnie Macaulay's toes. We were
undercuttin' one of 'is concerns an' 'e came round mob-
'anded ter put us out o' business. When 'e saw it was me 'e
couldn't get over it. Mind yer 'e still closed us down pronto,
but me an' Joey got work wiv 'im. It was small stuff ter
begin wiv, but 'e must 'ave seen that I 'ad somefing about
me an' I started gettin' important jobs ter do. It just went
from big ter bigger.'

'An' now you're the top man.'

'Yeah, yer could put it like that.'

'An' what about Joey Spain?' Sadie asked.

'Joey's still around,' Len said with a smile. ''E's one o'
Johnnie's minders.'

'Do you ever see your wife?'

Len shook his head. 'I told yer she was a Catholic, didn't
I?' Sadie nodded and he stared down at his hands. 'I can
never get me freedom, an' frankly I don't care a toss.
Marriage an' me don't work.'

Sadie looked sad. 'It would 'ave done, if yer'd met the
right person.'

'If I'd met you first it could 'ave bin different,' he said
quietly, 'but it's all water under the bridge now. We got it
tergevver, kid, an' let's enjoy it. Life's too short ter go
makin' too many plans.'

They left the park and walked back to the factory, and
Sadie stretched up on tiptoe to kiss him on the lips as he
clasped her shoulders.

'When can I see yer, Len?' she asked.

'I've got some business wiv Johnnie this evenin',' he replied, 'but I'll be free on Friday night. See yer at the same place?'

'Same place, same time,' Sadie said smiling. 'Take care, Len.'

Chapter Three

The Lockwood sisters shared the house at number 20 Carter Lane. They had lived together ever since the winter of '29 when Cynthia's husband Aaron Priestley went missing. Charity Lockwood had called in to offer her younger sister her support and comfort and never left.

Cynthia Priestley was not really in need of much comfort and support. In fact she was glad to see the back of her uncouth, lazy and lecherous husband. Aaron had had many bad habits, as Cynthia soon discovered, but being the dutiful wife she had devoted herself to his comfort and well-being and suffered him in silence for twenty-five years.

When Aaron went missing Cynthia was sporting a black eye, which she explained away by telling her neighbours that the wind had slammed the backyard door in her face. The neighbours nodded their heads in sympathy and concurred that Cynthia Priestley was a poor liar. They knew of Aaron's violent temper and his drunken habits, and they were all glad to see the back of him. Had Cynthia been a more robust woman, with perhaps a more volatile temper, they might even have suspected that the good woman had had something to do with his disappearance. As it was, they all knew that Cynthia was too meek and mild even to step on an insect.

Charity Lockwood was a little less meek, though she too was very mild-mannered and retiring. She had never married, and when she realised that her younger sister would be alone in the house at night, in a rough area such as Bermondsey, she rallied to her aid. There were things to be done and Charity took charge. She forced Cynthia to report her husband's disappearance to the police, and between the two of them they furnished the attending officer with a fine description. Charity told the police that Aaron Priestley was an ugly, lecherous pig and when Cynthia added that her husband was not too particular about changing his underclothes on a regular basis, the constable had to remind the sisters that this was not exactly the information he needed. A facial description, height and build, colouring and distinguishing marks on the body were the kind of details he required from them, and they duly obliged.

Aaron was never found, though there were a few reported sightings, to which the sisters reacted unequivocally when they got to hear.

'As long as the old goat doesn't come back here,' Cynthia would say to her neighbours.

'If he does you must send him packing with a flea in his ear,' Charity would remind her in front of them.

Now in their late sixties, the sisters were seen as sweet, quaint and eccentric by everyone in the street. They spoke very properly, dressed neatly and tidily, with their grey hair carefully waved and set, and they always went out together, be it to the market or to church on Sundays or the local park on warm balmy evenings to feed the ducks and pigeons.

With the coming of the war Cynthia wanted to go and live in the country but Charity decided otherwise. 'We have our friends and neighbours here,' she pointed out. 'In the country we wouldn't know anybody and when it snows we could be cut off from civilisation.'

Cynthia felt that they were hardly likely to be cut off in Clacton, and she said as much, but as usual Charity came back with an answer. 'Yes, but do you realise that Clacton is on the east coast? The Germans could come that way. We'd be in the front line, and at our time of life. We could be raped and pillaged.'

'We might get raped, though I doubt it at our age,' Cynthia remarked, 'but we certainly won't get pillaged. Property and belongings get pillaged.'

'Well all right, but I still don't think that Clacton is a good idea, especially at this stage of the proceedings,' Charity persisted.

With the decision made the sisters decided to visit the saloon bar of The Sun to drink to it, and as always they ordered sweet sherries.

Cynthia looked troubled as they waited for the drinks to be poured. 'Would you say you were as alert as me, Charity?' she asked. 'I mean, do you notice things, little things, things that don't look important but are?'

'Whatever are you getting at?' Charity said sighing, as Charlie Anson put the drinks down on the counter.

'On our way to the market this morning I noticed something about that pillar-box in Munday Road.'

'What about it?'

'A man was painting the top of it.'

'Well?'

'I was going to mention it to you,' Cynthia went on, 'but you started talking about poor old Mr Abel.'

'Cynthia, pillar-boxes do get painted occasionally,' Charity told her with a patronising note in her voice.

'Yes, red, not yellow.'

'Yellow?'

'Yes, yellow – well the top of the pillar-box anyway.'

'I didn't notice,' Charity said.

'No, you were too busy talking, but I noticed it,' Cynthia replied smugly. 'Postboxes are Government property and it's a criminal offence to interfere with a pillar-box.'

'Quite right too,' Charlie cut in. 'Pillar-boxes are Crown property ter be exact.'

'Then who gave that man the right to paint a pillar-box yellow I'd like to know,' Cynthia said indignantly. 'Pillar-boxes should be red. That's where the name comes from, pillar-box red.'

'P'raps 'e's a fifth-columnist an' 'e's tryin' ter disrupt fings,' Charlie remarked, trying his best to keep a straight face.

Charity Lockwood sipped her sherry. 'Come now, Mr Anson,' she said stiffly. 'You don't think things would be disrupted by someone painting the top of a pillar-box yellow, do you?'

'Ah but 'e might 'ave just started,' Charlie replied with due seriousness. 'P'raps 'e was gonna paint the 'ole of it yellow, then people wouldn't be too sure whether they could still post letters there or not.'

Cynthia nodded. 'Quite right too,' she said with a smile playing on her small lined face. 'Charity, I think we should report this to the police, just to be on the safe side.'

Charlie Anson did not have the heart to spoil their day by frightening them about the gas-detector paint, feeling that perhaps this was a classic case of ignorance being bliss. 'Good fer you,' he said, walking along the bar to serve a customer who had just come in.

Chief Inspector Rubin McConnell had been at Munday Road police station for more than twenty years now and there wasn't much he didn't know about the area and its denizens. The Lockwood sisters were well known to him and the large file he had devoted to them proved it. The pair had come in to report some pretty outrageous goings-on over the years and Rubin had learned to open his file and take their report down without comment, a ploy that got the two quaint women out of his hair as soon as possible.

On that Wednesday afternoon, according to protocol, the Lockwoods walked into Munday Road police station and demanded to see Chief Inspector Rubin McConnell. 'It's no disrespect to you, young man,' Charity told the duty officer, 'but this is very important and only for the inspector's ears. Besides, he always sees us.'

Hiding a smile the young policeman spoke to his sergeant, who pulled a face and went to let the inspector know that trouble had arrived in the guise of the batty sisters.

'Come in, ladies, and take a seat,' Rubin bid them. 'Now let me get my file out so we can get things moving.' Then putting on his glasses he took his pen and looked up at their intent expressions. 'Right, I'm ready,' he said with a resolute smile.

Cynthia knew the drill off by heart and she did the talking, encouraged by occasional nods from her older sister. 'This morning about nine fifteen exactly . . .'

'Just a moment,' the inspector stopped her, keen to show he was taking the report seriously. 'Was it about nine fifteen or nine fifteen exactly?'

'About,' Cynthia replied with a smile. 'About nine fifteen my sister and I were on our way to the market at East Street when we chanced to pass a pillar-box that is situated in Munday Road, a few yards away from this police station.'

'Yes, I know it,' the inspector said helpfully.

'My sister and I noticed that there was a workman, well he looked like a workman, painting the top of the pillar-box yellow.'

Charity smiled at being credited with the same powers of observation as her sister and she folded her hands in her lap contentedly.

'At first we took no notice, but then while we were having a morning sherry we got to thinking,' Cynthia went on. 'Pillar-boxes are Crown property and are always painted red. Why then should this man be in the process of changing the colour? Was it to confuse the public, and if so, why, we asked ourselves?'

Rubin McConnell was writing furiously, praying that he wouldn't start laughing. 'Why indeed?' he said quickly.

'The only answer we could come up with was that the man doing the painting was a fifth-columnist,' Cynthia continued. 'If he'd been from the IRA he would have more likely blown the box up.'

'Quite so,' Rubin replied. 'Right then, ladies, I have your report word for word and rest assured I will act on it forthwith.'

Cynthia and Charity looked pleased with themselves as

they went out of the police station, leaving in their wake a relieved detective who was thankful to have got off lightly. 'Honestly, Johnson,' he told his subordinate, 'I couldn't bring myself to spoil their day. Besides, it would only put the fear of God into the poor old things if they knew the Germans might be thinking of using poison gas.'

'But surely they would have heard about all the emergency precautions taking place,' the detective sergeant replied.

'Not those two,' the inspector assured him. 'They have the knack of closing their ears and their minds to everything they don't want to know. But nevertheless, they are public-spirited. You'd be surprised if you saw some of the reports in that file. Two months ago they came in to report that they'd seen a man who looked very much like the Hoxton Creeper, would you believe?'

'The Hoxton Creeper?' Johnson said grinning widely. 'He was a product of Edgar Wallace's imagination, surely?'

'Be that as it may, the sisters came in to report that a man who resembled the Creeper was working on the cat's-meat stall in East Street Market.'

'Do they ever come back to see what progress we're making?' Johnson asked.

'Never,' McConnell told him. 'Once they report an incident they forget it, or at least I hope they do, otherwise we'll be looking at the largest backlog of police work in England.'

The Wednesday evening meal at the Flynns' was eaten quietly and with little conversation. Dolly and Mick had been told by their lads that they had volunteered for the armed forces, and Mick drew comfort from the fact that

Frank and Jim had put in a request to serve together. He felt pleased too that Pat was going in the airforce, until the young man told him that he was volunteering for aircrew as soon as he could. There was no stopping them and Mick knew that it was useless trying to get Patrick to change his mind. Dolly had very mixed emotions. She felt a sense of pride in the gesture her sons were making but she was terribly fearful about what might befall them. She was also furious with them for treating the war like some adventure. They would soon learn otherwise, she thought fretfully.

'What about you, Sadie?' Pat asked after the meal was over. 'Are yer gonna go ter Bedford wiv the firm?'

She shook her head. 'No, I'm gonna stay round 'ere, if I can.'

'If yer can?' Dolly queried.

'I'm single, Mum. Me an' Jennie'll get called up fer war-work before long.'

'Well, you should both try an' get a war-work job local before they're filled up,' Dolly told them.

Jennie ran her fingers through her red hair and stretched. 'Well, I'm certainly not gonna stay at Jones and Whatleys fer the duration,' she said firmly. 'I might apply fer the services too. I fink I'd look good in a Wren's uniform.'

'Oh no you don't, young woman,' Dolly said sharply. 'It'll be bad enough wiv the boys away, wivout you joinin' up.'

Sadie pushed her chair back and gathered up the dirty crockery and Dolly followed her out into the scullery. 'Try ter talk Jennie out o' doin' somefing silly, Sadie,' she said sighing. 'I couldn't stand 'er bein' away too.'

'I'll try, Mum,' the young woman told her with a warm smile. 'But you know 'ow 'eadstrong Jennie is. Anyway it's early days yet. Anyfing might 'appen.'

'Yeah, all bad fings,' Dolly replied. 'It makes yer blood go cold when yer listen ter that wireless. This mornin' they was on about the amount o' shippin' that's bein' sunk by U-boats.'

Sadie poured the boiling water from the kettle into the stone sink. 'Go an' put yer feet up, Mum,' she said. 'Jennie'll 'elp me wiv the dryin' up.'

'Ain't you goin' out ternight?' Dolly asked.

'No, Len's just got back from some business in Brighton an' 'e's got too much on.'

'Won't 'e be gettin' called up in the forces?' Dolly remarked.

Sadie chuckled. 'Len, in the army? I don't fink so.'

Dolly sighed sadly. 'I know I must sound like a broken record but I do wish you'd seriously consider all the pitfalls in goin' out wiv someone like Len Regan.'

'Look, Mum, I know yer mean well, but I love 'im,' Sadie said quietly. 'I never came between 'im an' Ann. The marriage was over long before I came on the scene. Len was straight right from the start. 'E spelled it all out. She'll never give 'im 'is freedom an' there's no point 'im worryin' about it. The both of us are enjoyin' our lives. I couldn't be 'appier, Mum, believe me.'

'I wanted ter see you all 'appily married before I snuffed it,' Dolly replied defeatedly.

Sadie reached out and put her arms around her. 'You're the bestest Mum, an' we all love yer. Don't go gettin' all sad an' miserable. Not now, please.'

Dolly brushed back a tear as her daughter released her. 'The boys'll be all right, won't they?' she said fearfully.

'Course they will,' Sadie assured her, 'especially now that Frank an' Jim are goin' in the same regiment. Those two 'ave always taken care of each ovver. Remember when that bully set about Jim at school? Frank nearly killed 'im.'

'What about young Pat though?' Dolly fretted. 'I wish we could talk 'im out o' volunteering fer those aircrews.'

'It's no good, Ma,' Sadie replied. 'Pat can be the most cantankerous sod at times. We'll just 'ave to 'ope 'e changes 'is mind.'

Jennie came bounding into the scullery. 'Sadie, is there any chance o' borrowin' that nice black dress o' yours? I'd be grateful fer ever an' ever.'

Dolly left them to bargain and stepped outside into the backyard. The evening was balmy with a few stars showing between the gathering clouds. She saw the rusted tricycle that Pat used to ride as a kid and which she had never been able to get rid of, and she felt the tears coming again. There was the carving on the lavatory door and the old tin bath that all her brood had climbed into in front of the fire on Friday nights. Little things, ancient things, and things that would forever remind her of them all. She turned to go back into the house and Mick was there, standing in the doorway watching her.

'I was gonna offer a penny fer yer thoughts but I didn't dare,' he said with a warm smile on his large weatherbeaten face.

'I was just rememberin',' she said simply.

He stepped out into the yard and slipped his arm around her waist. 'Look, I know it's bin a terrible few days, but we're not alone, gel,' he said in a quiet voice. 'All over the country young men are preparin' ter go off an' fight. In almost every family 'ouse in the land there'll be spaces round the table an' bedrooms not bein' slept in. There's nuffink me, you, nor anybody else can do ter change it. It's up ter the politicians an' the warmongers ter realise that whatever 'appens, 'owever bitter the fightin', there'll come a time when they'll 'ave ter get tergevver round the table an' talk. All we can do is pray that it comes sooner rather than later.'

The stars had all gone in and the heavy clouds were full of rain. The sound of brass-band music drifted out from next door and a dog barked in the distance.

'Come on, gel, let's listen ter the news,' Mick said.

'Mick?'

'Yeah?'

'It doesn't matter.'

'Now come on, out wiv it.'

'Mick, do you still feel the same as yer did when we were young?'

'About you yer mean?'

'Who else d'yer fink I meant?'

'The answer's no.'

'What?'

Mick squeezed her waist and chuckled. 'I love yer fifteen bob more than I did then,' he told her.

'Well, that's all right then,' Dolly said sternly. 'Come on let's go in, I'll make a mug of cocoa.'

Chapter Four

The early days of the war were warm and sunny, with a frenzy of activity going on everywhere in an atmosphere that seemed unreal. Brick surface shelters were hurriedly erected in streets where children played, and in the parks people had picnics beside anti-tank trenches and concrete barriers. Railway stations became staging points for the services, and military uniforms mingled with the crowds of everyday commuters and families on weekend trips. Everyone learned the art of queuing and had to practise getting in line. Ration books and petrol coupons were issued and scientists and doctors worked out a basic diet guaranteed to sustain good health, while in the West End of London prime steak and lamb cutlets, pork chops and lavish cuts of beef were still on the menu at all the hotels and restaurants. Pubs saw a rise in trade as well and people danced to the big bands in the top night-spots of London.

The war at sea was raging and the toll of shipping sunk grew daily, but for the people at home it was a time of waiting and worrying, as their young folk left for the armed services. Constant reminders of the unseen dangers and patriotic exhortations were posted up at every vantage point.

It was a time to 'Dig for Victory', and to remember that 'Careless Talk Costs Lives'. Collections were made in back-streets and everyone was urged to bring out their old pots and pans and any other metal scrap that they might have in their gardens and backyards. More signs encouraged folk to 'Beat that Squander Bug' and 'Save for Victory'. Iron railings and metal gates were removed for the war effort, and even the children's playgrounds were stripped of everything metal.

The strictness with which the blackout was enforced was an ominous suggestion of things to come, and often a careless moment would be met with the cry, 'Put that light out!' Torches could be carried to light the way home, provided the beam was dimmed with a double layer of tissue-paper. Vehicles' headlights were restricted by the use of slitted metal caps and the road accident toll grew alarmingly. Directional signs were removed and premises were taken over for air-raid wardens' posts. In every area civil defence command posts were installed and cars were commandeered for stretcher-carrying. And while all the preparations and conversions, innovations and transformations went on, so did the waiting . . .

Frank and Jim Flynn passed their army medicals and were waiting eagerly for their call-up papers, and Patrick Flynn had no trouble being accepted for the RAF. His trade as a carpenter would help him become an air-frame fitter, so the recruiting officer informed him, and the young man nodded compliantly. First things first, he told himself. Like his two brothers he sailed through the medical, and along with them he waited for an official letter to drop onto the mat.

Big Joe Buckley was called up into the navy and the night before he left he sat talking to Bert Kenny in the parlour. 'I've really enjoyed lodging here, mate,' he said with a smile. 'I'm gonna miss the both of you. I couldn't have got better tucker anywhere and you two have made me feel like one o' the family.'

Bert smiled self-consciously. 'Me an' Liz look on you as one of our own,' he replied.

Joe shifted his position in the armchair. 'By the way, I'm sorry if I disturbed you both last night. I was with a few o' the berko buggers from the building site. We were on a bit of an elbow-bender.'

'So yer won't be goin' out ternight then?' Bert said grinning.

'Aw yeah. Tonight I'm gonna drown me troubles in a tubful o' Bermondsey brainrot,' Joe replied enthusiastically. 'But in a civilised sort o' way, and I'd be delighted to buy you and Liz a drink if you don't mind stickin' your heads in The Sun.'

'Liz 'as gone fer a chat wiv Dolly Flynn,' Bert told him. 'I'll see if she's game when she comes back. Anyway, what troubles 'ave you got? A young man like you wiv no ties can please 'imself where 'e goes an' what 'e does. You wait till yer get spliced. Yer'll see the difference then.'

'That's probably right, Bert, but I'd willingly give up all the old cobblers for Sadie Flynn. Now there's a beaut, if ever I saw one. I've been after asking her out for a drink but I ain't seen anything of her lately.'

''Ave you ever really spoke to 'er?' Bert asked.

'Nah, not really. Not a single bloody word, now I think of it.'

'I was gonna say why don't yer go an' knock at 'er door,' Bert said, 'but I s'pose yer can't unless yer on speakin' terms.'

'Nah, it'd be a bit ocker,' Joe agreed. 'Anyway as soon as I get some leave I'll put that right. I'll get to know her and see what a nice new uniform does for her. Like the old song says, all the nice girls love a sailor.'

'Well, I wish yer luck, but don't get yer 'opes up too much, Joe,' Bert warned him. 'Yer know she's goin' out wiv Len Regan.'

'Yeah, so I've heard,' Joe replied. 'He's a big man around here, according to the ole bush telegraph.'

''E's more of a front man really,' Bert remarked. 'It's common knowledge that Len Regan runs Johnnie Macaulay's affairs but Macaulay's the big fish. 'E owns pubs an' clubs, an' they say 'e controls all the mobs this side o' the river. You name it – 'e's into it. Gamblin', prostitution, protection, an' Gawd knows what else.'

Joe shook his head slowly. 'The Flynns seem a nice family. Why would Sadie Flynn wanna get involved with the likes of him?' he asked. 'The way I see it there's only bad times on the trolley for that sort. The bigger they are the harder they fall at the end o' the day.'

Bert shrugged his shoulders. 'It could be the excitement that attracted 'er in the first place. You know the sort o' fings, night-clubs, racin' meetin's, shows an' the like. A lot o' gels' 'eads are turned by that sort o' fing. But that's only one way o' lookin' at it. Yer gotta consider too that she might really love the geezer. I understand from what Liz told me that 'e's quite a bit older than 'er. Some gels are attracted to older men, not that I'm an expert on that sort o' fing.'

Joe laughed aloud. 'You could've fooled me, Bert,' he replied. 'Anyway I'm going for a shave. The rubbity-dub'll soon be open to all chunderers.'

While the big man was getting ready to go out Liz returned. 'Poor Dolly,' she said as she sat down in the armchair facing Bert. 'She's just 'ad a few tears. Those lads of 'ers are gonna be off very soon. It's bad enough one goin', let alone three.'

Bert nodded sadly, then his face brightened up. ''Ere, luv. Why don't we get Dolly an' Mick ter come up The Sun fer a drink wiv us? Joe wants ter buy us a drink anyway. It'll make a change, an' it might cheer the poor sods up fer a bit.'

Liz thought for a few moments, then she nodded. 'Sadie ain't out ternight, p'raps she might come up there as well. Joe's bin tryin' ter get ter know 'er. It'll be a chance fer 'im ter chat the gel up. By the way, if you wanna come too get yerself a shave. Yer look like Burglar Bill.'

Friday nights were music nights at The Sun public house and Blind Bob was already at the piano tinkling on the keys, a pint of beer within his reach. Joe was standing at the counter surrounded by the friends he had made in the short time he had lived in Carter Lane.

'We're gonna miss that ugly mug o' yours round 'ere,' the elderly Danny Crossley remarked.

'Yeah, me too,' Shorty Beaumont added.

'I know somebody who's gonna be glad ter see the back o' you, though,' Alf Coates piped up.

'So do I,' Danny chuckled into his beer. 'Since that night I don't fink anybody's seen 'ide nor 'air o' Sid Cafferty.'

'I 'ave,' one of the street's dockers said. 'Cafferty's usin' The Bull now.'

''E wants ter be careful in there,' another of the group remarked. 'There's a right crowd gets in there. They won't stand fer any nonsense.'

'Nor do we, come ter that,' Danny said rolling his bony shoulders.

The pub was gradually filling up and wreaths of cigarette smoke hung in the air as Blind Bob got into his stride on the ivories.

''Ere, Bob. What about, ''All the nice gels love a sailor''?' Lofty Knowles called out.

'What about it?' Bob called back, cocking his ear in the direction of the counter.

'Play it, yer daft git,' Lofty growled at him.

Everyone in the saloon bar joined in the ditty and Joe stood in the middle of the group feeling embarrassed as they sang to him with gusto. It was then that the Kennys and the Flynns walked in and Big Joe immediately noticed Sadie. She stood talking to her sister Jennie while Bert and Mick ordered the drinks and she glanced over at him and gave him a brief smile of recognition. Joe swallowed quickly and tried to pick up on the inane chatter passing back and forth around him but it was all going over his head. 'Excuse me, mates,' he said, moving away from the counter.

'Don't look now but Big Joe Buckley's lookin' over,' Jennie said, giving her sister a sly smile.

'I 'ope 'e don't come over,' Sadie hissed.

'Why? Don't yer like 'im?'

'It's not that,' Sadie replied. ''E just makes me feel uneasy.'

Jennie pulled a face. 'Sadie Flynn, Len Regan's gelfriend,

an' a bloke like Big Joe makes yer feel uneasy. You've gotta be kiddin' me.'

Sadie glanced furtively towards the counter. 'Joe's a decent sort o' bloke, I s'pose, but I've never actually spoke to 'im. I dunno what it is about 'im. It might be 'is size, or the way 'e looks at me when we pass in the street. Anyway don't keep lookin' over there.'

Jennie was not to be put off. 'I like 'em big an' 'andsome. Big Joe could chat me up for any day o' the week.'

Dolly Flynn and Liz Kenny were gossiping together round a small iron table and Bert was standing to one side with Mick, discussing football. Sadie went uncharacteristically quiet and Jennie began to feel a little bored as she sat sipping her port and lemon. 'As we were sayin'. It's nice in 'ere, ain't it?' she said with heavy sarcasm.

'Sorry, Jen, I was miles away,' Sadie said weakly.

'Len trouble?'

'Not really, but 'e's 'ere, there an' everywhere lately,' Sadie replied. 'It's that Brighton business I was tellin' yer about. I 'ardly see 'im. 'E's bin back an' forwards at least four times this week.'

'Look, there's Ken Bennett over at the counter,' Jennie said nudging her. 'Let's go an' stand up there, 'e might notice me.'

'You're a pushy little bitch,' Sadie laughed, smiling fondly at her. 'C'mon then.'

As they got up and made their way over to the end of the counter where it was less crowded Joe Buckley walked up. 'Er, excuse me,' he said, hesitantly, addressing Jennie. 'I'd like to buy your party a drink. Can you tell me what they're having?'

Jennie smiled up at him. 'That's very nice of yer, ain't it, Sadie? Now let me see, Mr an' Mrs Kenny are . . .'

'Yeah, I know what they're drinking,' Joe said quickly. 'I mean you an' your mum and dad.'

'I'll find out,' Jennie said, walking back to the table.

'What would you and your sister like?' Joe asked, giving Sadie a disarming smile.

'It's all right, I've still got this one,' Sadie said holding up her drink.

'Let me refill it for you. It's the last chance I'll get to buy my good neighbours a drink,' Joe told her as he leant one arm on the counter. 'I'm off tomorrow.'

''Ave yer bin called up?' Sadie asked.

'Yeah, I'm going in the Royal Navy,' Joe said proudly. 'I've gotta report to Chatham or I'll get shot.'

Jennie had memorised the order but delayed going back to the counter when she saw Joe and Sadie talking together.

'I wish yer luck,' Sadie said, averting her eyes self-consciously.

'I'm gonna miss this area,' he said sighing.

''Ow long 'ave yer bin 'ere now?' Sadie asked.

'Three months, but it seems much longer,' Joe replied.

The barman was looking at him expectantly. 'What'll it be, Joe?'

'What the lady's having and I'll have the usual overpriced rubbish,' the big man told him. 'The rest of the order seems to have got held up.'

'Mine's a port an' lemon, same as Jennie,' Sadie said.

'Do your worst, and one for yourself,' Joe said, laying a pound note on the counter.

Sadie drained her glass and set it down to be replenished.

'It must seem strange fer you,' she remarked, 'livin' in a small community I mean, after livin' in Australia.'

'As a matter o' fact I grew up in a little community back home,' Joe replied. 'It was in the suburbs o' Sydney.'

'But it's such a big country,' Sadie said.

'Yeah, but you don't really think much about that, till you grow up a bit,' Joe told her. 'It was only when I left home and travelled, went walkabout as we say, that I started to realise just how big it is.'

'What made yer come over 'ere in the first place?' Sadie asked, beginning to feel intrigued.

Joe shrugged his shoulders, giving her a wide smile. 'Now that's a big question. I suppose I had itchy feet by then, and I got to find out that my folk originally came from England. Things weren't going all that well in Oz and I was at a loose end, so I signed on as an engineer on a liner and worked me passage to the old country, as we call it.'

'What about yer family?'

'I never knew them,' Joe replied. 'I was brought up in an orphanage.'

'I'm sorry,' Sadie said, catching a fleeting look of sadness in his wide blue eyes. 'It can't 'ave bin the ideal way ter start out.'

Joe shrugged his shoulders again. 'Such is life. At least it taught me to look after meself. I left the orphanage when I was fourteen and they fixed me up at a marine engineering firm, where I got the chance to do an apprenticeship. There's not much I don't know about marine engines; which is a good thing really, 'cos I know bugger all about anything else. That's how I managed to get in the navy so quickly.'

The barman put two port and lemons down on the counter

along with a frothing pint of beer and Sadie chuckled. 'It seems Jennie's got somefing else on 'er mind,' she said, nodding over to where her sister was chatting away intently to a young man.

'That's my good luck,' Joe said, giving her a shy smile. Then he struggled with himself for a moment or two. 'Would you mind if I told you something?'

'It depends what it is,' Sadie replied, beginning to feel relaxed.

'Ever since I've lived in Carter Lane I've been wanting to talk to you, but I could never find the spunk to do it,' he confessed. 'You seemed different to all the other girls in the street. You have that proud walk and a sort of air about you that scared me off. Does that sound stupid?'

'Not really,' Sadie said smiling. 'You 'ad that effect on me.'

'Did I?' Joe replied, looking surprised. 'Ripper!'

Sadie sipped her drink. 'Anyway yer'll be gettin' some leave, won't yer, an' then we can 'ave a chat when we meet up wivout us feelin' scared of each ovver.'

'That'll be something to look forward to,' Joe said in a serious voice. 'This area's become like home for me and the Kennys feel like me own. Your mother and father are dinkum too and I've enjoyed a few true blue nights in here with your brothers. I know that you're going steady but it'll be nice if I can count on you as a friend as well.'

The drinks and the unexpected conversation had made Sadie feel a little light-headed and she held out her hand. ''Ello, friend.'

Joe took her hand in his much larger one. 'Pleased to meet you, friend,' he said smiling broadly.

Jennie finally walked over. 'Sorry to interrupt,' she said, giving Joe a big grin. 'I've got the order.'

'This is my friend,' Sadie said with a dignified expression. 'Jennie, meet Joe.'

The night was wearing on and Joe was pulled away for a toast, then Charlie Anson came round the counter to say a few words as Blind Bob took a breather. 'Joe, we're all sorry ter see yer go,' he began, 'but we know it won't be the last o' that ugly face round 'ere. Liz Kenny told me that 'er an' Bert are keepin' yer room for yer an' there's always a space at the bar fer you while me an' Tess are runnin' the gaff. This is a small backwater in a small country, but the people round 'ere 'ave got great big 'earts an' they've all taken ter yer. So 'ere's ter you, an' may whoever's bin smilin' down on yer keep doin' so. Gawd bless yer, son.'

Liz Kenny came up and gave the big man a hug and Bert shook his hand vigorously. People were slapping his back and Sadie suddenly noticed the tears forming in his large blue eyes as the demonstrations of affection overwhelmed him.

'Joe's a smashin' feller,' Liz said, wiping her eyes.

'One o' the best,' Bert agreed, swallowing hard.

''E's lovely,' Jennie sighed to her older sister.

'Yeah, 'e's nice,' Sadie said calmly, but she felt like kissing him.

Chapter Five

Albert Levy sat down on the stool behind the counter and opened his packet of sandwiches. When Abel was working at the shop Albert had been free to take a short break for lunch at the nearby cafe or the pub opposite, knowing that his old friend could cope with any customers who might come into the shop. Now though it was different. Bernard Shanks, the young man he had employed, was skilled enough in his trade but was not familiar with selling and lacked confidence, so Albert spent the whole day behind the counter and ate his make-do lunch when it was quiet.

Apart from the radios on show, Levy's Radio Store sold light bulbs and torch bulbs, as well as batteries, accumulators and electrical bits and pieces. Radio accumulators were charged in the shed out the back and in the two rooms upstairs Albert kept his stock. At first he and Gerda had lived in the cramped quarters over the shop but as the business developed he was able to get a mortgage for a Victorian terraced house in New Cross. It was only a short tram ride away and it suited him.

When he had finished the fish-paste sandwiches and eaten the rosy apple Gerda had put in his bag, Albert went into the workroom to make a cup of tea. He had finally got around to clearing Abel's personal things from the back of the cupboard and there was nothing there that he felt he wanted to keep. A few old receipts and radio magazines, along with some technical manuals which he had passed over to Bernard, was the sum total and it saddened Albert. 'There wasn't a lot to remember you by, was there?' he said, thumbing through a manual on valves and transformers. 'Still I've got the chess set and that's nice. I can see you now, Abel, when you looked up with that apologetic smile as you checkmated me. I'm sure you would have preferred me to win sometimes, but I know how your mind worked. You felt it might upset me if you treated me like some incompetent youth and pretended to make a little mistake or two. Like I said before, Abel, I was getting your measure. By the way, it's Gerda's birthday tomorrow. We're going over to Whitechapel to be with her family. They're doing something special for her fiftieth.'

Albert looked towards the front door of the shop, suddenly feeling a little self-conscious about talking aloud. If anyone walked in, he thought, they would probably assume he was going off his head. He turned back to stare at the paraphernalia on the bench and saw in his mind his old friend sitting hunched over a dismantled wireless with a soldering iron in his hand and a look of extreme concentration on his thin face. That was the time to avoid talking to him. A word or question would be met with a tut-tut and a nervous cough, and Abel would be in a bad mood for the rest of the day. Such was his dedication to his trade and his single-minded proficiency.

'The new technician seems quite all right, Abel, though

he's a strange lad,' Albert continued. 'Not very fit by the look of him. I'm sure he's undernourished. I was thinking earlier, if you can hear me you'll know how things are going with the war, but I'll keep you up to date with my assessment anyway. Do you know what I think? I think there'll be a stalemate now that the Nazis have got Czechoslovakia and overrun Poland. I think they'll be after settling for that. It's all quiet on the Western Front and they'll have their work cut out breaking through the Maginot Line. I shouldn't be too surprised to see things moving towards an armistice before long, certainly early in the New Year. We'll talk some more later, old friend. Bernard will be back from lunch in a few minutes.'

Daisy Harris had been putting off the task of cleaning Abel's rooms, but on Saturday morning she finally faced up to doing it. She had given all his clothes to the Salvation Army and Mr Levy had gone through the cardboard box containing his personal effects. The rooms needed scrubbing out and a good airing before she could consider taking in a new lodger. The doors and cupboards needed some fresh paint and the cracked oil-cloth would have to be replaced too.

Bill Harris did the painting, which took him well into the afternoon, and then Daisy pulled up the oil-cloth which she folded into manageable pieces for Bill to tie up and leave by the dustbin. The last piece of floor-covering that Daisy pulled up was around the fireplace, and on the lefthand side there was a small piece that had already been cut into an oblong shape, presumably by Abel. Beneath it a flap of wood was loose and Daisy prised it up with curiosity. In the recess she could see a brown paper parcel and, loath to touch it, she called out for Bill.

'It could be anyfing,' she said, stroking her chin.

'Well, there's only one way ter find out,' he said going down on his knees.

'You be careful,' she said fearfully.

Bill gave her a disdainful look and removed the small bundle. The wrapping was not tied and as he unfolded the paper he saw the diary. It was bound in leather with gold-leaf figuring on the front cover. Quickly he flipped through the pages and perused the tiny scribblings and figures. 'I can't make 'ead or tail o' this – it's in some foreign language,' he said, looking up at Daisy.

'You shouldn't be lookin' at it anyway,' she admonished him. 'That's Mr Abel's personal diary. I'd better let Mr Levy know about it.'

'Why should 'e wanna stick it away like that?' Bill wondered, scratching his head.

''Cos it's personal,' Daisy said pointedly.

'Yeah, so yer keep sayin',' Bill growled.

'I'll pop it in ter Mr Levy's shop before 'e shuts,' Daisy decided. 'I gotta go next door ter the shoemender's anyway.'

Jennie Flynn had grown more and more disenchanted with the idea of being a saleswoman, especially a saleswoman for the venerable company of Jones and Whatleys. Travelling to and from the West End every day was bad enough, without having to work on Saturdays. Then there was the system at the old Royally chartered establishment. The senior staff were all long-term employees who felt privileged just to be part of such a fine company, judging by the way they spoke and acted, and whenever any of the owners or directors appeared in the store they would grovel and bow and scrape in a way that left Jennie and some of the newer girls feeling disgusted at it all.

At first Jennie was pleased to be taken on, as she was led to believe that promotion would soon be awarded to staff showing the right initiative and motivation. 'The sky's the limit with Jones and Whatleys,' the personnel manager had informed her during her initial interview. Well it wasn't, unless the hopeful young sales assistant quickly learned the art of fawning and kowtowing. Now, with four years under her belt, Jennie was ready to seek pastures new.

'I should think it over very carefully,' Mrs Collins told her during the morning break as they sat together in the staff room. 'You could do a lot worse. The conditions here are not at all bad and there are openings for the right people. Take me – I've only been a senior saleswoman for two years and at the present moment I'm on the shortlist to take over a floor.'

'Well, I've bin 'ere fer four years now an' there's as much chance o' me gettin' a senior saleswoman's post as goin' ter the moon,' Jennie said dismissively.

Mrs Collins smiled. 'It's all about attitude and presentation,' she remarked smugly. 'Either you've got it or you haven't.'

'Yer mean I don't come over as a good saleswoman?' Jennie retorted quickly. 'I speak proper when I'm be'ind the counter an' I always try ter be all smiley an' 'appy.'

'Yes and you do very well,' the older woman replied. 'No one would question you on that score. But it goes much deeper than that, you see. This company is an old establishment with a

Royal charter. Those at the very senior level have worked very hard to get where they are and they expect to be treated accordingly. You take Mr Forbes as an example. He likes to be called sir by the staff, and whenever he makes an appearance on the floors he expects the staff to recognise and respect his position. He spent fifteen years on menswear and another five years in furnishings before he went upstairs as junior buyer. Now he's a senior buyer and whenever he requests anything he expects the staff to jump.'

'Well, you can say what you like about Mr Forbes, but ter me 'e's just a lecherous ole goat who could do wiv a little more soap an' water,' Jennie said with disgust. ''E reeks o' sweat, an' if 'e expects me ter call 'im sir, 'e can whistle.'

Mrs Collins secretly admired the young woman's pluck, but she dared not let her know. As it was, Jennie was right about her prospects for promotion. Mr Forbes had her pegged as a troublemaker and malcontent and he had been instrumental in ensuring that she would remain a junior saleswoman for as long as she worked at Jones and Whatleys.

'Well, if you won't bend a little and show a little more respect where it matters you can't expect to move upwards,' Mrs Collins said sighing.

Jennie picked up her bag from the chair beside her. 'It could all be up in the air anyway,' she said as she stood up to go back to the handbag and accessories counter.

'Up in the air?' Mrs Collins queried.

'Well, if this new law comes inter force single women are gonna be recruited fer war-work,' Jennie replied. 'If that's the case then 'alf o' Jones an' Whatleys' staff are gonna be leavin', an' who knows, they might even call up that ole goat Forbes.'

Mrs Collins shook her head slowly as the young redhead walked off. Jennie Flynn was incorrigible, but with a figure like that and her pretty face she needn't be tied to the likes of Jones and Whatleys.

On the fourth floor at the accessories section there was a minor crisis blowing up and Jennie walked right into it.

'Ah, Miss Flynn, just in time,' the effeminate salesman said, looking a little ruffled. 'The lady here wanted a grey crocodile-skin handbag and I'm afraid we're out of them at the moment.'

Jennie looked at the large woman dressed in green tweeds and immediately sensed trouble. She was a classic example of 'the predator', as the junior staff had named the breed of shopper who looked upon them as fair game. The woman was holding a grey crocodile-skin handbag under her arm and eyeing the young man with hostility.

'It's all right, Leon. I'll deal with it,' Jennie told him.

'Madam wants to change the bag for another of the same you see,' Leon went on.

'Yes all right, leave it to me,' Jennie said calmly.

'This handbag is defective,' the woman declared in a booming voice as she banged the item down on the glass counter.

'Let me take a look,' the young woman said, smiling as she pulled at the stitching.

'Inside. Look inside.'

When she opened the bag Jennie saw the split satin lining and noticed that it was stained.

'Could I ask what you have been carrying in this, madam?' she asked.

'Nothing. It was like that when I bought it,' the woman retorted in a louder voice.

'Madam, we always remove the paper packing from each handbag that we sell to check that the lining is in perfect condition,' Jennie told her.

'Are you calling me a liar, young woman?' the predator boomed out.

Jennie realised that she would have to change her tack. 'Could I see the receipt for the bag, please?' she asked.

'I haven't got it, but what if I had? You seem to be out of this type,' the woman said haughtily.

'If you have your receipt, then we can refund your money or order you a replacement.'

'Young woman, are you calling me a liar?'

'Certainly not, madam.'

'You seem to be implying so.'

'I'm sorry, but it's company policy,' Jennie tried to explain. 'Without a receipt showing that the bag was purchased here there's nothing I can do.'

'Now you listen to me,' the woman said menacingly. 'I've been shopping at Jones and Whatleys for many years and I've never encountered anything like this before. Go and fetch your superior at once. Do you hear me?'

Jennie took a deep breath to control her temper as it started to rise dangerously. Her job did not seem very important at that particular moment, and as for the old adage driven home daily to the staff that the customer was always right, it was all a load of hot air. 'Madam, it looks to me like you've been carrying a couple of housebricks in that bag by the state of the lining,' Jennie said in a measured tone of voice, 'but as you wish, I'll fetch the floor manager.'

The predator's eyes were bulging with disbelief at what had just been said to her and for a moment she was rendered speechless. Leon had been listening from behind a rack of scarves and, feeling sorry for Jennie, he had already hurried off to get the manager. On the way he bumped into the venerable Mr Forbes who was on one of his forays and decided to let him know what was taking place at the handbag counter.

'All right, Miss eh, Miss Flynn, I'll deal with this,' the senior buyer said in his superior manner. 'Would madam like to sit down first? Flynn, fetch madam a chair.'

'And where am I gonna get a chair from?' Jennie asked acidly, dropping her saleswoman's voice. 'If you fink I'm goin' all the way down ter the rest room yer've got anuvver fink comin'.'

'Miss Flynn,' Forbes almost screamed out. 'Do as you're told.'

'Get somebody else,' Jennie said spiritedly.

The awkward customer was beginning to attract the attention of other shoppers as she glared at the buyer. 'Look at this handbag. I purchased it here in this store, at this counter, only yesterday. The lining's damaged and stained.'

'I just told 'er she must 'ave bin carryin' bricks in it,' Jennie butted in.

'Go away, Miss Flynn,' Forbes told her, beginning to sweat profusely.

'I want that young woman sacked immediately. Do you hear me?' the virago snarled.

'You just leave that to me,' Forbes said, eyeing Jennie with venom. 'Now let us see. Have you the receipt?'

'I'm afraid I've mislaid it,' the woman told him.

'She's tryin' ter pull the oldest trick in the book an' you, yer silly git, are fallin' for it,' Jennie remarked, beginning to enjoy the confrontation now that she was certain to be sacked on the spot.

'Trick? What do you mean by trick?' the woman shouted.

'They buy imitation gear dead cheap at the markets an' then try ter say they bought the item at a West End store,' Jennie explained to Forbes. 'She 'ands in a bag werf four an' a tanner an' gets a three guinea bag as a replacement, if she's lucky, which she ain't this time. Shall I fetch the police?'

'Go away! Leave us!' the senior buyer screamed out.

'I'll fetch the police anyway,' Jennie said, giving the woman a piercing look.

Shoppers were standing around listening and many had smiles on their faces. The staff too had become aware of what was happening and they were watching the proceedings from vantage points throughout the fourth floor. A young soldier with his forage-cap shoved through his epaulette grinned at Jennie as she hurried by. 'Well done, luv,' he told her. 'You're a diamond.'

Once out of Forbes' view Jennie made a detour and worked her way round to the lift. The rest room was situated in the basement and when the young woman walked in still puffing from her exertions she was greeted with handclaps.

'What a gel,' the doorman said grinning.

'Well, if yer gotta go that's the way ter do it, out wiv yer 'ead up 'igh,' one of the elderly cleaners remarked.

Jennie had hardly sat down to catch her breath when Leon came hurrying in. 'Jennie, I thought I'd die when you stood up to that nasty woman,' he told her with feeling. 'I said to myself, Leon, she's just talked herself out of a job. I was trembling all over. I still can't stop shaking now. Look at me, I'm like a Hartley's jelly.'

Mrs Collins came in and sat down facing Jennie with a smile on her face. 'Well, you've finally done it, but I know it doesn't worry you. You'll make out, and perhaps that little episode, if you can call it that, might help blow some fresh air through the musty corridors of Jones and Whatleys.'

Mr Forbes had gone to lie down, fortified with a couple of Aspros, and the dire deed was left to the floor manager, who was strangely supportive when he came over to inform Jennie of her fate. At four o'clock that evening she left the store with her cards and a week's wages. The sun was still hot and the sky a clear blue, dotted with the silver barrage elephants. Khaki, navy-blue and airforce-blue uniforms contrasted with city suits and rolled umbrellas as Jennie strolled along Regent Street among the crowds. She felt elated, her step light and bouncy, and in a moment of euphoria she decided to go into Lyon's Corner House at Piccadilly Circus for a coffee. She had never been in the establishment before, and little did she know then that it was a decision she would look back on fondly for the rest of her life.

Chapter Six

On Saturday afternoon Daisy Harris collected her shoes from the menders and then called next door. Albert was serving a customer who seemed unsure about the torch bulb he was buying. 'It's a bit bright,' he remarked as Albert tested it on a battery.

'It's the one you'll want,' the shopowner told him. 'It'll be all right as long as you put tissue-paper over it.'

While Daisy waited she glanced around at the new wirelesses. Her old set was run from a large battery and grid bias and she had been getting on to Bill for ages now to fork out for one of those push-button sets. There was one on the top shelf which looked very smart.

'Afternoon, Mr Levy,' she said as the satisfied customer left the shop.

'Afternoon, Mrs Harris,' Albert said smiling. 'Not after a new wireless, are you?'

'As a matter o' fact I was lookin' at that push-button one yer got up there, but first fings first,' she replied. 'Me an' Bill 'ave bin cleanin' Abel's rooms out an' we found this.' She took the brown paper bundle from her large handbag. 'It was under the oil-cloth, well actually, under a loose floorboard.

We're changin' the oil-cloth yer see or we'd never 'ave found it.'

Albert took the small bundle from her and unwrapped it. 'A diary. Abel's diary,' he said excitedly, his dark eyes widening. 'That's very interesting.'

'Me an' Bill thought you should 'ave it, you bein' very close ter the poor man,' Daisy told him.

'I'm grateful to you for thinking of me,' Albert replied, flipping quickly through the pages. 'Abel wrote in Yiddish, as you probably noticed.'

'We never looked inside, Mr Levy,' Daisy said quickly. 'It wouldn't 'ave bin right. Diaries are very personal fings, as I told Bill. No, we wrapped it up again straight away.'

Albert laid it down reverently on the shelf behind him and turned back to Mrs Harris. 'I don't think Abel would mind very much if I read his notes, do you?'

'I'm sure 'e wouldn't,' Daisy replied.

'Now, Mrs Harris, about a new wireless. Let me show you this one. It's the latest Philips model and I could do you a reasonable discount.'

Daisy watched while Albert took the radio down from the top shelf and placed it in front of her. 'The case is made of strong Bakelite which wears very well,' he informed her as he quickly ran a duster over it. 'It's a mains set. You have got electricity in the house?'

Daisy nodded. 'Yeah, it was put in about five years ago.'

'Well then, this set also has a magic eye.'

'A magic eye?' Daisy echoed, looking confused.

'Let me show you,' Albert said, plugging the set into a power-point. 'There we are. Now when you find a station you watch that green light and when the two lights go into one that means that it's fine-tuned. In other words the reception will be nice and clear. There we are, can you see?'

'That's very clever,' Daisy remarked, stroking her chin.

'Now here's another feature,' Albert went on. 'These push buttons here. You get certain stations by just pressing them in, like so.'

'Well, I never did,' Daisy said, by now sold on the new radio.

'This new model is priced at twenty-two guineas, but I can knock two guineas off for you. How does that sound?'

'Do you do it on the book?' Daisy asked.

Albert nodded and made a few quick calculations. 'Let me see,' he said. 'If you can pay one pound seventeen and six down it'll work out at eighteen and a tanner per month over two years, that's with the interest as well. If you decide to buy the set on instalments your husband would need to sign the agreement.'

Daisy left the shop promising to fetch Bill straight away, and although he was alone once more Albert resisted the temptation to look inside Abel's diary. It would be better to wait until later, he told himself. It was something better broached in the quiet of evening with a large brandy at hand.

When Jennie walked into the Lyon's Corner House she saw it was fairly packed, but she managed to find a small table near the window and sat down to wait for the waitress to take her order. It had been a crazy day all in all, she thought, but the feeling of freedom, of having to plan what to do next was exciting and she smiled to herself. Suddenly she realised that a young soldier sitting alone a few tables away was eyeing her with amusement. She gave him a cold look and turned away to stare out of the window. After a moment or two she sensed someone next to her and turned to see him standing by her table. 'I'm sorry to disturb yer,' he said quickly, 'but I 'ad to admire the way yer dealt wiv that ugly ole witch this afternoon. I thought you 'andled it really well.'

'You were there?' Jennie asked in surprise.

'Yeah, I saw yer storm off an' I called out well done, or words ter that effect,' the soldier said grinning.

She grinned back at him. 'That's right, I remember catchin' a glimpse of yer.'

'I was in Jones an' Whatleys ter buy a present but I never got it,' he told her. 'By the way, I don't wanna interrupt yer if yer meetin' anyone.'

Jennie shook her head. 'No, I'm takin' a break before I catch the bus 'ome,' she replied. 'Sit down if yer like, unless you're meetin' someone.'

He shook his head as he sat down facing her. 'Fanks. I was beginnin' ter feel conspicuous on me own.'

'Yeah, I don't like comin' in these sort o' places on me own eivver,' Jennie agreed.

He smiled showing strong white teeth, and his eyes were laughing. 'I 'ope they didn't give yer the sack.'

'Jones an' Whatleys couldn't do anyfing else,' she replied mockingly, 'but I consider meself well out of it.'

'Well, I'm glad I didn't get that present there now,' he remarked. 'By the way, I'm Con, Con Williams, currently Private Williams of the Rifle Brigade.'

'Jennie Flynn, currently unemployed,' she responded with a smile.

'Really it's Conrad, but everybody calls me Con,' the young soldier told her. 'Gawd knows 'ow I ever got 'iked up wiv that moniker. Me dad must 'ave bin drunk at the time.'

'It's an unusual name but a nice one, though I prefer Con,' Jennie replied.

A tired-looking waitress came over and stood staring at them, and Con looked enquiringly at Jennie. 'I just wanted a coffee,' he said.

'Yeah, me too,' she answered.

'Two coffees it is then.'

As Con watched the waitress hurrying away Jennie looked at him. He couldn't be much more than twenty-two or three, she guessed. He had a smooth face with no sign of stubble and his fair hair was cut short. His nose was small and straight and he had a strong, square chin. His eyes were his most striking feature though, Jennie thought. They were a very pale blue, almost grey, and they shone kindly.

'Who were you buyin' the present for?' she asked as he turned to face her again.

Con's face grew sad. 'As a matter o' fact I was after gettin' a silk scarf fer me Gran. I live wiv 'er or I did, till I got mobilised.'

'Mobilised?'

'Yeah, I was in the territorials, an' as soon as the war started they called us inter the colours,' he explained. 'Most of my lot 'ave gone ter France already but I got delayed 'cos I 'ad ter take compassionate leave when me gran got ill wiv pleurisy. She's over it now but she's very miserable. I was gonna get 'er a scarf. It might 'elp cheer 'er up a bit.'

Jennie felt a sudden warmth towards the young man and she nodded in agreement. 'Your gran's a lucky woman to 'ave someone like you ter take care of 'er.'

Con looked out of the window for a few moments and

when their eyes met again she could see that he was still upset by it. 'She's looked after me since I was knee-'igh to a grass'opper,' he said quietly. 'My mum died when I was five an' me dad was in the merchant navy. I 'ardly knew 'im. 'E married again apparently an' last I 'eard 'e was livin' in Glasgow.'

''Ave yer got any bruvvers or sisters?' Jennie asked.

'There was a bruvver two years younger than me but 'e died o' diphtheria when 'e was two,' Con replied.

The waitress came over with a laden tray and Con quickly picked up the bill and slipped it into his tunic pocket. 'Wanna be mum?' he said grinning.

Jennie filled the two cups from the squat coffee pot and passed one across the table. 'Where d'yer live, Con?' she asked.

'Dock'ead.'

'I live in Bermon'sey,' she told him. 'Carter Lane, off the Old Kent Road.'

'That's not far from me, is it?' he replied.

'Only a stone's throw.'

''Ave you got a family?'

'Three bruvvers, one sister.'

'That's nice.'

'Me mum an' dad are really worried,' Jennie went on as she poured milk into the hot coffee. 'Me bruvs are all waitin' ter go in. They all volunteered soon as the war started.'

'The army?'

'Frank an' Jim the eldest two are goin' in the army but Patrick, the baby o' the family, signed on fer the RAF. 'E's dead set on bein' aircrew.'

'I'd sooner 'im than me,' Con replied as he ladled two

80

large spoonfuls of sugar into his cup.

'So yer still gotta buy a present,' Jennie said sipping her coffee.

'I dunno if a scarf's the right fing ter get, now I come ter fink of it,' he said sighing. 'What can yer buy fer an ole lady who never 'ardly goes out?'

'Does she take snuff?' Jennie said helpfully but Con shook his head. 'What about slippers? Carpet slippers?'

'I don't know 'er size,' the young soldier replied.

'Well, what about a nice shawl? A bright colour might 'elp ter cheer 'er up a bit.'

Con's eyes lit up. 'Of course. A shawl. She wears a shawl all the time an' it's really tatty.'

'Don't get it over 'ere though, yer'd pay frew the nose,' Jennie advised him. 'There's some good ones at the markets. East Street's the best, on Sundays.'

'I'd 'ave time,' Con said nodding. ''Er birfday's not till next Tuesday an' I don't go back until Monday mornin'.'

Jennie finished her coffee and glanced up at the clock. 'Well, I'd better be goin' or me mum's gonna be worried where I've got to,' she told him reluctantly.

Con nodded. 'Yeah me too, or Gran's gonna get all worried. There's me a fightin' soldier an' she's worried in case I get knocked down or somefing, would yer believe?'

Jennie laughed. 'It's bin really nice talkin' to yer,' she remarked.

'Yeah, it's bin really good,' he said. 'I 'ope yer boyfriend doesn't get to 'ear about it.'

She shook her head. 'No, I'm not courtin' at the moment.'

'Could I . . .' Con hesitated for a second or two. 'Could I ask yer somefing?'

'Yeah, sure.'

'Would yer like ter come fer a drink termorrer night?'

'Yes, I'd like that very much,' she told him with a smile.

His eyes flashed happily. 'Where shall we meet?'

'You could call round if yer like.'

'Yeah, I'd like to.'

'Number eleven Carter Lane.'

'Is eight o'clock okay?'

'That'll be fine,' she replied.

Con counted out some silver and put the coins on the small silver tray at his elbow, adding a shilling tip, and then as they stood up he chuckled. 'I fink we're goin' the same way 'ome, ain't we?'

Jennie nodded and gave him a quick shy smile as they walked out into the busy street. 'I usually get a fifty-three bus ter the Old Kent Road,' she told him.

'Yeah, I could do that an' change at the Bricklayers Arms,' he replied.

A large queue had formed at the bus stop but two buses came along together and they managed to get on the second one. They found a seat on the upper deck at the rear and chatted casually as the vehicle crawled through the heavy rush-hour traffic. All too soon it seemed the bus pulled up at the Bricklayers Arms, and as Con slipped out of his seat he laid his hand on her arm. 'I promise not ter be late,' he said with a grin, then he was gone.

Much later that evening Albert Levy took advantage of Gerda's trip to the women's meeting at the local synagogue by pouring himself a very large brandy. Gerda would have been horrified, he thought with a smile. She felt that brandy speeded up the heart rate too much and preferred him to confine his intake to a tiny glass with coffee after an evening meal. But this one he sorely needed. The diary was lying on the small table beside the divan as though mocking him, daring him to open it and peer into the very soul of his old friend Abel Finkelstein. Taking a deep breath, Albert settled himself and picked it up, certain that his heart was not beating faster because of the brandy.

At ten o'clock Gerda came home and sighed sadly as she sat down alongside Albert on the large divan. 'It was very depressing and it's left me with a splitting headache,' she told him. 'We were discussing the possibility of forming a group to try to help the Jewish people in the occupied countries and Germany itself, but it seems there's very little we can do except try to work with the Red Cross.'

Albert grunted a reply and Gerda kicked off her shoes. 'I need something for this headache,' she said, preparing to get up.

Albert grunted again and Gerda gave him a hard look. 'Normally you get me some tablets,' she complained.

'I'm sorry, dear, I was miles away,' he said quickly as he stood up. 'I'll get them for you, you just relax and put your feet up.'

When he came back with the medication Gerda noticed the worried look on his face. 'Is there anything wrong?' she asked. 'You don't look yourself.'

Albert sat down heavily and waited until his wife had swallowed the tablets. 'How long were Abel and I friends?' he asked her. 'Ten years? Fifteen years? No, we were friends from the first day at school, when we held each other's hand, friends until the day Abel took his life. A lifetime of friendship, true and steadfast throughout all the persecution, a friendship that would last beyond the grave, or so I believed.'

'Albert. What is it?' Gerda asked, beginning to feel frightened.

'It's all there. There in the diary that Abel left behind,' he replied. 'I just can't believe it. After all I did to obtain his release from that concentration camp, and the problems I faced in getting him over here, and to find out after his death that it counted for nothing.'

'Albert, please. Whatever's wrong?'

'Wrong? I'll tell you what's wrong,' Albert replied with his eyes flaring and his breath coming fast. 'My good, old friend of a lifetime, Abel Finkelstein, has been unburdening himself in his diary.'

Gerda slumped down in the divan. 'The diary?'

'The diary,' he repeated. 'It's all there, plain and simple. Abel has betrayed our friendship.'

'Where is it?' Gerda asked.

'It's in my desk drawer.'

'I want to see it.'

'Not tonight,' he said firmly. 'Tomorrow we'll look at it together and you'll see. Then it will be time for a decision. Do we go ahead with the memorial plaque? I don't see how we can. It would be sacrilege.'

'What was so terrible to make you talk like this?' she asked him. 'What has he said?'

'It's what he has done,' Albert said bitterly. 'Abel has been robbing me. Systematically robbing me. For years!'

Chapter Seven

Sara and Tom Jackman were a genial couple who worked long hours in their grocery shop on the corner of Carter Lane. Tom had taken over the business from his father more than fifteen years before when it got too much for the old man to manage. He was forty years old then and still single, but six months later he married a widow Sara Viney, the daughter of a local market trader, and people immediately started to talk. Many felt that Sara was marrying Tom for his money and believed the shop would fail with her working behind the counter of the old family concern. What they didn't know was that the shop was failing anyway and that Tom had inherited a lot of debt.

Sara proved everybody wrong and it was largely due to her shrewd management that the shop was finally transformed into a little goldmine. She worked very hard to win over the locals and from grudging admiration they came to genuinely like her.

Now in their mid-fifties the Jackmans were working harder than ever, what with food rationing and customer registration. Almost everyone in Carter Lane and the adjoining Brady Street and Munday Road registered at the corner shop and there was hardly a time when there wasn't a queue waiting to get served. It was only natural for people to chat while they queued, and it was at the corner store that the locals picked up all the latest gossip. Tom Jackman shut his ears to most of the chatter but Sara was inclined to store the juicy titbits in her head and pass them on to a select few whenever she could. There was no malice intended on her part, only a sense of being neighbourly and communicative towards her loyal customers.

Bill Harris knew all that was going on in the immediate area from listening to Daisy and he had dubbed the store 'The Ministry of Information'. He was always prepared for some bit of news whenever his wife came in with the groceries and normally it went in one ear and out the other. He ignored his wife's lengthy account of Mrs Bromilow's heartbreak at being forced to leave the leather factory and he didn't even raise his eyes from the paper when he heard about Alice Smithson's daughter leaving home, but he did show some interest when Daisy told him about the Conroys' boy. Ted Conroy was a drinking pal and many a time Bill had lent a supportive ear to his family problems, which mostly concerned Ted's son Alec.

'Rene Conroy's worried out of 'er life,' Daisy began. 'She said Alec's told 'er an' Ted that 'e's definitely not goin' in the forces an' if they want 'im they'll 'ave ter come an' get 'im.'

'That's exactly what they will do, make no mistake,' Bill told her.

'Rene said Alec's goin' on twenty-four an' 'e'll be in the first batch ter get called up,' Daisy went on. 'It's a bloody shame what 'er an' Ted 'ave 'ad ter put up wiv. Alec's never bin any good. 'E was in Borstal at twelve years old an' then 'e got two years fer that trouble over in Dock'ead. Sara said they might not take 'im, what wiv 'is prison record an' all.'

'They'll take 'im right enough, don't you worry about that,' Bill said firmly. 'If 'e refuses ter go they'll send a military escort, an' if 'e don't knuckle down to it they'll stick 'im in an army detention centre, an' then 'e'll know all about it. They're not as soft as civvy prisons, not by a long chalk.'

'Sara was sayin' about the shame Alec was bringin' down on Rene an' Ted,' Daisy continued. 'Rene said she wouldn't be able to 'old 'er 'ead up in the street, what wiv everyone else's sons goin' in the forces.'

'Well, it ain't 'er an' Ted's fault, not the way I see it,' Bill commented. 'They've tried ter do their best fer the boy but 'e's just a bad apple.'

Daisy had some more intriguing snippets for Bill but he'd heard enough for one day and he gave her one of his special looks which told her it was time to shut up and put the kettle on.

Albert Levy sat alongside Gerda in their comfortable living room and shook his head slowly as she read out the entry for the second of January in Abel's diary.

'An encouraging start to the year. Fifteen shillings is not much, but trade has been very slack since the Christmas break so I have to be careful. It's best that I carry on the way I left off last year.'

'Look at the end of January,' Albert told her. 'No, turn over again. Just there, look.'

'One pound seven and sixpence this week. Things are beginning to look up. Must still be on my guard though.'

Gerda glanced up and saw the sad look in her husband's dark eyes. 'It seems hard to believe,' she sighed. 'After all you did for the man.'

Albert took the diary from her and flipped the pages. 'Every week without fail,' he said. 'Look at this entry here. March the fifth.'

'It was a little distressing to hear Albert talk about that new automatic till on the market. If he does get one of them it'll make things very difficult. Apparently every transaction is recorded. He'll know his daily takings to the last penny.'

'I should have got one of those new tills,' Albert growled. 'That would have stopped his little game.'

Gerda took the diary back from Albert and turned some more pages. 'I'm not so sure about that, if you read this bit,' she pointed out.

'Albert's been going on again about the new till. Still never mind, there's more than one way to skin a cat, as they say. Customers don't always notice what's being rung up and if they did query the price it could always be put right. Have to be careful of the stocks though. Albert knows his stock. Very rarely runs out of anything.'

'According to that he's been filching my stocks too,' Albert

groaned. 'But I've never noticed any unaccountable shortages in the shop.'

'Well, I'm sure I don't know,' Gerda replied. 'I just find it
so hard to believe.'

'It's all there in black and white,' Albert told her. 'I've
totalled it all up until the last entry at the end of August. It
comes to almost forty pounds. Then there's the previous
years, or at least one year that he referred to. God knows
how much he's taken me for.'

Gerda got up and went over to the sideboard where she
poured her distraught husband a large brandy. Normally it
would have been a very small tot, but tonight he looked like
he needed more.

Jennie Flynn sat on the edge of Sadie's bed while her elder
sister rummaged through her wardrobe. 'What's the name o'
the club?' she asked her.

'The Black Cat,' Sadie replied. 'It's a big do ternight an'
Len wants me ter look me best.'

'Oh 'e does, does 'e,' Jennie said scornfully. 'Is that what
'e said? Well, I fink 'e's got a bloody cheek. You always look
yer best when yer go out.'

''E didn't mean nuffink by it,' Sadie was quick to point
out. 'There's a lot of important people comin' ternight an'
Len wants me ter circulate around. You know the fing, keep
'em topped up wiv drinks an' make small talk.'

'Who are these important people?' Jennie asked her.

Sadie hung the black dress she had picked out on the door
of the wardrobe and sat down on the dressing-table stool.
'They're mainly business people wiv money ter burn,' she
explained. 'Some are down 'ere from Glasgow an' Liverpool

an' it's all about puttin' money in the venture.'

'The Black Cat?' Jennie queried.

'Yeah. Johnnie Macaulay's turnin' it into a gamblin' club,' Sadie went on. 'Trouble is 'e can't get a gamblin' licence so it's all cloak an' dagger stuff.'

''Ow excitin',' Jennie said with sarcasm.

'You don't like Len Regan, do yer?' Sadie remarked, her eyes narrowing slightly.

Jennie shrugged her shoulders. 'I've only seen 'im a couple o' times when 'e's called round, but I worry fer you,' she said earnestly. 'It all seems like the roarin' twenties films ter me. Gamblin', nightclubs, an' Regan doin' the biddin' of the big man Macaulay who seems ter be runnin' everyfing round 'ere. The impression I get is that Macaulay's nuffink more than a gangster an' you're bein' drawn inter that way o' life by 'is messenger boy Len Regan.'

'Len's not a messenger boy, 'e's Johnnie Macaulay's manager, an' 'e's got respect round 'ere,' Sadie replied defensively.

Jennie stood up and went over to her elder sister. 'We've always bin close, Sadie, an' I'm concerned for yer,' she said, resting her hand on her shoulder. 'I don't want ter see yer get 'urt.'

Sadie stood up and gave her a quick squeeze. 'Don't worry, sis, I can look after meself. I'm a Flynn don't ferget.'

Jennie smiled and turned to view herself in the full-length mirror on the wardrobe door. 'D'yer fink I'm puttin' on weight?' she asked.

Sadie chuckled as she appraised her sister's trim figure and small firm breasts. She was at least half a stone heavier with large breasts and a more rounded figure. 'I wish I looked like you,' she remarked.

'Funny, I always wish I looked like you,' Jennie told her. 'Me breasts are too small. You've got nice curves an' yer legs look really shapely, 'specially in yer 'igh 'eels.'

'So do yours.'

'D'yer really fink so?'

'I wouldn't tell yer if it wasn't true.'

'D'yer like the way I've done me 'air?' Jennie asked.

Sadie nodded. 'I like it short, 'specially the way yer got it set round yer ears. Redheads can get away wiv short 'air.'

'Yours looks very nice too,' Jennie replied, admiring the black dress as she stroked the fabric.

'I'm lettin' it grow a bit,' Sadie told her. 'I want it shoulder-length, then I'm gonna get one o' those wavy perms.'

'Yer'll really be a roarin' twenties gel then,' Jennie said grinning. 'I 'ope you can do the Charleston.'

Sadie smiled and went over to the wardrobe again. 'I dunno about this dress. D'yer fink this one looks better fer a special occasion?'

Jennie pinched her lip as she looked at the silver-grey dress Sadie was holding up. 'Yeah, I like that one better,' she remarked. 'I like the way it's cut at the front.'

'Right then, I'll wear it,' Sadie decided. 'You can borrer the black one ternight if yer like. It'll fit yer. I 'ave ter squeeze into it anyway.'

Jennie shook her head. 'I'm only goin' ter the pub fer a drink,' she replied. 'I don't wanna shock 'im wiv that low front.'

Sadie sat down at the dressing table and picked up a nail file. 'What's this Con Williams like? Is 'e good-lookin'?'

Jennie nodded. 'I fink so. 'E's a bit taller than me an' 'e's stocky like our Frank. 'E's got a nice smile an' 'e's ever so friendly. Yer'll be able ter take a gander when 'e calls, that's if yer still 'ere.'

'What time's 'e callin' for yer?' Sadie asked.

'Eight o'clock.'

'That's all right. Len's pickin' me up at nine.'

'An' no oglin' 'im,' Jennie warned with a smile.

'As if I would,' Sadie replied with a sly look.

Jennie sat on the edge of the bed for a while, watching Sadie manicure her fingernails, and then she got up to look down into the quiet evening street below. 'It seems 'ard ter realise there's a war on,' she remarked.

Sadie nodded. 'I feel the same way when I'm out wiv Len. The places we go to are full o' people gettin' drunk an' chuckin' their money about. There's not a uniform in sight an' no one ever mentions the war.'

'It's all gonna blow up soon, I feel certain,' Jennie said quietly. 'People are gonna 'ave ter take notice then.'

'D'yer reckon we'll get bombed?' Sadie asked.

'I'm sure of it,' Jennie replied.

'Yeah, I fink so too,' Sadie said, studying her nails.

'By the way, 'as Len said any more about that job 'e was gonna try an' get yer?'

Sadie shook her head. ''E's bin so busy lately, but 'e won't ferget.'

'Long as it's not workin' in one o' those clubs of Macaulay's,' Jennie said. 'Still that wouldn't be classed as essential war-work, would it? Or would it? Comforts fer the troops.'

'Officers more like,' Sadie corrected her.

Jennie looked out again through the crisp net curtaining. 'There's Alec Conroy goin' past,' she said. 'Did you 'ear what Mum was sayin' about 'im?'

Sadie nodded. 'Not many round 'ere 'ave anyfing good ter say about 'im but I don't fink 'e's as bad as 'e's painted out ter be. All right, I know 'e's bin ter Borstal an' done time in prison, but 'e's kept out o' trouble fer some time now an' 'e's got a regular job.'

'The trouble is 'e ain't gonna endear 'imself ter people if 'e refuses call-up,' Jennie remarked.

'I s'pose there'll be a few white feavvers bein' sent frew the post before long,' Sadie said. 'Dad was tellin' me it was common in the Great War. They even sent 'em to people who weren't fit ter go in the army. If it 'appens again, I expect Len'll get one.'

'Will 'e be liable fer call-up?' Jennie asked.

'Well 'e's firty-five now so 'e's got a bit o' time yet,' Sadie replied. 'I fink it all depends on 'ow long the war lasts. If all 'ell breaks loose an' there's a lot o' casualties then they'll call up older men.'

'All this talk's beginnin' ter get me depressed,' Jennie groaned. 'Tell me somefing nice.'

Sadie chuckled at her childish expression. 'Get out of 'ere an' let me finish gettin' ready,' she said, pointing to the door.

Jennie was loath to move. 'Why? Yer've got till nine.'

'Shouldn't you be gettin' ready?' Sadie pressed.

'It's only twenty past seven,' her younger sister replied. 'I've only gotta slip inter somefing allurin'.'

''Ere, you watch yerself,' Sadie said, getting up from her stool. 'Now leave me alone an' go an' worry yer bruvs.'

As soon as she was alone Sadie sat down again at the

dressing table and stared at her image in the mirror. There was no chance of ever getting married as long as she was with Len, and lately it seemed to be hard work keeping his attention when they were socialising. He always had things to do, people to take care of and negotiations to be undertaken. Len's life wasn't his own, he was at the beck and call of Johnnie Macaulay twenty-four hours a day. At the moment everything was going well, but it could all change and the loyalty and dedication shown by Len would count for nothing if a scapegoat was needed. Donna Walsh had said as much when they were talking together not so long ago. Donna had been close to Len at one time and it was rumoured that they had been lovers. It mattered very little to Sadie. It was before her time and now Donna Walsh was bloated with drink and pushing forty. She worked as a barmaid in one of Macaulay's pubs, the Royal George in Rotherhithe, and whenever Len took Sadie there Donna made a point of waylaying her for a chat. Donna truly felt that Johnnie Macaulay was overstretching himself and the day would come when it would all blow up in his face.

Much as she wanted to discount Donna's predictions Sadie felt obliged to listen at least. Donna had the ear of many of the local villains and in her view it was not all sweetness and light within the Macaulay empire.

Chapter Eight

Con Williams felt a little awkward, fiddling with the knot of his striped tie while he waited on the doorstep of number 11, and when Dolly answered his knock he gave her a shy smile. 'I er, I . . .'

'You must be Con,' Dolly said cheerily. 'Jennie'll be down in a minute. Won't yer come in?'

The young man followed her into the parlour. 'It's a warm evenin',' he said as he returned Mick's nod.

'Take a pew, son,' the older man bade him as Dolly went to the foot of the stairs and called up to Jennie. 'Yer in the army then?'

'Yeah, the Rifle Brigade.'

Mick nodded. 'That's an old East End regiment. Are you from over the water?'

'No, I was in the territorials at the Dock'ead depot an' they mobilised us inter the Rifle Brigade,' Con told him.

Mick nodded. 'Jennie tells me yer goin' back termorrer an' you expect ter go off ter France very soon.'

'It's pretty certain,' the young man replied. 'We're gonna be part o' the British Expeditionary Force.'

'Well good luck ter yer, son,' Mick said as Jennie came bounding into the parlour.

'I 'ope yer've not bin grilled about the army,' she said smiling.

'It's a good job our lads are out or 'e would 'ave bin,' Mick said, turning back to Con. 'Me sons are waitin' fer their call-up, did she tell yer?'

'Yes, I did,' Jennie remarked. 'I'm ready, Con, shall we go?'

'Don't be too late,' Mick called out as she led the way out into the passage.

Jennie raised her eyes in mock horror. 'Don't they make yer sick,' she groaned. 'It's the weekend, fer God's sake.'

They walked out of the turning in the balmy evening and Con smiled at her. 'I was finkin' we could try The Boatman down by the river,' he said. 'It's pretty lively at weekends.'

'Why not?' Jennie replied lightly.

As they walked over the railway bridge towards Jamaica Road the young man turned to her. 'It's a bit of a walk. We could get a bus.'

'No, let's walk, it's a lovely evenin',' she replied. 'Can I take yer arm?'

Con's face lit up. 'Yeah, course. I wanted yer to.'

After a short distance she asked, 'Did yer manage ter get that shawl fer yer gran?'

He pulled a face. 'I fink I got the wrong colour,' he told her. 'She always wears black fings so I decided ter get 'er a nice bright one fer a change. Anyway I saw this green shawl on a stall at East Street so I took a chance. When I got 'ome I wrapped it up in some fancy paper ter put by 'er bed before I leave termorrer, but then I got finkin' – s'posin' she doesn't like the colour – so I gave it to 'er straight away.'

'An' did she say she liked it?'

'Oh yeah, but the look on 'er face gave 'er away.'

'She'll get used to it, I'm sure,' Jennie said, taken by the young man's thoughtfulness.

They crossed Jamaica Road and ambled on towards the river, breathing in the sour smell of mud and the pungent tang of spice and pepper seeping from the creaky old warehouses in Shad Thames.

''Ave yer decided what yer gonna do next?' Con asked.

Jennie shook her head. 'I might get some shop work fer the time bein',' she told him. 'There's a job goin' in the local baker's.'

They could hear piano music coming from the pub up ahead and Con smiled. 'They've started early by the sound of it.'

As they walked into the saloon bar Jennie looked around at the pewter pots and pans hanging from the tarred rafters and saw the old prints arranged along the walls. 'This is nice,' she remarked.

Con nodded towards the elderly woman pianist as they reached the counter. 'That's Sal Terry,' he said quietly. 'She used ter be on the stage.'

He ordered a pint of bitter for himself but Jennie only wanted a shandy, and after they had been served their drinks by an uninterested barman they found a vacant table in a dimly lit alcove. Old men sat around on the long padded bench by the wall, one or two with clay pipes hanging from their mouths, and younger customers lounged at the counter or sat in the other alcoves by windows.

'I like these old riverside pubs,' Jennie grinned.

Con looked at her, his eyes appraising her pretty face and shining red hair. 'Do you really?' he replied. 'I was wonderin' if it might be too scruffy for yer.'

She laughed, her white teeth flashing in the low light of the alcove. 'I always reckon it's not where you are but who you're wiv that counts,' she said with emphasis.

'I wish I 'ad more time ter get ter know yer,' he said, running the tip of his forefinger round the rim of his glass. 'I loved the way yer dealt wiv that woman in the store an' I wanted ter tell yer there an' then, but when yer marched off I thought, well Con, yer missed yer chance there, didn't yer? Seein' you again in that Lyon's corner 'ouse was like fate. It gave me anuvver chance ter make yer acquaintance, an' I wasn't gonna pass it up.'

'I'm glad yer didn't,' Jennie said quietly.

'Can I ask yer somefing?'

'Yeah, course.'

''Ave yer got any photos of yerself?'

'One or two, but not wiv me,' she replied.

He thought for a moment. 'Would it be askin' too much fer you ter give me a photo?'

She chuckled. 'You really want a picture o' me?'

'I really do.'

'I could send one on, I s'pose.'

He smiled happily. 'If you address it ter Rifleman C. Williams, Second Battalion, Rifle Brigade, BEF France it'll reach me. By the way, yer'll need me army number. I don't s'pose yer've got a pen, 'ave yer?'

She shook her head, then fished into her small handbag. 'Right, pay packet, lipstick,' she said triumphantly. 'Tell me your army number.'

Con rattled it off, shaking his head at her improvisation. 'You amaze me,' he said.

'Why?'

'Yer just do.'

Jennie was pleased with the compliment and she relaxed a little in her seat. He was nice to be with, and unlike some of the other young men she had dated he appeared to be more interested in her than in himself. ''Ave yer dated many girls?' she asked suddenly.

The question caused him to flush up a little and he shook his head. 'Not many,' he admitted. 'I seem to 'ave spent more time in men's company this last two years.'

'What made yer join the territorials?' she enquired.

Con studied his clasped hands for a few moments as he thought about how to explain properly. 'I'm not sure,' he began, 'an' I'm not avoidin' the question, but it's difficult ter put into words. Every night when I came 'ome from work the 'ouse was quiet. The ole lady was usually noddin' in the armchair an' the place seemed dark an' gloomy. There was little or no conversation, an' I gradually felt like I was losin' somefing. It wasn't like a family 'ouse where there's noise an' laughter, an' bruvvers an' sisters ter chat wiv. I used ter make us a meal an' clear the place up a bit, then I'd sit wiv 'er, listenin' while she talked about when she was a young woman an' all about the 'ard life she 'ad, an' slowly I got more an' more depressed. I was beginnin' ter feel like an ole man meself. Can you understand?'

She nodded. 'I fink I can.'

'A pal at work told me 'e'd joined the terriers,' Con went on. ''E told me all about the good time 'e was 'avin' an' I thought, that's fer me. So I signed on. I went ter the drill 'all two nights a week an' then there was the odd weekend camp. I was wiv ovver people my age an' it lifted me more than I can tell yer. It wasn't as though I was neglectin' me gran. I still took care of 'er an' there was the woman next door who I paid ter look after 'er personal needs. Course I didn't realise at the time that I'd be mobilised, well not at first, but I guessed it'd come, if fings did deteriorate. Now I'm in the regular army, but nuffink's changed. The woman next door still looks after me gran an' there's the welfare people who come ter see 'er every so often.'

Jennie had been staring into his pale blue eyes all the time he was talking and she was suddenly assailed by a strange sadness that seemed to flow through her. There was something there in the young man's eyes that burned like a beacon and it melted her heart. She heard the singer, the tinkling piano and the clatter of glasses but it seemed far away, a vague cacophony of sounds muted behind glass. It felt as if time was standing still, and she shivered to break the spell. 'Yer gran'll be all right,' she said, but the words sounded flat and cold, and she quickly added, 'I'm sure it was the right move back then, even though yer've bin mobilised. If you 'adn't joined the terriers you'd 'ave bin called up anyway sooner or later.'

He nodded, and suddenly he reached out his hand and gently touched hers. 'I'll be finkin' about yer all the time I'm away,' he said in a quiet voice. 'Will yer give me a thought now an' then?'

'Yes, I will,' Jennie replied with a smile.

The young man collected the two glasses and walked over to the counter and Jennie quickly straightened her dress before searching her handbag for her powder compact. The evening was going well, better than she had expected and there were so many more questions she wanted to ask him.

When he returned to the alcove and set the drinks down on the polished table he smiled at her. 'This one's on the 'ouse. Sammy the landlord knows I'm goin' back off leave termorrer.'

'That's nice of 'im,' she replied.

Con nodded. 'This is where I bring me gran sometimes, when she's feelin' able. She likes a milk stout. Ses it bucks 'er up.'

Jennie could see him now, holding on to the old lady, fussing over her and getting her comfortable in a seat and she smiled back at him. 'I fink your gran's very lucky to 'ave you look after 'er needs,' she told him.

'It's no more than she deserves,' he replied. 'She looked after me when I was a kid, when there was no one else. If it wasn't fer 'er I'd 'ave ended up in some children's 'ome.'

'You're a nice man, Con,' she said.

He flushed slightly, two spots showing on his pale cheeks and he averted his eyes for a few moments. 'I fink you're very nice too,' he said.

Sal Terry had been suitably fortified with her usual concoction and she pounded the keys with determination. People were singing loudly, and when Sal struck up with 'Knees up Mother Brown', two elderly ladies decided to demonstrate their dancing skills. Jennie and Con were forced to raise their voices over the din as they chatted happily, and in no time at all the bell sounded for last orders.

'I've really enjoyed this evenin',' Jennie said as they left the little riverside pub.

'I can't remember a better one,' Con replied.

'Can we go an' look at the river fer a while?' she asked.

A full moon hung in the velvet sky like an everlasting lantern and stars glimmered at the periphery of its pale glow. The dark river was at low tide, still and calm before its cold, muddy waters flowed back in again. From their vantage point at the river wall the young people could see Tower Bridge framed against the blacked-out City of London, and downriver a brace of barges rocked gently on their moorings in midstream, before the darkness deepened towards Galleon's Reach. The two held hands as they gazed out at the scene, sensing the fragility of this moment in time for their hometown, their homeland, and with a subtle movement Con turned to face her. Like gentle magnets their bodies slowly joined together and their lips met in the tenderest of kisses. Her sweet breath excited him and he pulled her closer and tighter, and feeling the controlled strength of his arms and the flat pressure of his hands on her back she let the hungry embrace possess her.

Con glanced up at the moon for a brief second or two as they moved apart and his handsome face was smiling. 'It was 'is fault,' he said. 'Just look at 'im grinnin'.'

As Jennie looked up into the night sky she saw the dusty cloud moving across the white face like a stage curtain at the end of a scene. 'Who d'yer blame on moonless nights?' she said smiling.

'The first star.'

'Can we do it again?' she asked, surprised at her own daring.

He pulled her gently to him and very slowly touched her lips with his. He could feel her warmth and the sweet taste of her, and he encircled her waist with his arms as the kiss grew in passion. He relished the sensation of her hands on his neck, her body pressed unashamedly to him and he knew then that he was holding the woman of his dreams.

As heavy cloud moved in, the blackness of a capital at war deepened around them, and now only the sour smell of river mud told them where they were. They finally set off, along the cobbled lane that led into Dockhead, and neither spoke as they enjoyed a silent reverie of their moonlight embrace.

Carter Lane was empty and quiet, and the two young people lingered for some time at Jennie's front door.

'Will you write to me?' he asked.

'Every day,' she said.

'Will you send me that photo?'

'The best one I can find.'

'Will yer fink of me sometimes?'

'All the time.'

It was time to say goodnight and they embraced, a soft, gentle kiss tingling with an electric emotion, then Con stepped back to look at her, to brand the image of her into his mind, and he took her by the hands. 'Do you believe in God?' he asked.

'I say my prayers every night,' she told him.

'Pray fer me, Jennie, an' I'll pray fer us,' he said.

They kissed again, briefly, then she waited at the door until his footsteps faded in the blackness, and that night, as she lay sleepless in her bed, Jennie marvelled at the way the evening had gone. She hardly knew him. It was a first date that she would have expected to end with a nervous peck that had to suffice for a goodnight kiss. But they had kissed as lovers, talked together intimately and discovered a bond that would span the distance between them, binding them together until the day when they could once again walk hand in hand by the river and challenge the mocking moon.

Chapter Nine

Early on Thursday morning the postman pushed two letters through the letterbox of number 11, and as Dolly Flynn picked them up her heart sank. The letters OHMS told her the worst and she put them on the parlour table. The kettle was singing loudly and the toast had started to char by the time she pulled herself together. It had to happen soon, she thought as she spooned tea leaves into the large enamel teapot.

'Was that the postman, Ma?' Frank asked a few minutes later as he came into the parlour yawning widely.

Dolly nodded towards the table. 'There's one fer you an' one fer Jim,' she said, trying to appear casual.

Frank tore his open. 'It's the Rifle Brigade,' he said. 'I gotta report ter Winchester next Thursday.'

Jim came into the parlour and looked at his older brother. 'Rifle Brigade, did yer say?'

'Yeah. There's one fer you there.'

Jim quickly tore the envelope open. 'Well, at least we'll be goin' tergevver,' he said grinning. 'I told the geezer at the recruitin' office I'd need ter keep me eye on yer.'

Dolly went out of the room brushing back a tear, and

returned with the teapot, cups and saucers and toast on a large tray. 'We're out o' marmalade but there's some strawberry jam left,' she told them, disappearing again before they saw her watery eyes.

Mick Flynn came into the room, closely followed by Patrick, who looked somewhat the worse for wear. They sat down at the table and helped themselves to the tea.

'Muvver ses yer got yer papers,' Mick said, glancing up as he stirred his cup. 'Rifle Brigade. That's the regiment Con's in.'

'Con?' Frank said frowning.

'Yeah, the young man who called fer Jennie last Sunday.'

'Ain't there no papers come fer me?' Pat asked, rubbing his forehead tenderly.

'It doesn't look like it, does it?' Frank said, smiling at Jim as he lifted his plate. 'They ain't under yours, are they?' he joked.

'Now don't piss-ball about,' Pat growled. 'I ain't in the mood fer frivolity this mornin'.'

'No, I shouldn't fink so, the way you come in last night,' Mick remarked with a shake of his head. 'You literally fell up them stairs. Gawd knows what young Brenda must fink of yer.'

'Frankly I couldn't care less,' Pat told him. 'We 'ad a ruck last night over me volunteerin' an' she stormed off. She thought I was gonna go chasin' after 'er but I got drunk instead.'

'That's charmin',' Mick replied.

Pat slurped his tea and reached for the last piece of toast. 'I tried ter reason wiv 'er but she wouldn't listen,' he said gruffly. 'I told 'er if I didn't volunteer I'd be called up soon anyway, an' the waitin' would only put a strain on both of us.'

'Well at least yer won't need ter buy 'er the engagement ring now,' Frank remarked with a smile.

'She'll come round,' Jim said supportively. 'Yer wasn't plannin' on gettin' engaged till next month anyway. There's plenty o' time yet.'

'It's the ole battleaxe who's stirred the poison,' Pat gulped as he washed down the toast with hot tea. 'She's always stickin' 'er oar in. Trouble is Brenda's scared of 'er. I've told 'er I ain't bendin' over backwards ter please 'er muvver. Bloody ole cow.'

Frank looked at Jim for support. 'They say that women become like their muvvers as they get older,' he said with a grin playing in the corner of his mouth. 'What d'you fink, Jim?'

'So they say,' he replied. 'What's Brenda's muvver look like, Pat? Is she ugly?'

Mick tried to catch Frank's eye but his son ignored him and glanced over at Patrick. 'If Brenda don't change 'er mind you could always work yer ticket, I s'pose.'

'Work me ticket?' Pat echoed in disgust.

'Yeah, you could act the queer, or balls everyfing up they tell yer ter do.'

'That's a good idea,' Jim remarked. 'They'd soon chuck you out if they thought yer was bent.'

Pat gave both his brothers a hard look in turn as he got up from the table. 'I ain't got time ter listen ter you pair o' dopey gits,' he growled. 'I'm off ter work.'

'Don't go fallin' off no ladders,' Frank called out after him.

Pat shouted an unintelligible reply and the front door slammed shut.

'You two do go on at 'im sometimes,' Mick said, trying to look stern.

'Pat's all right, 'e knows we're only jokin',' Jim told him.

Dolly came into the parlour as Mick and the boys prepared to leave for work. 'Yer better take yer big coats, it looks like rain,' she said.

When Frank and Jim had hurried off, Dolly turned to Mick. 'I'm really gonna miss those boys,' she said tearfully. 'I'm worried sick about 'em.'

Mick slipped his arm around her shoulders and pecked her on her cheek. 'They'll be fine, Ma, an' yer gotta be fankful they're goin' in the same regiment. They'll watch out fer each ovver, they always 'ave.'

'What about our Pat?' she went on. 'Who's gonna watch out fer 'im? Fancy 'im wantin' ter go in the aircrew. What's 'e finkin' about, puttin' that worry on me shoulders?'

'Our shoulders, gel.'

'Yeah well, 'e shouldn't be so Jack-the-lad.'

''Im an' Brenda's split up, did yer know?'

Dolly shook her head. 'When was this, last night?'

Mick nodded. 'That's why 'e got pissed.'

'I s'pose it was over 'im volunteerin',' Dolly replied. 'I can see 'er point o' view, what wiv 'em plannin' ter get engaged next month.'

Mick shrugged his shoulders. 'Well I can't stop, gel,' he said quickly. 'It's a quarter ter bloody eight.'

Carter Lane was coming to life and at number 20 the elderly sisters were making plans. 'I think it's a very good idea,'

Charity remarked. 'Mind you, we'll need to sound everyone out.'

'I suppose we could invite people here to find out their feelings,' Cynthia replied. 'We could use our best china and I can make a few rock cakes.'

Charity held back on a sharp reply. Cynthia's rock cakes usually came in a condition befitting their name, and she recalled the last time her sister was moved to do some baking. She had nearly choked on an iron-hard rock cake, and the jam tarts had been little better. 'We don't need to go to all that trouble,' she said diplomatically. 'We could buy a dozen or so jam tarts at the cake shop, and maybe a nice apple pie to cut up.'

Cynthia nodded. 'We could call our idea "Carter Lane Women's Comfort for the Troops Club".'

'It sounds a little long-winded,' Charity said, stroking her chin. 'I know – why don't we call it the "Knitting for Victory Group"?'

'What a good idea. You are clever, Charity.'

'You're the clever one,' her sister told her. 'It was you who thought up the idea.'

'Yes, I did, didn't I?'

Charity put her empty teacup down on the table and felt her neatly permed hair with the palm of her hand. 'I think we should get the chores done early and then do some canvassing, don't you?' she suggested.

Cynthia's face lit up. 'Isn't it exciting?' she said breathlessly.

Lunchtime in The Sun saw the return of Sid Cafferty, and his entry was met with a scowl from the elderly Danny Crossley.

'What's that no-good git doin' back in 'ere?' he growled.

Alf Coates took his clay pipe out of his mouth and tapped it on the heel of his boot. 'They must 'ave got fed up wiv 'im at the ovver pub,' he remarked.

''E wouldn't 'ave the nerve ter show 'is face in 'ere if Big Joe was still around,' Danny said with passion.

'No, yer bloody right.'

'Just look at the big flash git.'

'I 'ope that bloody pint chokes 'im.'

Danny leaned back in his chair and stared over at the counter. 'What's the matter wiv Charlie Anson? Why don't 'e tell 'im ter piss orf out?'

'Don't ask me,' Alf growled. 'I fink 'e's bloody frightened of 'im.'

The lumbering malcontent leaned on the counter as he talked to the landlord. 'I was in the wrong, Charlie, an' I'm the first to 'old me 'ands up,' he declared. 'Don't you worry though. I won't give yer no grief. I'm just gonna 'ave me pint or two an' keep meself ter meself.'

'As long as yer do, Sid,' the landlord warned him. 'That last turn cost me enough.'

'Well, I appreciate yer kindness, Charlie,' Sid said. 'Give us anuvver pint, an' one fer yerself.'

Danny Crossley shook his head sadly. 'All the boys are goin' off ter war an' there's that ugly great git enjoyin' 'imself,' he said disgustedly. ''E ain't too old ter go in.'

''E ain't too old, but they won't take 'im,' Alf replied. ''E's got gastric trouble.'

''E'll 'ave more than gastric trouble if Big Joe comes 'ome on leave an' sees 'im in 'ere,' Danny remarked as he refilled his pipe.

The public bar of the corner pub was filling up as usual at that time of the day and soon a group of building workers came in and spread themselves along the bar. Alec Conroy was amongst them and after he was served he detached himself from the rest and sat in a corner reading the *Daily Mirror*.

'What's the matter wiv 'im?' one of the newer members of the group asked the worker next to him.

'Take no notice of 'im,' he was told, ''e's just a miserable git.'

'Conroy lives in this street. I don't fink 'e wants the locals ter know 'e works wiv us crowd,' another worker cut in.

'Why?' the young man asked.

''Cos we're a rough tough mob who work 'ard an' drink 'ard.'

The answer pleased the new recruit to the building site and he stuck out his chest and tried to look as tough as the rest. 'Sod 'im then,' he remarked.

Alec Conroy was unaware that he was being talked about, but had he known it would not have troubled him unduly. He was a loner who preferred his own company, except when he was able to see Ada Monahan who lived a few streets away. Ada was married to a merchant seaman, and the long days and nights she was forced to spend apart from her husband were made bearable by her association with the young loner. With him she could talk about her fears and worries, her hopes and aspirations, something she could never do with her husband, on the odd occasions when he was around. With all his faults Alec Conroy was a good listener, and with her he was able to relax and be himself, something he found difficult with others.

Sid Cafferty had downed three pints by the time the building workers arrived, and spotting the young man sitting alone he ambled over with the fourth pint in his large hand. 'I made me peace wiv Charlie,' he said in a slightly slurred voice as he sat down at the table.

Alec looked up and nodded. 'That's okay then,' he replied.

'Mind you though, that big Aussie git was out of order that night,' Sid went on. 'All I was sayin' was, we should let ovver countries fight their own battles.'

'Yeah, that's right,' Alec replied, without taking his eyes from the paper.

'So you won't be volunteerin'?'

'Nope.'

'Yer'll just wait till they call yer up then?'

'Yup.'

'What's yer preference? Army? Navy?'

'None.'

'Yer gotta 'ave a preference.'

'Why?'

'Yer just 'ave to.'

Alec folded the paper and put it down on the empty chair beside him. 'Look, millions o' men died in the last war,' he said with emphasis, 'an' countless more frew the effects o' mustard gas. That was the war to end all wars, so they said. Now we're at it again. We don't make the wars. Politicians make the wars, but it's the ordinary people who 'ave ter fight 'em. Well, I ain't gonna be cannon fodder, not fer no bloody politician.'

'Gettin' involved in ovver people's wars is one fing,' Cafferty growled, 'but I'm sodded if I'd stand by an' let the Germans walk in 'ere an' take over our country.'

112

'Let me tell you somefing,' Alec replied sharply. 'If every ordinary man in whatever country said 'e was gonna refuse ter fight, what'd 'appen then?'

'They'd be put up against the wall an' shot in Germany,' Cafferty told him.

'That's a load o' balls,' the younger man growled. ''Ow many could they shoot? Ten, fifteen, twenty million?'

'So what 'appens when they come for yer?' Cafferty asked.

'I'll disappear.'

'They'll catch up wiv yer.'

'Well, we'll 'ave ter wait an' see, won't we?'

All the malice in Cafferty's resentful heart came rumbling to the surface as he eyed the thin, pale-faced young man. 'Yer know what I fink?' he sneered. 'I fink you're a yeller-livered, no-good bastard who'd let 'is mates do the fightin' an' dyin' for 'im. That's what I fink.'

'Well, you can fink what yer like,' Alec Conroy said as he got up, picked up his newspaper and walked smartly out of the pub.

Charlie Anson had been kept busy serving pints, but he caught the last of the exchanges between the two and he turned to his wife Tess. 'I was a bloody fool ter listen to 'im,' he growled. 'I should 'ave barred 'im fer good.'

'You still ain't lost yer chance,' she replied acidly.

In the relative quiet of the saloon bar Cynthia and Charity Lockwood sat sipping their sherry.

'Well, it wasn't too bad, was it?' Charity remarked.

'No, I was quite pleased really,' her sister replied, looking at the list of names written down in the small notebook lying on the table. 'We've got Mrs Harris, Mrs Flynn, Mrs Bromilow and Mrs Arrowsmith. Then there are some may-bes: Mrs Jones, Mrs Wilson and that woman from number fifteen. I can never remember her name.'

'Wickstead,' Charity reminded her.

'That's right, Mrs Wickstead,' Cynthia said smiling.

'We'll need to do some more door-knocking,' Charity said with enthusiasm. 'If we get twenty people we can get the wool and needles at cut price. It said so on the wireless. The lady on the programme said it was mainly socks and scarves the troops needed, especially with the winter coming on.'

'We could send little notes to the troops inside the parcels,' Cynthia suggested. 'You know the sort of thing. "Keep your pecker up, we're all thinking of you." '

'What a nice thought,' Charity replied. 'You do get some bright ideas, Cynthia.'

The younger sister smiled happily at the compliment and reached into her handbag. 'I know this is being very daring, but I think the situation calls for it. I'm going to have another sherry. Would you like another?'

Some time later the two elderly sisters walked back along Carter Lane arm-in-arm and smiling to all and sundry.

'I feel positively tiddly,' Cynthia sighed.

'I feel like I'm walking on air,' Charity remarked.

'Don't let me go, will you?'

'And you hold on to me too.'

'Charity?'

'Yes?'

'Can you knit socks?'

'I've never tried.'

'Nor have I.'

'All I know is you have to use four needles.'

'Charity?'

'Yes?'

'I can see two of everything.'

'That's funny, so can I.'

'Aren't we awful?'

'No, just a little tipsy,' Charity replied with a lop-sided smile, 'but doesn't it feel good?'

Chapter Ten

The weather had suddenly turned cold, with a chill wind threatening a severe winter, and in Carter Lane chimneys belched smoke as people hurried about their business, eager to get back indoors. A few wore sad and worried expressions. Dolly Flynn had seen two of her sons go off to war and Mrs Jones, Mrs Wickstead and Mrs Bromilow had each said goodbye to a son during the same week. Mrs Wilson's boy Dennis had joined the navy the previous week and her daughter Claire had gone off to work in the Land Army.

The Sun public house on the corner of Carter Lane had become a kind of bastion for the local families and it was there in the cosy public bar that the locals took heart and gained support from each other.

'I'm not worried too much about my Dennis,' Mrs Wilson lied to Mrs Jones. ''E's always bin able ter look after 'imself. 'E makes friends easily an' 'e's a good swimmer. 'E got a certificate fer swimmin' a mile when 'e was at school.'

'I wish I didn't worry about my Jerry,' Ivy Jones replied as she picked up her Guinness. ''E's always bin such a little daredevil. D'yer remember that time 'e fell in the water down by Tower Pier? Tryin' ter climb inter one o' those barges, 'e was.'

'Yeah, I remember that time, Ivy,' Mrs Bromilow cut in. 'My Freddie came runnin' 'ome ter tell me that your boy was drowned.'

'The little cow-son nearly was,' Ivy went on. 'They fished 'im out the water down by Chamber's Wharf. 'E'd floated right down under Tower Bridge an' the lighterman who pulled 'im out said it was a miracle 'e never drowned, what wiv the currents an' all.'

That Sunday lunchtime Danny Crossley and his old drinking partner Alf Coates were sitting nearby, listening in on the conversation.

'The boys'll be all right,' Danny said, giving the women a smile of encouragement. 'Anyway, the war might not last long. Old 'Itler knows we ain't no pushover fer 'im or anybody else. 'E'll be suin' fer peace next year, you wait an' see.'

'Yeah, an' I'm a Dutchman,' Alf growled under his breath. 'This is goin' on fer a long while yet, you mark my words.'

'I feel the same,' Danny told him, 'but yer can't say that ter them, now can yer? Poor ole Dolly Flynn's just seen two of 'er boys go off an' young Pat's waitin' ter go any day now.'

Alf nodded and tapped his clay pipe against the leg of the table. 'Did you 'ear Cafferty goin' on at young Alec Conroy the ovver day?' he asked.

Danny shook his head. 'Nah, I'd left 'ere before it started, but I did 'ear from Lofty that Cafferty was right out of order.'

'Too bloody right 'e was,' Alf went on. 'All right the 'ole

street knows the boy's feelin's about goin' in the forces, but that don't give that loudmouth git the right ter go shoutin' 'is mouth off. I tell yer somefing, I'd never 'ave let 'im talk ter me like that, old as I am. I'd 'ave crowned 'im wiv a quart bottle.'

'Yeah, me too,' Danny agreed.

Alf filled his pipe thoughtfully. 'Cafferty's bin strongin' it wiv the booze lately,' he remarked. ''E's staggered out of 'ere pissed out of 'is brains the last few nights. I just 'ope 'e don't run inter Big Joe. Yer'd see the sparks fly then.'

''Old up, talk o' the devil,' Danny Crossley said quickly.

The old friends sat watching as Sid Cafferty walked unsteadily towards the counter, and Charlie Anson puffed irritably as he faced him across the polished surface. 'Sid, I ain't gonna serve yer,' he said boldly. 'You've 'ad enough. Why don't yer go 'ome an' sleep it off. Come back ternight when yer more steady on yer feet.'

'Yer mean yer barrin' me?' Sid growled, his bleary eyes trying to focus on the landlord.

'No, I ain't barrin' yer,' Charlie replied. 'I've just said yer'll be welcome 'ere ternight, but not now, not in that state.'

'I can 'old me beer,' Sid slurred. 'I won't be a nuisance to anybody.'

'Look, pal, yer got stroppy the ovver day when you was pissed an' I was gettin' ready ter bar yer then. I would 'ave done too if young Alec Conroy 'adn't 'ad the sense ter get out of 'ere before it went too far.'

''E's a yeller-livered coward an' I told 'im so,' Cafferty snarled as he slouched over the counter. 'You should be barrin' the likes of 'im, not me.'

'I ain't barrin' yer, Sid,' Charlie sighed, 'but I ain't servin' yer now, not while yer in that state.'

'If that's the case I'll take me custom elsewhere,' the big man scowled as he turned on his heel.

'Yeah, you do that, Sid,' the irate landlord told him.

Bernard Shanks checked the soldered connection with the meter contacts and then eased the metal chassis back into the casing. It was nearly five o'clock and he had been working for the last two hours on the difficult repair. 'It's fixed, Mr Levy,' he announced as he put his head round the door. 'It needed a new diode.'

'Well done, lad,' the shopowner told him. 'Mrs Fredricks'll be lookin' in again first thing Monday morning. You might as well go now. I'll be closing in half an hour.'

After Bernard had left Albert Levy counted the day's takings and put them into a large brown envelope which he then folded and slipped into his coat pocket. He turned the open sign on the front door round to closed and went into the workroom to gather up his overcoat and Homburg. All that week he had deliberately not sat down at the bench, for if he had he would have felt bound to deliver a few home truths to Abel. Tonight though he knew that he could not face another weekend with the knowledge of his old friend's deceit eating into him. Things had to be said and now was the time.

'Abel, I don't know if you'll turn away from me tonight, but I hope you won't,' he began. 'God knows, you and I have been lifelong friends and that has to count for something. Why? Why I ask myself? Was it something bad that compelled you to rob me? Gambling, women? That I could understand, but not you. I knew you too well to believe it could be something like that. What then, I've asked myself a thousand times? I paid you good wages and I always looked out for you. My house was always open, as far as you were concerned, and how many times has Gerda wanted you to call round for a meal? It's driving me mad, Abel. You of all people to rob the hand that fed you. Did I ever harp on the time I saved you from that death camp? Did I ever mention how much money it cost to buy your freedom? No never, and you know it. What could have turned one old friend against the other?'

Albert sat down wearily and leaned his head in his hands on the wooden bench. 'If only you could give me a sign, let me know and put me out of the misery I face every day now. It's destroying me, Abel. Can't you see, or are you gloating from wherever you are? Listen to me, my old friend. Three weeks ago I spoke to Rabbi Bloomfield. I told him I would like to have a plaque put up in the synagogue in your memory and he agreed it would be a fitting epitaph to a friendship that spanned the many years we shared. I'm to see him again soon to go over the details, but how can I go ahead with it now? It would be a sacrilege. Why, Abel? Why did you see fit to rob me in such a way, and then to mention the sordid details in your diary? Was I meant to see it? No, I'm sure I wasn't. The diary was well concealed, and only discovered by chance. But then that was typical of you, wasn't it? Secretive to a fault. Even when you took your life you never left me a letter of farewell. Nothing, Abel. You left me nothing, nothing that would explain the reasons for the terrible and tragic decision you took. All right, I knew how you felt about war coming, we'd discussed it so many times, but to leave no goodbye, no farewell old friend, only the terrible thing you did to me that has now come to light.'

Albert got up slowly, buttoned up his heavy overcoat and reached for his hat. 'I'm tired, Abel,' he sighed. 'I'm tired and dispirited beyond your understanding, because I'm still living. Maybe one day the truth will out. Maybe you'll send a sign, and show me why you did this to me. Maybe never. Maybe I'm destined to carry the burden of this mystery to my grave. Good night to you, Abel, and sleep the long sleep. I'll talk to you again, when my heart is not so heavy.'

Rene Conroy cut thick slices from the crusty loaf and coated them liberally with salted margarine. The hunk of cheese was going mouldy at the edges and she carefully pared it before cutting slices and laying them on the bread. Cheese or brawn sandwiches with pickles was the regular supper in the Conroy household and Alec would be in from the pub soon.

Rene worried over her only son, and lately she had had good reason to. He had openly told her and Ted that under no circumstances was he going to put on a uniform. Ted had tried to get to the bottom of it but failed. Alec was not one to open up and have a lengthy discussion of the whys and wherefores, and to say merely that the war was wrong and people shouldn't be made to fight was not enough to satisfy her or Ted. Alec had shrugged his shoulders and clammed up when they tried to delve, and his true reasons for the stance he was taking remained locked in his head.

The kettle was coming to the boil when the young man came in the house and Rene glanced up at the clock. He was earlier than usual and she gave him a searching look as he slipped off his coat and hung it behind the scullery door.

'I left a bit early,' he said. 'It was gettin' a bit silly.'

''Ere take yer sandwich in the parlour an' I'll bring yer tea in soon as it's brewed,' she told him.

Ted Conroy was sitting by the fire reading the evening paper and he looked up as his son walked into the room. 'You're early,' he remarked. 'They ain't run out o' beer, 'ave they?'

Alec ignored the joke. 'What's the news?' he asked. 'I 'aven't seen the paper this evenin'.'

Ted passed it over without comment and Alec settled himself into the armchair facing him.

Rene heard it first as she poured the boiling water into the teapot, and she went into the passage to listen. The shouting got louder and it carried into the parlour.

'It's Sid Cafferty, take no notice,' Alec said quickly, putting his supper plate down on the table.

'Alec Conroy. You're a coward,' the voice called out. 'Come out an' let us all see yer.'

Ted got up quickly but Rene took him by the arm. 'Don't you dare go outside,' she said anxiously.

'Can you 'ear me, Conroy? I know yer in there. Come out an' let us all see what a yeller-livered coward looks like.'

'I'm not gonna put up wiv this,' Ted growled as he tried to break Rene's grip on his arm.

Alec got out of his chair with a deep sigh. 'Leave it, Dad,' he said calmly. 'It's me 'e wants, not you.'

'You stay right where you are,' Rene told him. 'I'll see ter this.'

'No yer can't, Mum,' Alec said shaking his head. 'Sid Cafferty's bin lookin' fer a confrontation so I might as well face 'im.'

'You're no match fer that ugly great git,' she shouted at him.

'It's not a question o' matchin' 'im, it's about facin' 'im,' Alec told her. 'Just leave me ter sort this out in me own way.'

People were coming to their front doors to find out what was going on and in the light of the moon they could see the large figure of Sid Cafferty standing in the middle of the cobbled roadway with legs splayed apart and hands hitched into his belt.

'Just look at that drunken git,' Bert Kenny remarked to his wife Liz. ''E looks like someone out o' one o' those western pictures.'

'Well 'e certainly ain't no Billy the Kid,' Liz growled.

Cafferty ambled further along the turning. 'Can you 'ear me, Conroy?' he bawled.

Both Cynthia and Charity Lockwood had been curious to see what the rumpus was about and they looked a little frightened as they stood by their front door with coats over their flowered dressing gowns.

'Come out an' face me, Conroy,' Cafferty bellowed. 'Let's see what yer made of.'

The sisters saw that their neighbours were at their front doors and Charity was moved to respond to the taunting. 'Why don't you go home, you silly man,' she called out.

'Charity, do be careful,' her sister warned. 'The man's drunk.'

'I know very well that he's drunk, Cynthia,' she replied. 'All the more reason he should go home and let us get some sleep.'

'I don't know if I could sleep now,' Cynthia said shivering.

'Why don't you piss orf an' go ter bed,' Bert Kenny shouted out.

'Keep out o' this,' Cafferty snarled back. 'This is between Conroy an' me.'

Suddenly the harangued young man stepped out from his house into the cobbled roadway and walked very slowly towards the bigger man. 'I don't know what yer beef is,' he told him, 'but you're out of order. Why don't yer go 'ome an' sleep it off.'

'Leave it, Alec,' Bert Kenny called out to him. 'Get back indoors.'

Alec was only a few feet away from his tormentor when Cafferty lunged at him. The first blow grazed the young man's cheek but the next one landed full in the face, dropping him to his knees. A trickle of blood ran down from his nose onto his chin and Alec shook his head as he staggered to his feet. Cafferty grabbed him in a bear hug, his head going backwards as Conroy tried to press his fingers into the bigger man's eyes. The attacker was roaring like a bull and Alec felt the life being slowly squeezed out of him. With his remaining strength he brought his knee up sharply and caught Cafferty full in the groin. He was free as the big man gasped and fell down on one knee.

'Go 'ome, Cafferty,' he gulped.

'I'm gonna tear you apart, yer little rat,' the drunkard snarled as he climbed painfully to his feet.

Bert Kenny had pulled away from Liz's restraining grip and he hurried over to the combatants. 'Right, that's enough,' he bawled as he got between the two of them.

Cafferty swung round and caught Bert with a quick blow

to the chin and the older man staggered back into the kerb. Alec Conroy immediately went for the bully and rained blows on him, most of which were parried. People were screaming out for an end to it and suddenly Mick Flynn ran over and grabbed the young man by the waist, lifting him off his feet and swinging him away from the bigger man. Women ran out to remonstrate and Dolly held a rolling-pin menacingly in her hand.

'It's over,' she said. 'Now go off 'ome, Cafferty, or as sure as Gawd made little apples I'll open yer 'ead wiv this.'

Cafferty looked at the rolling-pin held up in front of him and he backed off. 'This ain't over, Conroy,' he called out as the young man was led away. 'I'll finish yer next time.'

Dolly raised the rolling-pin over her head and moved forward, only to be grabbed by Mick. 'Come on, luv, it's all over,' he urged her as Cafferty turned on his heel and walked unsteadily out of the little turning.

A dazed Bert Kenny was led into his house by Liz who sat him down in a chair and gently pressed her fingers around his chin. 'You was lucky,' she told him. 'That ugly great slummock could 'ave busted yer jaw.'

'That would 'ave kept me quiet fer a while, wouldn't it?' Bert said, grinning painfully.

'Just you wait till Big Joe comes 'ome on leave an' I tell 'im what's 'appened. 'E'll go bloody bananas.'

'You just keep yer mouth shut, d'you 'ear me?' Bert said sharply. 'I don't want 'im in any more trouble.'

'Big Joe finks the world o' you, Bert,' she told him. ''E'll slaughter that ugly big git when 'e does find out, an' believe me 'e will. All right, I won't say anyfing to 'im but yer gotta remember there were plenty o' people who saw what 'appened ter yer ternight, an' someone'll tell 'im, make no mistake about that.'

Bert nodded slowly. He knew only too well that in a small community like Carter Lane it would be impossible for Big Joe not to find out, and knowing the Australian's temper he feared the outcome.

Chapter Eleven

Life went on for the families at war as the bad weather closed in, and in Carter Lane the prospect of the young servicemen coming home on leave was one of the main subjects of conversation. Like many of their neighbours, the Flynn family were eagerly awaiting the homecoming of their three sons. Patrick Flynn had finally gone off to join the RAF and like his two brothers in the army his basic training was coming to an end.

Jennie Flynn had found herself a job at a bakery in the Old Kent Road and her sister Sadie was still hopeful of getting some war-work in the area. She had despaired of Len Regan coming up with anything, although he tried to convince her that there was time yet. He had been increasingly preoccupied during the last two months with the establishment in Brighton, and now that it was up and running successfully Sadie hoped that he would have a little more free time. Jennie however was a little concerned about her elder sister and she was quick to voice her opinion when the two were together in the scullery on Saturday morning.

'You should be out enjoyin' yerself on Saturday nights,'

she remarked, 'but you 'ardly ever go out lately.'

'I'm seein' Len ternight,' Sadie told her. 'An' you're a fine one ter talk.'

'It's different wiv me,' Jennie responded. 'Con's over in France an' I'm not interested in playin' around while 'e's away.'

'Yeah, but you 'ardly knew 'im before 'e left,' Sadie went on. 'Surely it don't 'urt goin' out wiv ovver lads, as long as it don't get too strong. There's plenty round 'ere who'd be only too glad ter take you out.'

'I'm just not interested,' Jennie said. 'Con writes ter me all the time an' we're gettin' ter know each ovver pretty well from the letters. Besides, most o' the presentable young men are away in the forces now.'

Sadie shrugged her shoulders as she got up to check the cake baking in the oven. 'Well it's up ter you, it's your life,' she sighed.

Jennie took out the small photo of Con from her handbag and studied it. 'Don't yer fink 'e's a bit like our Pat in looks?' she asked.

Sadie leaned over her sister's shoulder. 'Yeah, I can see a likeness, around the eyes.'

''E's got lovely eyes,' Jennie drooled. 'They make me go all soppy when 'e looks at me.'

Sadie picked up a tea towel and went over to the oven. 'I'd better take this out before it gets burnt,' she said, moving back as the heat billowed out. 'There we are, perfect.'

Jennie picked a roasted almond from the top of the fruit cake and nibbled it. 'There's no end ter your talents, is there?' she joked. 'When yer gonna cut it?'

'This is goin' away till the boys come 'ome on leave next

week,' Sadie replied quickly. 'Mum's found me a tin ter keep it in, so keep yer 'ooks off.'

Gerda Levy had become increasingly worried about her husband and she took it on herself to visit Carter Lane.

'I'm sorry to trouble you, but I'm Albert Levy's wife,' she told Daisy timidly when the Harrises' front door was opened to her. 'I wonder if I could have a few words with you?'

'Of course yer can. Come in,' Daisy said pleasantly.

Gerda walked into the tidy parlour and stood by the table. 'It's about my husband really,' she began.

'Look, you take a seat an' I'll get us some tea,' Daisy told her. 'I've got some brewin'.'

She was soon back and she gave her visitor an encouraging smile as she handed over her tea. 'I always find a cup o' Rosy Lee goes down well in the afternoon.'

Gerda took a small sip and looked up at Daisy. 'You remember the diary you found under the floorboards in Abel's room?' she said without wasting time. 'Well, it contained something which has upset my husband very much. In fact it revealed that Abel was robbing the till at my husband's shop. He actually made notes about it. There were dates, amounts and certain remarks written down which upset Albert terribly, and it's got to the stage where I'm beginning to fear for his sanity.'

'Good Gawd!' Daisy said quickly. ''Ow shockin'.'

'I don't know if you're aware that Abel was in a concentration camp in Germany before the war,' Gerda remarked.

'Yes, I did know that as a matter o' fact,' Daisy replied. 'I only found out when I saw the number printed on Abel's arm. 'E told me that your 'usband managed ter pay fer 'is release.'

'That's true, which makes this business all the more terrible,' Gerda said sadly. 'Never once did my husband ever remind Abel about what he did. They were childhood friends and he felt it was only his duty to save him from the camp. It was almost impossible to get out of one of those camps, and Abel was one of the lucky ones, thanks to Albert.'

Daisy shook her head slowly. 'Your 'usband's a very nice man. 'E was always pleasant when 'e called ter play chess wiv Abel an' we often joked about different fings. Abel seemed ter worship 'im. It seems so out o' character that 'e should end up robbin' 'im, after all that was done fer 'im.'

'This was going on for some time by the look of it,' Gerda told her. 'Although there was only one diary Abel did make references to the previous year and he even had a total that he carried over.'

'Now yer've told me this, I wish I'd never discovered the diary,' Daisy said with sadness etched in her voice. 'I did take a look inside ter tell yer the truth but it was written in a foreign language an' I felt that your 'usband should 'ave it, considerin' 'ow close they were.'

'I don't put any blame on you, Mrs Harris,' Gerda was quick to remark. 'You did the right thing. But Albert's suffering over what he discovered. The knowledge has been eating into him and he's taken to talking to himself. He doesn't sleep either. Many a night I've woken up and found him sitting in the lounge mumbling to himself. He's on tablets that his doctor prescribed but they don't seem to help much.'

'I'm so sorry,' Daisy said with compassion. 'I wish there was somefing I could do.'

'As a matter of fact there is,' Gerda told her. 'Can you

search your memory and think of anything Abel might have told you concerning his life or anything he might have mentioned about Albert? Any little thing, however trivial it may seem, might hold the key.'

Daisy thought for some time then she shook her head again slowly. 'Abel was a very private person, an' we respected 'is privacy,' she replied. ''E never spoke much about 'imself nor your 'usband, apart from mentioning when 'e'd call round ter play chess.'

Gerda finished her tea and put the cup and saucer down on the table. 'If anything does come to mind I'd appreciate it greatly if you would contact me. There's my address. Maybe your husband might recall something.'

'I'll certainly speak to 'im,' Daisy said, glancing down at the slip of paper Gerda had handed her, 'an' if eivver of us remembers anyfing I'll definitely get in touch.'

'You are very kind and I do appreciate it,' Gerda said as she got up.

Daisy saw her visitor to the door, and she was still shaking her head and frowning as she went back into the parlour. It beggared belief that Abel would do such a thing, she told herself. Such a nice, quiet, inoffensive man who would jump at the slightest sound. He hadn't the nerve nor the inclination to resort to robbing his friend. That she was sure of.

Len Regan was looking a little harassed when Sadie arrived at The Swan off the Walworth Road. 'Look, I'm up against it ternight, kid,' he told her as he took their drinks to a secluded table in the saloon bar. 'There's a party down from Glasgow an' we've got anuvver team from Kent who are interested in puttin' some dough in a project Johnnie's got lined up. I gotta get down ter The Black Cat later, but I'm s'posed ter meet the Glasgow boys first. We've gotta look after 'em while they're in London.'

'So bang goes our quiet evenin' tergevver,' Sadie said with irritation in her voice.

'I'm sorry, kid, I really am,' he said.

'It's not good enough, Len,' she told him. 'Our time tergevver seems ter be gettin' less an' less.'

'I know, an' I'm gonna make it up ter yer very soon,' he replied. 'In the meantime I wanna ask yer a big favour. Yer can say no if yer like, but it would be a great 'elp if yer'll do it for me.'

'What is it?' Sadie asked sighing.

'If I get Nosher ter run yer down ter Kent can yer act as 'ostess ter the Kent mob till I get there?'

''Ow long are yer gonna be?' she asked. 'I can't be expected ter nursemaid 'em all night. I don't know 'em anyway.'

'I should get down there by eleven or thereabouts,' he estimated. 'All yer gotta do is introduce yerself as Len's assistant an' make sure they get all the booze they want. Tell 'em I'm due soon an' just make small talk. I know yer can do it. The barman's already bin primed up an' 'e'll give yer all the drinks yer need. There's a table reserved as well. Say yer'll do it.'

'An' what if I say no?' Sadie replied.

'Well it's fer you ter decide, kid, an' I wouldn't dream of askin' yer if I thought yer wasn't up to it. Yer've 'eld the fort before remember.'

''Ow many's comin'?' Sadie asked.

'Four.'

'An' yer promise me yer won't leave me roastin'?'

'I promise.'

'All right then, just this once,' she sighed.

'Yer a diamond an' I love yer, Sadie.'

'Yer could 'ave fooled me,' she told him with a grudging smile.

Frank and Iris Ross had lived in Carter Lane ever since their wedding back in nineteen eighteen when Frank came back from the war. Two years later their daughter was born, and due to complications at the birth when Iris almost died the couple decided that Brenda would be their only child. They doted on their precious gift and spoiled her in the process. Neighbours remarked that Brenda was the best-dressed child in the street and at Christmas and on her birthdays she would always have the most expensive toys. Iris and Frank always sought the very best for her and when she won a scholarship to St Olave's Grammar School for Girls they were delighted. They saw a good future for her and hoped and prayed that one day she would marry a wealthy businessman who would worship her and give her everything her heart desired.

To Brenda's credit she did not take advantage of the privileged position she was in. In fact she was sometimes embarrassed to witness the struggles of the families around her, especially during the years of the depression as she was growing up. Her family seemed to manage quite well in contrast and her father's job as chief clerk in the Council wages office was never in jeopardy. Her mother worked too as a welfare officer and all in all things were prosperous for them throughout the bad years.

Brenda grew into a beautiful young woman, dark-haired

and with large hazel eyes, and the boys soon came calling. Her parents watched her progress with due concern and they kept a tight rein on her activities, often warning a young buck off or vetting a prospective boyfriend until Brenda began to rebel. The young men who came calling or tried to chat her up did not turn her head or make her pulse race overmuch, for Brenda had already lost her heart, to the one young man in the street who did not seem to realise that she was now a very desirable young woman.

As children Brenda Ross and Patrick Flynn had played together. They were often seen hand in hand going off on some big adventure or sitting together at the kerbside chatting away, as Pat showed her his new penknife or instructed her in the art of woollen rein-making on a cotton reel with four nails punched into one end. Brenda would in turn teach him the words of the latest songs and show him how to play four-stones, which the lad found hard to master. A childhood full of fun and happiness, while the world about them was moving ever closer to conflagration.

Frank and Iris Ross saw no harm in the childhood friendship. Patrick Flynn was a fine lad from a good hard-working family, but a few years later they became worried when their teenage daughter started to make her feelings felt. It was obvious to them that Brenda was very fond of her childhood friend and as far as she was concerned their association had taken on another dimension.

'It's only natural fer Brenda ter like the lad,' Frank remarked. 'After all, they grew up tergevver in the street.'

'Yes, but it's obvious 'e don't feel the same way about 'er,' Iris replied. 'Patrick's bin out wiv quite a few gels lately.'

'Only one or two,' Frank said.

'Well all I'm sayin' is, Brenda's gotta realise that there's plenty o' fish in the sea,' Iris answered irritably, 'an' she shouldn't be wastin' 'er time pinin' over the likes o' Patrick Flynn.'

On the day when the Prime Minister Neville Chamberlain returned from Munich waving a piece of paper to declare that it was peace for our time, Brenda Ross went to a dance at the local palais and met Patrick there. He had been stood up and he had decided to drown his sorrows at the bar. From where he stood looking down on the dance area on the floor below he could see the beautiful young woman he had grown up alongside moving with gossamer grace to the big-band music and he forgot his drink. Men were cutting in to dance with her and she seemed to be in constant demand. Not being a very confident dancer himself he was loath to approach her, but he thought of their childhood together and knew that she would be nice enough not to criticise him for his shortcomings.

Brenda and Patrick danced all evening to the exclusion of the other young hopefuls and then they walked home together, deep in conversation. Brenda's heart was light and pumping excitedly while Patrick cursed his stupidity at not noticing how beautiful Brenda had become until that evening. They slipped furtively into the dark doorway of a warehouse in Brady Street and kissed goodnight, a young, innocent kiss that lasted until they were breathless, and they arranged to meet again. Their new-found love soon became obvious to everyone, and even Iris and Frank had to agree that Patrick Flynn was the man their daughter would one day marry.

It was a time for love, for planning, for looking at rings and wedding gowns, but it all paled in the shadow of an army on the march. When the Germans moved into Poland it was clear to everyone that war was imminent, and Brenda and Patrick's plans were thrown into disarray.

'I've gotta join up,' Patrick told her as they sat by the river on a balmy night a few days after war was declared.

'You can't, Pat,' she said. 'I won't let yer go.'

'I can't not go,' he persisted. 'Look, darlin', I'll be called up soon anyway an' I won't 'ave much choice then. It'll be the army more than likely.'

'I thought I meant somefing to yer,' she said with a break in her voice.

'You mean everyfing ter me, but I just can't sit back while all the ovver young blokes are signin' on.'

'You men are all the same,' Brenda rounded on him. 'You fink this is a game. "Look at me, mate. Look at all the medals I've got." '

'Don't trivialise it, Brenda,' he said quietly. 'It's not a game an' you know it. If we don't fight the Germans'll overrun the country, an' where would we all be then? In slavery – that's where.'

'Well, if that's the way yer feel then at least wait till they call yer up, please,' Brenda pleaded.

'I can't. I gotta do it now, luv,' he said sighing. 'The sooner we all get into it the sooner it'll be over.'

'An' the sooner yer'll get yerself killed.'

'Don't fight me on this, darlin'.'

'I will an' I'll keep on till yer see sense.'

'It won't matter 'ow long yer go on about it, Brenda, me mind's made up,' Pat said firmly.

'Well, in that case yer better make the choice,' she told him with tears of anger filling her eyes. 'If you volunteer then me an' you are finished.'

A few days later Patrick Flynn joined the Royal Air Force, and Brenda Ross put his photograph face down in her dressing-table drawer.

Chapter Twelve

Nosher Smith had said very little during the journey down to The Black Cat nightclub which was situated on the outskirts of Maidstone. He was an ex-fighter who had never reached the heights, but rather been the one all the rising young pro boxers were expected to get past on their way to fame and fortune. Now employed as a chauffeur, minder and general handyman to Johnnie Macaulay, the ageing ex-pugilist did as he was told and found it a good policy to keep his thoughts to himself.

'You are waitin' around, Nosher, aren't yer?' Sadie queried as the car swung off the road into a long, curving drive lit only by the light of the full moon.

'Yus, miss,' he grunted in reply. 'Mr Regan told me someone else'll be bringin' 'im down later.'

Sadie gathered up her calf-long dress as she got out of the Daimler and pushed open the door of the darkened nightclub. Inside the air was tainted with tobacco smoke and she could see in the low lights a crowd assembled round the long bar. The stocky-looking barman smiled at her as she walked up to him and nodded towards the far end of the counter. 'The party's arrived, Sadie,' he told her.

'The table's reserved, the one by the stage.'

As the young woman walked over to the group of well-dressed men she noted that one looked far younger than the other three and he seemed to be doing the talking. Two of the others were grey-haired and wore spectacles, while the third was completely bald, the dome of his skull shining as though it had been polished.

'Ah, this must be Sadie Flynn, if I'm not mistaken,' the young man said cheerily as she reached them.

'In person,' Sadie said in her best voice, smiling at each of them in turn. 'I hope you're all being looked after.'

The young man held up his drink. 'Yes thank you, and we're looking forward to the show. I understand there's a good singer here tonight.'

'Yes, Alma Deane sings with the big bands and she's just done some cabaret work with Debroy Summers,' Sadie told him.

'Very good,' the bald man cut in. 'And what about you? Are you in the entertainments business?'

'Of sorts,' Sadie said smiling. 'I'm Len Regan's assistant and I look after his clients while he's on other business.'

'And very well too, I'm sure,' the man replied with a leer that Sadie found repulsive.

'I understand Mr Regan's coming down later tonight,' the young man said.

'Yes, he'll be down as soon as he can,' Sadie told him.

'Well, I think I'd better do the introductions,' he said. 'I'm George Barton, and this is James Carrington and Jowett Howland of Howland Enterprises. And this is Warren Tate who has business interests along the south coast from Brighton to Portsmouth.'

The handshakes from the two grey-haired men were quite perfunctory but when the bald Warren Tate grasped her hand his flesh felt cold and clammy, and reminded Sadie of holding a slippery fish. The contact was slightly longer than it should have been and the look in the man's dark puffy eyes made her skin creep. She guessed that he was in his mid-forties, his build turning to fat around his jowls and midriff. His face was flat and there was no sign of stubble. In fact his features seemed to be as smooth as his large head, glistening with sweat.

'We have a table reserved for you,' Sadie told them. 'Are you ready or would you prefer another drink at the bar? There's time yet, the show doesn't start until eleven.'

George Barton looked around for guidance. 'I think we might as well take the weight off our feet,' he concluded.

Sadie led the way to a round table set out with cutlery and wine glasses sprouting red table napkins which had been expertly folded. The waiter took the drinks order and then Warren Tate took out a flat gold case from his coat pocket and extracted a coloured cigarette with a gold tip. 'This is certainly very nice,' he remarked, looking around. Then turning to George he added, 'Macaulay seems to have done well here.'

The drinks were served and the men chatted amongst themselves, occasionally turning to Sadie so as not to seem impolite.

'There's a gaming room here, I understand,' Carrington remarked to her.

'Yes, it's to the right, by the palm,' she told him with a smile.

Warren Tate constantly glanced in her direction and Sadie

found herself wishing that Len Regan would hurry down and take the sorry bunch off her hands.

The waiter came back to take the food order and Sadie suddenly noticed George Barton acknowledging a very suggestive smile from a young man sitting with an elderly group of jewel-bedecked women and tired-looking old men. The young man stood out in the group and his manner left little to the imagination. He was openly flirting with Barton, who appeared to be enjoying it.

The soup was followed by fish and vegetables which were presented in large silver tureens, and as the party tucked into the delicious meal the cabaret got under way. Scantily clad dancing girls kicked their way through an exerting routine, and as they side-stepped off the club manager climbed up onto the stage to introduce the main artiste. Loud applause greeted her appearance and Alma Deane did not disappoint. Her repertoire contained both new and old songs, and while her voice mellifluously soared as purely as a nightingale Warren Tate sat staring like an alley cat eager for its prey. His mouth hung open and his dark brooding eyes never left the singer. The cigarette in his hand was forgotten till it seared his flesh and even then he stubbed it out on the plate without removing his gaze from the stage. Loud, lengthy applause rang out at the end of the performance and Alma Deane obliged with two more songs before she made her final exit.

Sadie looked round as the waiter came over to take the dessert order and saw that George Barton was missing from the table. She had not noticed him get up and she turned to Jowett Howland. 'I didn't see George leave,' she remarked.

'He's otherwise engaged, my dear,' the elderly man

replied, giving his colleague a knowing glance. 'It seems he's found a friend and they've moved to the gaming room.'

'Yes, and I think I'll try my luck there too,' Carrington declared.

With the meal over and the band pianist playing a medley of bland melodies Carrington got up. 'Are you going to join me, Jowett?' he asked. 'And what about you, Warren?'

'I think I'll stay here for a while,' the bald man replied, much to Sadie's distaste. There were two hostesses available in the gaming room to assist any novice and encourage the more daring player and she would not be expected to follow the men into the salon, but she felt obliged to sit with Warren Tate as long as he stayed at the table.

'The same again?' Tate asked as he motioned to an attendant waiter.

'No, just some water, thank you,' Sadie replied.

'Nonsense. Have another gin and lemon,' he said firmly.

'All right then, but just a small one,' she told the waiter pointedly.

Warren Tate fixed her with an intent stare as he spoke at length about his early days and his rise to becoming a very successful businessman, then suddenly his manner changed. He started to delve and pry into the lives of Johnnie Macaulay and Len Regan, and some of his questions shocked the young girl. 'Are you his woman?' he asked brazenly.

'I'm his girlfriend as well as his assistant,' Sadie replied, trying to maintain a smile.

'Do you like the water?' he asked, and seeing her puzzled frown added, 'Sailing?'

'I've never tried it,' she answered.

'I've got a powered sailing sloop moored at Hayling Island,' he announced. 'You should come down some weekend and I could take you out on it. I have a crew to man it, and I'm sure you'd enjoy yourself. Len Regan too, though I'd prefer it if you came alone. I understand from talking to Mr Regan that he's a landlubber. His words, mind.'

I bet you would, Sadie thought, giving him a noncommittal smile.

The barman was making signs and Sadie excused herself to go over to him. 'What is it, Sam?' she asked.

'Mr Regan's just been on the phone,' he told her. 'Something's come up and he can't make it tonight. Can you pass on his apologies to the guests and make sure they're looked after while they're at the club? Oh and will you see to it that Nosher drives them to the Manor Hotel when they're ready.'

Sadie cursed her luck as she nodded to the barman. Warren Tate was doing a good job of making her skin crawl and she had been praying for Len to come and take him and his cronies off her hands. Now it seemed that she was stuck with them for the next few hours.

Before going back to the table she went into the gaming room and sought out her charges. Carrington was standing beside Jowett Howland who seemed to be on a winning streak and she passed on the message.

'Never fear, my dear, I'm on a roll,' Jowett told her.

'Have you seen Mr Barton?' she asked him.

'He left some time ago,' Jowett said winking.

I wish Tate would, she thought as she went back to join him.

The bald man was keen to learn more about her and his questions became more personal as the late night drifted on into the early hours. He had consumed a large amount of whisky but he still appeared to be alert and no less searching in his manner.

A few minutes after two o'clock Carrington and Howland came out from the gaming room and walked over to the table. 'We've had a very nice evening,' Howland told her, patting his breast pocket. 'We're ready to leave now, my dear. Are you coming, Warren?'

'No, I think I'll stay on a while,' Tate said, glancing over to where couples were dancing together to the dreamy music. 'I might even be able to coax the young lady into dancing with me,' he added, smiling and showing his small tobacco-stained teeth.

Sadie excused herself while she saw the elderly men out to the courtyard where Nosher was sleeping behind the wheel of the large grey Daimler. 'Don't ferget ter come back fer me, Nosher, whatever yer do,' she whispered to him as the men climbed into the back seats. 'I can't wait ter get out of 'ere. I'm still lumbered wiv that bald-'eaded lecher. Just wait till I see Len Regan.'

Nosher smiled and drove off, and Sadie took a deep breath of cold night air before she went back inside, desperately wishing the time away.

For the next hour she was subjected to Warren Tate's objectionable chatter which was growing more and more suggestive. The whisky had given him the courage to pursue his objective, which Sadie knew only too well was to get her into his bed.

'I think it's time we left,' she finally told him. 'People are going home now.'

Tate had a fixed grin on his face as he stood up. 'By the

way, I've something important for Mr Macaulay,' he slurred. 'Can you see that he gets it?'

'Yes, of course.'

'It's a folder and it's back at my hotel.'

White mist was rising from the fields and crows cawed from the coppice beside the frosty driveway as they walked out into the cold fresh air, Tate holding her arm whilst warning bells sounded furiously in Sadie's head. The reliable Nosher was sitting huddled behind the wheel and he gave the young woman a questioning glance as she climbed into the car. Tate got in after her and sat down heavily, his bulk pressed against her as Nosher eased the car out onto the deserted highway. The journey was short, and Tate drummed his fingers on his leg nervously as the Manor Hotel loomed up out of the thickening mist.

'Wait for me, Nosher,' Sadie said as she climbed out onto the gravel driveway. Tate leaned back into the car and said something to the ex-boxer, and as he turned to Sadie the car drove off.

'What are you doing?' Sadie asked him sharply. 'I need that car.'

'It's all right, I couldn't expect you to make the journey back to London at this time of the morning,' he replied. 'I told the chauffeur to come back around ten o'clock. It'll give you time for a few hours' sleep and a freshen-up. Don't worry, you can have the bed, I'll sleep on the divan.'

'But I want to get back to London,' Sadie persisted irritably. 'This isn't what I'd planned.'

'Nonsense,' Tate said dismissively as he took her arm and shepherded her into the warm interior of the hotel. 'You've been taking care of us all night and now it's my turn to look after you.'

Sadie saw the knowing look on the night porter's face as he handed Warren Tate the key to his room and she gripped her hands into tight fists as they entered the lift. Unless she was very much mistaken Warren Tate had designs on her, and from the impression she had got he was not a man who took no for an answer.

He led her into the room and she saw him put the 'Do not disturb' notice on the outside doorknob. 'A livener to take away the chill,' he said as he hunched his shoulders over the drinks cabinet.

Sadie put her handbag down on the chair by the door and pretended to look down into the courtyard below, all the time watching his movements closely. She had heard stories from Len Regan about clients spiking drinks and she felt sure Tate was up to something of the sort.

'There we are,' he said as he handed her a very large gin and tonic. 'This'll take care of any worries and fears you might have.'

'I beg your pardon?' Sadie said quickly.

'Come now, Sadie, you are a little wary of me, aren't you?'

'Not at all,' she replied with a frown. 'I just want to get home right away.'

'It's nice and warm in here and I can make you glad that you accepted my offer of a bed,' he said, moving towards her and taking her by the forearm. 'Go on, drink it down.'

Sadie put the glass to her lips and immediately detected a faint acrid tang. She was right. He had spiked her drink. 'Look, I'd better go,' she told him as she backed away. 'Give me the folder an' I'll phone for a cab.'

'At this time in the morning?' Tate said incredulously. 'All the way to London?'

'Len Regan can pay,' Sadie answered with spirit. 'It's 'is fault I'm 'ere anyway.'

'You disappoint me, Sadie,' Tate said, coming towards her again. 'Regan told me that you were a woman of the world. Hostesses usually are. I expected more from you.'

'Like takin' me ter bed?' she charged him angrily.

'It would be very nice, and I'm sure you'd enjoy the experience,' he said leering.

'That's it,' Sadie declared quickly as she grabbed her handbag from the chair. 'I'm leavin'. You give Regan the folder.'

'Oh no you don't, you little tramp,' Tate snarled as he made a grab for her. 'You knew the score when you came up here with me. Was the drink not to your liking? I only added a little something to heighten your natural desires. You would have enjoyed the feeling it produced.'

'Let me go,' she shouted as he slipped his arms around her waist.

'Relax and just let it happen,' he gasped as his wet blubbery lips sought out her neck.

With a supreme effort she pressed his chest backwards and at the same time brought her knee up sharply. Tate screamed and doubled up, his eyes bulging as he gasped for breath. 'I'll kill you, you ungrateful bitch,' he spat out hoarsely.

Sadie did not stop to watch him recover. She left the room as fast as she could and dashed down the stairs, to the surprise of the night porter who watched open-mouthed as she ran out into the mist clutching her handbag to her bosom.

As she hurried headlong down the path she heard the crunch of tyres on the gravel behind her. 'Nosher! I thought yer'd gone back ter London,' she gasped as he pulled up beside her.

'I take orders from Len Regan, nobody else,' he replied with a dignified air.

'Nosher, you're a diamond,' she said with feeling as she slipped into the seat beside him. 'That bald-'eaded ole coot told me 'e 'ad some information fer Johnnie Macaulay in 'is room an' I'm afraid I fell fer it. 'E tried it on but I managed ter get out before any 'arm was done, ter me at least.'

Nosher pulled the car up sharply at the end of the drive. 'Maybe I should go an' 'ave a quiet word wiv the geezer,' he said, clenching his large fist suggestively.

'No, leave it,' Sadie said quickly. ''E didn't feel too well when I left, an' anyway Len Regan can sort this mess out.'

Nosher drove back to London carefully with diffused headlights, through a thick mist which seemed like a solid wall in front of them. Sadie leaned her head back against the seat and tried not to let herself get too angry. Len had gone too far this time though, she told herself. He had used her as a plaything for his unsavoury clients while he swanned about back in London. She betted that he had had no intention of coming down to the nightclub and had left her holding the candle. Well he wasn't going to get away with it, she vowed. And she wasn't going chasing after him either. If he wanted to know how things had gone he would have to contact her.

As Nosher drove into the outskirts of London Sadie

reached into her handbag and took out the little notebook she always carried with her. Slipping the tin pencil from the binding coil she scribbled a few words down and tore out the page. 'Nosher, can you go past Len Regan's place?' she asked. 'I wanna slip this frew 'is letterbox.'

'Sure,' he replied.

Soon they were carefully negotiating familiar backstreets to emerge into the New Kent Road, and Nosher swung the car into a side turning and pulled up outside a row of large Victorian houses. 'Stay there, I'll put it frew,' he told her.

As he walked up the flight of steps to the front door Sadie leaned across to his side of the car and glanced up in the breaking dawn at Len's bedroom window. She saw the curtains move slightly, sending out a shaft of light, then they closed again. Len had seen the car.

'Right then, let's get you 'ome,' Nosher grunted as he slipped back behind the steering wheel.

When the Daimler finally pulled up in Carter Lane Sadie turned sideways and kissed the ex-pugilist on his stubbled cheek. 'Fanks, Nosher,' she said affectionately. 'I wish everybody was as reliable as you.'

He smiled, embarrassed at her show of gratitude. 'No sweat, Sadie,' he replied. 'That's what I get paid for.'

The young woman let herself into the house and crept carefully up the stairs to her bedroom where she quickly undressed and slipped between the cold sheets. Sleep would not come, after everything that had happened that night. In her troubled mind she pictured over and over again the way the curtains had moved, and she could not get the feeling out of her head that Len Regan had not been alone in that bedroom.

Chapter Thirteen

Another week of war had passed and Carter Lane seemed full of khaki and navy blue. Frank and Jim Flynn were home on leave from training and their younger brother Pat was due home the following week, while Mrs Wilson's son Dennis was home from the navy, looking the part in his tight-fitting top and bell-bottoms. His younger sister Claire had managed to get home from her job in the Land Army to see her brother before he went back to Chatham and Mrs Jones' son Jerry was home too. Mrs Bromilow was very proud of her son Freddie, who looked every inch a Grenadier Guardsman. Mrs Wickstead too was feeling very proud of her boy Chris who was in the Royal Fusiliers. He carried the uniform well, with the distinctive feathered plume on the front of his beret.

The Sun public house did a roaring trade that week and Charlie Anson lost no time in telling everyone who was interested that he had finally barred Sid Cafferty for good.

'Well, ter be fair 'e couldn't do much else, could 'e?' Danny Crossley remarked to Alf Coates. 'Big Joe's due 'ome any day now an' when 'e gets ter know about Cafferty smackin' ole Bert Kenny 'e's gonna wipe the floor wiv 'im.'

'Yeah, an' there'll be more than a few glasses broke this

time if Joe catches Cafferty in 'ere,' Alf agreed.

'I bin finkin' about what 'appened last week,' Danny went on. 'If Alec Conroy's the coward Cafferty makes 'im out ter be, why did 'e stand up to 'im? I mean ter say, the ugly git must be four stone 'eavier at least.'

'Search me,' Alf replied.

''E'll 'ave ter go in the end, or they'll lock 'im up,' Danny said.

'P'raps 'e'll register as a conshie.'

'Yeah, 'e might do.'

''Ere, I know what I was gonna ask yer,' Alf remarked suddenly. ''As your ole woman joined that knittin' fer victory fing?'

'Yeah, she 'as,' Danny told him. 'Mind you, she ain't much of a knitter. Yer wanna see the navy scarf she's makin'. It's about six foot long an' she ain't finished it yet.'

'My ole woman wanted ter join but she can't knit,' Alf said shaking his head. 'Those Lockwood sisters said they'd teach 'er, but I fink they're wastin' their time. Anyfing like that an' she's all fingers an' fumbs. I tell yer somefing. The ovver day me braces' buttons come orf me strides so the ole gel sorts frew the ornaments where she keeps all the bits an' pieces an' she finds these two buttons. Grey they were. Anyway, she sews 'em on, after a fashion, an' when I come ter put me braces on I can't button 'em up. Know what she done?'

'No.'

'She'd sewed two poxy overcoat buttons on me trousers. They must 'ave bin two bloody inches wide. They looked like a couple o' dustbin lids stuck on. I ses to 'er, '''Ere, Flo, 'ow the bloody 'ell am I expected ter button these up?'' Went orf alarmin' she did. Told me I was never satisfied. Then she finds me a poxy safety pin. I told 'er I could 'ave done that in the first place. Bloody useless where sewin's concerned she is.'

Despite a few negative responses the Lockwood sisters had succeeded in recruiting enough of their neighbours to form a fair-sized knitting group and they applied for wool and knitting needles from the WVS and other agencies. The idea had been for the women to meet up at the Lockwood home and work together over cups of tea and rock cakes, but it never quite worked out like that. Mrs Bromilow, who was an expert knitter, declined to become that sociable. 'I'll knit scarves an' socks, no problem,' she said to her friend Ivy Jones, 'but I couldn't sit there all the time. Yer gotta watch yerself in their gaff. When I drop a stitch I'm inclined to eff an' blind an' yer can't do that wiv them around, they go all funny. Besides, 'ave you ever tasted their tea? It's like cat's piss. An' those rock cakes they make! Gawd almighty, I 'ave enough trouble wiv me choppers as it is, wivout tryin' ter bite frew them bleedin' fings. Rock's the word. I fink they must 'ave got the bakin' powder mixed up wiv cement.'

Dolly Flynn knitted for the group whenever she found the time, and Daisy Harris became the street's fastest sock knitter. Mrs Wickstead went to the Lockwood house on a couple of occasions but found it hard work trying to knit while the sisters chatted about their early lives and Cynthia's brute of a husband, who had mercifully disappeared from the scene some ten years ago.

Mrs Bromilow found the ideal solution. She took her knitting bag to The Sun at lunchtimes and sat knitting over a glass or two of milk stout. Ivy Jones soon realised that Amy Bromilow had the right idea and she joined her. At first the clicking of needles irked Charlie Anson but he soon got used to it, and when his wife Tess decided she would have a go at making socks he could only shake his head in resignation.

Frank and Jim Flynn were due to catch the late train back to Winchester that Sunday evening and Dolly wanted the dinner to be just right. Frank liked his Yorkshire pudding crusty while Jim liked plenty of roast potatoes on his plate, but they both revered her meat stock gravy, and as she stirred in the beef cube Dolly dipped her finger in the thick mixture to sample it. She had chopped the cabbage and shelled the peas, mixed the Yorkshire and made the mustard for Mick, and she felt pleased that it was all under control and on time. Normally the girls would help her get the Sunday meal ready, but today everything had to be perfect and she did not want them getting under her feet.

Up in Sadie's bedroom the two girls were taking advantage of their release from scullery duty by chatting about one or two things that their parents were not privy to.

'So yer've not seen 'im since?' Jennie queried.

'Nope.'

'Yer mean 'e didn't reply ter yer note?'

'Nope.'

'So what yer gonna do then?'

'I dunno, but one fing's certain,' Sadie replied with gusto. 'I ain't gonna go runnin' after 'im.'

'I should bloody well fink not.'

'I wouldn't 'ave minded, but it was as though 'e was usin' me as some ole prosser,' Sadie went on.

'You should've let Nosher give that geezer a goin'-over,' Jennie said.

'I couldn't very well,' Sadie replied. ''E was one o' Johnnie Macaulay's clients after all. It would've only got Nosher inter trouble an' 'e's a really nice bloke.'

'Anyway I reckon Regan'll come callin' before long,' Jennie remarked. ''E's done it before when yer've given 'im the elbow.'

'Well, 'e can please 'imself,' Sadie said sharply. 'I might not answer the door to 'im. I might let you do it, an' you can tell 'im I'm out.'

'Good fer you,' Jennie told her, bouncing up on the edge of the bed. ''Ere, s'posin' yer bump inter Big Joe while 'e's 'ome on leave an' 'e asks yer out. Would yer go?'

'I might,' Sadie said, shrugging her shoulders.

'You like 'im, don't yer?'

''E's all right. 'E's a nice enough feller.'

'I could tell 'e finks a lot o' you.'

'I 'ardly know 'im.'

'What difference does that make?' Jennie pressed. 'I 'ardly know Con but I fink 'e's a dream.'

'All your fellers are dreams,' Sadie scoffed.

'Not the way Con is,' Jennie said sighing as she cuddled the pillow. 'As a matter o' fact I fink I'm in love wiv 'im. Do you believe in love at first sight?'

'It can 'appen, I s'pose, but it's never 'appened ter me yet.'

'You told me yer loved Len.'

'Yeah, but it sort o' grew on me.'

'D'yer still love 'im?'

'I dunno. I dunno what I feel at the moment.'

'After the war I'm gonna marry Con an' 'ave 'is babies,' Jennie drooled on. 'We'll get a nice place in the country an' the kids can grow up in the fresh air wiv fields ter play in.'

'It sounds lovely, but it can only be a dream while this war goes on,' Sadie reminded her.

They heard their mother's voice calling them down to Sunday dinner and Jennie sighed deeply as she slid from the bed. 'I say me prayers every night,' she confided quietly, 'an' they say that if yer pray 'ard enough dreams do come true.'

'Yeah, course they will,' Sadie replied, giving her a warm smile.

Another week and the khaki and navy blue had gone from the lane, where a sprinkling of snow now lay on the cobblestones. An icy wind promised more and it cut through the young airman's greatcoat as he hurried along the turning. He had written a letter to her saying when he would be home on leave, asking her to meet him at midday on Saturday. The little tea bar in the Old Kent Road was the place where they had often sat chatting together in happier days, but as he strode on the young man was prepared for the worst. Brenda was a beautiful woman with a passion that sometimes surprised him, and he had spent many lonely hours back in camp wondering about her. Not all the local young men were in uniform yet and there were a few who wouldn't be slow to come calling, given the opportunity.

The cafe was warm and welcoming and the smell of bacon frying drifted out from the kitchen. Pat carried a large mug of tea over to a window seat and loosened his greatcoat as he made himself comfortable. Brenda was never one for punctuality and while he waited patiently for her to put in an appearance he watched the passers-by and the fairly heavy traffic through a circular space he cleared on the steamy window. It had been a long six weeks and he wondered how the parting had affected her. At least she would have had time to think clearly, though knowing Brenda she might have pushed it all into the background and decided to have a good time.

He suddenly saw her pass the window, and as she came into the cafe Pat was on his feet. ''Ow yer doin', Brenda?' he asked as casually as he could.

'Fine. An' you?'

'Yeah, fine.'

'Yer look like yer lost weight, Pat.'

He smiled awkwardly as he led her over to his seat. 'Can I get yer a cuppa?'

'I'd like a coffee please. Milky.'

They sat facing each other, hardly knowing what to say, and it was Brenda who finally made a start. 'You never wrote ter me while you were away, before askin' if we could meet terday,' she said, flicking her eyes up at his.

'I wanted to,' he sighed, 'but I thought we'd said everyfing before I left ter join up.'

'You could 'ave let me know 'ow you were gettin' on, told me about the trainin',' she remarked.

He shrugged his shoulders. 'If I 'ad done would you 'ave bovvered ter reply?'

'I dunno,' she said, staring down into her cup. 'Yer made it quite clear you were gonna volunteer an' I could like it or lump it.'

'I didn't say it like that,' he replied defensively.

'Not in as many words, but that's what yer meant,' Brenda

159

told him. 'It was as though it was a big adventure an' what I wanted fer us didn't matter.'

'But it does,' Pat said quietly. 'The fing was, I wanted ter get it over wiv, joinin' up I mean. Frank an' Jim decided ter volunteer instead o' waitin' ter be called up an' we talked about it. I agreed wiv 'em. It made no sense to 'ang around scratchin' ourselves.'

'Yeah, but it's all right fer them,' Brenda retorted. 'Neivver of 'em's got a steady girlfriend. Wiv you it was different. We were talkin' about gettin' engaged. We could 'ave done it before yer got called up, but no, you couldn't wait. I was so mad. It seemed ter me I didn't count fer anyfing. You just made yer mind up wivout talkin' it over. Surely I 'ad the right ter be told of yer feelin's before yer made the decision.'

'Maybe yer right,' Pat conceded. 'But please don't fink I treat this as some schoolboy adventure. I know what war means from listenin' ter me dad an' people of 'is age. It's terrifyin' an' bloody, but we're in a war an' that's that.'

Brenda looked up into his eyes. 'I was 'opin' yer wouldn't 'ave ter go,' she said quietly. 'There's plenty o' people in reserved occupations. I wanted you 'ere wiv me, not in the firin' line.'

He smiled. 'I'm not exactly in the firin' line, Brenda. At the moment I've passed out o' basic trainin' an' I'm gonna be trained up as an aircraft frame fitter.'

'You told me you was gonna volunteer fer aircrew,' Brenda reminded him.

'So I am, but there's no guarantee I'll be accepted.'

'But why?' she pressed him. 'I just can't understand. Surely you're doin' yer bit bein' a fitter or whatever, wivout volunteerin' fer a dangerous job like that.'

He sighed deeply, struggling for an explanation which he could put into words. 'Don't ask me fer reasons, Brenda,' he replied helplessly.

She pushed her empty cup away from her, her eyes flaring angrily as she stood up and leaned across the table towards him. 'No, course not,' she said coldly. 'You put yer name down fer one o' the most dangerous jobs yer can find an' yer don't know the reason? Well, I know the reason. It's that manly fing. "Look at me, everybody. Ain't I big, ain't I smart, ain't I brave?" You men are born wiv it. You 'ave it as kids an' it never leaves yer. You be big, Pat. You be smart an' brave too, but don't expect me ter sit at 'ome prayin' fer yer next letter an' worryin' meself sick every time a plane goes missin'. I've got a life too, an' I wanted it wiv you. I wanna be seen in a white weddin' dress, not mournin' black.'

Pat saw the tears welling up in her eyes as she turned away from him and stormed out of the cafe. People were looking over and he felt his face grow hot. He got up quickly, and as he hurried towards the door an old lady sitting alone at a table grabbed his arm. 'She'll come round in time, luv,' she said quietly. 'It ain't easy fer anybody these days.'

It snowed again that week and a general feeling of depression settled over Carter Lane. The servicemen had all returned from leave, Claire Wilson had gone back to Wiltshire and Mrs Jones' daughter Alma had left to join the WAAF. Even the corner shop couple, Sara and Tom Jackman, seemed to have lost some of their cheeriness. The queues grew longer and food supplies became short as the toll of shipping sunk mounted daily, and while the Jackmans refused to engage in what had now become known as the black market, certain foodstuffs were available 'under the counter' at many shops. If a customer could afford the price and knew where to go they could buy almost anything. Silk stockings were almost impossible to get hold of unless a person had the right contacts, and thereby a much-used epithet entered the English language. The 'spiv' always seemed able to lay hands on even the most scarce of commodities, and if the money was forthcoming so were the goods.

It was a bitterly cold morning when Big Joe Buckley finally walked back into the turning and knocked on the Kennys' front door.

'Oh my good Gawd, it's you!' Liz gasped.

'It was, the last time I copped a squiz at meself in the mirror, Liz,' Joe said grinning widely. 'Well, are you gonna let me in or what?'

'Come in, son,' she said, hugging him as he stepped into the passage. 'Bert, it's Big Joe.'

Liz's husband hurried down the stairs and grabbed the Australian by the hand. 'Blimey, you look well,' he remarked. 'We thought yer'd fergot about us.'

'Not a chance, mate,' Joe replied as he walked into the parlour.

'Sit down by the fire, son,' Liz said quickly. 'Bert, give 'im that cushion. Cup o' tea, Joe? Blimey, it is good ter see yer. Yer look smart in that uniform. Doesn't 'e look smart, Bert?'

''E certainly does,' Bert replied.

162

Joe smiled. 'You are now looking at Leading Seaman Joseph L. Buckley, no bloody less,' he declared drolly, pointing to the red anchor sewn into the arm of his uniform.

Liz fussed and Bert had many questions, and the big Australian settled back in the armchair with a huge mug of sweet, steaming hot tea.

'I've bin out wiv the flu,' Bert told him. 'I'm goin' back on Monday though. I'm glad I was 'ome when yer knocked. Bloody 'ell it's good ter see yer, mate.'

'And it's good to see you two,' Joe said, his smile growing even broader.

''Ave you 'ad anyfing to eat this mornin'?' Liz asked him.

'Yeah, I had some breckie before I left the barracks.'

'Don't tell me yer couldn't manage egg an' bacon,' Liz persisted.

Bert got up from his armchair. 'I won't be long, son, I'm just gonna go fer the mornin' paper,' he said.

'You stay where you are,' Joe told him. 'It's colder than a polar bear's arse out there. I'll get it.'

'She likes the *Daily Sketch*,' Bert reminded him. 'She only gets it fer the bloody 'oroscope.'

In a small community such as Carter Lane it would not have taken long, and fifteen minutes later Big Joe came back with the paper under his arm and a look of thunder on his handsome face. 'I want a word with you two,' he said sternly.

Chapter Fourteen

The cold weather was not likely to prevent the likes of Danny Crossley and Alf Coates from making their usual trip to the corner pub, and at ten minutes past eleven on Tuesday morning they stepped into the public bar to announce that it was cold enough to freeze the balls off a brass monkey.

Charlie Anson had got the fire going and the intrepid two took their pints over to a nearby table and stood for a few minutes by the hearth warming themselves.

'By the way, Big Joe's 'ome on leave,' the landlord called over as he poured Mrs Bromilow's milk stout. 'My missus saw 'im at the paper shop this mornin'. 'E told 'er 'e'd got 'ome yesterday.'

'That's nice to 'ear,' Danny replied. ''Ere, 'e ain't on the wagon, is 'e?'

'I shouldn't fink so. Why d'yer ask?'

'Well, I would 'ave thought 'e'd 'ave looked in 'ere last night.'

'No sweat, 'e told Tess 'e was gonna pop in this lunchtime.'

The two elderly gents made themselves comfortable at the table and sat watching Amy Bromilow unravelling a skein of thick navy-blue wool as she sat a little way away.

Alf took out his stained clay pipe from his top pocket and examined it before getting out his penknife to scrape the bowl into the hearth. 'Better than a briar,' he remarked to Amy. 'When yer burn 'em in they taste as sweet as a nut.'

'You could 'ave fooled me,' Amy said sarcastically. 'That stuff you smoke in that pipe smells like 'orseshit.'

'Nah, it's dark shag,' Alf told her. 'It don't burn away as quickly as that light stuff.'

Amy was struggling with the wool. ''Ere, Danny, give us an 'and will yer?' she asked him. 'Come an' 'old this while I wind it.'

The elderly man reluctantly went over and sat facing her while she slipped the skein over his outstretched hands and proceeded to make a ball. 'Now keep yer 'ands still,' she said, 'an' don't let it slip off or I'll be all day unravellin' it.'

Just then Big Joe made his appearance wearing his uniform, and he stood inside the door taking in the scene. 'Now that's what I call a nice picture,' he said grinning. 'I wish I had a camera. The folk back in Oz wouldn't believe it.'

Danny grinned sheepishly and Alf got up to pat the young man on the back. 'Nice ter see yer, son,' he said. 'Come on, let me buy you a pint.'

Big Joe put his arm around the old man's shoulders. 'I wouldn't bloody dream of it,' he replied. 'I'm gonna buy you one, digger.'

Charlie Anson shook the big man's hand vigorously. 'Yer look very well, Joe,' he said. ''Ow long you 'ome for?'

'Seven days,' Joe told him.

'It ain't long.'

'It's enough to sort a few things out,' the Australian said as he watched the landlord pour the drinks.

Charlie glanced up quickly at the tone of his voice and saw the steel glint in Joe's deep-blue eyes. 'You just take it easy, son. Yer 'ome ter rest, remember.'

Joe insisted on buying Charlie a drink as well as Amy and the two pub fixtures, and when he had settled himself at the table beside them he took a long draught. 'I got to hear about the barney with the Conroy boy and that boofhead Cafferty,' he remarked, glancing at each of the old gents in turn.

''E was well out of order,' Alf said quickly. 'Whatever the rights an' wrongs there's no call fer the bloody ox ter go pokin' 'is nose in ovver people's business.'

'I s'pose you 'eard about Bert Kenny gettin' clocked?' Danny queried.

'Yeah, I did,' Big Joe growled, 'and Cafferty's gonna 'ave to see me about that. That dingo's gonna be as scarce as rockin'-horse shit round here when I've finished with him.'

'You can't afford ter get involved, Joe,' Alf warned him. 'If yer come up in front o' that beak again 'e'll chuck the book at yer.'

'Don't you worry about me,' Joe replied. 'I'll flush that nong down the dunny before the blue boys get here.'

'You just be careful,' Danny added. 'Bert Kenny finks the world o' you an' 'e wouldn't want yer gettin' inter trouble on 'is account.'

Joe took another gulp from his glass. 'I understand the Flynn boys were home on leave a couple o' weeks ago,' he said, changing the subject.

'Yeah, but it was a pity Frank an' Jim missed young Pat,' Alf replied. 'As they went back so Pat comes 'ome. 'E went back last Sunday. 'E was in 'ere on Saturday night wiv some of 'is pals an' 'e ended up gettin' as pissed as an 'andcart.'

167

'How's the Flynn girls?' Joe asked casually.

'Young Jennie's got a job at the baker's in the Old Kent Road,' Amy cut in, 'an' Sadie's started work at the gasworks offices up on Canal Bridge. Oh an' as you can see I've joined the Lockwood sisters' sewin' club.'

'Good fer you, Amy,' Joe said grinning. 'Is that a scarf you're knitting?'

'Looks more like a bed blanket,' Alf chuckled.

'None o' your cheek neivver,' Amy growled at him. 'This is fer a sailor, an' those navy boys need long scarves ter keep 'em warm while they're at sea.'

'Our Amy's a good ole knitter,' Danny remarked. 'Yer should've seen the pair o' socks she's just finished. The bloody size of 'em. I ses to 'er, ain't those socks s'posed ter be worn under their Wellin'ton boots. I thought I was gonna end up wearin' 'er glass o' stout.'

'I wouldn't waste it on the likes o' you,' Amy said disdainfully.

Joe studied his near-empty glass for a few moments and then he leaned over the table. 'Have either of you seen anything o' Cafferty lately?' he asked quietly.

Alf shook his head slowly as he filled his pipe. 'I expect Bert Kenny told yer that Charlie barred 'im from 'ere, and I've 'eard 'e's usin' The Dun Cow now. Apparently Cafferty's the yard foreman in the Council buildin' depot just round the corner in Lynton Road.'

'Yeah, one o' the buildin' lads was tellin' us,' Danny cut in. ''E said Cafferty's there every lunchtime shootin' 'is mouth off about one fing or anuvver. The guv'nor at The Dun Cow won't stand too much o' that, mark my words.'

Joe looked from one to the other, a smile forming on his

broad features. 'Do you still go on those little walkabouts?' he enquired.

'Yeah as long as it's dry,' Alf told him. 'The cold don't worry us, does it Danny?'

'Nah, long as we're well wrapped up.'

'Apart from Cafferty are you two known at The Dun Cow?'

'Nah, we never go in there,' Alf replied.

'How would you like to do me a big favour?'

'You name it, son,' Alf told him.

'Right then, here's the plan, but first let's get some more drinks in,' Joe said, smiling slyly.

At five o'clock Sadie walked out of the gasworks office and waved goodnight to her workfriends, pulling her coat collar up around her ears as she turned into Lynton Road. After a few yards she felt a hand on her arm and turned quickly to see Joe Buckley smiling at her. 'Hello, Sadie,' he said cheerfully.

'Well I'll be . . .' Sadie said in surprise. 'What are you doin' up 'ere?'

'Time was on me hands and I suddenly got this idea that maybe you might be a bit bored walking home with no one to talk to,' Joe said smiling.

'Well, it's very nice, but 'ow did yer know where I worked?' she asked.

'How do you keep a secret in a place like Carter Lane?' he replied.

Sadie smiled back. 'An' I s'pose yer've caught up wiv all the ovver news?'

He nodded nonchalantly. 'Yeah, this and that,' he said.

'Well, I 'ope yer not gonna get yerself inter trouble over that set-to in the turnin',' she remarked.

Joe was still holding on to her arm as they walked up the rise that led over the railway lines, feeling the chill wind on their faces. 'Nah, I've gotta be a bit careful after last time,' he said with a sigh. 'Still, I'm sure that big bully'll get his comeuppance one day soon.'

'Yeah, 'e will, that's a dead cert,' Sadie replied. 'So you just let it rest. Bert's fergot about it I'm sure.'

'Yep, sure thing, Sadie,' Joe said blithely.

She looked into his eyes, a smile playing on her lips. 'Try not ter ferget yerself when yer've got a few pints inside yer, won't yer?' she told him. 'Just mind what yer doin'. Liz Kenny won't take kindly ter bailin' yer out again.'

He winced noticeably. 'Yeah, best behaviour,' he said with a sheepish smile.

'I wasn't gettin' at yer, Joe,' she said quickly. 'It's just that people in Carter Lane like yer an' they wouldn't wanna see yer gettin' into any more trouble.'

'Does that include you too?' he asked.

'Yeah, me too.'

'Sadie, are you still with that feller?'

'Well, if yer must know it's bin an off-an'-on fing lately, but I'm still seein' 'im occasionally.'

Joe looked pleased with her answer. 'Look, is there any chance of coming out for a drink with me?' he asked. 'Tonight maybe?'

'Well, I was gonna wash me 'air an' do some ironin',' she told him.

'Aw, your hair's not dirty yet,' he replied. 'And ironin' ain't very exciting.'

'An' comin' out fer a drink wiv you would be?' she teased.

Joe pulled a face. 'I'm not very good at this sort of thing,' he said solemnly. 'But if you decide to come out for a drink I'd be honoured.'

His serious expression looked very comical and her heart bounded. 'You're on,' she said smiling.

Joe's face lit up. 'Ripper,' he said, punching the air.

They turned left into Munday Road and left again into Carter Lane whereupon Joe let go of her arm. 'Is eight o'clock okay?' he asked as they reached her front door.

'Yeah, fine. See yer then,' Sadie said, giving him a smile as she let herself into the house.

On Wednesday morning Alf Coates and Danny Crossley wrapped themselves up against the inclement weather and took a stroll along the Old Kent Road to The Dun Cow. 'I understand Sid Cafferty drinks in 'ere,' Alf said to the barman as he waited for his glass to be filled.

'Yeah, that's right,' the barman said, eyeing the elderly man curiously. 'Why d'yer ask?'

'It's just that we don't like ter see trouble where it can be avoided, do we, Alf?' Danny cut in.

'Trouble?'

'Yeah, it seems that Sid Cafferty's card's bin marked.'

''Ow d'yer mean?'

'Well, me an' my mate 'ere was 'avin' a livener in The Sun public 'ouse down in Carter Lane yesterday,' Danny went on, 'an' we 'eard this geezer called Alec Conroy shootin' 'is mouth off. 'E was sayin' that Sid Cafferty was a no-good git an' a yeller-livered coward ter boot, an' if 'e ever showed 'is face around Carter Lane again 'e was gonna get

171

sorted out good an' proper. This Conroy bloke said that it was only the neighbours interferin' that saved 'im last time but the next time round they wouldn't get the chance. 'E went on ter say that Cafferty 'ad better keep ter The Dun Cow or 'e'd do 'im over bad.'

'Yeah, that's right,' Alf said. 'We're on our way ter Peckham ter see me daughter so we decided it might be a good idea ter pop in 'ere while we was in the area an' warn Cafferty off from goin' anywhere near Carter Lane. I can't stand ter see people bashin' each ovver up. It's bad enough wiv the bleedin' war.'

''E'll be in around twelve,' the barman told them. 'Why don't yer 'ang about.'

'Nah, I'm afraid we ain't got time,' Alf replied. 'Me daughter 'as ter go out at twelve. P'raps you could warn 'im. We wouldn't like ter see the bloke get duffed up, would we, mate?'

Danny shook his head as he put on his most stern expression. 'This Conroy bloke seems like 'e means it. 'E was slaggin' Cafferty off unmercifully. Best if yer warn 'im ter keep well away from The Sun.'

As the two old friends walked back to Carter Lane they could not help looking a little pleased with themselves.

'You know somefing, Alf,' Danny said grinning. 'I make you out ter be one lyin' ole git.'

'You ain't so bad yerself,' Alf replied.

Big Joe Buckley was wearing his civilian clothes as he sat alone at a table in The Sun waiting for the two to arrive back. Last night had been a very nice evening, he thought dreamily – a few drinks in The Anchor, an old timbered pub by the river, sitting by a log fire and chatting away non-stop about almost everything. He had told Sadie more about his life back in Australia and she had spoken about her childhood days in the street. They had laughed and joked together, and she had told him a little bit about her relationship with Len Regan. She had been light-hearted about it but he had sensed an undertow of discontent. He had gained the impression that Regan wasn't taking things seriously enough and she needed more from their relationship. He also got the message that Sadie had no intention of cheating on him. To her the evening was nothing more than a friendly chat between two neighbours and he should read nothing into it. Okay fair go, he thought, but as far as he could work out, the door had been left ajar, and it was up to him to make his mark, let her see that he was truly pretty mad about her, despite Len Regan. How he was expected to achieve anything though, what with the war and being away most of the time, was beyond him and the problem left him feeling a little frustrated.

The look on both Alf and Danny's faces as they walked into the pub told Joe that things had gone according to plan and his heart pounded with anticipation.

''E'll get the message,' Alf said grinning.

'Cafferty's gonna be fired up like a mad bull,' Danny added. 'You'd better be careful, Joe.'

Come lunchtime, the pub was filling up, which suited Joe very nicely. If Cafferty did take the bait and come calling he would be on his opponent's ground and be unlikely to have a cohort nearby to back him up, should things not go his way. It was also important to the big Australian that Cafferty should be shamed away from the area once and for all.

173

Time moved on. Twenty past the hour, twenty to two, and still no sign of Sid Cafferty. Joe was beginning to feel that his plan had failed and he considered getting another drink, but at fifteen minutes to two a young workman came into the bar looking a little agitated. 'Is Alec Conroy in 'ere?' he asked the elderly man sitting just inside the door.

Joe heard the remark. 'Who wants him?' he asked.

'A big geezer across the street,' the workman said timidly.

Joe looked through a clear gap in the figured glass of the door to see Sid Cafferty leaning against the wall opposite. He was wearing a duffle coat with a scarf loosely tied around his bull neck. Suddenly he straightened up and cupped his hand to his mouth. 'Come out, yer mouthy git, I know yer in there,' he bellowed out.

Joe took a deep breath, threw out his chest and stepped out into the street. 'You never learn, do you, Cafferty,' he called back.

The bully's face grew dark. 'I should 'ave suspected somefing like this,' he growled as he stepped into the roadway. 'Keep out o' this, Buckley. I got no beef wiv you. I'm lookin' fer Conroy.'

'He's not been in the pub for a couple o' weeks,' Joe told him calmly.

'Yeah, that figures,' Cafferty said, gritting his teeth. 'Yer set me up, didn't yer?'

'Well, it wasn't hard,' Joe told him with a laugh. 'You ain't got enough brains to give yerself a headache. An' now you're gonna answer to me for Bert Kenny.'

'Bert Kenny? Who's 'e?'

'The man you conked when he tried to stop you beating the Conroy lad up,' Joe replied. 'Bert's a good mate o' mine,

174

so when I've finished you won't work in an iron lung.'

Cafferty realised there was no way out of the straits he found himself in and he got ready by slipping out of his heavy coat and unravelling the scarf from around his neck as Joe moved closer to him. Still holding the scarf he suddenly lunged forward, attempting to get it round Joe's throat but the Australian was too quick for him. A short right in the midriff made Cafferty gasp but he swung round smartly and planted a left hook on the side of his opponent's head. For a moment Joe saw flashing lights and he realised that Cafferty was not going to be a pushover. He turned, his fists held up in front of his face, and when the bully darted forward he was ready. The first blow smacked full into Cafferty's face and the looping left hit him behind the ear. The hulking bruiser spat blood from his split lips as he staggered back, then with a roar he rushed forward and grabbed Joe round the waist. With his hands pinned to his sides and the breath slowly being pressed out of him Joe butted Cafferty in the face, at the same time bringing his knee up sharply into his groin.

They moved back from each other, circling like dogs looking for an opening, oblivious of the cries of people watching the fight.

'For goodness' sake stop them somebody,' Charity Lockwood called out.

'Let 'em fight,' Alf Coates called back, dancing from one foot to the other with excitement.

'Why don't somebody do somefing?' Mrs Wickstead shouted.

'What d'yer suggest, gel?' another chuckled. 'A bucket o' water?'

Fists smashed out with sickening thuds and both men were beginning to spill blood. Cafferty's nose was broken and his eyebrow cut, and Joe had a gaping gash on his cheekbone. They circled once more, breath coming in rasping gasps and then as Cafferty rushed forward in a last desperate effort a swinging right with all Joe's force behind it slammed home and it was all over. Cafferty went down as though he had been poleaxed and lay prone on the cobblestones, dead to the world.

Joe made his way painfully back to the pub, and as he glanced back he saw Bill Harris in the process of dowsing Cafferty with a bucket of cold water.

'I don't fink we'll see 'im round 'ere any more,' Alf Coates remarked to Danny.

'Good riddance, I say,' his friend replied.

Later that evening as soon as Alec Conroy got home from work Rene told him about the fight. 'Joe slaughtered the ugly git,' she said with passion. 'Me an' yer dad was sayin', we've never seen a fight like it.'

Alec slumped down in the armchair and kicked off his shoes. 'Yeah,' he said flatly.

'I thought yer would 'ave bin well pleased,' Ted remarked.

Alec looked up at his mother and father in turn. 'What did it solve?' he asked them. 'Tell me what it solved.'

'It put a bully in 'is place, that's what,' Ted said sharply. 'It's what this war's all about. About standin' up against the bully. You stood up ter Cafferty, so why won't yer stand up ter the biggest one of all?'

'Well, if it makes yer both feel any better, I volunteered fer the army this mornin',' Alec told them.

Chapter Fifteen

1940

The first Christmas of the war had been a very quiet affair for the people of Carter Lane. With so many empty spaces around the festive tables it had been almost wished away as people looked forward hopefully to a New Year that would bring peace. A freezing January and snow in February gave way to seasonal March winds, and with them a general realisation that the war was not going to end that soon after all. With news coming through of naval activity off the coast of Norway and the massing of the German army in the Baltic ports it seemed to almost everyone that it was only just beginning to hot up.

Riflemen Frank and Jim Flynn were now serving in France with the British Expeditionary Force along with Con Williams, and so too was Chris Wickstead of the Royal Fusiliers. Amy Bromilow's son Freddie was sent to France in January with his battalion of Grenadier Guards and Ivy Jones' son Jerry was serving with a Royal Marine brigade which was making ready to land in Norway. Big Joe Buckley had used his special knowledge of marine diesels to get selected for a secret and elite force, and in the early new year he was training at a remote base somewhere in Scotland.

Early in April the German army swept into Denmark and Norway and within twenty-four hours Denmark was in German hands. Its ports and inlets were now available for an assault on Norway, and as the depressing news filtered through, Ivy and Ben Jones had good reason to worry when they heard that the Royal Marines were amongst the British forces which had landed in Narvik. Ben Jones kept a map of Norway and he was able to follow the military movements as the German army swept down from the north of the country. Reports were coming through of heavy casualties, and when the army was evacuated from Norway on the third of April Ivy and Ben said a special prayer that their son Jerry would be amongst the survivors.

As the weather changed for the better at the end of April people felt that maybe the summer would bring some good news for a change, but their hopes turned to nightmare when in early May the German army swept through the Low Countries and attacked France through the Ardennes. Their units pushed back towards the coastline, the sons of Carter Street were now fighting for their lives.

Sadie Flynn dried the last of the plates and hung the wet tea towel over the line above the gas stove. For some time now there had been a strained atmosphere between her and her parents and when she complained to Jennie she had got little support.

'It's understandable when yer stop ter fink,' Jennie reminded her as they sat together in Sadie's bedroom. 'Frank an' Jim are fightin' in France and Pat's away, an' there's you swannin' it wiv that wide-boy Regan.'

'What am I s'posed ter do, pack 'im in, just 'cos 'e's not out there fightin' as well?'

'I'm not sayin' that,' Jennie replied, 'but it don't 'elp when yer told Muvver the ovver night about that party at the nightclub. I mean, champagne an' all the best food, while people round 'ere are 'avin' ter pay frew the nose fer under-the-counter stuff. It ain't on, is it?'

Sadie sighed sadly. 'I can understand 'ow people must feel, but as I tried to explain ter Mum, not everyone can just put on a uniform. Life 'as ter go on at 'ome. Lots o' young men are in reserved jobs an' they're doin' their bit, even though people tend ter slag 'em off fer dodgin' call-up.'

'I fink it's all right fer people in reserved occupations,' Jennie went on, 'but it's people like that Johnnie Macaulay an' your feller who are takin' advantage by dealin' in the black market. 'Ow d'yer fink our bruvvers'd feel if they were riskin' their lives on those convoys bringin' food in an' then they 'eard about all this dodgy business that's makin' certain people rich.'

'I don't fink Macaulay's in the black market,' Sadie said defensively. 'All right, so they buy stuff under the counter like a lot of ovver people but as fer dealin' in it, I don't believe they do.'

Jennie shook her head slowly. 'What you're really sayin' is yer don't wanna believe it,' she corrected her. 'Face up to it, Sadie. Johnnie Macaulay an' Len Regan run this area, an' from yer own admission they control almost all the goin's-on. They just use ordinary people, an' if yer want my opinion I fink they're usin' you. Look at yerself. Last year there was this fing you got about Len playin' fast an' loose.

You felt sure that 'e 'ad someone else, an' what 'appened? Soon as 'e contacted yer you came runnin'. 'E's a sweet talker an' you're lettin' yerself be swayed by it. What future can you 'ave wiv a bloke like 'im? There's no chance o' you ever gettin' married, yer said so yerself. Are you always gonna be at Regan's beck an' call? What 'appens when you're older, inter middle age? There's all yer friends married an' wiv their kids growin' up, an' there's you, still single an' lookin' over yer shoulder at every young sort who comes on the scene in case she turns 'is 'ead.'

'There's a war on an' I'm not lookin' that far ahead,' Sadie replied, her sister's words of wisdom weighing more heavily than she cared to admit. 'We could all be dead before the war's over.'

'Well, if that's all yer can say then I feel sorry for yer,' Jennie said with irritation.

'You don't 'ave ter feel sorry fer me,' Sadie answered quickly as she swung round on the dressing-table stool and snatched up her hairbrush.

Jennie sighed deeply, thinking that she had perhaps gone too far. 'Look, Sadie, I'm yer sister, the only one yer've got, an' we've always bin close, able ter tell our secrets to each ovver, talk to each ovver about the lads we went out wiv, an' that's the way it should be. Lately though yer've become very defensive, sharp if yer like, an' that's why there's an atmosphere in the 'ome. Well, it's part of it anyway. You seem ter jump lately when anyfing's said about where yer goin', what yer doin'. I don't fink you're 'appy, the way fings are wiv Len Regan. In fact I'm sure you're not.'

The remarks hit home and Sadie gulped back a tear as she turned again to face her younger sister. 'Last year, when I suspected Len o' seein' somebody else,' she said quietly, 'I decided to 'old fire instead of accusin' 'im outright. After all, I didn't 'ave any proof that anyfing was goin' on. It was just a lot o' little fings that began ter trouble me. Anyway I decided ter pull meself tergevver an' act as though I didn't 'ave a clue. So after a few days I came runnin', as you described it. I thought that if anyfing was goin' on I'd find out fer sure sooner or later, but d'you know, from then on fings got much better between us. Len got really attentive an' I was gettin' involved in more an' more of 'is business. I even done some work on the firm's books. Then last month Len 'ad ter go down ter Brighton, ter that place they set up.'

'The brothel,' Jennie said helpfully.

'Yeah, the brothel,' Sadie continued smiling. 'It's a posh set-up wiv a lot o' senior officers an' professional people amongst its clients. Len was gone fer a whole week an' when 'e came back 'e seemed different. I can't describe it, but I could feel it. Fings started ter slip back ter the way they were before an' now when we get tergevver we find it 'ard ter relax wiv each ovver. D'you understand what I'm sayin'? We both seem ter be on a short fuse an' I don't like it. I'm pretty certain now that Len 'as got someone else.'

''Ave yer fronted 'im about it?' Jennie asked quickly.

'Yeah I did, an' 'e denied it of course,' Sadie told her.

'But yer still don't know fer sure?'

'I can tell. I can tell when we make love,' Sadie said, picking away at the brush hairs. 'It used ter be good, really good, but now it's as if 'e's preoccupied all the time, an' ter be honest 'e's not that keen any more, not like 'e was.'

'It could be the pressure of the job 'e's doin', or 'e might not be 'undred-per-cent fit,' Jennie suggested.

Sadie shook her head. 'I'd know if it was that.'

''Ow?'

'I just would.'

'So what yer gonna do?'

'I'm gonna play it cagey an' wait fer 'im ter make a mistake. They do, they always do.'

'Come back, Big Joe,' Jennie said, raising her hands to the ceiling. 'Come 'ome on leave an' sweep my big sister off 'er feet.'

'Yeah, it'd be nice ter see 'im again,' Sadie agreed, smiling at Jennie's pose. 'But don't get any wrong ideas. Me an' Joe are just good friends.'

'Do just good friends write lots o' letters?' Jennie asked with raised eyebrows. 'Don't worry – I ain't bin rootin' frew yer drawers. I've got ter recognise the 'andwritin' on those letters ter you that keep droppin' on the mat. Big Joe must be writin' to yer four times a week at least. God, what can one good friend keep on writin' about to anuvver good friend?'

'Jennie, yer've just outlived yer welcome,' Sadie said, making a threatening gesture towards her.

'All right, all right, I'm leavin',' Jennie giggled as she got up from the edge of the bed. 'I bet 'e's writin' poetry an' sayin' lovely fings, ain't 'e? Can I see one o' those letters?'

'Get out,' Sadie growled as she threw the hairbrush at her fleeing sister.

Down in the parlour Dolly leaned back in her armchair and screwed her face up against the tiredness inside her. The wireless had been left on and soft music drifted through the room, lulling her to sleep, but it was suddenly interrupted when Mick came home from the pub. 'Good news, gel,' he said loudly. 'The Joneses 'ave 'eard from young Jerry. 'E's safe. 'Is unit landed in Iceland an' 'e's managed ter send 'em a letter.'

'Fank Gawd fer that,' Dolly said with feeling as she straightened herself in the chair. 'Turn the wireless up a bit, luv, the news'll be on soon.'

Across the narrow strip of water that had thwarted many an army and at least one armada, an army was massing at the coast around Dunkirk, tired, disorganised and fighting for its life. Moving in to crush the remaining resistance were the well-trained and disciplined German divisions, and in reserve a Panzer regiment and the dreaded SS corps waited to perform the coup de grâce.

The Rifle Brigade had taken heavy casualties as it fought to keep the road to Dunkirk open, and now the remnants were being rallied for a last-ditch stand. The battalion commander had been killed and the adjutant severely wounded, leaving the senior officer Captain Morgan in charge. His first duty was to send a runner to summon the B company commander, and amid the din of battle with shells flying overhead and machine-gun emplacements picking off anyone who showed themselves above the redoubt, Second Lieutenant Garry Baker slid down into the trench to be told that B company was to fight a rearguard action until their ammunition ran out, in an effort to allow the rest of the battalion to get to Dunkirk. There was no time for an explanation as to why B company had been chosen, and Lieutenant Baker did not dream of asking for one. The truth was, his company had taken fewer casualties than the other companies and they would be able to provide the best cover available.

'Sergeant Brody, take your squad up to the rise. Corporal Williams, take your squad over to the farm. Hold your fire as long as possible,' Baker told them. 'Make every round count. When you have to fall back make for the road and then it's a question of fighting our way down to the sands. Good luck.'

Frank Flynn looked around the dust-covered members of C company as they slithered down into the redoubt and to his immense relief he saw his brother Jim who raised his hand in greeting. Frank slid over to him, careful to keep his head down and Jim grinned, his white teeth standing out against his blackened face.

'Okay, bruv?'

'Yeah. You?'

'B company's makin' a stand at the farm by all accounts.'

'Poor bastards.'

''Ave yer got a fag?'

'Right out,' Frank told him. 'If yer wait a minute I'll pop up ter The Sun an' get a packet.'

'What wouldn't I give ter be sittin' in there right now,' Jim said sighing.

The noise of battle increased and the men of C company knew that their pals in B company were locked in battle, giving them the chance to make the dash to the sands of Dunkirk.

'Fall in, you beautiful shower,' Sergeant Stanford bawled out. 'Let's go, an' keep those stupid 'eads down.'

A firm favourite with the company and a veteran of the First World War, Stanford was believed to be immortal and the men would have followed him right into hell if he had led the way. But hell was already gaping all around them, here in this once green and serene landscape, a charnel-house of corpses,

184

both human and animal, where bullet and shell, machine gun and grenade, had turned the flatlands into a bloody, battle-scarred, dust-caked nightland which defied belief.

The men trudged on, weary beyond caring. Hungry, thirsty men who less than a year ago were practising their trades, dating young women, swilling pints and tucking children into bed. They could see the town of Dunkirk ahead with its church spire still intact, and they knew that there on the beaches was the rendezvous point, where they would be fed and watered and then taken off by luggers and ships' boats to the vessels anchored in deep water. What they didn't know yet, although they heard the din and roar, was that Stuka dive bombers were strafing the beaches and sinking ships, turning the beaches into another hell-hole, another place to die, cut to ribbons by the planes' machine guns as they made their runs, flying low above the dunes.

As night fell and the enemy aircraft left to rearm and refuel, C company were herded together and Sergeant Stanford spelt it out. 'We're to assemble by the upturned wreck,' he told them. 'We've been allocated one large ship's boat and a few dinghies. Some of you will have to go in the water and be towed out, but I don't want any panic, understood? Too many in the boat and it'll capsize. Take orders from the matelots and don't over-fill those dinghies neither. You know your capabilities. The strongest swimmers will give up their places and the wounded get first priority in the boat, which goes without saying. Right then, my merry little men. Let's go.'

Dawn was breaking as the empty boat returned to the prearranged spot, and as the men waded out up to their waists and were hauled aboard, the Luftwaffe returned.

Those in the water had no chance and puddles of blood spread in the sea as the cannon and machine-gun fire sprayed down amongst them. The two matelots were cut down and the boat reduced to splinters as it took a direct hit from a plane's cannon. Men who had survived swam out towards the ships, towing their wounded comrades, while those still on the beach ran headlong into the dunes.

Jim Flynn felt the wetness on his arm and realised that a bullet had ripped through his tunic and cut a deep furrow in his upper arm. Frank was next to him and looked unscathed.

'What did I always tell yer,' Jim said as his older brother quickly ripped the top of his tunic and applied a field dressing to the wound. 'Did I or did I not tell yer it was important yer learnt ter swim well.'

'Shut up, kid, yer sound like me,' Frank replied grinning.

'It's nuffink ter laugh at,' Jim went on. 'I told yer I'd 'ave ter take care of yer. You just stay close ter me when we go in the water. If yer get tired just relax an' let me tow yer, all right?'

'I can make it on me own,' Frank insisted.

'It's a bloody mile ter those ships,' Jim growled. 'All you could ever do was a width at the baths, an' yer splashed an' struggled like some beached whale.'

'Fanks fer the vote o' confidence, bruv,' Frank replied as the roar of aircraft grew louder.

Bullets cut into the sand as dive bombers screamed like a tribe of banshees, then just as quickly it grew quiet again.

'Come on, it's now or never,' Frank shouted.

The brothers dashed to the sea and dived into the surf, struggling to get into deeper water. They realised that the planes were concentrating on the men still trapped in the dunes and they said a silent prayer. Suddenly Jim saw a figure rise up out of the surf and fall back onto the sand. 'It's Stanford,' he shouted. 'You go on, I'll catch you up, an' swim easy, don't tire yerself too quickly.'

As he waded back Jim saw that Stanford had taken a bullet in his left shoulder and his arm was hanging useless at his side. 'Come on, Sarge. Put yer good arm round me an' let me do the work,' he told him firmly.

'Don't you go orderin' me about, young Flynn,' the sergeant roared. 'I'll 'ave you on a charge before you can blink.'

'Shut yer stupid row up,' Jim growled as he pulled the wounded sergeant into the sea.

The water was very cold and Stanford was losing consciousness as Jim turned him on to his back and towed him by his shirt collar into deeper water. Up ahead the nearest ship seemed miles away, and the distance impossible to close as the survivors desperately swam on. Frank was further out by now and seemed to be swimming well enough, though hampered by his thick uniform. Bombs hit the beach and the screams of wounded and dying men reached hauntingly across the sea as the captain of the Thames paddle steamer searched the water through his binoculars.

'There, two points to starboard. Men in the water,' he bawled out. 'Loosen the painter.'

Frank and Jim were finally pulled aboard the ship's boat, along with the unconscious company sergeant and a few other troops swimming alongside.

An elderly man with white hair and a handlebar moustache stood in the prow wearing a fawn duffel coat, sea boots and a rollneck jumper. 'Keep your heads down, lads, the Boche are coming back,' he shouted in a cultured voice as his younger companion turned the boat back towards the paddle steamer. 'Any more for the *Skylark*? Two and six-pence for a one-way trip to jolly old Blighty.' Then, to everyone's amazement, he began to sing with gusto.

'Comrades, comrades, ever since we were boys.
Cheering each other's sorrow,
Sharing each other's joys.
Comrade's a man to be born with,
Faithful what ere may befall.
And when I'm in danger my daring old comrade
Is there by my side.'

Stanford had regained consciousness and he groaned with pain as he tried to move.

'Lie still, it won't be long now before we're aboard ship,' Jim told him.

The company sergeant looked up at Jim Flynn and nar-rowed his eyes. 'If I remember rightly you gave me some lip, son,' he growled.

'It must 'ave bin the pain, Sarge,' Jim said smiling.

Stanford smiled back. 'It must 'ave bin. You wouldn't 'ave dared bawl me out,' he said through chattering teeth. 'I'd 'ave 'ad yer guts fer garters.'

At eleven o'clock that morning the S.S. *Medway Queen* docked at Newhaven with her human cargo, bedraggled remnants of the British Expeditionary Force, and Jim and Frank Flynn gratefully tucked into plates of sausage and mash, washed down with mugs of hot sweet tea.

Chapter Sixteen

Through the last days of May and into June as the exhausted British and French troops were being lifted off the beaches of Dunkirk, continuous wireless broadcasts kept the Carter Lane folk huddled by their sets, their faces white and gaunt with the anxiety and fear. Was my son amongst those taken off? Will he make it back, or is he one of those already fallen, left alone in the dirt beneath a foreign sky?

Throughout the whole country news of survivors was patchy, and the people of Bermondsey suffered the same uncertainty as everyone else. Hurried letters were sent to loved ones as soon as possible after debarkation and police stations, libraries, corner shops and businesses took phone calls and relayed the good-news messages. 'Your son is safe.' 'See you soon, Ma.' 'Back in Blighty.' And for some, no message came.

The Flynn household got their news from Sara Jackman at teatime. The shopkeeper had taken the call from Frank herself and she came running, her face flushed with excitement. 'The boys are safe, Dolly,' she gasped. 'Your Frank phoned just now. 'E said ter tell yer Jim's bin a pain in the arse but they're fit an' well. They don't know if Con got away.'

Dolly cried and Mick strolled out to the backyard to hide his overflowing emotion. Jennie and Sadie hugged each other, and then when the first flush of happiness and relief subsided a little Dolly put her arm around Jennie. ''E'll be all right, you'll see,' she said encouragingly.

''Is gran'muvver might 'ave 'eard somefing,' Jennie replied.

'D'yer know 'er address?'

'Only that she lives in Dock'ead.'

'Keep yer pecker up, luv. Con's gonna be all right,' Dolly told her.

'I wonder if Amy or Ivy's 'eard anyfing yet,' Sadie remarked.

'They'd 'ave come over ter tell us,' Mick replied.

'I must go an' tell 'em the good news,' Dolly said, slipping into her coat.

As she hurried across the cobblestones she saw Amy Bromilow standing in her doorway sobbing, with Ivy Jones holding on to her hand.

'A policeman's just bin,' Ivy told Dolly as she came up to them. ''Er Freddie's safe.'

'I can't stop cryin',' Amy gulped. 'I'm so 'appy.'

The good news travelled fast, but there were those who still had to wait, and for many the waiting was ended by an official communication, a telegram or a War Office letter to say that their son or husband had been killed in action.

Later that evening Jennie sat alone in her tiny bedroom on the bend of the stairs going through the letters she had received from Con. Where was he now, she wondered, her stomach churning as she recalled the news broadcast earlier that evening. Had he been taken as a prisoner of war, or was he at this very moment just lying there, dead on the beach? Perhaps he was badly wounded and could not write a letter or use the phone. There were still many soldiers on the beaches and they were being lifted off nonstop. That was it. He would be one of the last ones to leave. That was Con sure enough.

'Are you all right, Jen?' Sadie asked as she put her head round the door.

'I was just sittin' 'ere finkin',' Jennie replied.

Sadie came into the room and sat down on the edge of the bed. 'That's all there is fer us to do,' she sighed. 'Just sit an' wait, an' fink.'

Jennie quickly gathered her letters together and re-tied them with their silk cord. 'I know it sounds silly, but when I read those letters I can imagine it's Con talkin' ter me,' she said smiling. 'I can 'ear 'is voice an' see the expression in 'is eyes. I take comfort from it.'

'It's not silly at all,' Sadie said kindly, weighing the bundle of letters in her hand. ''Ere, I've got a bundle like that.'

'Do yer reply to 'em?' Jennie asked.

'I 'ave a couple but I find it difficult.'

'Why?'

'I dunno,' Sadie said shrugging. 'It's funny really. I work in an office an' I'm quite used ter puttin' letters tergevver when customers' bills are overdue or when I 'ave ter send out some information, but when it comes ter writin' personal letters I find it very difficult.'

'Take anuvver look at Big Joe's letters an' answer in the same vein,' Jennie suggested.

'It's not as easy as that,' Sadie replied. 'Joe makes

everyfing so interestin', like when 'e describes what it was like fer 'im as a young lad, I feel as if I know the places 'e writes about. I couldn't write fings down like 'e does.'

'Yeah, but yer don't 'ave to,' Jennie persisted. 'Fer instance, just sit down quietly like I do an' fink about 'ow the day went, what the weavver was like, who yer met, what yer did. There's no end to it.'

'Oh, 'e wouldn't be interested in all that chit-chat,' Sadie said dismissively.

'That's where yer wrong,' Jennie told her. 'This is Joe's new 'ome. 'E's missin' it, an' if yer write about all the little fings around yer it'll keep 'im in touch, 'elp 'im ter remember everyfing back 'ere.'

'I s'pose I could do that,' Sadie replied, rubbing her chin, 'but I gotta be careful. I don't wanna give 'im any wrong ideas, like lettin' 'im fink I wanna get serious.'

'That wouldn't be such a bad fing,' Jennie said. 'Yer'd get a lot more attention an' lovin' from 'im than Len Regan.'

'Don't go on about that,' Sadie pleaded. 'I'm all mixed up as it is. I fink about Len, an' I go over in me mind what I'm gonna say next time I see 'im, an' then when we do meet it's like it's all sweetness an' light. Then there's times when one o' Joe's letters drops frew the letterbox. I get excited as I open it, an' I ask meself why. Christ, Jennie, I've only bin out wiv 'im once an' 'e never forced 'imself on me or anyfing like that. We just talked.'

'But didn't yer feel anyfing when you was tergevver?' Jennie asked.

'I felt comfortable an' sort o' cosy. Joe's easy ter talk to an' 'e was interested in what I was talkin' about too, I could tell.'

'I know just what yer mean,' Jennie remarked. 'When I first saw Con in the cafe an' 'e came over ter my table an' got talkin' I found meself studyin' 'im, watchin' 'is eyes an' the way 'e 'as of grinnin' out the corner of 'is mouth. It was little fings I noticed, an' I felt comfortable too. There was no bells ringin', no earth-shakin' moment when me life changed, just a nice cosy feelin' inside, an' I could 'ave sat there all day just talkin' to 'im.'

'An' now?'

Jennie sighed. 'A bundle o' letters later an' I take 'im ter bed wiv me at night. I cuddle the piller an' make out it's 'im. Does that sound terrible?'

Sadie laughed aloud. 'Nah, that sounds like true love.'

'I do love 'im, Sadie. I love 'im more each day.'

''Ow d'yer cope?'

'What d'yer mean?'

'Well, yer've always bin like a flitterin' butterfly,' Sadie explained. 'At least that's what Mum used ter say about yer. You was always flyin' from one lad to anuvver an' never in the 'ouse fer five minutes. It was eivver dancin' or the flicks, or trips up West. Now you never go out. Ter be honest, if someone 'ad told me a year ago you'd be quite 'appy ter sit in a corner wiv a book or magazine I'd 'ave said they were mad. Since yer've met Con yer've changed so much.'

'Contentment, Sadie, that's what it is,' Jennie told her. 'War changes everybody an' I'm no exception. I'm not interested in ovver fellers. I want Con, an' I know 'e feels the same way about me. The war's parted us, but in some strange way it's brought us closer tergevver, an' as time goes by I know that the feelin's we 'ave fer each ovver can only get stronger. Can you understand?'

'D'yer know somefing,' Sadie said, 'I envy you. I was always lookin' fer the glamorous life, goin' places, seein' fings, 'avin' a smart 'ome, wiv good clothes ter wear an' money in the bank. I wanted out o' this place, I wanted ter get away from Bermon'sey an' its factories, wharves an' smells, an' 'ard-up people livin' in run-down 'ouses an' damp, ramshackle buildin's. I told meself there 'ad ter be somefing else, somefing better.'

'Don't you fink we all feel like that?' Jennie said quickly. 'I'd like to 'ave lots o' nice fings an' plenty o' money, but yer gotta look at the ovver side o' the coin. Take the people, fer instance – yer won't find better anywhere yer go. An' yer talk about the smells, but I love 'em. I love ter walk along Tower Bridge Road when 'Artley's are boilin' the Seville oranges an' I love the smell of leavver tannin' an' the lovely aromas from the spice ware'ouses down Shad Thames. An' there's the sharp tang of 'ops from the brewery an' sour vinegar as yer pass by Sarson's, not fergettin' the river o' course. I love the smell o' the river an' the grey mud down below when I walk along the embankments. That's Bermon'sey, an' that's what makes it so different from anywhere else yer could name. All right, it might all disappear. If the bombin' starts a lot o' factories'll move out o' London or be destroyed, an' the old buildin's an' little 'ouses won't last fer ever. It'll all change, but while fings are as they are you can keep anywhere else, Bermon'sey suits me just fine.'

'Jennie, you amaze me, you really do,' Sadie declared with feeling. 'The way you just described it makes Bermon'sey sound like paradise. I'd never 'ave guessed you felt so passionate about it.'

'Well, there you are,' Jennie said smiling. 'An' that's the sort o' stuff you could put in that letter ter Big Joe.'

'I'm gonna write to 'im,' Sadie said enthusiastically. 'I'm gonna write to 'im ternight.'

'Good fer you.'

Sadie got up from the bed and went to the door. 'By the way,' she said, turning back on her heel. 'Fanks fer the chat, an' fanks fer makin' me feel shallow an' selfish.'

'Sadie, I'm sorry. I didn't intend ter make yer feel bad,' Jennie replied, looking concerned.

'Don't apologise, sis. It was just what I needed. It was better than a kick up the backside,' Sadie told her, grinning broadly.

Across the Channel the last of the British forces were fighting a rearguard action, back through hedgerows and fields, through muddy lanes and country roads to the beaches. Remnants of the Royal Fusiliers and Rifle Brigade were amongst the exhausted troops who finally reached the sands as night fell, and in the failing light they came upon the carnage. Most of the large ships had left but some small boats of various description were struggling against the tide to reach the shore. Men clambered aboard and others swam alongside, hoping to be picked up once they were out at sea. The bodies of their dead comrades had to be left on the sands along with the badly wounded, but those who could still walk were helped down to the water and into the small overflowing craft.

Fusilier Christopher Wickstead had taken a bullet in his chest and was left for dead in a dune. Fortunately two privates from the decimated Northamptonshire Regiment sheltering nearby heard him groaning and they managed to drag him to the water and into a small launch.

Corporal Conrad Williams and his depleted squad had held out at the farm until they were almost out of ammunition and they withdrew under heavy fire to the road. The four survivors only covered a short distance before they came under more fire from both sides. Two men died instantly and Con dived into a ditch alongside the only other survivor, Rifleman Cohen from Bethnal Green. They could hear heavy footsteps running and shouted commands in German, then it went quiet. For a while they remained where they were, and finally Abe Cohen eased himself across to Con. 'I'm out of ammo, Corp,' he said.

'I've got a few rounds left,' Con told him. 'I fink we'd better make a move before we're overrun.'

The rifleman grabbed Con's arm. 'Save the last one fer me, Corp,' he said matter-of-factly.

'What you on about?' Con said irritably.

'If we're captured put yer last bullet in me, an' make sure yer do a good job,' Cohen told him.

'Don't piss-ball about,' Con growled. 'Let's go, an' keep close.'

'I'm bein' serious,' Cohen hissed. 'If we're captured they'll take our army books fer identification, you know that.'

'So?'

'What chance d'yer fink I'll 'ave wiv a name like Abraham Cohen? They'll shoot me on the spot. I'd sooner you do it.'

Con grabbed Abe Cohen by his shoulder webbing and shook him. 'Now you listen ter me,' he muttered. 'You an' me are goin' up on the road an' we're gonna make it ter the beach, understood? Now c'mon, let's go.'

The dark country lane seemed deserted as the two soldiers hurried along with their heads held low, and at a curve of the track they nearly stumbled over a dead soldier lying twisted on the ground, his rifle still at his side. Con checked the weapon and released the magazine to find that there were still some rounds left in it. ''Ere, take this,' he said, throwing it to Abe Cohen.

'This feels better,' Abe said, slipping the safety catch of his rifle.

Ahead the town of Dunkirk was lit up with flames and smoke was rising high up into the night sky. The two soldiers followed the lane round as it veered sharply and suddenly they found themselves looking down gun barrels.

'You two left it a bit late, didn't yer?'

Con saw it was Sergeant Brody and his blackened face relaxed into a wide grin. 'Yer made it then, Sarge.'

'Yeah, four of us,' Brody said bitterly.

'We're all that's left of our squad,' Con told him as he shouldered his rifle.

'It's not a pretty sight on that beach,' Brody puffed, 'but there's no option. If we're not away ternight it'll be a prison camp fer the rest o' the war.'

The remnants of B company moved down into the port, passing the burning buildings and installations on their way to the dunes.

''E wasn't jokin', was 'e?' Cohen remarked as they saw the results of the constant strafing.

Bodies were everywhere, broken and lifeless, and back from the water the badly wounded had been laid together and covered with greatcoats, their heads resting on army packs. There was no moon, but the burning port lit up the dunes and cast a hellish red reflection on the sea for some distance, till the blackness swallowed it up.

'The boats 'ave bin comin' in waves,' Sergeant Brody told his men. 'They've bin usin' megaphones to announce their arrival. Flares would only alert the German gunners up above the town.'

'What about those poor sods over there, Sarge?' Abe Cohen asked, pointing to the wounded.

'There's nuffink more we can do,' Brody sighed. 'We've just gotta 'ope the Germans'll look after 'em.'

'I just 'ope the SS units don't get 'ere first,' Cohen mumbled to Con.

That night under cover of darkness the last of the fighting rearguard put to sea in a small river launch, piloted by an elderly man who like hundreds of other pleasure-craft owners had answered the call for boats. An off-shore wind had made the operation difficult, but with considerable skill and detailed knowledge of his particular boat the skipper of the *Lady Luck* had managed admirably.

''Ere, Corp, if we'd bin captured would you 'ave done what I asked?' Abe Cohen wanted to know.

Con shrugged his shoulders, beginning to feel queasy as the small boat bobbed up and down like a cork in the heavy swell. 'I dunno, I might 'a' done.'

'Sergeant, can you take the wheel while I rustle up some soup?' the skipper asked. 'Just keep it on this course.'

As the smell of tomato soup rose up from the tiny cabin below deck Con felt his stomach turn over. Abe Cohen was sitting next to him and he smiled. 'Not feelin' too good, Corp?' he asked casually.

'Leave me alone,' Con growled.

'I'll 'ave your soup if yer don't want it,' Cohen said grinning.

'If you don't shut yer trap I'm gonna put that last bullet in yer 'ead right now,' Con scowled.

'Promises, promises,' the irrepressible young soldier said as he wedged his feet against the bulwarks to counter the roll and pitch.

As the dawn light filtered into the sky the *Lady Luck* docked at Newhaven and a party of very sick landlubbers came ashore. They were given huge mugs of steaming tea and dry clothes, and then taken to a makeshift canteen where they were served with the inevitable sausage and mash.

'What, no roll-mops?' Abe Cohen remarked.

'What the bloody 'ell's roll-mops?' the soldier next to him in the queue asked.

'Soused 'errin's,' Cohen told him.

Con was standing behind the soldier and felt his stomach move again. 'Will someone loan me a rifle, now?' he growled. 'An' make sure it's loaded.'

Chapter Seventeen

On a bright June morning a letter arrived at number 11 and Dolly Flynn's face lit up as she picked it up off the doormat. 'Mick, it's a letter from our Frank,' she shouted up the stairs. 'I can tell it's 'is 'andwritin'.'

'Well, go on then, open the bloody fing,' Mick growled as he hurried down.

Dolly read it and tears welled up in her eyes as she passed it to him. 'The boys are comin' 'ome on leave soon,' she told him.

Mick read the letter and then looked up. 'Con's company 'ad ter stay be'ind 'em, accordin' ter Frank,' he said sadly. 'Young Jennie's gonna be upset. Still we mustn't look on the black side, 'e could be a prisoner o' war.'

Dolly took the letter from her husband and studied the postmark. 'This letter's three days old,' she said. 'Frank must 'ave wrote it the same time as 'e phoned. Jennie's young man might 'ave got back after the letter was sent. It said on the wireless that soldiers were still bein' picked up from Dunkirk.'

'It's quite possible,' Mick said encouragingly, though he knew what a rearguard action meant. In his time it was a case of sacrificing a few to save many and it wouldn't be any different now.

When Sadie came in with the shopping and read the letter she was overjoyed, but her heart went out to Jennie. On the surface her sister was being calm and contained, but she was not fooling anyone. Inside they knew she must be in turmoil. 'I wonder if Con did get back an' phoned 'ome,' Sadie said.

''E might well 'ave done,' Dolly replied. 'Trouble is there's only 'is ole gran, accordin' ter Jennie, an' she couldn't be expected ter let us know. She don't even know where we live fer a start. An' it's quite possible that Con ain't even told 'er about Jennie.'

'There's only one answer,' Sadie said quickly. 'We've gotta find out where the ole lady lives.'

'An' 'ow yer gonna do that?' Dolly asked.

'Jennie said she lives in Dock'ead, an' let's face it Dock'ead ain't that big,' Sadie remarked.

Early that evening when Jennie got home from her job at the baker's shop and read the letter from Frank she broke down in tears. Sadie put her arm round her and Dolly hurried out to the scullery and came back with a cup of tea. 'Now drink this, an' try not ter worry too much,' she told her kindly. 'We was only sayin' this mornin' that Con could 'ave got back since that letter was sent.'

As Jennie sipped her tea in the armchair Sadie knelt down beside her. 'Do yer know if Con told 'is gran'muvver about you?' she asked.

'I don't know,' Jennie replied. ''E never said.'

'Right then, we're gonna find the ole lady.'

''Ow we gonna do that?'

'When you an' Con went fer that drink where did yer go?'

'A little pub down by the riverside,' Jennie told her.

'In Dock'ead?'

Jennie looked up smiling and sniffed back her tears. 'Of course,' she said quickly. 'Con takes 'is gran there some-times. People in the pub would know where they live, wouldn't they?'

'Yeah, I'm sure they would,' Sadie replied. 'Right then, my gel, after tea me an' you are goin' fer a stroll.'

'But you're goin' out ternight wiv Len.'

'Not any more.'

Rabbi Friedman leaned back in his armchair and joined the tips of his fingers together in contemplation. He was a diminutive individual with thick grey hair, well known for his sometimes acid-sharp tongue as well as his wicked sense of humour. He was held in high esteem by Bermondsey's Jewish community, who felt that he was a man who would listen and sympathise with their problems and generally administer sound advice. On Saturday evening though, Rabbi Friedman was feeling slightly irked by Albert Levy's change of mind. 'Only a few weeks ago you came to me and asked me to consider your request for a bronze plaque to be installed in the synagogue to the memory of Abel Finkel-stein,' he reminded him, 'and now it seems you don't care to remember him. Tell me, Albert, has he come back to haunt you or something?'

The shopkeeper cringed in his armchair facing the rabbi. 'Many a true word is spoken in jest,' he replied. 'Actually, the simple truth is I can't bring myself to honour his name, and Gerda agrees with me.'

'I'm sure she does,' Friedman said sarcastically. 'But then

your devoted wife Gerda knows more about this than I do. Maybe I'll agree too, once you have explained yourself fully.'

Albert Levy shifted uncomfortably in his seat. 'Rabbi, do you believe we can communicate with the dead?'

Friedman smiled. 'I have to, at some of my services. There are times when I feel that half my congregation are dead, or well on the way out, judging by the expressionless look on their faces. But to be serious, no I don't believe in communication with the dead.'

'I've been speaking to Abel for some time now,' Albert told him. 'At quiet moments I go to the back of my shop, to the workroom where Abel used to mend the wireless sets, and I speak to him, or I used to, until recently.'

'I think we all tend to speak our thoughts when we're troubled,' the rabbi replied. 'But it's not communicating as such, it's more of an exercise in getting things off our chest. Things left unsaid. Angry thoughts, and questions that need answering. It's a part of bereavement. Do you understand what I'm saying?'

'It's finished now though,' Albert Levy said sadly. 'My old friend bit the hand that fed him. He betrayed me, the man who loved him like a brother, and I told him so, the last time I spoke to him.'

Friedman raised his hands in front of him in puzzlement. 'Now, let's get this straight,' he said. 'You found this out after Abel died?'

The shopkeeper took Abel's diary from his coat pocket and passed it over to Friedman. 'It's all in there,' he told him. 'See for yourself and then tell me, if you can, what could have possessed Abel to do such a thing.'

As he thumbed through the pages the rabbi's face creased in a smile and he looked up at his visitor. 'Quite a bit of money,' he said, raising his eyebrows. 'Have you been able to put a figure on it?'

Levy nodded. 'Taking the carry-over figure from last year at the front of the diary and totalling up the entries, I made it almost one hundred and twenty-seven pounds, give or take a few shillings. To rob an old friend of all that money! Why, rabbi? Why?'

Rabbi Friedman held Albert in his deep gaze for a moment or two. 'When Abel first came to talk to me about his plan I was a little unsure of how to advise him,' he said finally, the smile still lingering in his eyes. 'You of all people know that Abel Finkelstein was a very meticulous man. Unfortunately for him he could not be completely exact in this instance, which troubled him. It had to be guesswork. You see there was no rate of exchange available for the old German Mark against the pound because of the roaring inflation in Germany during that time. It could only be calculated by the cost of comparable items in both countries at that period, but even that was very difficult. As you know, even the price of a loaf of bread changed daily in the worst times. I could only surmise, and I felt that the figure should be around two hundred pounds, which Abel concurred with.'

Albert Levy sat with his mouth hanging open, his eyes popping like organ stops. 'You mean to tell me you were in on this?' he gasped. 'You advised him? You set a figure? I don't believe it. I'm dreaming. Tell me I'm dreaming.'

Rabbi Friedman felt a wave of pity for the shopkeeper and he raised his hands in front of him again. 'Now listen to me, Albert,' he began. 'The figure Abel Finkelstein and I agreed upon was the amount we estimated you would have paid in pounds for his release from that prison camp. Now you've done your sums and come up with the figure of one hundred and twenty-seven pounds, which leaves a shortfall of seventy-three pounds.'

'A shortfall of seventy-three pounds!' Albert exploded. 'The shortfall is one hundred and twenty-seven pounds, the total Abel took from my till.'

The rabbi smiled indulgently. 'What I'm saying is, if Abel had lived the shortfall would have been rectified in time.'

'Am I hearing this right, or am I going stark raving mad?' Albert said in consternation. 'You're telling me that if Abel had not taken his life the figure would have reached two hundred pounds. And what then?'

'That would have been the end of it,' Friedman replied.

'I am going mad,' Albert Levy wailed. 'You, a respected rabbi, in league to systematically rob one of your own.'

'No, not rob,' Friedman said calmly. 'Reimburse is the word you're looking for. All those figures in Abel's diary refer to the money he slipped into the till when he could. He was paying you back, Albert, paying you back what he hoped would be every penny of the money you spent to obtain his release. It was the only way. He knew that you would refuse to take it if he offered it to you. That's why he came to me with the plan. To get my approval, which I was happy to give him.'

Albert Levy lowered his head and his shoulders heaved. 'I loved him, rabbi,' he sobbed. 'I loved him like a brother, and I ended up cursing his memory.'

'Many a harsh word is spoken in anger and in haste,' Friedman said rising from his chair. 'You were not to know the truth of it and the wording in the diary led you to believe the worst.' He laid his hand on Albert's hunched shoulders. 'Let's talk some more of the memorial plaque, shall we?'

Sadie led the way into the busy little riverside pub, ignoring the curious glances from the locals, who were not used to seeing unaccompanied young women enter the bar.

'Yes, ladies?' the landlord asked. 'What can I get yer?'

'I'm sorry ter take up yer time while you're busy,' Sadie began nervously, 'but d'yer know a Mrs Williams who comes in 'ere sometimes wiv 'er gran'son Con, who's in the army? We're tryin' ter contact 'er. It's very important.'

The landlord looked from one to the other and then he walked along the bar and put his head through some bead curtains. 'Got a minute, Vi?'

A buxom blonde wearing heavy make-up came through from the saloon bar, and after the landlord mumbled a few words in her ear she came up to the two young women and gave them a quick smile. 'Could you come frew?' she said as she lifted the counter flap.

Sadie and Jennie looked at each other in surprise as they followed her through the curtains and into a small back room that led off the saloon bar. It was sparsely furnished with a table and four chairs and some shelves around the walls.

'Sit yerselves down,' the woman told them, pulling up a chair facing them. 'I know yer can't be related ter the ole lady or yer'd know 'er name wasn't Williams. It was Franklin, Ida Franklin. I say was, because I'm afraid they found 'er dead in 'er chair yesterday mornin'.'

'Oh my God!' Jennie gasped. 'Poor Con.'

'I remember yer face now,' the woman said. 'I saw you in 'ere wiv young Conrad once.'

'Con's my boyfriend an' 'e's in Dunkirk, yer see,' Jennie said anxiously. 'That's why we were tryin' ter locate the ole lady. We thought she might 'ave 'eard somefing.'

The buxom woman smiled sympathetically, showing a row of large white teeth. 'I never ferget a face. I remember sayin' ter my bloke what a nice couple yer made. Anyway, I fink yer'd better speak ter Mrs Crosier. She did the cleanin' an' ran a few errands fer the ole gel. She may know somefing. She was the one who found 'er. Must 'ave bin a terrible shock; after all, Mrs Crosier ain't no chicken 'erself. She lives in St Saviour's Buildin's by the way, by Shad Thames. D'yer know the place?'

'We'll find it,' Sadie said. 'D'yer know Mrs Crosier's number?'

'Nah, I don't, but she lives on the ground floor facin' the street, next ter the rubbish chute,' the blonde told her.

'We're very grateful, an' sorry to 'ave taken up yer time,' Sadie said smiling as she and Jennie stood up to leave.

'It was no trouble,' the woman replied. 'I do 'ope you 'ear some good news. Con's a very nice lad. 'E'll be upset when 'e finds out about the poor ole gel.'

The two sisters linked arms as they walked through the river mist towards Shad Thames, an ancient riverside byway noted for its pepper and spice warehouses. The ramshackle tenement block loomed up ahead and Sadie shivered. 'It gives me the creeps round 'ere.'

'This must be the flat,' Jennie said, lifting the doorknocker.

'What yer want?' a scratchy voice called out from within.

'My name's Jennie Flynn. I'm Con's gelfriend,' Jennie

called back through the letterbox. 'Can I talk ter you fer a minute?'

Bolts were slid back and the door opened slowly to reveal a tiny woman in an apron with a black shawl over her shoulders. Her feet were clad in carpet slippers and she was wearing metal-framed spectacles. 'Are yer sisters?' she asked.

'Yeah, we are,' Jennie told her. 'I'm Jennie an' this is Sadie.'

'Yer look very much alike,' the woman said, screwing her eyes up behind her glasses. 'Yer'd better come in. It's too late ter stand gassin' at the street door.'

They followed her into a small front room lit by a gas lamp and warmed by a low fire.

'It's nice an' cosy in 'ere,' Sadie remarked as she looked around.

'I need a fire,' the woman replied. 'It gets damp an' chilly at night, bein' so near the river. Can I get yer a cuppa?'

'No, it's all right,' Jennie said quickly. 'We were told in the pub that Con's gran'muvver 'ad died an' you was the one who found 'er. I'm really sorry. The landlady told us you was the lady who did 'er cleanin' an' run errands for 'er, so we took a chance an' called round. I'm worried about Con. I wondered if yer'd 'eard any news yet.'

Mrs Crosier shook her head. 'No, I 'aven't, but as soon as Con gets back 'ome 'e'll phone The Boatman, I feel sure. They knew Ida Franklin very well in there. Look, yer might as well make yerselves comfortable by the fire an' 'ave a cuppa, it's no trouble.'

Sadie and Jennie exchanged glances and Sadie nodded to the old lady. 'All right then. Fank you.'

'I can't 'ave the fire too 'igh, not till I get that chimney swept,' Mrs Crosier told them. 'Trouble is I've just not 'ad the chance. It's a bloody day's work clearin' up after our ole chimney-sweep.'

'It must 'ave bin a terrible shock findin' the ole lady,' Jennie remarked.

Mrs Crosier nodded her head slowly. 'She looked very peaceful though, an' she 'ad that new shawl round 'er shoulders, the one young Con bought 'er. There was a Bible restin' in 'er lap, open at the twenty-third Psalm it was. "The Lord is my Shepherd." The wireless was on as well. She must 'a' bin listenin' ter the news an' no doubt sayin' a few prayers. She was a God-fearin' woman was Ida.'

' "Yea, though I walk through the valley of the shadow of death, I will fear no evil," ' Jennie quoted. 'I remember that Psalm at school. We all learned it off by 'eart. Mrs Crosier, d'yer fink Con will phone the pub?'

'I'm sure 'e will, an' soon as 'e does I'll try an' let yer know,' the old lady replied, 'if yer'll give me yer address.'

'We live in Carter Lane off the Old Kent Road,' Jennie told her. 'It's a bit of a way from 'ere. We'll go back ter the pub an' leave 'em the phone number of our corner shop. I'm sure they won't mind phonin' if they 'ear anyfing from Con.'

'There's no need fer you two ter go runnin' back there this time o' night,' the old lady said. 'I'll take the phone number there meself termorrer mornin'. I usually go in fer me bottle o' Guinness at openin' time.'

'That's very nice of yer,' Jennie said smiling.

Mrs Crosier put her empty cup and saucer down on the table. 'Ida Franklin wasn't Con's real gran'muvver,' she remarked, 'although 'e always called 'er gran. She was only a neighbour, but when the boy was left on 'is own she took 'im in ter save 'im goin' in one o' those children's 'omes. Poor as Lazarus she was, an' wiv no ole man neivver, but she managed ter make a nice 'ome fer the boy. That's the sort o' woman she was. Con loved 'er like 'is own, an' she took great comfort in that.'

Sadie and Jennie thanked the old lady for her hospitality and hurried back home through the dark empty streets.

'There's nuffink else we can do now except wait,' Jennie said sighing.

'I honestly don't fink yer'll be waitin' very long,' Sadie told her comfortingly. 'I bet yer'll get some good news termorrer or Monday.'

When they arrived home their mother had some other news for them. 'Mrs Wickstead knocked while you two were out,' she said excitedly. ''Er boy Chris is safe. A copper come ter tell 'er. 'E was wounded but 'e's sent a message 'ome from the military 'ospital ter say not ter worry 'e's doin' well. An' Freddie Bromilow's back 'ome too wivout a scratch.'

'Fank God fer that,' Sadie replied.

Jennie bit on her bottom lip to control her emotions. The men of Carter Lane were gradually returning home. Would her prayers be answered too?

Chapter Eighteen

Jennie turned over on to her back and opened her eyes to bright sunlight streaming through the window. For a moment she lay there gathering her thoughts, and then she sighed thankfully when she realised it was Sunday morning. Before the war started the church bells would have been pealing but now they were silenced, to be rung only in the event of an invasion. Some things had not changed though, she thought. The smell of bacon frying for one, and the noise her father made in the backyard where he dubbined his workboots and polished his Sunday best. The distant sound of a passing train was familiar and comforting and the young woman turned over for a few more minutes, until she heard knocking and excited voices.

'Jennie. Are you awake?'

'Yeah, I'm just gettin' up.'

'It's Con. 'E's safe,' Dolly shouted from the foot of the stairs. 'That was Sara Jackman. A pub in Dock'ead just phoned 'er. Con phoned the pub late last night.'

Jennie's face glowed with happiness as she hurried down the stairs to hug her mother. ''E must 'ave phoned just after we left,' she said. 'A bit earlier an' we'd 'ave bin there. What exactly did Mrs Jackman say?'

'All she said was the pub got a phone call from Con ter say 'e was safe an' well an' comin' 'ome terday on a seventy-two-hour pass.'

'Terday!'

'That's what she said.'

'I wanna meet 'im,' Jennie said quickly as she followed her mother into the scullery and saw her father framed in the backyard doorway with a big smile on his wide face.

''Ow yer gonna find out about the trains?' Dolly asked her.

'Frank phoned from New'aven,' Jennie recalled. 'That's where they're landin' all the soldiers I should fink. Now let me see. That's the Brighton line. 'E'll be comin' in at London Bridge. Maybe Frank an' Jim too.'

'They didn't say anyfing about that in the letter,' Dolly reminded her.

'Yeah, but it was only a rushed letter,' Mick cut in. 'They most likely didn't know when they were gettin' leave.'

'Mick, I gotta get prepared, just in case,' Dolly said quickly. 'I'll need ter put anuvver tray o' spuds in the oven an' one Yorkshire won't be enough.'

'Don't build yer 'opes up too much,' Mick warned her. 'Our two might not get leave till later, maybe next week.'

'Nah, they'll be 'ome terday along wi' Con,' Dolly said confidently. 'I can feel it in me water.'

'I can't let Con go straight 'ome,' Jennie fretted. 'The people at the pub might not 'ave 'ad the chance ter tell 'im about 'is gran'muvver. It was more than likely a rushed call anyway. At least I can break it to 'im gently.'

'Before yer fink o' goin' up the station yer'd better get this down yer,' Dolly said as she ladled a fried egg onto a plate with rashers of crispy streaky bacon.

Albert Levy went to his shop on Sunday morning, something he had never done before. Today though he felt a compelling need to go. Only there could he be really close to Abel, in the little workroom where his old friend had sat day after day, humming tunelessly when things were going well, cursing when they were not. Only in that little backroom, which was now orderly and tidy, could he say the things he needed to say.

'It's been a while, old friend, but you know the reason,' Albert said as he sat down at the bench. 'The last time I spoke to you was an occasion I deeply regret, but I take comfort in knowing that what I said didn't hurt you nor trouble you in any way. Pain and anger can't touch you now and I know you suffered my angry outburst because you understand the weaknesses and frailty of us mortals. I deeply regret that I misconstrued your actions but fortunately for me I was able to talk to Rabbi Friedman, and although he let me roast for a while, it was no more than I deserved. In hindsight I should have put the diary into the fire and refused to believe that you could ever have taken it on yourself to deceive me. You couldn't, and I should have known that, but as I said, I am mortal and suffer all the frailties of mortality. Don't think ill of me, old friend. You still are my friend, and that could never change. I know you would never forsake me, not in your world, where the grass is always green and where the roses hold their scent forever.

'I'm going to say goodbye for now, old friend, but before I go I must tell you that everything's underway with regard to the bronze plaque. I know it'll make you smile, but I've decided to have one made like the Rosenblum plaque that's just inside the entrance to the synagogue. You know the one I mean. It will cost a good few shillings more but I feel that the original round plaque wouldn't do you justice. You'll be pleased with this one and the extra cost will be my penance for having doubted you. Farewell, Abel. Gerda sends her love as always.'

Albert Levy locked up his shop with a light heart. He was happy to have gone some way to restoring the bond. It would be even stronger from now on, he thought as he crossed the main thoroughfare.

The tram was gathering speed and there was no way the driver could have prevented the accident. People gathered round the figure lying prone in the gutter and one young man bent down to feel for a pulse.

'I saw it 'appen,' a man said in a shocked voice. ''E just walked straight inter the tram. It wasn't the driver's fault.'

'Yeah, I saw it as well,' another remarked. ''E was sent flyin' an' 'e whacked 'is 'ead against the kerb. It sounded fer all the world like the crack of a whip.'

'Is 'e dead?' an old woman asked fearfully.

A policeman pushed his way through the crowd. 'Don't move 'im,' he ordered. 'I'll phone fer an ambulance.'

Jennie was determined to go to the train station at once, ignoring any objections. 'They could be arrivin' any time, Mum,' she said quickly. 'I've got to be there.'

With her heart beating excitedly she hurried out into the Old Kent Road and caught a number 21 bus, which would take her directly into the station forecourt. The short journey seemed to last forever and she closed her eyes and said a silent prayer that she wouldn't be too late.

London Bridge Station was busy on that sabbath morning, with servicemen and women milling around or standing waiting by mounds of suitcases and equipment. Military police patrolled the concourse in pairs, strutting officiously with their hands clasped behind their backs and their eyes obscured and inscrutable beneath the stiff peaked caps they wore. Porters pushed luggage on large two-wheeled barrows and children ran excitedly from one empty chocolate machine to another while steam hissed from huge tenders and bored-looking train drivers and firemen leaned on the footplates idly watching the feverish activity.

'Er, excuse me, but 'as the troop train come in yet?' Jennie asked a passing porter.

The man eyed her with some amusement. 'Which one would you be referrin' to, miss?' he enquired.

'The one from New'aven,' she said quickly.

'Well, we've 'ad one in – no, come ter fink of it, it was two this mornin', countin' the milk train,' he told her. 'They stuck a couple o' Red Cross carriages on the milk train yer see. Stretchered wounded.'

'Is there any more due in terday?' she asked anxiously.

'Yer know I shouldn't be givin' yer that sort of information,' the porter said, trying to look serious. 'I mean ter say, you could be a fifth-columnist fer all I know.'

'My bruvvers were at Dunkirk,' Jennie replied puffing, 'an' me boyfriend too. They're comin' 'ome terday. That's why I'm askin'.'

The porter smiled and took her arm. 'Let's see now,' he said as he steered her away from an approaching truck full of baggage. 'See that RTO office over there? They'll be able ter give yer some information. Actually there is a troop train due in very shortly from New'aven, that I can tell yer. It's comin' in on platform four. I should get yerself a platform ticket. If yer loved ones aren't on that train go over an' make some enquiries at the office. An' good luck, miss.'

Jennie thanked him and hurried to get a ticket from a machine, her heart beating even faster as the minute hand on the large clock above the concourse climbed towards the hour. Other people were waiting, looking anxiously up at the clock and down the empty track to where the rails arced away out of sight. Beyond the ticket gate more people were standing around, and when the first puff of steam was seen in the distance everyone moved impulsively a little closer to the edge of the platform. It was coming in now, the large locomotive belching steam, its fireman resting his arm on the brass rail of the footplate while the burly driver wrestled with the levers.

As the train ground to a halt at the buffers the carriage doors sprang open. Servicemen jumped down looking haggard and unkempt. Some wore their berets at a rakish angle, others had their tunics undone and cuffs turned back. Normally the military police would be ready to pounce at such flagrant disregard of prescribed military dress code, but this was a train carrying men straight back from hell and no one was going to demand any strict applications of the regulations at such a time.

Jennie saw Jim first, and then Frank. They were chatting together and when they spotted her they rushed up to lift her off her feet. 'It's great ter be back 'ome,' Frank sighed.

'Yeah, great,' Jim echoed. 'Con's in the end carriage.'

She saw him now, walking beside another soldier who had a bandage covering one eye. Jennie squealed out and Con's face lit up as he spotted her.

Frank caught Jim's eye and turned to Jennie. 'We'll wait for yer by the clock,' he said.

Con came up and threw his arms around her, gazing eagerly at her as if at a vision. 'You're even prettier than the picture I've carried round inside me 'ead,' he laughed.

'I thought I'd never see yer again,' Jennie croaked as she hugged him tightly. 'Especially when Frank told us you were in the rearguard.'

'Did yer pray for me every night?' he asked with a smile.

'Of course. An' you?'

'Every night.'

'I'm so 'appy,' Jennie said, almost choking.

Con released her and moved back a pace. 'By the way, 'ow did yer know I was comin' in this mornin'?'

'Me an' Sadie went ter The Boatman an' they agreed ter phone our corner shop soon as they 'eard anyfing,' she told him.

He smiled. 'I see. You wanted ter be in on the kill, did yer?'

Jennie's face suddenly became serious. 'Con. There's somefing I gotta tell yer,' she began. 'You obviously 'aven't 'eard.'

'It's me gran, isn't it?'

'Yeah I'm afraid so.'

'She died?'

'Yeah. I'm terribly sorry.'

He nodded his head slowly and saw the questioning look on Jennie's face. 'I 'ad a bad dream last night,' he said quietly. 'All I could see was these miserable faces comin' right up ter me. There was wailin' an' groanin' an' I tried ter move away but I was fixed ter the spot. I could see me gran but I couldn't reach 'er. She was callin' fer me wiv 'er arms 'eld out, an' then I woke up in a pool o' sweat. I knew then that somefing 'ad 'appened to 'er.'

As they walked slowly from the platform Jennie told him what Mrs Crosier had said, and she chanced to remark upon the old lady not being his real grandmother.

'She was as good as a granny ter me,' Con replied with a sigh. 'She loved me callin' 'er gran. It was a game we played an' she loved it. So did I, come ter fink.'

'I wish I'd 'ave got ter know 'er,' Jennie said sadly. 'Me mum wants yer ter come 'ome fer Sunday dinner terday. Yer will, won't yer?'

'Yeah, I'd be delighted,' he told her, his face brightening.

Frank and Jim were standing together sharing a cigarette, and when Jennie told them about the old lady they each put an arm on Con's shoulders. 'Yer better come 'ome wiv us fer a while,' Frank said.

'I've already asked 'im,' Jennie said quickly.

'She's a pushy little cow, Con,' Jim warned him. 'Still I expect yer know the way ter deal wiv that sort.'

Jennie gave him a sisterly look. 'Watch it, Jimbo, or I'll tell Con a few of your secrets.'

'I didn't fink I 'ad any,' Jim countered.

'An' what about the teddy bear you . . .'

'All right, all right, I'll be'ave,' Jim replied quickly, grinning at Con.

Gerda Levy sat by Albert's bedside at Guy's Hospital, her

eyes never leaving the ashen face of her husband. The doctors had informed her that he had a fractured skull and was in a coma which could last indefinitely.

'I know you can hear me, Albert,' she said softly. 'I've told the rabbi, and do you know what he said? He told me that it was preoccupation that caused your accident. How many times have you told me to look both ways before I cross the road? You treat me like a child, but I don't mind. That's your way of showing that you care for me, but you should have practised what you preached. I know it was to talk to Abel that you went, but you could have talked to him at home. He can hear you wherever you are.

'I've spoken to the doctor, Albert. He said there's no knowing how long you'll be in the coma. Open your eyes and talk to me soon, dearest. When I was talking to Rabbi Friedman about your condition he smiled and said that I shouldn't worry. What a sense of humour! He said I must talk a lot, worry you into waking up, it was the only way. He said that I should remind you about the shop. He said if I did you'd most likely spring up in bed and ask for your clothes.'

Just then Albert's mouth seemed to twitch and Gerda reached out and took his hand. Suddenly she felt a slight movement in one of his fingers.

'It's a very encouraging sign,' the doctor said when he looked in on his rounds. 'It's much too early to say yet, but it does indicate that he may be moving towards consciousness. Just keep talking to him.'

In the late afternoon, as the sun dipped down and a fresh breeze sprang up, the two young people walked hand in hand through the cobbled lane that led towards the river.

'It seems like I've known you ferever,' Jennie said quietly.

Con tightened his grip on her hand. 'That's exactly the way I feel. Those letters you sent me told me everyfing I wanted ter know. It was almost as if I'd known you as a child. I got ter know yer likes an' dislikes, I understood a little bit about 'ow you saw fings, an' best of all I knew you cared fer me. Did my letters tell yer what you wanted ter know?'

She nodded and smiled at him. 'I always put the latest letter under me piller when I went ter bed,' she told him. 'I 'eld it in me 'and when I said me prayers.'

He turned towards her, gazing at her pretty face, her impish smile and her hazel eyes glowing with life. He saw how she carried herself, the way her red hair danced on her shoulders and the natural sway of her hips and he sighed deeply. 'I gotta tell yer, Jennie, you're a very lovely woman.'

'Well fank you, kind sir,' she said smiling broadly.

They stopped in the deserted lane and he took her in his arms. The kiss was gentle and sweet and he could feel the warmth of her young body against his. This was a moment to savour, to remember, come what may.

Strolling along to where the ancient stone steps led down to the water's edge, they stood for a few moments watching the turning tide and the swirling eddies.

'They'll be reformin' the brigade,' Con told her. 'I'm gonna be made up ter sergeant so they told me.'

'What does that mean?' she asked.

'Well I'll be involved in trainin' the new intake,' he replied. 'Then when the battalion's ready we'll ship out.'

'To where?' Jennie asked anxiously.

'It's all a big secret at the moment an' I'm not sure if it's bin settled yet,' Con answered, 'but the whisper is it's the Middle East. Don't go repeatin' this though, will yer, Jennie?'

'Of course not.'

'Anuvver battalion's standin' by in this country in case of an invasion,' he went on. 'I could be wiv that one. It's all in the lap o' the gods.'

They found a secluded place by the river wall and held each other close, watching the rise and fall of the moored barges midstream. They saw the gulls dipping and soaring, the still cranes and the shuttered wharves and Jennie fretted. 'I'll never get used ter sayin' goodbye,' she sighed. 'I'll always choke on the words.'

He smiled and squeezed her to him. 'War will always be about goodbyes,' he replied. 'But we'll cope, 'cos there's nuffink none of us can do about it. We 'ave ter be strong, an' I'm sure each of us'll gain strength an' win frew, as time goes by.'

Chapter Nineteen

The summer streets of Bermondsey were quiet now after the few hectic days that followed Dunkirk and the homecomings of the servicemen. In Carter Lane women chatted on their doorsteps much as they had before, but they were often sad-faced and serious.

'Poor Mrs Dunkley's out of 'er mind,' Amy Bromilow told Ivy Jones. 'She got a telegram two days ago.'

'So did Mrs Bentley from Brady Street,' Ivy replied. 'Tommy was 'er only son.'

'At least Chris Wickstead's doin' well,' Amy went on. 'Ada told me 'e looked more 'is ole self last weekend when 'er an' Jacko went ter see 'im. Apparently they're gonna send 'im down ter Wales ter recuperate. It must 'ave bin terrible fer those poor lads. My Freddie didn't say too much about it all, but I could see 'ow it must 'ave affected 'im. One night 'e woke up screamin'. Frightened the life out o' me it did. I wondered what the bloody 'ell it was. In a pool o' sweat 'e was.'

Ivy shook her head slowly. 'Gawd knows what lastin' effect it's gonna 'ave on those boys,' she sighed.

Dolly and Mick Flynn had deliberately refrained from

asking too many questions when their two sons came home, but Dolly could not fail to notice the bandage on Jim's upper arm while he was washing at the scullery sink. He passed it off as a scratch that had got a little infected and was now healing nicely, though it still made his arm a bit stiff. Frank was non-committal when she asked him about his brother's wound, but he stressed that it was really nothing to make a fuss about, considering the injuries some of the lads had suffered. The usual banter between the two that had become second nature over their years as brewery draymen was still in evidence but both Dolly and Mick realised that it was now a little contrived, as if put on for their benefit. They felt that of the two Frank seemed the more affected, and at times when he had that faraway look in his eyes Dolly wanted to hug him in the way she had when he was a child. She knew that the scars of war were already indelibly there, seared into both her sons' minds, as they were for all the other sons and husbands who had fought their way back from the maw of death across the narrow Channel, and aware of her inadequacy she suffered in silence.

The wartime summer was warm and balmy, but now the clear August skies over Southern England were criss-crossed with tracer streaks, cannon fire and duelling aircraft darting and diving as the Battle of Britain raged. Airfields and coastal installations were targeted in the fight for supremacy between the Royal Air Force and the German Luftwaffe, and all the time an armada was being prepared across the Channel. An invasion date had been set by the German High Command and ill-prepared and undertrained battalions of British troops were rushed to the coastline to join up with a fully mobilised Home Guard, as ready as they would ever be to defend the country against an imminent landing. Everything hinged on the fate of Fighter Command. The skies above the landing points had to be made safe first, but the Spitfire and Hurricane pilots were proving to be more than a thorn in the side of the German forces. Losses on both sides were high, and on every placard outside every newsagent and paperstand battle scores and losses were printed in bold lettering. People rushed to buy the newspapers, reading the accounts and noting the scores as they might those of a cricket match in more peaceful times, but this game was deadly serious. Everyone knew that their whole future existence was in the hands of a few brave and exhausted pilots, who were slowly whittling down the might of the Luftwaffe and winning the battle of the skies.

It was some time before anyone on this side of the Channel realised that, due to their huge losses, the German war machine had decided the invasion of England would have to be postponed. However, a new and terrible plan was slowly taking shape. England had to be forced into submission one way or another, and where once the airfields in Northern Germany and occupied France had been full of fighter aircraft, they now became bases for the heavy bombers.

Saturday the 7th of September 1940 was to be a day that no one in London would ever forget as long as they lived, but on the eve of the cataclysm people went about their business and got on with their lives as they had always done. The women queued for food and prepared meals, holidaying children played in the warm streets and people came home from work looking forward to a restful weekend.

In the Flynn household it was a normal Friday evening, and with the meal over Sadie hurried up to her bedroom to get ready to go out. As usual Jennie looked in and sat chatting with her, curious to find out why Sadie had suddenly changed her plans. 'I fink Len Regan can twist you right round 'is little finger,' she said, pulling no punches. 'Only this afternoon you was goin' on about not bein' put upon an' then 'e shows up in that flashy car an' you start jumpin' frew the 'oop.'

Sadie sighed indulgently as she brushed out her fair hair. She felt very close to Jennie and generally tended to put up with her forthright remarks, knowing that they were said out of love and concern rather than malice, but this evening she took the bait. 'You just don't understand, Jen, so don't start goin' on. This is important business. Len's got some problems an' it's only right 'e should ask me fer some 'elp.'

'It must be serious if 'e couldn't say what 'e 'ad ter say in the 'ouse instead o' draggin' you out ter the car,' Jennie answered regardless. 'What must people fink?'

'Frankly I'm not interested in what the neighbours fink,' Sadie said quickly. 'Sod 'em, that's what you always tell me.'

Jennie shrugged her shoulders. 'Is this a big secret, or are yer gonna let me in on it?' she asked, her face assuming a saucy smile.

Sadie swivelled round to face her younger sister. 'It's this Brighton business,' she began. 'Apparently there's bin some disagreement wiv the people Johnnie Macaulay was cultivatin' an' it looks like the big deal's gonna fall frew. It seems that the people from Glasgow 'ave pulled out as well, an' that was where most of the backin' was comin' from.'

'It's all above my 'ead,' Jennie sighed.

'It's a question o' raisin' enough money ter buy inter the gamblin' set-up on the south coast,' Sadie explained. 'Macaulay's invested 'eavily in that Brighton business an' now 'e's lookin' ter raise some money by gettin' some new backers.'

Jennie's irritation was obvious as she pulled a face. 'So 'ow does all this concern you, apart from bein' involved wiv Regan?' she asked.

'There's a big meetin' ternight at Brighton an' some important business people are invited,' Sadie went on. 'Len wants me to 'elp 'im take care of 'em.'

'An' you're gonna stand fer that?' Jennie said incredulously. ''Ave you fergotten what 'appened at that club down in Kent? Yer gotta be mad.'

'It's nuffink like that,' Sadie told her. 'Len's gonna be there all the time an' 'e won't let no one take liberties.'

'I thought yer said yer wouldn't be seen dead in that place,' Jennie remarked. 'Yer said yerself it's nuffink more than a brothel.'

'I was angry at the time an' I went over the top when I told yer that,' Sadie replied. 'Actually it's a smart 'otel that doubles as a dinin' an' gamblin' club. There's some 'ostesses employed there an' they encourage the customers ter drink an' gamble. It's their job an' they get commission. If they fancy a customer an' the customer fancies them, so what? If there wasn't any bedrooms there they'd book in somewhere else anyway.'

'Oh I see,' Jennie said sarcastically.

Sadie picked up her hairbrush once more. 'I don't fink yer

do,' she sighed. 'Anyway I've agreed to 'elp out ternight so that's that.'

'Just as long as yer not expected ter play the 'ostess game,' Jennie persisted.

'What d'you take me for?' Sadie said angrily.

'I'm just concerned for yer, that's all,' Jennie told her in a sincere voice.

Sadie smiled. 'I know you are, but stop worryin'. I know what I'm doin'.'

'By the way, 'ave yer replied ter Big Joe's latest letter yet?' Jennie asked.

Sadie shook her head. 'I was gonna do it ternight. I'll do it termorrer fer sure.'

'Yer wouldn't want Joe ter fink out o' sight means out o' mind, would yer?' Jennie pressed.

'I said I'd do it, didn't I?'

'Yeah all right, touchy Lill.'

'Well you do go on at times.'

'Sorry fer breavvin'.'

Sadie put down the brush and let her shoulders slump. 'If yer must know I'm findin' it a bit difficult answerin' Joe's latest letter,' she said. 'It wasn't a problem replyin' ter the ovver ones, after me an' you 'ad that little chat. I just told 'im about what it was like growin' up round 'ere, like you suggested, an' I told 'im all the little chit-chat from the street, an' 'is replies were in the same vein, but this last letter from 'im seems different.'

'Different? 'Ow d'yer mean?'

'I dunno really. 'E just seems more serious.'

''As 'e asked yer ter be 'is gelfriend?'

'No, it's just the general tone o' the letter.'

'Well unless I read it I can't offer any opinion,' Jennie said with a wry smile. 'But don't fink I'm pressin' fer you ter show me it. I know it's private.'

'You're welcome ter read it,' Sadie replied, opening the dressing-table drawer and taking it out. 'There's nuffink soppy in it.'

Jennie read the two pages carefully and then handed them back to her sister. 'I must admit it does sound a bit serious,' she remarked. 'That bit about you bein' special to 'im an' 'opin' that you feel the same way, and the bit about rememberin' 'im wiv love if fings go wrong. It seems as though 'e expects somefing to 'appen.'

'That's what I thought,' Sadie agreed. 'The problem is, 'ow do I reply wivout committin' meself? Big Joe knows the score wiv me an' Len. I just can't tell 'im I love 'im.'

Jennie looked thoughtful as she studied her sister's anxious face. 'I don't fink 'e used the word love in that way,' she said quietly. 'Just fink about it. Joe's trainin' up in some remote part of Scotland, an' the location suggests ter me that this is all preparation fer a dangerous job. If that's true, then 'e most likely feels 'e might well end up gettin' killed when it goes off. That could be why 'e's askin' you ter remember 'im wiv love. Someone to 'old on to, someone special who'd keep 'is memory alive, that's what 'e's sayin', Sadie, I'm certain of it.'

'You could well be right,' Sadie replied. 'After all, Joe's thousands o' miles away from the country where 'e was born and raised. Back 'ome people'd mourn 'is passin' an' 'ave their own special memories of 'im, but over 'ere 'e prob'ly still feels like an outsider ter most people.'

'I fink yer'll write that letter now,' Jennie said smiling.

'What's more, I'll be willin' ter bet that even wivout committin' yerself yer'll make 'im a very 'appy man.'

Albert Levy opened his eyes and stared fixedly for a few moments at the shadowy figure by his bedside. Slowly, as his vision cleared, he saw Gerda smiling down at him. 'Where's Abel gone?' he croaked.

Gerda felt her heart sink. His brain's damaged, she thought. He can't remember. 'Abel went some time ago,' she faltered.

Albert smiled wearily and slid his hand across the crisp white bedsheet. 'Abel was standing there,' he replied. 'I saw him at the foot of the bed and he told me I'd been very careless. Is it true I was knocked down?'

Gerda nodded as the tears came. 'Abel wouldn't lie,' she gulped.

'No, of course not.'

'Close your eyes now and rest,' she told him. 'I'll be back soon.'

'Abel was there all the time,' Albert said, his voice hoarse with emotion. 'He listened to all my ravings and he understood. I asked his forgiveness for ever doubting him and he said there was nothing to forgive. He came to tell me, Gerda. He gave me the sign. At last I can be in peace.'

'Close your eyes, dearest. Sleep deeply and when you wake up I'll be at your side,' she whispered.

'Of course, my dear,' Albert answered. 'You always are.'

The doctor smiled as he patted Gerda's hand. 'He'll be fine now,' he said.

Liz Kenny made her usual call on Dolly Flynn and the two

sat sipping their tea while they filled each other in on the street's developments.

'Big Joe sent us a nice long letter,' Liz said. ''E's such a carin' young man. 'E was concerned about my Bert. You remember Bert wasn't very well when Joe was 'ome on leave.'

'Our Sadie's 'ad a few letters from 'im too,' Dolly told her.

'I'm so glad,' Liz remarked. 'Wouldn't it be nice if those two got tergevver.'

'Yeah, it would,' Dolly replied. 'I don't like 'er bein' wiv that wide-boy Regan. 'E's nuffink but trouble if you ask me.'

'Does your Sadie answer the letters?' Liz asked.

'Yeah, I'm sure she does.'

'That's nice. Big Joe finks the world of 'er, yer know.'

'Yes, I know.'

''Ere, while I fink of it,' Liz said suddenly, 'I bumped inter Rene Conroy down the market this mornin'. 'Er Alec's due 'ome on leave very soon. Apparently 'e's in the Royal Engineers. Who'd 'ave thought it?'

'Yeah, it was strange 'ow 'e just went an' signed on, after all 'e'd told 'is muvver,' Dolly replied. 'The poor cow was goin' out of 'er mind over 'im. She said she wouldn't be able ter stand the shame of the police comin' fer 'im.'

Liz Kenny put her empty cup and saucer down on the table. ''Ave yer done any more knittin' lately?' she asked.

Dolly shook her head. 'Nah, I ain't 'ad the time, what wiv the boys bein' 'ome an' all. I'll get back ter doin' it again though. Those Lockwood sisters don't let up, do they?'

Liz grinned. 'What a strange couple they are.'

'Yer tellin' me,' Dolly agreed. 'Mind you though, yer

gotta feel sorry for 'em. Poor Cynthia got knocked from piller ter post by that ugly git of an ole man, then 'e pisses orf an' leaves 'er wiv debts up to 'er eyeballs.'

'Strange about the way 'e disappeared,' Liz went on. 'Everyone was very surprised. 'E led a life o' Riley wiv Cynthia. She used ter do everyfing fer 'im. 'E even 'ad 'er puttin' 'is bets on, the lazy bastard.'

'Mind you, she's 'appy wiv Charity bein' there wiv 'er,' Dolly remarked. 'They're very close an' she does fuss over 'er. It makes a change fer someone ter fuss over the poor cow.'

'Didn't she ever marry?' Liz asked.

'Nah, it was the ole story,' Dolly explained. 'Someone told me once that she looked after 'er sick muvver until the ole gel was in 'er nineties, an' by then it was too late.'

'Bloody shame.'

'Yeah, what some people 'ave ter put up wiv.'

'Well I s'pose I'd better get back or Bert'll fink I've left 'ome.'

'Anuvver cuppa 'fore yer go?'

'All right then. 'E'll be snorin' 'is 'ead off anyway.'

Sapper Alexander Conroy wiped the sweat from his brow and blinked quickly. The loose earth had been cleared from around the bomb and its grey wet surface glistened in the light of the portable lamp.

'So what now?' the voice crackled over the wireless set.

'I'm about ter remove the detonator,' Alec answered in a whisper through the mouthpiece.

'Don't jerk the spanner, ease it. Message understood?'

'Loud an' clear,' Alec replied.

The evening felt chill as the last of the light faded and the young sapper shivered as he picked up the large spanner and slipped the end onto the protruding nut. Slowly he applied pressure, lightly at first, then with more force when the nut resisted movement. It was turning, coming out easier now and Alec paused for breath. The rest could be done with his fingers and he slowly turned the nut until it came away from the casing.

'Report,' the command crackled down the line.

'Detonator removed. Goin' fer the wires.'

'Check the wiring first.'

Alec shone the torch into the recess and saw that the red wire was connected to a small metal case and the blue wire ran into the darkness of the bomb casing. 'Cuttin' the blue wire,' he said, his throat suddenly dry.

'Why the blue?'

'Red wire booby-trapped.'

'Proceed.'

Alec gingerly eased the blue wire up until he managed to get a proper grip on it with the snippers, then with a silent prayer he cut the wire clean through. The ugly buzzing made him jump back in fright against the wall of the crater, and he looked up fearfully to see the sergeant approaching.

'You bloody fool. You just killed yourself, Conroy,' he bawled.

'I saw that the red wire was attached ter the condenser,' Alec said taking a deep breath. 'That's why I cut the blue.'

'Without checking where the blue ended up,' the instructor growled. 'If that'd been a real unexploded bomb you would have blown yourself and your assistant to kingdom come. In future don't take anything for granted. You can't afford to in bomb disposal. The red wire attached to the condenser was a decoy and you fell for it. The blue was booby-trapped.'

Alec rubbed his grimy hand across his sweaty forehead and the sergeant gave him a sympathetic smile. 'Come on, Conroy, let's get back to the truck. I don't think you'll make that mistake again.'

Chapter Twenty

Simm's bakery in the Old Kent Road ran out of bread as usual around midday on Saturday and the last bake was snatched up as soon as it came out of the ovens, which pleased George Simm as he had a wedding function to attend that evening. He chased around cleaning the mixing equipment, while his wife Addie scrubbed the wooden worktops in the back of the shop. Jennie took her cue from the rush and dash around her and cleaned the shelves, tidied up in general and counted out the till.

'I fink we broke the record terday,' Addie smiled as she wiped the sweat from her forehead with the back of her hand.

'Four o'clock, that's not bad,' George remarked. 'We can close up early. You might as well get off, luv,' he told Jennie. ''Ave a nice early night fer a change.'

Jennie needed no persuasion and she hurried out into the sunlit thoroughfare, looking forward to another letter from Con. She normally received one on Saturday morning but the postman invariably came after she had left for work, and her mother would put it on the mantelshelf in front of the chimer for her to find as soon as she got home.

As she turned into Carter Lane she saw Liz Kenny standing on her doorstep and the woman beckoned to her. 'Got a minute, luv?' she asked.

'Yeah, course.'

'We got a letter from Big Joe this mornin' an' it seems 'e won't be able ter write fer a while,' she said as she led the way into her parlour.

'Did 'e say why?'

'No, but I don't s'pose 'e could very well,' Liz remarked. 'I fink it's somefing very secret if you ask me. The last couple o' letters 'ave bin a bit different, like 'e was tryin' ter tell us somefing. Well, that's what my Bert seems ter fink.'

'It's funny you should say that,' Jennie replied. 'Sadie gets letters from Joe, as yer know, an' she said the same fing.'

'Yeah, well I wanted ter catch yer comin' 'ome from work ter let yer know so you could pass it on ter Sadie,' Liz explained. 'I wouldn't want the gel ter fink that Joe wasn't bovverin' ter write. 'E finks the world of 'er. 'E's always askin' after 'er in 'is letters.'

'Sadie finks a lot of 'im too, but she's not sure of 'erself at the moment,' Jennie told her. 'That Len Regan's a pain in the arse as far as I'm concerned. 'E seems ter be able ter twist 'er round 'is little finger, an' I told 'er too. I wish she'd give 'im the elbow.'

'She'll learn the 'ard way,' Liz sighed. 'I know yer mum worries over 'er. We were only talkin' about 'er an' 'im the ovver day. Regan's a right spiv. 'E seems to 'ave 'is fingers in everyfing.'

Jennie nodded. 'Regan's s'posed ter be Johnnie Macaulay's right-'and man but from what Sadie tells me it seems that Regan's the one who's runnin' the show.'

'D'yer want a cuppa while yer 'ere?' Liz asked.

Jennie looked up at the clock and saw it was twenty-five minutes past four. 'No, I'd better get off, fanks all the same,' she replied. 'Claire Wilson's 'ome fer the weekend an' me an' 'er are goin' ter the pictures ternight. I got me 'air ter wash an' some ironin' ter do.'

When Jennie let herself into the house Dolly pulled a face and jerked her head towards the stairs. 'Sadie's in 'er room but be careful what yer say to 'er,' she warned. 'She's in a violent temper. Nearly bit my 'ead off when she walked in. All I said was that she looked a bit peaky.'

Jennie climbed the stairs and knocked gently on Sadie's bedroom door. 'Are yer takin' visitors?' she said quietly.

'Don't be funny, come in,' Sadie growled.

'Man trouble?' Jennie said with a disarming smile as she took her usual place on the edge of the bed.

'If yer call him a bloody man,' Sadie replied.

'Phew. 'E didn't leave yer ter . . .'

'Don't ask,' Sadie said, gritting her teeth with temper. ''E never.'

'Tell me, Jennie, do yer really fink I'm shallow an' stupid?'

'Course I don't,' the younger sister said quickly. 'Yer not still broodin' over that little chat we 'ad the ovver day, are yer?'

'I've decided,' Sadie declared with a serious look on her face, 'I'm gonna go inter nursin'.'

'You, nursin'?' Jennie said in surprise.

'Yeah, me. Don't yer fink I'm up to it?'

'I fink yer'd make a very good nurse,' Jennie replied quickly. 'But why the sudden decision? Is it anyfing ter do

239

wiv what 'appened last night?'

'Ter be honest I've bin toyin' wiv the idea fer some time,' Sadie told her. 'I can't sit back an' do nuffink till the powers that be decide I should be in war-work. I thought about nursin' after I saw the boys back 'ome an' sittin' round the dinner table. I knew then that I 'ad ter do somefing, but last night really made me mind up once an' fer all. I'm gonna try an' get in the Queen Alexandra's Nursin' Service.'

'They're army nurses, ain't they?'

'That's right.'

'Well, good fer you, sis,' Jennie said getting up and putting her arm around Sadie's shoulders. 'Yer'll make a crackin' nurse.'

'D'yer really fink so?'

'I know so.'

Sadie swivelled round on her stool at the dressing table and clasped her hands together as Jennie resumed her place on the bed. 'Me an' Len are finished,' she announced, as if to put the seal on it.

'So what 'appened?' Jennie asked.

'The evenin' started off very well, funnily enough,' Sadie began. 'Len was all charm when we were goin' down ter Brighton. Nosher drove us an' me an' Len chatted away in the back, all nicey nicey, then when we got ter the 'otel 'e introduced me ter those clients of 'is. They were the usual sort yer'd expect. Smart suits an' gold watches an' rings, wiv money comin' out o' their ears. Len seemed ter be gettin' on famously wiv 'em an' then after a while 'e left 'em talkin' ter Johnnie Macaulay, an' me an' 'im went inter the gamblin' room. I was surprised ter see a few uniforms there. Army officers they were. One of 'em was just a young lad really, couldn't 'ave bin no more than twenty-two, twenty-three, an' 'e 'ad the shakes, literally. One o' the 'ostesses was 'angin' on to 'is arm an' encouragin' 'im ter place bets. All over 'im she was. Len told me that the feller was the son of a local businessman an' the family were stone rich. Anyway, I watched the goin's-on while Len placed a few small bets. Didn't win anyfing, but 'e was on form, chattin' away to everyone. Then we went ter the bar fer a drink an' we stood talkin'. Apparently this young officer 'ad bin at Dunkirk, an' Len said 'e'd just come out of a military 'ospital. 'E was sufferin' from shell shock. Honestly, Jen, it was pitiful ter see. The lad 'ad a bulgin' wallet an' this tart was actually takin' the notes from it ter buy more chips. The poor sod didn't know what day it was. I'm sure she pocketed some of 'is money, but when I mentioned it ter Len 'e just laughed. "'E won't miss it," 'e said. I felt sick ter me stomach. I could see our Frank an' Jim in me mind an' I thought, this could be them. This could 'appen ter them, given the same circumstances.'

''Ow 'orrible,' Jennie said, shaking her head sadly.

Sadie stared down at her hands for a few moments. 'Len was drinkin' double whiskies an' 'e began ter get very sarcastic as the drink took effect. 'E told me that the war could be a godsend if yer knew yer way around the obstacles an' 'e said 'e wanted some o' the action. Course I made the mistake o' tellin' 'im that if it was action 'e wanted why didn't 'e join up like me bruvvers. Blew 'is top 'e did. I felt so embarrassed. People could 'ear 'im goin' on an' I'm sure they were laughin' at me. 'E started ter tell me about the money bein' made on the black market an' all about the goin's-on at Brighton. What done it fer me was when 'e told me they were settin' up a club fer servicemen near this big army camp somewhere on the south coast. It's gonna be a cheaper version of the 'otel, fer ordinary soldiers wiv less money who wanna apply fer membership. I just lost me temper completely an' I told 'im that all 'im an' Macaulay were doin' was takin' advantage of young men who were away from their loved ones an' feelin' lonely. "Too bad," 'e said. "An' who are you ter criticise? Are you turnin' inter some Bible-thumpin' campaigner?" '

'So yer told 'im straight you was finished wiv 'im?'

'No, not then,' Sadie went on. 'This young officer was at the roulette table an' 'is number came up. 'E started ter get very excited an' this 'orrible tart who was wiv 'im persuaded 'im ter let it ride. You know, stay on the same number. Now the chances o' that givin' yer a result are one in a million, but the young man didn't seem ter know where 'e was, let alone what 'e was doin', an' 'is face was all distorted. It was so sad ter see. Then the people round the table started ter laugh at 'im. I just saw red. I walked over an' in a loud voice I told 'em all that they should be bloody well ashamed o' themselves. This tart told me ter piss off an' the next fing I remember was grabbin' an 'andful of 'air an' tuggin' on it. She started ter scream an' Len came over an' yanked me away.'

'Wow!' Jennie exclaimed. 'I wish I'd 'ave bin there ter see it!'

'It wasn't very pretty,' Sadie said with distaste. 'Anyway, Len marched me outside an' started ter lay the law down an' I told 'im a few 'ome trufes. I told 'im 'e could go back ter whoever 'e was knockin' off an' 'e nearly exploded.'

''E didn't touch yer, did 'e?' Jennie asked quickly.

'Nah, 'e never actually slapped me, but 'e did shake me. I just kicked 'im in the shin an' stormed off. Nosher brought me back, an' me an' 'im 'ad a very good chat on the way 'ome. Apparently there's a lot o' trouble brewin' between Macaulay an' those businessmen I 'ad to entertain at the club that time, an' Nosher reckons I'm well out of it an' should stay well clear of the lot of 'em.'

'It must be serious if Nosher warned yer,' Jennie remarked. ''E's bin drivin' fer that crowd fer years, so you said.'

'Yeah, that's right,' Sadie replied, 'but me an' old Nosher get on very well, an' 'e treats me sort o' like 'is own daughter. 'E knows 'e can trust me not ter repeat anyfing 'e tells me, an' I've decided I'm gonna take 'is advice.'

'Good fer you, sis.'

'I mean it, Jen.'

'I know yer do,' Jennie said smiling. 'It just wanted somefing like this to 'appen ter bring yer ter yer senses. By the way, Liz Kenny stopped me on the way 'ome from work. She got a letter from Big Joe this mornin'. Apparently 'e can't write any more fer a while. Liz said 'e didn't explain why but it follows on from what we were sayin' about 'is last letter bein' a bit different. After listenin' ter Liz I reckon Joe's goin' on somefing very dangerous.'

Sadie nodded thoughtfully. 'I'm gonna write 'im a letter ternight,' she declared suddenly. 'I'm gonna tell 'im I'll be finkin' of 'im an' I'll say a prayer fer 'im every night.'

'That's lovely,' Jennie said, sighing extravagantly.

'I'm not committin' meself, mind,' Sadie said quickly, 'but it will 'elp give 'im somefing to 'ang on to if 'e is goin' on some dangerous mission.'

'Will yer tell 'im yer ditched Regan?'

'I might.'

'Course yer will.'

Sadie turned to face the mirror once more, feeling her cheeks flushing slightly, and then suddenly the air-raid siren wailed out. The young women looked at each other and Jennie smiled as she fought to stay calm. 'It's probably just one o' those try-outs,' she said dismissively.

They soon began to hear the drone and distant thumping and they jumped up at the window and peered out. A few people were standing at their front doors and pointing skyward.

'Somefing's 'appenin',' Jennie said, hurrying out of the bedroom.

Sadie followed her down the stairs and they found their parents already standing on the pavement outside.

'What is it?' Jennie asked.

The azure sky was full of aircraft, flying high in formation. Shells were bursting amongst them and Mick Flynn let out a sudden yell. 'Get inside! It's an air raid!'

Dolly and the two girls ignored him, all three rooted to the spot as they gazed up at a sky dark with planes. Explosions could be heard now and the drone became deafening. Large palls of smoke and flames rose high above the rooftops and the din of engines and destruction grew so loud it almost drowned out the whine of the air-raid siren.

'It's the docks!' Bill Harris screamed out from across the street. 'They're bombin' the Surrey Docks!'

'Oh my good Gawd!' Dolly gasped, her hand held up to her face.

A man carrying a service gas mask over his shoulder and

wearing a steel helmet marked ARP dashed into Carter Lane. 'Get inside! Take cover!' he yelled, blowing on a whistle.

'Don't you shout at me like that,' Charity Lockwood told him sharply as he dashed past her front door.

'I thought it was very strange a little while ago,' Cynthia remarked to her sister. 'The wireless went dead and I knew it wasn't the accumulator. I only changed it yesterday.'

'I didn't know,' Charity replied.

'No, you were having a snooze and I didn't want to disturb you.'

'Look at those flames and all that smoke,' Charity almost shouted.

'It's the Surrey Docks,' Ted Conroy told them. 'The place is crammed full o' timber. Gawd 'elp the poor sods who live Downtown.'

Downtown Rotherhithe was an island, formed by the natural loop of the River Thames. The one main road around the island followed the bank of the river and led over bridges which spanned the canals and creeks that linked the chain of docks. The rising and swivelling bridges were the only land access to what had become known many years ago as 'Downtown' by the residents, mainly dockers and factory workers who lived in old tenement blocks and two-up, two-down houses and prided themselves on their isolation, and the area was cut off when the bridges were operating and a freighter was passing into or out of the dock system in the centre of the island. The dockyards were always stacked full of timber brought from Russia, Finland and Scandinavia, and in the local pubs in Downtown Rotherhithe weird and wonderful concoctions of drinks could be had and a dozen different languages heard. Around the perimeter of the island riverside factories and small warehouses abounded, storing or processing supplies and produce dropped off in barges and small freighters. It was a vibrant and busy area, and an obvious target for the raiding Luftwaffe which visited a hellish punishment upon it that balmy Saturday afternoon.

It didn't take long for the fire chief to assess the situation and he quite simply called for as many fire tenders as possible. Appliances were brought across the river and rushed up from Kent and Sussex and still they could not cope. A sea of resin melted the firemen's boots and the iron sheds were twisted into grotesque shapes by the heat. The people who lived Downtown were trapped on their prized little island. Bridges had been blasted and those still in place were burning fiercely, making it almost impossible for the fire crews to get to many of the blazing yards. It was growing hotter by the minute as the oxygen was sucked out of the air, and as more fire tenders arrived exhausted firemen took a short breather before going back to tackle the conflagration once more.

As the evening wore on the light from the raging inferno could be seen as far north as Hertfordshire and from the Kent–Sussex borders. It also acted as a beacon, lighting up the heartland of London, and most people realised only too well that the Luftwaffe would be certain to make good use of it before the night was out.

In Carter Lane, as in other Bermondsey backstreets, people had to make a decision. If, as seemed likely, there was another raid that night, should they use the public shelters, or should they sleep under the stairs or in the downstairs rooms?

'I couldn't possibly go in one of those public places,' Cynthia groaned.

'No, nor could I,' Charity agreed. 'There's no privacy and what about our bodily needs?'

Amy Bromilow put it more crudely. 'I couldn't piss in one o' those buckets,' she said firmly. 'Besides, everyone can 'ear yer.'

'What about the tube?' Ivy suggested. 'They say it's safe down there.'

'Yeah, unless yer go sleep-walkin',' Amy replied.

'Ada Wickstead said that the jam factory was bein' used as a shelter. Mind yer, that's a bit of a trek every night.'

Amy was adamant. 'I'm gonna take me chances under the stairs an' if it's the Lord's will that I go, then it don't matter what shelter I use, does it?'

Dolly and Mick Flynn had made up their minds to stay in the house for the time being, but should the raids get worse then it would have to be a public shelter.

Liz Kenny and Daisy Harris stood talking to Dolly beneath a blood-red sky as the all-clear sounded, speaking quietly as though fearful of reawakening the devils of destruction.

'I was wonderin' what the workmen were doin' ter that empty 'ouse next ter the factory,' Liz said. 'It turns out it's gonna be a command post fer the ARP. That's what Mrs Jones told me.'

'Did yer notice they've started sandbaggin' it?' Daisy cut in.

'I looked in this mornin' on me way back from the

market,' Dolly said. 'The men were puttin' big wooden posts up ter support the ceilin'. Now that's the place ter shelter.'

As it grew late the sky still threw back the orange glow of the fires, making the streets as bright as day, and fretful children puzzled by it all found it hard to sleep. Families sat together round their wireless sets, and as the Grimethorpe Colliery Band struck up with 'It's a Long Way to Tipperary' hundreds of aircraft at airfields in France and Northern Germany were roaring into life and moving onto the runways. Soon they would be back, flying over the Kentish fields and up the Thames estuary towards London, carrying in their bellies a metal cargo of death and destruction. The first night of the London Blitz was about to begin, and it would be seventy-six consecutive nights before any respite came.

Chapter Twenty-One

Very few people were surprised when the air-raid siren blared out on Saturday night. Danny Crossley and Alf Coates refused to leave the public bar of The Sun until they had finished their drinks and Charlie Anson decided to let the pub stay open for a while to see how things went. Many people had already gone to the public shelters to make sure of getting a place, but most of the Carter Lane folk had decided to stay at home, at least for the time being.

Soon the roar of the anti-aircraft guns in the local parks and open spaces became deafening and then came the dreaded sound of falling bombs. Explosions shook the very foundations of buildings and ceiling dust and plaster fell like snow. Never before had there been anything like it. Dogs howled and cats scurried under beds, children wailed and adults prayed as the din increased and explosions got louder. Windows cracked, but for the most part stayed in their frames due to the protective strips of brown paper that had been stuck on them. Ornaments toppled from shelves as houses shuddered, and shouts and running footsteps could be heard as the ARP services went into action.

For what seemed an eternity the deafening noise of bombs

and guns reverberated, then there was a brief lull before the second wave of bombers flew over the burning capital. Fires were raging everywhere, and as the onslaught continued relentlessly families moved out of their parlours to shelter under the stairs. All night long it went on, until four-thirty the following morning, when people gradually emerged from their homes to inspect the carnage. The pre-dawn sky was lit up with an orange and red glow and a strong, acrid smell of cordite and charred wood filled the air. The factory at the end of Carter Lane was burning fiercely, defying the efforts of the exhausted firemen. Shattered roof slates and glass splinters lay on the cobbles, and from the reinforced house next door to the stricken factory two ARP personnel with blackened faces emerged to take a well-earned rest.

'That was a close one, Miss Watson,' the male controller remarked to his female colleague.

'I thought it was our lot, to tell you the truth, Mr Bayley,' she replied.

Nigel Bayley jutted out his square chin and took stock. By day he was employed on the London Underground, where his organising skills helped to keep the vital service running on time, and at night he was the controller responsible for linking the local ARP resources. 'I think we'd better have a general clear-up and then catch some shut-eye. What say you, Miss Watson?'

Karen Watson was in charge of a large City typing pool by day and like Nigel she gave up her nights to supervise the volunteer ARP runners, whose job it was to carry messages to and fro when the lines were down. Shapely, attractive, and with wide grey eyes, Karen took her work seriously. To all intents and purposes she was the ultimate professional, maintaining a formal rapport with her superior officer yet friendly and outgoing to those working under her. 'Right-o, Mr Bayley,' she replied. 'Shall we get started?'

As they went back inside, Ted Conroy emerged from his house with a large jug of tea, accompanied by Rene who had scrounged some large mugs from her neighbour Amy Bromilow, and the firemen received the refreshment with much gratitude.

When the last of the volunteers had gone and the re-inforced control room was looking a little more clean and efficient, Karen turned to Nigel. 'At last, darling.'

'I think we did well, dearest.'

'Hold me, Nigel.'

'There there, don't let this get to you.'

'I feel that nothing can harm me when I'm in your arms, Nigel darling.'

'You were very brave, Karen.'

'Was I?'

'Umm. I was very proud of you.'

'And I of you.'

'We make a good team, don't we, darling?'

'We certainly do.'

At six o'clock that Sunday morning the controller and his assistant emerged from the control post and locked the front door.

'Good day to you, Miss Watson.'

'Good day to you, Mr Bayley.'

As they walked off in opposite directions the Sunday morning dawn light rose in the ragged orange sky and the people of Carter Lane took to their beds for a very welcome, if all too brief, slumber.

★ ★ ★

Vehicles from the Royal Engineers bomb-disposal squad drove into Southwark Park early on Sunday morning and the sappers began to set up a base inside a fenced-off area which contained hurriedly constructed huts. Later that morning the commanding officer introduced himself to the soldiers assembled outside the mess hut. 'I'm Captain Joseph Fairburn, officer commanding Baker Company, which is what this squad will be known as from now on,' he began. 'Our area of control will be the Bermondsey and Rotherhithe district, but we are to be flexible, should the need arise. Now you men are all fully trained for the hazardous operations you will be required to perform and the situations you will encounter in bomb disposal, but for my money the term of reference does not fully do credit to the service you will be providing. Disposal of unexploded bombs and devices is the easy part. Before that comes the little task of rendering them impotent.'

The men gathered before him smiled and nodded in agreement, and a young Bermondsey lad was already feeling a little more confident that his commanding officer was not going to be a complete and utter bastard.

'Now we are lucky, inasmuch as we have two sappers amongst us who know the area very well. Sergeant Kilbride and Sapper Conroy will be able to get us to the job in hand without too much map work, saving valuable minutes. Conversely, I have to tell you that we have drawn the short straw to some extent, being based in what is considered to be the eye of the storm. As you will all be aware, this area is a prime target for the Jerries, and as such it is currently looking forward to a considerable pounding. I don't need to tell you that the Surrey Docks is still burning out of control as I speak, and when stock is finally taken we will be set to work there, make no mistake. It will be your blooding, and I want nothing less than a one-hundred-per-cent commitment from you all and no six-foot boxes ending up down the post office. Remember my words. Promotion comes quickly in the bomb-disposal section of the Royal Engineers, and so does death. Kingdom come is at our elbow all the time, and only your expertise and know-how can prevent an early and rather energetic shuffling off of mortal coils. A brutal and callous assessment you might say, but then I am a brutal and callous man. So bear with me and remember, never take the Jerries for fools. Never underestimate them, nor their specialists, who will constantly pit their wits against yours. Good luck, men, and may your particular gods go with you always.'

Enthusiastic applause broke out and the captain gave a salute of acknowledgement before climbing into a waiting car.

'Well, 'e couldn't 'ave put it more plainly,' Sergeant Kilbride remarked.

Alec Conroy smiled as he glanced over to the bandstand and the gun emplacement further on. 'This used ter be a nice park at one time,' he said. 'It's gone ter the bloody dogs now.'

Kilbride put his hands on his hips as he looked around the encampment. 'Come on, lads, let's get workin',' he yelled. 'We're expected ter be operational by this time termorrer.'

Sunday dinner at the Flynns' was eaten with very little talking. Mick had been to The Sun for a pint and learnt that

253

one of his workmates and his wife had been killed by a blast which had brought the front of their house down. He had also found out that one of his drinking pals, Vic Slater, had lost his son when his ship was torpedoed in the North Atlantic. Dolly was quiet and thoughtful, having been told by Sadie that morning of her intention to join the army nursing service. True to form Jennie had also sprung a surprise.

'There's no way I'm gonna sit in some shelter while ovver women do their bit, Mum,' she had said firmly. 'I'm gonna see about joinin' the ARP.'

Dolly knew better than to argue with her youngest daughter when her mind was made up and she worried in silence. Mick had already told her that the men in the street were planning on getting themselves organised into a fire-watching team and that didn't exactly detract from her worries. 'I can see I'll be talkin' ter me bloody self wiv all you lot doin' yer bit,' she had said.

Dolly was feeling decidedly better now though. Liz Kenny had called in with her own little plan that afternoon and cheered her up.

'I was talkin' ter Mrs Spencer this mornin',' Liz began. 'Yer know 'er ole man's a fireman, well, she said they want women volunteers ter back up the fire crews. I'm finkin' of givin' it a go.'

'Yer don't mean 'elp 'em fight the fires, do yer?' Dolly asked incredulously.

'Course not, yer silly mare,' Liz said grinning. 'When the firemen are at a big blaze an' they can't leave it, canteen vans go round wiv tea and food. That way the blokes can take a short break in turns wivout leavin' the fire.'

'Sounds a good idea,' Dolly remarked.

'Yeah an' I'm gonna volunteer,' Liz said proudly.

'What does Bert fink about it?' Dolly asked her.

''E wasn't too keen at first,' Liz replied, 'but like I told 'im, while 'e's out fire-watchin' I ain't stayin' in the 'ouse on me own. Besides, as I said to 'im, lightning don't strike the same place twice. If a place 'as bin bombed I'll be safer there than cowerin' under the bloody stairs in our 'ouse. Let's face it, Dolly, a bleedin' good shove would knock our 'ouses over, let alone a bomb!'

'When yer gonna volunteer?' Dolly enquired.

'Termorrer mornin'.'

'Where?'

'At the fire station in the Old Kent Road.'

'Give us a knock an' I'll come wiv yer.'

'That'll be nice,' Liz said excitedly. 'Me an' you'll make a bloody good team.'

''Ere, who's gonna drive the canteen van?' Dolly asked.

'They've got drivers already,' Liz told her. 'It's servers they're short of.'

'Don't rush inter this, Mum,' Sadie implored her when she found out what her mother intended to do.

'Now listen 'ere,' Dolly said resolutely. 'It's all right you lot decidin' ter do yer bit an' then springin' it on me, but I'm s'posed ter stay 'ere on me own wiv the bombs fallin' all round. Well, you can bloody go an' whistle. I'm gonna do my bit an' that's that.'

'It could be dangerous, luv,' Mick remarked. 'A lot o' firemen get killed on the job. Walls fall on 'em an' floors give way.'

'Be sensible, Mick, fer Gawd's sake,' Dolly said sighing

255

with impatience. 'They won't park canteen vans under dangerous walls, now will they?'

'You'd be safer in a shelter, Mum,' Jennie told her.

'I see,' Dolly growled. 'Yer want me ter sit twiddlin' me thumbs all night worryin' about all o' you an' 'avin' ter listen ter the likes o' the Lockwood sisters goin' on about their aches an' pains. No fear! What's good fer the goose is good fer the gander, so that's the end of it.'

Mick and the girls were worried but they had to admit defeat, and they glowed with pride inside when they envisaged Dolly in a steel helmet, braving the air raids while serving tea and buns to hardy firemen.

The Sunderland flying boat took off from the remote base in Scotland and flew due south, hugging the coastline. At first light on Sunday morning it landed near the submarine base in Portland and four Royal Navy personnel, as well as supplies and equipment, were transferred to the submarine *Porbeagle*. At midday the submarine left port and sailed in a south-westerly direction, staying on the surface to conserve power. Once past the Scilly Isles it dived to ten fathoms and steered a more southerly course, still keeping well clear of French waters. A storm was brewing in the Bay of Biscay, but after coming up to periscope depth and scanning the area, the captain decided to surface and the four men who had joined the crew were able to go up on deck briefly.

'Bloody nectar,' Big Joe remarked as he drew in deep gulps of air.

Petty Officer Stone nodded as he quickly filled his pipe. 'All being well, we'll be in Gib by tomorrow night,' he said.

The other two passengers, Petty Officer Chivers and

Leading Seaman Preston, stood a few feet away on the slippery deck chatting together, but any chance of further relaxation was abruptly curtailed when the lookout suddenly shouted out, 'Clear the decks!'

The last man down the Jacob's ladder spun the wheel of the hatch and the submarine dived steeply.

'The aircraft might have been friendly but we couldn't afford to wait and find out,' the executive officer told the startled team as the vessel levelled off below the surface.

Leading Seaman Joe Buckley sat down in the cramped mess, sipping a mug of disgusting coffee while he re-read Sadie's letter. He closed his eyes, trying to evoke a vivid image of her in his mind but it eluded him. He put the letter back into his breast pocket and tapped it meaningfully as he made his way along the companionway and climbed up into his bunk. There was little to do except rest and he took advantage of the free time by sleeping as much as he could while the submarine was in transit to Gibraltar.

The last two days had been very hectic, with the dress rehearsal on Saturday afternoon which went on late into the night, then a de-briefing before sleep, which was cut short by the arrival of the flying boat. Joe had had no access to a wireless and was unaware that London had been bombed, until he heard two ratings discussing it.

'There were lots of people killed, according to the reports on the news broadcasts,' one said. 'I'm glad my folk don't live in London.'

'They say the place took a fair old bashing,' his mate added.

'When was this?' Joe interrupted him.

'Saturday afternoon,' the sailor replied. 'The Surrey

Docks in London were destroyed and there were hundreds of casualties.'

The rest of the journey to Gibraltar was a nightmare for the young Australian. Was Sadie all right? And what about the Kennys? Would they all have been caught up in the bombardment?

A whole day in Gibraltar was needed before confirmation came through that the mission was on, and during that time the four men on special service spent their time looking around the Rock and visiting the busy bars where they sat in the sun sipping ice-cold beers. At the appointed hour they returned to the dockside and were immediately summoned to the submarine's wardroom.

'Right, men, we've got the go-ahead,' Captain Fellows told them. 'We set sail at twenty-one hundred hours and our destination is Oran on the Algerian coast. Your target is the German surface raider *Kaiser Wilhelm*, which intelligence informs us has just arrived there.'

The four looked at each other excitedly. All the training, all the preparation was over and done with. Now it was the real thing and very soon they would be slipping into the night waters of the Mediterranean and setting off into the unknown.

'Our roundabout route will bring us ten miles off the Algerian coast by tomorrow evening and we'll stay submerged until darkness,' the captain went on, 'then we'll surface and move in closer. You will then set off at twenty-two hundred hours. Assuming that all goes well, and I'm sure it will, you will make your way in an easterly direction, following the coastline to this point, about a mile from the port.'

The men leaned forward over the table as the captain stabbed his forefinger down on the chart. 'It's a deserted spot with a small cove that's inaccessible by land but easily recognised by two large rocks here and here. The locals call them the Sentinels. You will wait there until 04.30 hours when you should see our signal. There'll be two flashes at ten-second intervals and you'll reply with two flashes. Our acknowledgement will be three flashes and you will then take to the water. Okay so far?'

The men nodded quickly and the captain looked from one to another. 'Now if for some reason we don't get your acknowledging signal we will wait for one hour. Here are the maps for you to study before you leave. You'll see that there's another rendezvous point marked further along the coast. Failing contact at the initial rendezvous, we'll be waiting off this point the following night between twenty and twenty-three hundred hours. I hope this back-up point will not be needed but study the map and digest the information very carefully – your survival depends on it. Good luck, men. I'll be seeing you again at your departure time.'

Joe Buckley wrote two letters that night as the submarine made its way beneath the dark waters towards a hostile coast, and after arranging with the ship's bosun to have them forwarded should anything go wrong the big Australian settled down to sleep.

Chapter Twenty-Two

During the first few days of the Blitz people walked around as if dazed, hardly believing what they saw. Buildings, factories and homes that had been an intrinsic part of their lives were now piles of rubble. They rushed home from work to eat their evening meal and get prepared before night fell, gathering up bundled blankets and flasks of tea for the nightly trek to the local shelters. Whether it was the London Underground system, factory shelters or the public shelters of the backstreets which they hurried to, it made no difference. The idea was to get there early for a place before dark and to pray for rain and cloudy skies, for a blanked-out moon and for providence to spare them and their homes.

Many families who had previously ignored the call for children to be evacuated now sought to get their young ones out of London as soon as possible, while others still resisted the urge, taking the fatalistic view that if a bomb had their name on it then they would all go together. Some people, distressed by tales of bad treatment meted out to evacuees, decided that they did not want to subject their own children to such a risk, and tired nervous children joined their parents on the nightly trek.

Not everyone was happy about using the shelters, feeling that they were unhygienic, and that it was a risk in itself being crowded into a restricted place which could receive a direct hit. Under the stairs or in the cellar of their own or their neighbours' home was the choice of many at first, but as the fury of the Blitz increased and more and more homes were hit by the blast from nearby bombs so public shelters became the only sensible choice. At least there, people could feel less exposed to the dangers of blast and injury from flying glass and debris.

During the first week of the Blitz the folk of Carter Lane reluctantly accepted that the shelter in the adjacent Brady Street offered the best protection and they booked their nightly places with the warden in charge, who was coming under increasing pressure to limit the number of people using the place for safety reasons.

'You can see fer yerself,' he said to Amy Bromilow and Ivy Jones when they approached him one evening outside the entrance. 'The shelter's split inter two arches an' each one can't take no more than one 'undred people. At the moment there's only wooden benches but soon they're gonna put bunks in. If I allowed more than that number o' people ter shelter 'ere, what's gonna 'appen when the bunks arrive? Some would 'ave ter be turned out.'

'Ain't yer got no room fer us two then?' Amy asked.

'Yeah, there's still a few spaces left,' he replied, 'but don't go tellin' all yer neighbours there's room for all o' them when there ain't, that's all I'm sayin'.'

Amy and Ivy booked their places, as did Mr and Mrs Wickstead and the Harrises. Liz Kenny and Dolly Flynn had never considered the shelter as an option, expecting to be otherwise engaged with the fire service, and as for the Lockwood sisters their philosophy was that it would be better to be buried under a few timbers and roof slates rather than tons of reinforced concrete.

'But yer'd be safer there than under yer stairs,' Mrs Wilson told them. 'These old 'ouses ain't very strong. A bomb in the street could bring 'em all down.'

Charity and Cynthia had already discussed their options in detail and they were adamant. 'That's as it may be but we're prepared to take a chance,' Charity said for both of them. 'We fit in nicely under the stairs and we've got our palliasse and a couple of warm blankets. We'll manage quite nicely, thank you very much.'

On Friday of that first week Sadie Flynn went to the local Labour Exchange and made enquiries about becoming an army nurse, while Jennie called in to the Town Hall and was enrolled as a trainee ARP warden.

'They gave me a tin 'elmet, a gas mask an' an armband, oh an' a whistle too,' she told her sister that night. 'I gotta report every evenin'.'

'I've got this big form ter fill in,' Sadie said, pulling a face. 'I 'ope this ain't gonna be all drawn out. I'm impatient ter get started.'

'I don't fink it'll take long,' Jennie replied. 'I should imagine they'll be cryin' out fer nurses.'

'Well, nobody can say this family's not doin' their bit,' Dolly reminded them all. 'Even yer farvver's joined the fire watchers.'

'We're worried about you though, Mum,' Sadie remarked. 'Are you sure you're doin' the right fing?'

'Don't you go worryin' about me, my gel,' Dolly said indignantly. 'I ain't exactly confined to a rockin' chair wiv a rug roun' me yet awhile. I can do me bit. Me an' Liz Kenny'll be reportin' fer duty on Monday night.'

'What we gonna do, still stay under the stairs?' Jennie asked.

'Yeah, I fink it's as good as anywhere,' Dolly told her. 'Besides, Amy Bromilow said we'd 'ave ter book places in the shelter an' we won't be needin' 'em, will we?'

'I'm still a bit concerned about you though, Mum,' Jennie persisted. 'You could . . .'

'Fer Christ's sake, don't keep goin' on about it,' Dolly cut her off quickly. 'What's done's done an' I don't wanna 'ear any more on the subject, is that clear?'

Jennie nodded. When her mother adopted that tone of voice there was no use arguing with her.

Late on Friday night, with the Blitz at its height, a high explosive bomb fell in the yard of Gleeson's leather factory in Munday Road, just round the corner from Carter Lane, causing a large crater which uncovered a grisly relic. It was discovered by the fire crew who had just shut off the water pouring from the exposed fractured pipes.

'What the bloody 'ell's that?' a fireman said to his colleague, pointing into the moonlit crater.

'What? Where?'

'Look, there, just below the pipes.'

The two scrambled down into the hole to take a closer look.

'It must 'ave been there fer some years,' the fireman said as he shone his torch on the skeletal remains of a human hand.

''As it got a body attached to it, I wonder?' his colleague remarked.

'We'd better not go pokin' about,' the first fireman replied.

'The bomb could 'ave uncovered an ole burial ground,' the second fireman went on.

'I'll go an' let the chief know.'

''Ang on, I'm comin' wiv yer. This place is givin' me the willies.'

On Saturday morning a police team, under the local pathologist's supervision, removed a complete skeleton from the crater.

'It's early yet,' the pathologist told the police sergeant, 'but from a preliminary examination I'd say that the body has been in the ground about ten, twelve years.'

The *Porbeagle*'s captain scanned the sea above him through the periscope and then issued the order to surface. The night was clear, with a waxing moon casting a silverish sheen on the calm waters of the Mediterranean, but the two small black rubber dinghies and their crew in wet suits and masks blended in with the surface as they paddled steadily away in a south-westerly direction, the leading one some ten yards in front.

All the advice and well wishing had been expended and now there was an ominous silence, broken only by the sound of the paddles and the soft slap of water against the flimsy rubber craft. Ahead was the Vichy-controlled port of Oran with its flotilla of French navy ships and the visiting surface raider, the *Kaiser Wilhelm*.

The four men paddled steadily, conserving their strength for whatever might befall them, and every fifteen minutes they took a short rest while Petty Officer Chivers in the leading dinghy checked the position with his compass. After two hours the dark shape of the raider loomed up dead ahead and Chivers raised his arm, steering the craft portside of the target. At a certain point the leading crew stopped paddling and the rear dinghy drew alongside. A loop was attached to keep the craft together and a killick anchor dropped overboard. Chivers made a downward movement with his thumb, donned his breathing apparatus then picked up two small metal discs from the well of the dinghy before slipping backwards into the water. The others followed suit and together they swam beneath the surface until they saw the dim outline of the raider's hull directly in front of them.

The operation had been rehearsed many times and without having to think the teams set to work. Chivers and Preston dived under the hull and placed their magnetic charges on the starboard side while Big Joe and Petty Officer Stone placed theirs on the port side. The operation took barely a couple of minutes and then keeping close together the four underwater saboteurs swam away from the raider. Suddenly Preston found it difficult to breathe, and he motioned to Chivers to check his tank. There was nothing for it but to surface. The leak in the breathing tube leading from the oxygen tank was sending a stream of bubbles towards the surface and very soon the air would be gone.

The underwater conversation was conducted in swift hand signals and clearly understood. Preston and Chivers would continue up above while Stone and Buckley carried on submerged. By the time the first pair reached the surface Preston had swallowed mouthfuls of sea water and was choking into his mask as Chivers tore it off his face, supporting him while he coughed and spluttered and glancing anxiously behind them.

The dinghies were finally reached and the distressed saboteur was helped aboard. As they slipped the joining attachment and cut the anchor rope the beam of a strong searchlight sliced through the dark night and arced towards them. The crews fought desperately to put some distance between themselves and the doomed raider but Chivers was at a disadvantage. His partner Preston was hanging over the side choking up water. Stone and Buckley paddled in unison, making quick progress, and seeing the problem Joe threw Chivers a rope so that he could tow the dinghy away faster. Chivers would have none of it and bravely battled on alone, like a Red Indian in a war canoe, using the paddle on both sides of the craft to keep a straight course.

Joe looked back again and saw to his horror that the following dinghy was bathed in light, and then the sound of gunfire split the silence. Bullets sprayed along the water and Chivers suddenly fell backwards overboard. Preston seemed to be moving about in frantic confusion and Joe saw him start to paddle furiously before he too was cut down. There was nothing to be done – nothing could be done – and Joe gritted his teeth as he threw all his energy into paddling away.

The searchlight was probing in an arc some distance behind and any second it could rise and pinpoint them. Stone nudged Joe and pointed to the water. He was right, it was their only hope. Still towing the dinghy they swam below the surface, with Stone checking their progress on his sub-aqua wristwatch. Experience told him how much distance they could cover in a specific time, and when he signalled Joe to surface he was spot on. There, looming up from the sea and leaning slightly shorewards, were the two Sentinels. The sound they had heard underwater came more faintly through the air but it was growing closer, and they guessed it to be the powerful engine of an E-boat hunting them. Stone led the way ashore and the two men hauled the dinghy after them onto the smooth wet sand.

'The charges should be going off any second now,' Stone gasped as he threw himself down some way from the water's edge.

'They'll find the two bodies,' Joe remarked, aware that the air inside the wet suits would keep them afloat.

Petty Officer Stone nodded. 'If they figure there was only one dinghy we've got a better chance,' he replied. 'If not they'll be searching the coastline. Come on, we'd better get this boat out o' sight.'

Together they dragged the dinghy up to the sheer cliff and covered it with broken branches and leaves from withered vines that dotted the high rock-face. Suddenly the night sky was lit up and a split second later a loud explosion rent the air, followed immediately by two more. There in the cove the two men could not witness their handiwork but the explosions and light in the sky told them all they needed to know. They punched the air and hugged each other exultantly for a few moments, then Stone turned to gaze out to sea. 'Well done, lads,' he said sadly.

'Yeah, good on you, shipmates,' Joe said quietly.

They finished camouflaging the dinghy and then Stone unzipped the top of his rubber suit and took out a bar of Fry's chocolate. 'This is all we'll get for supper, I'm afraid,' he said grinning.

The noise of the hunting powerboat had faded away but now it grew louder again, getting nearer this time.

'If it comes too close we'll need to be out of here or we'll get picked off,' Stone growled.

'How?' Joe said looking puzzled. 'We can't take to the water.'

Stone glanced up at the cliff face. 'It'll have to be the water,' he replied. 'We can't scale that without ropes and climbing gear.'

The noise of the E-boat was still getting louder and the two men looked anxiously at each other. They could see it now some way westwards, its powerful searchlight scanning the coastline.

'Come on, let's go,' Stone said, dashing down to the water's edge.

They swam on the surface to conserve their dwindling air supply and a few hundred yards to the east they paused to see the E-boat settle down in the water outside the cove. In the light of the moon they could clearly see a small boat being launched and armed men piling into it.

'That's our dinghy gone for a burton,' Stone said, cursing aloud.

Joe took the lead and the two continued swimming along the coast towards their back-up rendezvous. Midway between the two points they waded ashore into a rocky inlet. 'This'll be as good as anywhere to hole up for a while,' Stone remarked.

Joe started to smile and then his smile turned to a low chuckle.

'What's so funny?' Stone asked him.

'It all looks so neat and tidy on paper, doesn't it?' Joe

replied. 'If the first rendezvous is out use the second and see you the following night – and now here we are stuck between the two, a couple of shark's biscuits with an E-boat hunting us down.'

Stone nodded slowly. 'The question is, now what do we do?'

Joe looked out to sea. 'I reckon it all depends on those buggers,' he replied.

'Yeah, if they leave we can go back to the cove,' Stone went on, 'but if not we're caught between the monster and the clashing rocks, to paraphrase the ancient Greeks.'

Suddenly they saw another light further out to sea and then heard the familiar roar of powerful engines.

'They've sent another boat out,' Stone growled. 'It seems to be searching further along the coast.'

'Yeah, right by our second bloody rendezvous,' Joe puffed.

Stone settled down with his back against a hard rock and Joe eased himself down beside him. Water lapped around their feet and above them the moon smiled down mockingly.

'D'you ever question yourself and your motives?' Stone asked after a period of silence.

'Yeah,' Joe replied with a laugh. 'I've just been asking myself the question I reckon you've been asking yourself. Why the hell did I volunteer for this?'

'What answers did you come up with?'

'Nothing as useful as tits on a bull.'

'That's okay then,' Stone grinned. 'At least I don't owe you a sensible answer, if you're as crackers as me.'

Joe leaned his head back against the rock and smiled. 'Yep. Two mad bastards in the moonlight. Ship? What bloody ship? I reckon it'd make a good song.'

The sound of the searching boat got gradually louder and the two hunted men looked at each other, their hearts sinking. The E-boat was dropping anchor directly offshore. If it stayed there until the rendezvous time of 04.30 the submarine would abort the pick-up, which meant another twenty-four hours dodging the enemy.

'What do we do now?' Joe hissed.

Stone shook his head. 'Outside of praying, nothing I guess.'

Chapter Twenty-Three

The factory in Carter Lane was now a tangled mass of charred timbers, blackened iron girders and brick rubble. Next door the ARP post had survived, but only just. The wall adjacent to the factory had cracked from the heat and blast and the ceilings were missing plaster, showing the bare ribs of wooden laths in places. The Sun public house had fared much better, which one or two elderly locals at least uttered a prayer of thanks for. Charlie Anson had already boarded up the large plate-glass windows, leaving a smaller square for light which he covered after closing time. The Jackmans' grocery shop was left in a sorry state, however, with glass from the two broken windows scattered amongst the tins of food and packets of tea and sugar that the blast had swept from the shelves.

'This'll take us a week ter clean up,' Sara groaned.

'We ain't got a week,' Tom reminded her firmly. 'It don't make no difference ter the customers what state we're in, they'll still expect ter get served.'

The Jackmans set to work clearing up the shop, with the help of Alf Coates, who had little else to do until the pub opened.

'I should've knocked at Danny's,' the elderly man remarked to Sara. ''E'd be only too glad ter give us a bit of 'elp.'

'We can manage between us, Alf,' Sara told him quickly, realising from experience that once the two pub fixtures got together nothing would get done.

The gruesome discovery in Munday Street was reported to the local press and everyone was talking about it.

'It could be one o' those victims o' the plague,' Danny Crossley remarked to Alf Coates over a beer.

'Could be,' Alf replied. 'They say there's fousands o' plague victims buried in Bermon'sey.'

'I shouldn't fink so,' Charlie Anson cut in. 'Yer talkin' about four 'undred years ago. There'd be nuffink left of 'em by now.'

'It's a bit creepy though,' Danny said. 'If that bomb 'adn't landed there the bones would never 'ave come ter light.'

'It just shows yer,' Alf remarked, studying his pint. 'Yer never know what yer walkin' over.'

'You never know what you're walkin' frew,' Danny said grinning. 'If there's any dog shit on the pavement you'd step in it.'

Alf was not to be sidetracked. 'They'll soon find out who it was,' he went on. 'They've got ways an' means.'

'Yeah, it's bloody clever the way they work fings out,' Charlie agreed.

Very soon the findings of the pathologist were on the chief inspector's desk, and they made interesting reading. Tests revealed that the body had been that of a male, five feet seven in height and aged around fifty at the time of death.

The jaw contained a full set of large teeth, less the two front ones, and there was some wear on the hip joint. A square hole in the right side of the skull indicated that the man had been dealt a heavy blow, with possibly a lath hammer, which although a roofer's tool could be found in most households. Lath hammers had a square head with a sharp, flat blade for levering up tiles, and were used domestically for chopping wood. They also had a groove at the side for levering out nails. One other interesting discovery was that the two joints were missing from the skeleton's left ring finger.

The first task confronting Chief Inspector Rubin McConnell was to check back through the missing persons files, and again the results proved interesting. In nineteen twenty-nine Aaron Priestley had been reported missing by his wife Cynthia. Her description was very precise. He was five feet seven, stockily built, and missing two front teeth due to a fight some years earlier. Aaron was reported as having a permanent limp, which Cynthia put down to arthritis, and she had been able to produce a photograph of her husband standing beside her as she sat in a chair, with his left hand resting on her shoulder, and what was more a large ring could clearly be seen on his third finger. The inspector was pleased with the progress so far, but now came the task of finding out just how the victim had come to be buried below a series of water pipes in a factory yard.

Working on the assumption that the body had been placed there during the time the pipes were installed, the inspector assigned his detective sergeant to make the necessary enquiries. A visit to the Town Hall planning department revealed that the leather factory in Munday Road was erected at the turn of the century, which disproved the initial theory. The next stop was the Metropolitan Water Board, which was quick to point out that their records for repairs to water pipes going back more than five years were stored at the local office at Rotherhithe, but they had all been destroyed in a fire on the first night of the Blitz.

Feeling disheartened by the lack of progress Sergeant Johnson stood up to leave, and then the chief clerk made a suggestion. 'Look, it might not lead anywhere, but you could have a word with Albert Banks. He's been with us for over thirty years and he used to be on maintenance gangs. You'll find him in the yard, or I could send for him.'

'No, it's all right, I'll have a word with him on my way out,' the sergeant said, smiling his thanks.

The elderly man was sweeping the yard when the sergeant approached him.

'Yeah, I'm Albert Banks, son. What can I do yer for?'

'Can you recall ever doing any work on the water pipes in Gleeson's leather factory, Munday Road?' the sergeant asked him.

Albert rested his broom against the wall. 'Funny you should ask that,' he replied as he led the way over to a stack of thick wooden shorings. 'Firty years I've worked 'ere an' I've lost count of 'ow many repair jobs I've done. Most of 'em I can't even remember, but I can remember that one. That one was different.'

'Different? In what way?'

Albert sat down on the shorings and proceeded to fill his pipe. 'It was back in the winter o' twenty-nine. I'd just bin made ganger an' that was me first job in charge. What's more I was pissed as an 'andcart the night before. My eldest daughter 'ad presented me wiv me first gran'child an' I was out celebratin'. Anyway the next mornin' me an' the lads 'ad ter fill the 'ole in an' tidy up like. It'd bin pissin' down 'eaven's 'ard all night an' yer can imagine what it was like. I was still feelin' the effects an' the pile of earth was all clay an' stuck ter the shovels fer a start, then the bloody 'ole was full o' water up ter the bottom o' the new pipes. Anyway we set about fillin' it in, an' yer gotta remember that when there's water in an 'ole an' it gets filled up wiv earth there's always a bit of subsidence as the water drains away. Now when it's dry yer just use the road roller ter flatten it but we 'ad ter wait till the next day fer it ter dry out before we could finish the bloody job, an' there's me the new ganger all keen ter show 'ow quick me an' me boys could work. Mind you they couldn't very well blame us fer it pissin' down wiv rain, could they?'

'That's really helpful, Albert,' the sergeant told him. 'Now can you give me the exact day?'

Albert studied his filled pipe for a few moments. 'My Betty's lad's goin' on eleven. 'Is birfday's the twenty-fourth o' November. As I say I remember it well. It was a Sunday, so we must 'ave filled the 'ole in on Monday the twenty-fifth o' November.'

The sergeant shook the helpful old Water Board man by the hand and made his way back to the station. Things were starting to fall into place. The victim would most likely have been thrown into the hole on Sunday and ended up submerged in the mud and silt at the bottom. The next step was to find out the exact date Aaron Priestley was reported missing.

'That's good work, sergeant,' the inspector said, thumbing through the file. 'There we are. Priestley was reported missing on Monday the ninth of December, two weeks later. It all ties in nicely.'

'So we're working on the theory that he was murdered,' the sergeant remarked.

'The shape of the wound backs it up,' the inspector replied. 'If he'd gone into the yard to relieve himself, for instance, and had accidentally fallen into the hole and cracked his head on the pipes there would have been a compressed fracture of the skull, not a square, clean hole. As for the motive, it might well have been robbery, considering the two missing joints, but that could have been an afterthought on the part of the attacker. The record says Mrs Priestley stated that her husband didn't have any enemies, as far as she knew, but he didn't have many friends either. Anyway, we can close the missing person file on Aaron Priestley and open a murder file, but I'm of the opinion that the new file's going to collect just as much dust. Let's face it, the murder took place more than ten years ago and now there's a war on. People are getting killed every night and a lot of locals have been evacuated. We're going to need nothing short of a miracle to solve this one, I'm afraid.'

The night was black to the east but westwards the fire-glow from the stricken German cruiser lit the sky. On the dusty roads above the shoreline troop carriers spilled out their human cargo and lit up the rocky terrain with powerful searchlights, and the hunt began.

'We've got to think of something,' Stone said after a while. 'Come first light that E-boat's going to resume the search.'

'Well, we can't go back to the original rendezvous,' Joe replied.

Stone eased his back against the hard rock. 'There's no time now anyway. It's turned four. The sub'll spot that E-boat through the periscope soon and abort the surfacing.'

'We'll never last out for another twenty-four hours,' Joe said quietly, 'even if we did manage to make the second pick-up point.'

'I think we should wait until after four thirty and then take to the water,' Stone suggested. 'We'll swim as far westwards as we can and then try to get away overland.'

Joe nodded. 'The next time I get the silly idea to volunteer for anything I'll bite me bloody tongue off instead,' he growled.

'You'll be there, just like me,' Stone replied. 'It's in our blood.'

'Are you married, Sam?' Joe asked, realising that it was the first time he had used Stone's Christian name.

'I was, but she took off with a sub lieutenant about a year ago,' Stone told him. 'What about you?'

'I got a girl back home, well sort of,' Joe said smiling to himself.

'That doesn't sound very positive,' Stone said.

'We write letters to each other and we've been out for a drink together,' Joe explained. 'Trouble is she's going out with the local wide boy, as they call them, and I'm hoping I don't turn out to be the spare dick at a wedding.'

'Doesn't it figure,' Stone said bitterly. 'While we're away fighting, the spivs and shysters are coining it. Not only that, they can't keep their dirty little hands off our women.'

'Sadie's not exactly my woman,' Joe said. 'Not yet anyway,

but give the ole Buckley charm a bit more time.'

Stone grunted as he moved his cramped legs. 'While I was on destroyers I got pally with a chap called Peter Simmons. Crazy over this woman he was. Had her photo pinned up in his locker and her name tattooed on his forearm. He used to write a letter to her every night and posted the lot together soon as we docked anywhere. Never seen anything like it. Anyway we pulled in to Chatham one night for repairs and they gave us all a forty-eight-hour pass. Simmons came back in a terrible state. Apparently his girlfriend had taken up with one of the wide boys and she was pregnant by the bloke. There was nothing any of us could do or say that would help poor old Peter. The second night out he went missing. He'd obviously gone overboard. It turned out that he'd clobbered the spiv to death and strangled his girlfriend and he just couldn't live with it.'

Joe shook his head. 'Everyone's got their breaking point, Sam,' he said quietly.

Captain Fellows had seen the stricken raider through the periscope lying low in the water and burning out of control, and now he checked the chart and gave the order for the sub to come up to periscope depth again. Stooping he gripped the cross handles and carefully scanned the moonlit surface of the water, then with a grunt of annoyance he straightened up. 'Take her down.'

The executive officer stood by the chart table waiting as the captain turned to him. 'There's an E-boat anchored offshore by the pick-up point,' he growled. 'It's a damned nuisance but at least it suggests that the men have eluded capture.'

'Let's hope so, Cap'n.'

The captain stroked his beard. 'The boat will have scoured the coastline and will no doubt resume the search at dawn. The Jerries will know that the cruiser was safe from attack by torpedo behind the anti-submarine nets and they'll be looking for frogmen. They have to decide whether the attack originated from land or sea. Did the frogmen set off from shore or were they dropped from a sub? It's my opinion that a sub chaser will be arriving on the scene before long and if we hang around here for another twenty-four hours we'll certainly be picked up on their sonar.'

'It's a tricky situation right enough,' the executive replied.

'What would you suggest, James?' the captain asked.

'I'd be reluctant to use torpedoes on such a small target at this distance, Cap'n, and if we move closer we'll be picked up on their instruments.'

'Go on, James.'

'I'd surface as arranged at 04.30 and bank on the element of surprise,' the executive officer continued. 'I'd use the guns, going in head-on and if need be run the boat down.'

Captain Fellows nodded. 'We'd quite possibly sustain damage for'ard and have to rely on our stern tubes.'

'Considering there's four ratings depending on us I'd deem it worth the risk.'

The captain smiled. 'That's the way I see it too,' he said, turning towards the intercom. 'Gun crews forward.'

Sam Stone glanced at his wristwatch. 'It's almost time,' he said, looking out into the darkness.

At that moment the alarm sounded on the E-boat and all hell broke loose. The two stranded men saw the tracer bullets rip into the boat as the submarine bore down on them. Engines roared as the E-boat tried to take evasive action then suddenly the night was lit up as a loud explosion violently blew it apart.

'They hit the magazine!' Joe shouted out. 'It's a bullseye.'

Stone was already signalling with his torch and answering flashes came from the sub's conning tower. 'They've seen us!' Stone shouted. 'C'mon, Joe, let's go!'

The submarine swung broadside on, perilously close to the shallows as the two men swam towards it, Stone still using his torch when he could to signal their position. A rope ladder was thrown over the side and as the men clambered up it Stone grabbed a helping hand. 'The other two didn't make it,' he gasped.

'E-boat approaching!' the lookout shouted.

Bullets sprayed the sub's hull as the second boat came in fast, and the answering fire from the gun crew deafened the two saboteurs as they clambered down through the hatch. Joe laid eyes on the captain and his face broke into a grin. 'Ya blood's worth bottling, mate!' he exclaimed.

The E-boat swung round to make another run and the gun crew scurried down the hatch and slammed it shut. 'Dive! Dive!' the command rang out.

A steady 'ping' on the radar sounded loudly at first but then diminished as the submarine put distance between itself and its adversary, and the captain smiled at his executive officer. 'It went well, James,' he said.

Down in the mess two exhausted men sat with blankets round their shoulders, sipping hot cocoa. They did not speak for some time, both dwelling on their two comrades who had not made it back, and when his trembling subsided somewhat Stone glanced up at Big Joe, struggling for something, anything to say. 'We should be in for some leave after this,' he said finally. 'I suppose you'll be seeing this girlfriend of yours.'

'Bet your boots on it,' Joe replied positively.

Chapter Twenty-Four

There was no let-up. Every night the air-raid sirens wailed and the bombers came. People huddled together in the shelters or under their stairs, all convinced that their neighbourhood and indeed all of London was slowly and systematically being pounded to rubble. Every night they endured the endless explosions, emerging tired and fearful in the dusty morning light to witness the results. Rest centres were opened for homeless people and non-serious casualties were bedded down in hospital corridors. Exhausted ARP volunteers took a well-earned breather before going off to their place of work, if the office, shop or factory still existed, and firemen stayed until the fires were finally extinguished.

One night the spice warehouse in Shad Thames was hit by an oil bomb, and as the firemen staggered away to take a short respite the canteen van was ready and waiting.

'Come on, lads, get this down yer,' Dolly said smiling encouragingly as she handed out mugs of steaming hot tea, her steel helmet pushed back on her head.

Liz Kenny worked alongside sploshing tea in mugs and slapping down hot meat pies on the counter, and she seized upon the chance to exercise her wit. 'There yer go, son, that'll put some lead in yer pencil,' she said grinning as she handed a steak and kidney pie to a young fireman. The driver of the canteen, Ben Chadwick, was an ex-firefighter himself and he had come out of retirement to drive the vehicle. ''Ow's the water goin', gels?' he asked.

'It's gettin' low,' Liz told him.

Ben came back with a brimming bucketful which he poured into the propane gas boiler. 'That should do it, gels. Five more minutes an' we've gotta be off ter Long Lane. There's a big 'un there.'

With Liz and Dolly sitting beside him Ben hurled the canteen van through the rubble-strewn streets to the next fire.

'Oi! Take it easy, Ben,' Dolly shouted at him. 'You ain't drivin' a bloody fire tender now yer know.'

'Yeah, my arse is bleedin' sore bouncin' up an' down,' Liz complained.

Ben grinned. 'Never mind, gels, you can 'ave yer feet up in a couple of hours.'

'Yeah, I should fink so,' Dolly growled. 'I got ironin', washin' an' me bloody shoppin' ter do.'

'Yeah, me too,' Liz added. 'You men fink we've got it easy, but you ain't got a clue. 'Ow's the boys, Doll?' she asked between bumps.

'We've 'eard from 'em all,' Dolly told her. 'Frank an' Jim are back at Winchester an' our Pat's goin' fer trainin' soon.'

'Aircrew yer said, didn't yer?'

''S right.'

'I bet you're worried sick.'

'Not 'alf. I don't know why 'e couldn't stay where 'e is. It's a bloody sight safer on the ground.'

''E'll be all right, Doll.'

'Yeah, course 'e will.'

Another fire, another exhausted crew to take care of, and as the general public made its way to work through the battered streets, two tired but satisfied women hung up their gas masks and steel helmets and brushed out their hair before leaving the fire station to manage their families.

Jennie Flynn had spent her first night as an ARP runner at the command post in Carter Lane and it had been one she would never forget.

'Good evening, Miss Flynn. I'm Nigel Bayley, the controller, and this is my assistant, Miss Karen Watson.'

Jennie smiled. 'Pleased ter meet yer.'

'Can you ride a bicycle, Miss Flynn?' the controller asked her.

'I used to 'ave one as a kid,' she told him. 'I s'pose I still can.'

'Righty'o. Now this is Miss Peggy Freen and this is Mrs Irene Copley. They're runners too. I'm sure you'll all get on like a house on fire.'

'Mr Bayley,' Karen said, speaking with some amusement as a teacher might to a naughty child.

'Sorry about that,' the controller said, grinning sheepishly. 'It was probably a little too apt, wasn't it? Never mind, to the job in hand. Throughout the air raids we need to have a clear picture of what's going on in the area, as you no doubt are aware from your initial training. The runner's job is to carry messages to other posts that we can't reach by phone and to report unattended fires and bombed ruins where people might be trapped. A lot of your work is going to be dangerous and not very nice to say the least. However, you'll acquit yourself very well, I feel sure, as Miss Freen and Mrs Copley invariably do. Now I suggest you get to know your co-runners and we'll talk some more once I've a few minutes to spare.'

Irene Copley smiled as the controller walked out of the side room. She was a thick-set woman in her forties with a ruddy complexion and pale blue eyes. 'I'm widowed and on my own,' she explained, 'so I thought why not? I find this better than spending my nights in some horrible shelter.'

'My boyfriend's in the navy,' Peggy said proudly.

'Mine's in the army,' Jennie replied. ''E was at Dunkirk.'

Peggy smiled. She had a small elfin face and longish fair hair tied at the neck with a ribbon, and looked rather childlike.

Nigel Bayley came back into the room. 'We've received the standby message,' he said, his square chin jutting out. 'We should be getting a red alert shortly, ladies, so prepare yourselves.'

Five minutes later he was back again. 'It's a red alert, team,' he announced.

Jennie followed the other two runners into the control room and saw Karen sitting by a small telephone switchboard. On the large table a map was spread out and dotted with coloured pins.

Nigel beckoned for the runners to gather round the table. 'Now as you can see, the places marked with the yellow pins are business properties,' he began, 'but here and here the blue pins indicate residential areas. The red pins show where properties have already been bombed. Thus, should we get a report through of a bomb in this street marked red then we call it low grade priority, whereas a bomb in a blue grade has to be top priority for fire and heavy rescue services. This will all be very familiar to you, Peggy and Irene, but we have to introduce the set-up to Jennie, so bear with me. Now when you come across a house or a block of buildings that's taken a direct hit you must first try to establish with the local ARP teams or street wardens whether there are any people buried, then you must relay to us the location and situation by whatever means at your disposal. A phone call using our special number is the ideal way but not often very feasible. On most occasions it's all about cycle power, as I like to describe it. You will be exposed to shrapnel as well as all the other obvious dangers, so it is vital to wear your steel helmets at all times.'

'Don't forget about the gas masks, Mr Bayley,' Karen piped in.

He gave her a quick look. 'Oh yes, the gas masks. Now when you cycle through streets that have just been bombed there may be fractured gas-pipes so it makes good sense to carry your gas masks at all times while on duty. They will offer you some protection and they do not mist over as quickly as the civilian type.'

Jennie had visions of pedalling like mad through back-streets wearing her gas mask and frightening the life out of everyone, and she looked at her two runner colleagues and saw that they were both smiling demurely. She was to learn later that Irene Copley carried her make-up and sandwiches in her gas mask case. Peggy Freen also confessed to a pretty cavalier attitude to her gas mask, saying that she would sooner die than be forced to wear one.

The air-raid siren began to wail about the usual time that

night and soon the anti-aircraft guns opened up. A loud explosion suddenly rocked the command post and ceiling dust fell down onto the large map. Karen seemed unperturbed as she sought to establish contact with the local fire station and Nigel Bayley calmly checked the position of the coloured pins. A policeman looked in, his face streaked with soot, to say that Sumner Buildings had taken a direct hit and been reduced to a pile of rubble. 'This is one for you, Jennie,' the controller said quickly. 'Take care now.'

Feeling that at last she was doing something important the young woman pedalled off as fast as she could, wincing every time a gun fired, and soon she arrived in Sumner Road to see the damage wrought. The street was full of brick dust and the strong, acrid smell of cordite hung in the night air. Fires were flaring nearby and the buildings themselves were unrecognisable, as though a giant and malevolent force had stamped them into the ground with its foot. An old man was being helped along by a warden and Jennie cycled up to them. 'Will there be many trapped under that lot?' she asked urgently.

The warden shook his head. 'This was the only one. The cantankerous ole git wouldn't do as 'e was told an' go ter the shelter like all the ovvers. No, 'e decided ter stay where 'e was an' lucky fer 'im 'e was blown out inter the street. Good job 'e lived on the ground floor or 'e wouldn't 'ave survived.'

The old man looked dazed and disorientated. 'I 'ad all me comforts in the flat yer see, miss. I got bad legs an' they give me what for if I 'ave ter sit up all night.'

'Well, yer goin' down the shelter now, Sharkey, like it or lump it,' the warden told him.

Jennie cycled off towards a fire that was raging in nearby Crawford Street. It was a factory that had been reinforced with sandbags at ground level and as she drew closer she could see that the fire was confined to the top two floors. The building faced a railway line and stood apart from a row of houses, separated on one side by a bomb ruin and on the other by a Council builder's yard. She looked around in vain for a telephone box and decided to pedal back with the report but just as she was about to remount her heart missed a beat. There over the sandbags she saw the shelter sign with its arrow pointing towards the end of the factory. She hurried along, pushing her cycle, then a loud rumbling seemed to shake the ground under her feet. Part of the roof and top level crashed down in front of her, showering her with brick dust and sparks. She felt a sharp stinging pain in her cheek and brushed at it as she picked herself up. A giant mound of bricks and burning timbers covered the shelter entrance at the far end of the burning factory and Jennie guessed that this would be the one occupied by the tenants of the nearby Sumner Buildings.

She pedalled as fast as she could and arrived back at the command post a few minutes later, gasping for air. She staggered through the door and fell into the arms of Nigel Bayley. 'Sumner Buildin's are gone! All the tenants are trapped in the shelter under the burnin' factory in Crawford Street!' she gasped as a red mist started to swim before her eyes.

Karen sent the message through and then helped Nigel lift the young woman onto a wooden bench. 'Here, drink this,' she urged her.

The strong spirit burned Jennie's throat and made her

cough and she opened her eyes. 'That was a silly fing fer me ter do,' she said when she gathered her thoughts.

'No, it wasn't,' Karen told her. 'In fact you did very well. I should think you'll have earned a vote of thanks from the people of Sumner Buildings come morning. Here, use this.'

Jennie took the handkerchief Karen held out to her and wiped her forehead. 'Is there a mirrer 'andy?' she asked.

Nigel grinned and was about to say something but Karen cut him short with a stern look. 'Just a moment, I've one in my handbag,' she replied.

Jennie studied her face and saw the nick on her cheek. 'I fink I'll survive,' she said smiling as she dabbed at it.

'I think you'll do very well as an ARP runner. Welcome aboard,' Nigel remarked with a grin.

Another dawn, another day to recover, and the day for Chief Inspector McConnell to break the news to Cynthia Lockwood about her missing husband.

'Why, if it isn't the nice inspector,' Charity said smiling. 'Do come in.'

McConnell walked into the tidy parlour and saw Cynthia sitting by the fire working on a piece of embroidery.

'Good morning, Miss Lockwood,' he said, knowing that she preferred to be addressed as such. 'Bad one last night, wasn't it? Actually, I've called about quite an important matter.'

Cynthia put down her embroidery and Charity motioned him into an armchair by the fire. 'Can I get you some tea?' she asked.

'No, I'm fine, thank you very much,' he replied, and

looked from one to the other. 'I suppose you've seen the report in the papers about the find in Munday Road.'

'The skeletal remains,' Cynthia said. 'Yes we have, inspector.'

McConnell looked down at his clasped hands for a few moments. 'We have reason to believe that it's most certainly the remains of your husband.'

'Oh my God!' Cynthia gasped, bringing her hand up to her face. 'How awful.'

'Deary me,' Charity added. 'After all this time. You are sure it is Aaron?'

'Without doubt,' McConnell replied.

'My goodness, you people are so clever,' Cynthia remarked, still with her hand up at her face. 'It's remarkable.'

'I don't wish to distress you, ladies,' the policeman went on, 'but the evidence seems incontrovertible. The jaw contained large teeth, minus the two front ones. There were signs of damage to the left hip, possibly some bone disease, and the pathologist was able to establish that the remains were those of a man about five feet seven tall and around fifty when he died, some ten to fifteen years ago. So you see it all matches the very thorough description of Aaron which you supplied us with.'

Cynthia took out a small lace handkerchief from her dress sleeve and dabbed at her eyes. 'I know it was a long time ago that Aaron went missing,' she sighed, 'but you coming here today brings it all back, you see.'

'I'm very sorry but I am obliged to follow these things up,' McConnell explained.

'We understand implicitly, inspector,' Charity cut in. 'As a matter of fact Cynthia's not feeling too bright today and your news has come as a shock. It's all this bombing. We hardly get any sleep and my sister's feeling utterly exhausted.'

'I appreciate that, Miss Lockwood,' he replied. 'Look, I'll leave you now. Maybe you might both like to call in the station when your sister's feeling better. There are a few loose ends to tie up.'

'We certainly will,' Charity said. 'And thank you for being so understanding. I'll see you to the door.'

McConnell bade goodbye with a pleasant smile as he stepped out into the street and Charity suddenly took him by the arm. 'Do you suspect he was murdered?' she asked in a low voice.

'It appears that he was dealt a fatal blow to the head,' the policeman replied.

'My goodness, that's terrible,' Charity remarked, covering her mouth with the tips of her long fingers.

'We'll talk some more when you call in,' the inspector said.

Back in the house Cynthia was pacing the room. 'I'm all of a quiver,' she said painfully.

'Now look, there's no need to distress yourself,' her sister told her sternly. 'You sit yourself down and I'll make us a nice strong cup of tea. I believe we still have some of that Lyons strong brew left.'

'You are a comfort to me,' Cynthia said sniffing.

'Nonsense. You're very brave,' Charity replied encouragingly. 'And remember dear, we stand or fall together.'

Chapter Twenty-Five

The air raids were getting worse each night and more and more people started to use the shelters, many after experiencing terrifying hours huddled under the stairs while their little homes were blasted and shaken. In Carter Lane, windows replaced during the day were blasted out again at night and on some of the roofs tarpaulins now covered the missing slates. The strain was showing on everyone's faces and the lack of proper rest and sleep was becoming a real problem. Homeward-bound workers often fell asleep on buses, trams and trains and found themselves two or three stops down the line. People fell asleep at their place of work and many began to develop the technique of 'cat-napping'. Ten minutes at mid-morning break and a half-hour sleep at lunchtime got them through the day, and in the shelters people developed the knack of sleeping soundly while sitting upright on uncomfortable benches.

Sadie Flynn had had the house to herself for a few nights, with her father fire-watching, her mother working on the canteen van and Jennie at the ARP command post, but the need to be with someone during the bombing led her to take up Daisy Harris's suggestion that she stay with her and Bill during the raids. Daisy was an enthusiastic member of the Carter Lane knitting circle and she put her expertise to good use by instructing her young neighbour, who was a self-confessed muddle of fingers and thumbs where knitting was concerned. One week saw a marked improvement, with Sadie managing to progress from plain and purl to cable stitch, but any further honing of her new skill was cut short when the letter came from the Woolwich Military Hospital instructing her to report for initial training.

The young woman took up residence at the nurses' quarters and began her new career with a single-minded determination that was severely put to the test during the traumatic experience of training on wards full of badly wounded servicemen.

For the Lockwood sisters the shelters were still out of the question, and they both decided to remain in what they had come to see as their impregnable position under the rickety stairs. Charity was as ever the prop for Cynthia, whose nervousness and timidity had not been helped by the visit from the police inspector bearing the news of the discovery of her missing husband's body. Still facing her was the ordeal of going over it all at the station and she baulked at it as long as she could.

'Look, I know it must be terrible for you, dear,' Charity said kindly, 'but it has to be faced sooner or later. Why don't we get it over with. You'll feel much better once you've been to see the nice inspector.'

Cynthia had to agree, and on a bitterly cold morning she and Charity presented themselves at the police station.

'We'll try not to keep you too long,' McConnell told them with a smile. 'There's just one or two questions I need to ask. Now I know it was a long time ago, but I want you to think back to round about the time your husband went missing. Did he act any differently? Did he seem worried or concerned about anything?'

'No, nothing,' Cynthia said, shaking her head slowly. 'He was being very nasty to me though about that time.'

'Was he violent towards you?' McConnell asked.

'He most certainly was,' Charity cut in. 'Cynthia doesn't like to paint too bad a picture of him, she's still too loyal, but I can tell you that he was physically abusive to her.'

'I see,' the policeman said, scribbling into a notepad. 'Was he a betting man?'

'Yes, he liked a bet, on the greyhounds as well as the horses,' Cynthia told him.

'Did it come as a shock when your husband went missing?' the inspector probed. 'What I mean is, did you suspect there was someone else in his life, another woman?'

Cynthia shook her head again. 'I don't think so, inspector,' she replied.

'Another woman wouldn't have had him,' Charity said forcibly. 'He was a pig of a man. Do you know that a couple of days before he went missing he . . .'

'Please, Charity, the inspector doesn't want to know . . .'

'Well, I'm going to tell him anyway,' the older sister said firmly. 'Every bit of information might prove helpful, wouldn't you say, inspector?'

'Yes, anything might help.'

'It was a Sunday evening,' Charity went on, 'and I called round to see if Cynthia wanted to join me for the evening service at St Margaret's. Aaron was out, but I could see that my sister was in a terrible state. Her wrists were bruised and her eye was almost closed where he had punched her.'

'Charity, please.'

'No, it has to be said, dear. Aaron had tied Cynthia in a chair, inspector.'

'Look, can I get you some tea?' the policeman offered.

'That would be very nice,' Charity replied.

McConnell left the room for a few moments to order the tea, and to pull himself together. This looked like it was going to take some time, but overworked as he was he felt sympathy for Cynthia Lockwood, wondering what had made her fall for such a brute in the first place.

Sitting comfortably in the warm office with cups of sweet tea, the Lockwoods listened attentively as the inspector resumed his questions.

'Do you happen to know if your husband was in the habit of taking a lot of money out with him?' he asked.

'The only time he had much money was when the horses or dogs came up,' Cynthia replied.

McConnell stroked his chin thoughtfully. 'You see, we're working on the theory that your husband was robbed, Miss Lockwood, after which he was thrown into the hole that the Water Board men had dug in the factory yard.'

'But surely his body would have been discovered by the workmen the next day?' Cynthia queried.

'It happened to be pouring with rain all night and we have to assume that the body was immersed in water and mud.'

The sisters exchanged quick glances and Charity put down her empty cup and saucer and rested her hands on top of the handbag in her lap. 'Tell me, inspector, is there any doubt in your mind that the remains were those of Aaron?' she asked.

'None whatsoever.'

'Well, I'm not saddened by it. I think he got his just deserts.'

'To be fair, Charity, he wasn't always a brutal man,' Cynthia said quickly.

'Not at the very beginning, granted, but it didn't take him long to show his true colours, dear.'

McConnell looked from one to the other, and although he wanted to mention the missing finger joints he thought better of it. Both women looked very upset as it was, without having to hear more gruesome details, and besides, the photograph of Aaron Priestley wearing a large jewelled ring already answered his question. 'I think that will suffice for now, ladies, and thanks very much for calling in,' he told them. 'Should there be any developments I'll certainly keep you informed.'

Back in their home Charity made a pot of tea and fussed over Cynthia, who was feeling the effects of all the strain. 'Now, you drink this and try to get some sleep before the raids start,' she encouraged her.

'I've tried so hard to forget everything,' Cynthia said tearfully, 'but today brought it all back. Was it me that made Aaron into the monster he became? Was I lacking in something? Was I that bad a wife?'

'I won't listen to that sort of talk, Cynthia,' her sister said firmly. 'No one could have been a better wife than you, and well you know it. Now finish that tea and close your eyes for a while.'

The house was quiet, with only the low sounds of light

music coming from the wireless and the rattle of the wind on the window frames, and as Charity sat sewing she felt very uneasy. Cynthia was showing signs of cracking, she realised, and the effects would be far reaching, for both of them.

Sadie slipped a few toiletries and clothing into a small case and took her first leave of the nurses' quarters for a weekend at home. The first week of practical patient care, of learning to take temperatures, blood pressures and pulses, perfect the noble art of regimental bed-making and change dressings on terrible wounds, as well as all the classroom work, left her feeling exhausted but filled with a deep sense of fulfilment. At last she had found her vocation. Intrigue, villainy and the seedy side of life were now a world away, and so was the boring, soul-destroying nine-till-five existence of totalling figures, answering telephones and office small talk. Now at last she could hold her head up high and face a new day without any self-recrimination, and it felt good.

She sat on the upper deck of the number 38 tram as it rattled through Woolwich, Greenwich and past New Cross into the Old Kent Road. Bomb-blasted shops, ruined homes and piles of rubble swept back from the pavement could be seen all along the route but her fellow passengers seemed not to notice, and she marvelled at their indifference. She noticed how they sat, erect in their seats, heads inclined as they read a newspaper or else stared dispassionately at nothing, at the void that had opened up around them. Maybe if she had to make a regular journey through once-familiar streets that had been blown to pieces she would do the same, she thought. Pretend that nothing's changed. Ignore the destruction, the shop that was there yesterday, the gap in the tall building. Think on good thoughts, thoughts of years ago when the son or daughter in uniform was the child who whipped tops, jumped in and out of twirling skipping-ropes, or chased coloured marbles along the gutters.

Sadie Flynn stepped down from the tram and made her way home through the war-torn backstreets. Just one short week away and how different it all looked. As she turned from Defoe Street into Carter Lane her heart rose. It was still there, battered, scarred but sweeter in its rawness, more than ever a part of herself.

''Ello, gel, nice ter see yer back,' Amy Bromilow said cheerily.

'There she is, our little Miss Nightingale,' Ivy Jones remarked smiling warmly.

As she stepped into the house Sadie was grabbed by Dolly and Jennie who hugged her in turn, while her father stood back with an amused smile on his face. ''Ere, give us a chance,' he grinned as he too hugged her.

'Guess who's 'ere,' Dolly said when she had regained her breath. 'Oi, Pat, come down an' see our little nurse.'

The young man bounded down the stairs and hugged his sister. 'Yer lookin' good, sis,' he said grinning.

'Yer look good yerself, bruv,' she replied, holding him round the waist.

'Guess what else,' Dolly said, motioning with her eyes to the two letters resting side by side on the mantelshelf. 'That's from Frank: the boys are comin' 'ome on embarkation leave termorrer. An' that one's from Big Joe.'

Sadie flopped down in the armchair and tore the letter open. 'Joe too,' she said happily. 'Some time next week.'

Mick rubbed his hands together and licked his lips. 'I fink

I'd better warn Charlie Anson ter get some extras in,' he joked. ''E's likely ter run dry when the lads get 'ome.'

Dolly's head was swimming with all the excitement. ''Ere, I'd better get down the market before all the best o' the stuff goes,' she announced.

'Sit down an' catch yer breath, Mum,' Jennie told her. 'I'll make us all a cuppa then me an' Sadie'll come down the market wiv yer, all right, sis?'

As Jennie left the parlour there was a knock at the door and she answered it to a flustered Liz Kenny who grabbed her arm and dragged her back to the others.

''As anyone seen the papers this mornin'?' she asked, her face flushed with excitement.

Mick shook his head. 'Only the racin' page,' he told her.

'Read that,' Liz said, taking the *Daily Sketch* from under her arm and pointing to a prominent article. Mick proceeded to read it aloud.

'It can now be confirmed that the German surface raider *Kaiser Wilhelm* was sunk by limpet mines and not torpedoes as at first reported.

The limpet mines were attached to the hull of the cruiser by a pair of two-man teams of Royal Navy divers. Unfortunately two of the divers failed to return from the mission and they can now be named as Petty Officer Peter Chivers of King's Lynn and Leading Seaman David Preston of Luton.

The surviving team of Petty Officer Samuel Stone and Leading Seaman Joseph Buckley spent the night evading patrols before being picked up by a submarine whilst under heavy fire.

The First Sea Lord added his congratulations at yesterday's War Cabinet meeting, saying that this heroic action was in the highest tradition of the Royal Navy.'

'I just got this letter from 'im,' Sadie said excitedly, 'an' 'e never mentioned a fing about it.'

''E wouldn't be allowed to, not till the story got released,' Mick told her.

'I'm all of a twitter,' Dolly said, dabbing at her eyes.

'Me too,' Liz Kenny replied. 'I nearly fainted when I saw it in the paper. I knew from Joe's last letter that somefing was in the wind.'

Sadie stared down at the neat handwriting of Joe's letter and felt a warm glow inside, then, worried that her feelings might show, she folded it away and stood up. 'I fink you should let me an' Jennie get yer shoppin' this mornin', Mum,' she said.

'Nah, I'll be all right,' Dolly told her. 'Me an' Liz are frontliners now, ain't we, gel? We can take it.'

'Too bloody true,' Liz said with spirit. 'Ole Jerry can't get us down.'

Mother and daughters trudged through the damaged backstreets to the East Street market, where the sarsaparilla man told everyone that his potions were guaranteed to sweep away the shelter blues and ward off bombs; a shopkeeper hung a sign over his damaged store that read, 'Get your rubble here. Bricks going at half price'; and a stallholder announced in a sing-song voice that 'Yes, we have no bananas, we have no bananas today.' Further along a trader stood on an upturned crate telling passers-by that his

303

restorative was good for bile, piles and stomach ulcers, as well as for growing girls and undernourished children and other afflictions. It prevented the common cold, flu and lumbago, and in short was now recognised to be the greatest medical breakthrough this century, the only sure alternative to the restorative on sale at the other end of the market.

The few potential customers stood listening suspiciously to the rhetoric, and a small dog spoke for most of them by cocking his leg against the crate before briskly trotting off.

The day was cold, and ahead a night filled with danger, death and destruction awaited, but for the present moment life went on as it always had, and stalls were beginning to display their wartime Christmas decorations. Nathaniel Bone had given up though. For years he had walked through the market with his banner stating that 'The End Is Nigh'. Now, cursing the Germans for upstaging him, he had resigned himself to handing out a few tracts on Saturday mornings, before using the rest of the day to get steadily drunk.

Chapter Twenty-Six

Jennie Flynn had not been too worried about not receiving a letter from Con on Saturday, believing that as he was now a sergeant instructor at the Winchester depot he would not be sent abroad on active duty, but she was wrong. On Monday morning his letter dropped on the mat and Jennie felt a cold shiver run down her back as she read it.

'Where d'yer fink they'll be sent?' Dolly asked her husband that evening.

'Gawd knows,' Mick said shrugging his shoulders. 'There's bin fings said on the wireless lately about sendin' more troops ter the Middle East, but yer never know. We got troops stationed all over the place. Africa, the Far East.'

'I dunno, it's one load o' worry, what wiv one an' anuvver of 'em,' Dolly said sighing. 'There's our Pat an' all. 'E'll be finishin' 'is trainin' soon an' goin' on them bombin' raids. I dunno about goin' grey, I'll end up bloody white before long.'

'What's 'appenin' about 'im an' young Brenda?' Mick asked.

'I fink it's all off,' Dolly told him. 'I saw Iris Ross down the market the ovver mornin' an' she said that the two of 'em 'ad a row last time Pat was 'ome. From what I gavvered from Iris it was over Pat volunteerin'. Brenda felt 'e should 'ave applied fer exemption frew 'is firm. I can understand 'er point o' view. They were plannin' on gettin' married next year, wasn't they?'

'Yeah, but yer never know fer sure wiv Pat,' Mick replied. ''E's never bin one ter let yer know much. 'E keeps 'is cards very close to 'is chest, does that one.'

'Pat prob'ly finks Iris Ross was be'ind it all,' Dolly went on. ''E don't go a lot on 'er, yer know, 'e let as much slip. 'E reckons she's a very dominant woman an' Brenda takes too much notice of 'er. It's a sad business when yer come ter fink of it. They seemed made fer each ovver, them two. Even as kids they were never apart. It's the bloody war. It's ruined so many people's lives.'

'Fings'll work out fer 'em, given time,' Mick said supportively.

'They won't if they're not seein' each ovver, will they?' Dolly retorted. 'Pat ain't got much time before 'e goes back an' I don't s'pose Brenda's gonna sit at 'ome pinin' fer 'im. She's a very pretty gel an' she can take 'er pick o' the fellers.'

Both Dolly and Mick would have been heartened had they been privy to a particular conversation at the Ross household a few days previously.

'Ter be honest, Brenda, I'm gettin' a bit tired o' you mopin' around the 'ouse,' Iris told her sternly. 'You've said yer piece an' made yer decision. No one forced yer ter split up wiv Pat.'

'No, that's right,' Brenda replied quickly. 'No one forced

306

me, but you never offered any advice or gave me your opinion. In fact I fink you were secretly pleased. You an' Pat don't exactly see eye to eye, yer never 'ave done.'

'That's not true,' Iris said sharply. 'We've always made 'im welcome.'

'Yeah, but you would 'ave preferred me ter get involved wiv someone wiv a good job an' plenty o' money,' Brenda replied. 'You told me that yerself when me an' Pat started ter get serious.'

'P'raps I did, but me an' yer dad were only tryin' to advise yer o' the pitfalls,' Iris went on. 'What future is there fer carpenters? All right, it's a trade an' there'll always be work around, but when yer married an' children come along there's lots of extras needed. I could just see you wiv a tribe o' kids, spendin' the best years o' yer life scrimpin' an' scrapin' like everyone else round 'ere. Me an' yer farvver felt you deserved better, that's all.'

'I couldn't get better than Pat Flynn,' Brenda responded. 'Anyway, money's not everyfing. I'd sooner be poor an' 'appy than rich an' miserable.'

'Well, it's your life,' Iris said sighing. 'Me an' yer farvver never stood in yer way. We understood that if it was Pat yer wanted, then so be it. But yer gotta get yerself sorted out. Eivver get back wiv 'im or accept it's over once an' fer all. The way fings are you're just wastin' yer life sittin' in every night mopin' around. You could always 'ave a night out wiv that Barry at work. You said yerself 'e's keen on yer.'

Brenda shrugged her shoulders, appearing noncommittal, but deep down inside her she knew what had to be done. She had been selfish, thinking only of herself and not trying to understand why Pat would want to jeopardise their future by volunteering to go off and serve his country, but it was different now. The Blitz had helped her see things in a new perspective, made her realise that there would be no future for her, Pat, or anyone else, until the war was won, and that seemed a long way off. Pat had done what he thought was best and she should really have given him the chance to explain himself instead of flying off the handle and getting angry with him.

'Don't worry, Mum, I'll sort fings out,' she sighed, not knowing just how she was going to begin.

The week wore on with nothing changing: days full of dread and nights of mayhem from the skies. The moon was full and lit the way – a bomber's moon they called it – and the carnage grew nightly. On Monday night there were no survivors when a block of buildings in the New Kent Road took a direct hit, and as more backstreets were reduced to rubble many more people never saw the dawn.

On Tuesday night the synagogue off the Old Kent Road was destroyed and Albert Levy despaired. At lunchtime the following day, when his mechanic was taking his break, he sauntered out into the workroom. 'Hello, old friend,' he said. 'First time I've had the chance of a chat since coming back to work.' He sat down at the bench with a tired sigh. 'Of course you know the synagogue's gone. A nice square plaque just inside the entrance, that's what I had in mind for you, but it won't happen now, not till we can rebuild the place, and we will one day. Anyway, you know that the bronze wouldn't have gone up right away, not while the war's on. They would have reserved the space and entered it in the book. Rabbi Friedman will be heartbroken. The synagogue was his life, and I must go to see him this evening to offer my support and help. Poor Friedman, I really feel for him. By the way, Gerda often speaks of you and I know she would send her love if she knew I talked to you, but I can't very well tell her, can I? She'd put it down to that knock on the head I got.'

Albert drew breath as he eased himself onto the high stool. 'It was nice of you to be with me at that time, old friend. I took great comfort in seeing you standing there at the foot of the bed. Mind you, I was a bit scared at first. I thought they'd sent you to collect me. Times are very bad now, Abel: the bombing seems never ending and it's getting worse. The news is very bad from the Continent too. More and more of our people are being rounded up and taken off to the camps. We're getting reports from our friends in the occupied countries that the Nazis are building many more of these places. God only knows what terrible things go on there. I feel so sad and angry about it all. I'm tired and depressed, and untroubled sleep is something I can only remember enjoying when I was a young man with big ideas. You too will remember those days of yore. How we planned and schemed. Now it seems that everything is dark and gloomy. But enough of that. I have to carry on like everyone else. After the war there will be so much to do, so much rebuilding and making good. We will rise again as a people and we elders will need to be at the forefront, should we live as long, God willing. Wish me luck, old friend, and keep me in your thoughts.'

The control post at Carter Lane was working as efficiently as the situation permitted. Land lines were constantly down and the three women runners were stretched to the limit. Karen Watson manned the switchboard without a break throughout the nightly raids and Nigel Bayley tried desperately to keep abreast of the ever-changing situation in the area, poring over the large map that was now covered with coloured pins. Not a square inch was left bare and he knew only too well that a square inch represented just a few backstreets or a mere factory or two. It was getting out of control. The whole borough seemed to be collapsing beneath the tons and tons of high explosive and incendiary bombs.

Occasionally there were short lulls during the air raids and on Wednesday night just before midnight it became quiet. Karen took off her headset and swivelled round in her chair to catch sight of Nigel sitting at the map table with his head resting in his hands. Irene Copley was sitting in the far corner fast asleep, snoring gently with her head against the wall.

'Nigel, are you asleep?' Karen said quietly.

He looked up, his eyes red-rimmed with fatigue, and he gave her a tired smile. 'Almost,' he sighed.

'Let's get some air,' Karen said getting up.

They walked out into the night and stood by the wall of sandbags, gazing at the glow in the eastern sky. 'That'll be the Stepney area,' Nigel remarked. 'They've certainly been getting their share.'

Karen reached out and clasped Nigel's hand in hers. 'You look all in, darling,' she said.

He nodded. 'I feel so inadequate,' he sighed.

'Inadequate, never,' Karen replied with spirit.

'I am,' he said. 'The whole borough's slowly turning into a giant ruin and there's me plotting the progress with those ridiculous coloured pins. I feel like some kind of ghoul looking down on the world, watching it grinding itself to dust.'

'You'll feel better after a rest, darling,' she told him kindly. 'We all will.'

'How do you do it, Karen?' he asked as he took her by the shoulders. 'You never lose that cool calmness, even at the height of the bombing. I look at you and see a very attractive young woman, unperturbed and unafraid. I listen to your voice on the switchboard and there's never a quiver. You're amazing.'

She smiled. 'A woman can take great comfort from the company she keeps. With you around I feel safe and secure. Nothing can harm me, nothing can touch me, as long as you're near.'

'Darling,' he said, pulling her to him in a tight embrace.

Their lips met and she slipped her arm around his neck, and there in the empty street, lit by a bomber's moon, time stood still.

'I want to make love to you,' he whispered.

'I want you to, but you know I can't,' she told him. 'Even though nothing would make me happier.'

'Yes, I know,' he sighed. 'We can have our dreams though.'

'And we can share these precious moments,' Karen added. 'Let it be our staff, our strength, and let these all too short moments serve to remind us that there is another time, a time for us.'

'I live for that,' he smiled.

'It fills my waking hours,' she said.

They heard the drone of aircraft and saw Peggy Freen

pedalling furiously into the lane.

'Come on, Miss Watson, we have work to do,' he said stoutly.

Jennie Flynn had taken a message to the fire chief at nearby Lynton Road and was pleased to see her mother and Liz Kenny there, busily serving tea and hot pies to the exhausted fire crew who had been tackling a blazing warehouse.

'You should be wearin' that tin 'at,' Dolly reprimanded her.

'It's all quiet at the moment,' Jennie replied.

''Ere, grab this,' Liz said quickly, handing her a large mug of steaming hot tea.

The young woman gulped it down gratefully. 'I've gotta check on the command post at the Borough,' she said. 'We can't raise it on the phone.'

'That's a bit of a way,' Dolly remarked. 'Yer'd better get goin' then while it's quiet.'

Jennie set off, pedalling energetically through the rubble-strewn streets, fearing that the command post at Lindsey Street had taken a direct hit. On the way she heard the ominous drone and winced as the anti-aircraft guns opened up once more. When she steered her bicycle into Lindsey Street she was relieved to see that the post was still intact. The controller, an elderly man with grey hair and a ruddy complexion, smiled at her concern. 'It's only the lines, luvvy,' he told her. 'We're tryin' ter link in to anuvver line. When we do we'll give you a call. Give my regards ter Nigel.'

Jennie started back, and as she turned the corner by the Children's Hospital there was a deafening crash and dust

rose in a billowing cloud from the adjacent bomb ruin. At
first she thought it was a wall that had collapsed but then she
saw the hole. Something had fallen into the basement of the
ruin and the young woman got off her bicycle to take a
closer look. Down in the gloom of the debris she could see
moonlight glimmering dully on the cone-shaped metal
object and her heart missed a beat. There, only yards away
from the hospital, was a very large unexploded bomb.

The large tea urn was kept constantly hot in the Royal
Engineers' mess hut at the Southwark Park camp and as
Sapper Conroy refilled his mug he saw Sergeant Kilbride
coming towards him. The man's face was lined with strain
and tiredness and he seemed to have aged years in the last
two weeks.

'Conroy, we've got a bad one. Sergeant Fletcher'll be your
NCO. 'E's outside briefin' the back-up. Five minutes, okay?'

Alec nodded. Already that night he and Kilbride had
steamed out an unexploded bomb at Dockhead and he had
been looking forward to a few hours' sleep, but when
Kilbride said it was a bad one all thoughts of sleep vanished.
The sergeant was not one to exaggerate. If he said it was
bad, then it was bad.

Sergeant Fletcher stood over six feet four in his socks,
with a build to match. A regular soldier and one of the best
in the bomb disposal business, he had a cool head and the
ability to transmit his unflappability to his assistants. Conroy
was happy to be teamed up with him, especially when he
learned of the task ahead.

'Jump in the truck, Conroy,' Fletcher told him quickly.
'I'll brief you on the way there.'

The fifteen hundredweight Bedford swung out of the park and along the Jamaica Road, swerving now and then to dodge the rubble lying in the roadway.

'Sergeant Kilbride said this was a bad one,' Alec remarked as he hung on to a tarpaulin strap in the back of the truck.

'Yeah, it is,' Fletcher told him. 'The bomb was found by an ARP runner who reported its whereabouts immediately. Apparently it's lying in the cellar of a bomb ruin. There are no residential properties in the immediate vicinity but here's the rub: next to the bomb ruin is the St Stephen's Children's Hospital.'

'Lindsey Street,' Alec replied.

Fletcher nodded. 'The runner warned the hospital and there's an evacuation taking place at this moment. That's the good news.' Conroy gave him a questioning glance as he drew breath. 'The bad news is they've got an emergency there. A five-year-old with a burst appendix. The surgeon said if he delayed the operation the child would surely die. He'll be washing up now and while we're playing with another of Jerry's toys he'll be doing his best for the lad. He's a brave man, son. He knows that if we make a mistake the blast will bring down half the hospital. Apparently the only functional operating theatre's located at the end of the building nearest the ruin. So now yer know.'

Alec Conroy felt the familiar trembling in his hands and the pain at the pit of his stomach but he did not dwell on it. It had always been that way, from his first assignment to the present one, and this would be his thirteenth.

Sapper Pete Swift stopped the Bedford at the end of Lindsey Street and Sapper Steve Fowler ran a phone line to the bomb ruin. Fletcher and Conroy walked across the bombsite and the sergeant shone his powerful torch down into the cellar. 'It's an ugly-looking bastard. A thousand-pounder by the look of it. If we get this one wrong that hospital's going to end up much the same as this place.'

The two set to work, occasionally reporting their progress to the back-up team, and Fletcher soon had his plan ready. 'Now look, we can't fiddle around using securing chains on this one,' he said matter-of-factly. 'For a start it's jammed tight between the foundation timbers, and secondly it ain't going nowhere. Right now we'll prop this torch up like so, and you can pass me the large wrench as soon as I squeeze round to the bastard's nose cone.'

Slowly and carefully the securing nuts on the mechanism housing cover were loosened, but as Fletcher was about to reposition himself a bomb fell in the roadway midway between the truck and the ruin, knocking the two back-ups out cold with the blast. The cellar shuddered and the unexploded bomb moved with a loud grating noise.

'My arm!' Fletcher shouted. 'I'm pinned! I can't move!'

Conroy cursed as he eased himself round to see the extent of the sergeant's injury. The man's forearm was crushed between the bomb casing and a supporting wall. 'I'll get some 'elp,' he said quickly.

'There's no time. You're on yer own, son,' Fletcher told him between clenched teeth. 'Just remember that kid in the operating theatre and you'll do okay.'

Alec Conroy picked up the phone to report the situation but found that the line was dead. He said a silent prayer and set to work, removing the nuts one by one. With a sweating hand he reached for a long screwdriver and used the tip to prise off the housing plate, and as it came away a steady tick

315

started deep down in the dark heart of the bomb.

Fletcher cursed aloud. 'That's all we want,' he growled. 'This is one of their latest delayed-action bombs and we don't know a lot about them. Bugger all, in fact.'

Alec shone the torch into the hole and saw the three wires, two red and one blue. A red and a blue wire snaked down into the darkness and the remaining red led off to the left and disappeared into a small black box. Without taking his eyes from the bomb's insides he relayed his findings to the sergeant, and when he heard a groan he glanced sideways and shone his torch across to see a trickle of blood running out from under the metal. Fletcher must have fainted from the loss of blood, he thought, suddenly feeling utterly exposed and alone. The back-up team must have been caught up in the blast too or they would have come onto the site when they realised the phone link was down.

There was no time to speculate, and as he picked up the snippers Alec remembered the training session. 'You've just killed yourself, Conroy,' the sergeant had said. It was different now. One wrong move and there would be a few more people joining him in the hereafter. 'Think, man, and for God's sake don't get it wrong,' he mumbled aloud. The red lead to the small box would act as an earth lead, he reasoned. Ignore it and concentrate on the two longer leads. Which one first? The blue. No, the red. God, don't let me get this wrong. How long was there? The ticking seemed to have been going on for ever. A minute before the detonator activated? Thirty seconds? Don't delay. Make the cut.

The snippers shook as he fought to control himself and then with a sudden flash of inspiration he moved to the red lead that stretched to the box and quickly applied pressure. The lead was severed but still the ticking went on. It was now a fifty-fifty chance. A wrong guess and it would be over for all of them. His hand moved to the red lead, then over to the blue one. He was about to make the cut when something warned him to stop. He reached his fingers into the hole and gently pulled on the blue lead. It was long and looped round, and about two feet along its length it forked, with a spur leading back to the concealed side of the black box. A classic Dubrovny short-circuit. 'So you're the decoy, you little bastard,' Alec growled as he quickly snipped the red lead. The ticking stopped, and he turned away and vomited on the dusty floor.

It took the heavy rescue team over an hour to free Fletcher, and as he was being stretchered from the bombsite he gave Sapper Conroy a weak grin. 'You did well, son,' he said.

The back-up team were recovering at the roadside and Alec sat beside them to have a cigarette, but he found that he could not pull one from the packet for the shaking of his hands.

'Here, let me do that for you,' a tall man said, bending down over him.

'Fanks, pal,' Alec said with a dry throat.

'I think the thanks are owed to you,' the man said. 'Mind if I join you?'

'Take a pew,' Alec told him. ''Ave a fag.'

The man took one out of the packet and lit it from the glowing tip of the cigarette held in Alec's shaking hand. 'It was touch and go tonight, but it turned out well in the end,' he said.

'Yeah, sometimes important decisions 'ave ter be made on the quick,' Alec remarked.

'That's very true,' the man replied. 'I couldn't delay or the child would have died, but I knew we were in good hands.'

Alec looked up at the man with a glint in his eye. 'I'm sure that lad was in good hands too,' he replied.

'That lad's doing very nicely as it happens,' Sir Roger Carmody told him.

Chapter Twenty-Seven

It was not until Saturday afternoon that Brenda Ross heard Pat Flynn was home on leave, and then it was only through a chance meeting at the market between her mother and Dolly Flynn. The letter she had written to Pat would not be needed now, thankfully. It had been hard enough as it was to put her true feelings down on paper, and even then the words did not fully convey what she felt inside. She had intended nevertheless to slip it through the Flynns' letterbox with an attached note asking Dolly to forward it on, but now there was the chance to meet face to face.

Brenda started to write another letter, a brief note asking Pat to call round at six o'clock and saying that she would be ready and on the doorstep, realising how he felt towards her mother and not giving him the excuse to avoid her for that reason. She sealed it up and suddenly threw it on the fire. This was stupid, she told herself. She would have to go round to Carter Lane to deliver it anyway. Better to swallow her pride and knock at the door instead. After all, he could only say no.

When she arrived at the Flynns' front door Brenda took a deep breath before knocking, and with her heart pounding she raised the knocker and let it fall lightly, as though fearful of what might happen.

Pat himself answered the knock and her spirits leapt as she caught his reaction.

'Brenda. You're the last person I expected,' he said with a nervous smile.

'Was you expectin' someone else?' she replied.

'No, I wasn't expectin' anybody,' he said quickly. 'Come in.'

'Is it a good idea?' she responded. 'I mean . . .'

'It's all right, there's no one in. Well, only Jennie an' she's takin' a nap,' Pat told her. 'Mum an' Sadie are out shoppin' an' me dad's gone ter the football match.'

Brenda walked into the warm parlour and loosened her heavy winter coat. 'I wrote you a letter, Pat,' she said, 'but I tore it up. It's better fer us ter talk.'

'I thought we'd exhausted the talkin',' he replied quickly, then bit his tongue. 'Anyway let me take yer coat. Sit down by the fire. Can I get yer a drink? Tea, coffee?'

'No, I'm all right,' she replied as she took a seat.

Pat sat down facing her, leaning forward in the armchair with his hands clasped. 'You look very well,' he remarked.

'So do you, except I fink yer've lost a bit o' weight.'

He sighed. 'An' there's me finkin' I'd put some on.'

'Is yer trainin' over?' she asked.

'Almost.'

'Then yer'll be . . .'

'Joinin' a bomber squadron as a tail gunner.'

'That's a dangerous job, isn't it?'

He shrugged his shoulders. 'Not really – well, no more dangerous than any ovver flyin' job.'

'When's yer leave up?'

'Termorrer.'

'I only found out you were on leave this afternoon,' Brenda said. 'I wish I'd known sooner.'

'I've bin finkin' about yer,' he said shyly.

''Ave yer?'

'Yeah, quite a lot.'

'Me too. Pat, I've bin so stupid,' she said with a break in her voice.

'Yeah, me too.'

'No, you did what you 'ad ter do an' I wasn't big enough to accept it.'

'Why should yer?' he replied. 'It must 'ave seemed like a selfish fing ter do an' you 'ad the right ter do yer nut, I s'pose, the way I told yer about it.'

'It was just that I could see all our dreams an' plans goin' up in smoke,' she said sadly. 'I thought that if yer waited till you was called up we might 'ave 'ad the time ter get married.'

'I know,' he sighed. 'I thought about that too, but can't yer see 'ow it would 'ave bin. We'd just be gettin' settled in a place an' then I'd 'ave ter leave yer all alone. At least now you're livin' wiv yer family.'

'I could 'ave gone back to 'em while you was away,' she replied.

'No, yer wouldn't. Yer'd 'ave made the place nice an' cosy an' spent yer time alone, waitin' fer the odd letter an' fer me ter get some leave.'

'Fousands o' newly married couples are doin' just that,' she reminded him.

'Yeah, I know,' he replied.

Brenda looked down at her clasped hands and squeezed them until the knuckles showed white. 'Tell me the trufe, Pat,' she asked him. 'Do you still feel the same way about me? I mean, is it different now that we've bin apart?'

'I feel more for yer than I've ever done, an' that's the God's honest trufe,' he said quietly. 'In fact I wrote you a letter too.'

''Ave yer still got it?'

'No, I tore it up.'

'Why?'

'Fer the same reason that you tore your letter up, I s'pose,' he told her. 'I just couldn't put me feelin's inter words.'

'It's so difficult,' she sighed.

'I was gonna send you a poem too,' he went on. 'There's a bloke in our billet who reads a lot o' poetry an' we've got friendly. As a matter o' fact, I was talkin' to 'im about you, about 'ow close we were an' 'ow the war caused us ter split up, an' 'e showed me a poem. It's a bit deep but it some'ow ses what I wanted ter say but couldn't.'

'An' yer tore that up too, I s'pose,' Brenda said.

'No, I've still got it.'

'Can I see it?'

He hesitated and then reached into his back pocket. 'Look, I'd prefer it if yer wait till yer get back 'ome before yer read it,' he remarked. 'I'd feel embarrassed.'

'Whatever for?' she smiled. 'D'yer fink it's bein' sissy ter like poetry?'

'No, it's just that I . . . sort of . . .'

'Patrick Flynn, 'ow could I ever fink that you're a sissy,' she said, smiling broadly as she took the folded sheet of paper. 'All right, I won't read it now.'

322

'I'd like ter see you again before I go back termorrer mornin' but Frank an' Jim 'ave just come 'ome on embarkation leave,' he explained. 'I've promised to 'ave a drink wiv 'em ternight. There won't be anuvver chance an' I may not see 'em both fer some time.'

'I understand,' she replied. 'You should spend some time wiv 'em. Maybe I could come ter the station ter see yer off.'

'I'd like that,' he said.

'Look, I'd better go,' she said quickly. 'I'd feel a bit embarrassed if I'm still 'ere when yer family come in.'

'It's all right,' he assured her.

'No, I'd better go,' she insisted. 'What time termorrer?'

'I was gonna leave 'ere about 'alf ten,' he replied. 'I'm catchin' the eleven forty-five from Liverpool Street.' He saw her hesitate. 'You could meet me on the corner o' Defoe Street at ten if yer like. It'd give us a bit o' time ter talk.'

'That'll be fine,' she said as she stood up to leave.

Pat got up and took her gently by the shoulders. 'I know this must 'ave bin a bit difficult for yer, Bren, but I'm very grateful yer did call round.'

'I just 'ad ter see yer, Pat.'

'I've missed yer so much,' he told her quietly.

She stood on tiptoe and planted a soft kiss on his lips, feeling him squeeze her arms. 'Termorrer at ten o'clock. Corner o' Defoe Street.'

He stood at the front door until Brenda turned the corner, then went inside feeling elated. Tonight at The Sun was going to be a night to remember, he thought.

At number 20 Carter Lane an intense conversation was in progress, and Charity Lockwood expressed her shock in no uncertain terms. 'I just don't understand you, Cynthia, really I don't,' she said sharply. 'What purpose will it serve? After all this time too. Goodness gracious me, I've never heard such a feeble, senseless reason. No, I can't let you do it. I won't let you.'

'I'm sorry, Charity, but my mind's made up,' Cynthia told her. 'You may think it's feeble but to me it's not. Sometimes we are given a sign from heaven. Last night was a sign.'

'Don't be so ridiculous,' Charity retorted smartly. 'That shell cone that fell in the backyard didn't come from heaven, it came from the sky, from the anti-aircraft shell, and well you know it. Go out in the street after an air raid and you'll see lots of pieces of shrapnel lying around; yes and shell cones too. It was just that last night one happened to fall in our backyard.'

'Yes, but it was just as I was coming in,' Cynthia reminded her. 'I could have been killed. In fact I nearly was. It just missed my head.'

'So you feel it's a sign, do you?' Charity said mockingly. 'It's been more than ten years now and you feel that God finally got round to giving you a sign. Deary me, Cynthia, don't you think the good Lord's got enough to do with all the problems of the war, without suddenly remembering to give you a sign. It's pathetic.'

'Maybe, but there's something I haven't told you,' the younger sister went on. 'I prayed for a sign. I've been praying for a sign for a while now, and at last it's come.'

'I suppose you did consider my feelings and my future when you decided on your course of action,' Charity remarked. 'Maybe not. No, she's the strong one, she can survive. She doesn't need me to wipe her nose or powder her bottom.'

324

'Don't be cruel, Charity,' Cynthia replied. 'You know I always think of you in every decision I make, which isn't many. Usually it's you who decides for us, and I'm not complaining. I'm happy for you to show your caring side and your compassion, but there comes a time when I have to do the thing I know is right.'

'Then you must understand that sometimes I too have to do what I feel is right, despite what others might think.'

Cynthia looked up at her sister and saw the determined look in her eyes. 'I don't quite know what you're trying to tell me, Charity,' she said, 'but please don't think there's anything you can do that will dissuade me from doing what I have to. I've made my decision and I'm sticking to it.'

Charity sat down with a deep sigh and shook her head slowly as she reached for the paper. 'We shall see,' she said craftily.

All day Saturday it had been damp and cold, with a light fog that would normally have prompted most people to remain by their fireside rather than visit the public house. On this particular Saturday night, however, it was different. It was a time for families to gather together while they could, despite the threat of the bombing. Normally in winter people would yearn for the balmy days of summer and the cool bright evenings, but again it was different now. Everyone prayed for a thick fog on Saturday night, and it appeared early on in the evening that their prayers were being answered.

'It looks like it might be a quiet night ternight,' Danny Crossley remarked as he took possession of his first pint of the evening.

'Gawd willin',' Alf replied. 'As long as the rain don't come.'

Another customer came in to announce that the fog was thickening and Danny ordered another pint for him and Alf. 'We'd better drink ter that,' he said grinning.

By eight o'clock the visibility was down to a few yards and Tess Anson began to feel that providence had intervened. 'They won't be over ternight,' she told Charlie confidently.

'I do believe you're right,' he replied.

'I 'ope yer got enough booze in,' she said.

'Plenty,' he assured her.

The customers and the landlord and landlady of The Sun public house had never known a night like it. Both bars were packed from early on in the evening and in the saloon bar it was difficult to reach the counter. Pints flowed endlessly from the taps and the pianist was kept busy from the moment he showed his face in the bar. The whole of the Flynn family joined with Bert and Daisy Harris and the Kennys in drinking to the health and good fortune of the young men of Carter Lane who would soon be going off to war again.

Ivy Jones' son Jerry looked resplendent in his Royal Marines uniform as he stood talking with Grenadier Freddie Bromilow, who had managed to get a forty-eight-hour pass so that he wouldn't miss the going-away party for his childhood friends.

'So are you on a forty-eight-hour pass too then, Jerry?' Freddie asked.

Jerry nodded. 'I'll be 'ome again soon on embarkation leave,' he replied. 'We're paintin' all the unit vehicles a shitty yellow an' we're due ter be kitted out next week wiv tropical gear. A lot o' the lads fink we're bound fer Egypt, or at least somewhere in the Middle East.'

'Well good luck, pal,' Freddie said clinking glasses.

Everyone was determined to relax and enjoy the evening while they could, knowing full well that when the weather broke the raiders would be back in force.

Sadie was home for the whole weekend and she was feeling excited as she chatted to Jennie. 'It's very 'ard an' they don't give yer much time ter get acclimatised,' she was saying. 'In the first week I 'ad to assist in changin' dressin's on amputees an' then I 'ad ter learn 'ow ter give injections.'

Jennie shuddered. 'Sooner you than me, Sadie, but everyone's proud o' yer. Who'd 'a' thought it? Our Sadie a nurse.'

'It's what I wanna do, Jen. I'm really 'appy at the 'ospital. I like the practical stuff better than the classroom work.'

'An' yer got no regrets about givin' Len Regan the elbow?'

'No, none whatever,' Sadie said positively. 'I'm sure 'e was two-timin' me, though I could never prove anyfing. The woman works in one o' Macaulay's pubs in Rovverhithe. She's a piss artist, ter tell yer the trufe, an' she looks every bit 'er age, but she was a good looker before the drink got to 'er. Len was dead keen on 'er but they fell out before I come on the scene.'

'An' yer fink 'e's back wiv 'er?'

'Yeah, I'm pretty sure.'

Jennie took a sip from her glass. 'Anyway, let's ferget that crowd. Joe's gonna be comin' in soon an' yer gotta look pink an' lovely.'

'Does me 'air look all right?'

'Yeah, course it does.'

'What about me make-up?'

'Just perfect.'

'An' this dress . . .?'

'Sadie, will yer shut up an' relax? I'm goin' over ter rescue Con from our bruvs.'

Bert Kenny had slipped back to the house and on his return he made his way over to Charlie Anson. ''E's out the tub an' dressed,' he reported. ''E'll be 'ere any minute now.'

Everyone who needed to had replenished their glasses and when Big Joe finally walked into the crowded pub wearing his freshly pressed uniform he was greeted with a big cheer. The pianist started up with 'For He's a Jolly Good Fellow' and the customers almost brought the roof down.

'Aw, you shouldn't have made a fuss,' Joe said, his face flushed with embarrassment.

'Shut yer noise, Joe,' Jerry called out. 'Charlie wants ter say a few words.'

The landlord made his way round the counter and held his hands up for attention. 'Now this is a special night fer all of us,' he began. 'We all know about Big Joe's little adventure not so long ago, an' I say little adventure because 'e'd be the last ter make a big fing of it. Nevertheless, it's blokes like 'im who make it certain that the Jerries will never beat us.'

''Ear 'ear,' voices called out.

'This country stands alone now an' we're gettin' a right ole pastin' every night,' Charlie went on, 'but we can take it, because we 'ave to. It's not in our nature to 'old up our 'ands an' surrender. We'll take it all, every last bomb they drop on us, an' then our turn'll come. We'll give it back tenfold, an' one day in the not-too-distant future the Jerries'll be the ones ter put their 'ands up. In the meantime we can feel safe, safe an' proud that our freedom an' a future fer our kids are in the 'ands o' people like Big Joe, the Flynn boys, Freddie Bromilow an' Jerry Jones, Alec Conroy, Chris Wickstead an' Dennis Wilson.'

'Good ole Chris.'

'Cheers, Denny.'

'Gawd bless all of 'em, I say,' an elderly woman remarked, raising her glass of stout.

Charlie Anson held his hands up for silence. 'A lot of us remember these lads kickin' a tin can in the turnin' or cheekin' the market traders, an' I would imagine Big Joe was doin' the same down under, but now they've got a job ter do – kick the Jerries right back where they came from – an' they'll do it. So I ask you all ter raise yer glasses to our lads in uniform, an' may the good Lord go wiv 'em.'

The pub suddenly erupted and in the din and hubbub of the moment Joe sought out Sadie. The Flynn boys and Con were in a huddle when Jennie went over to them. 'Will yer just take a look at our Sadie,' she said happily.

The brothers looked across the bar and saw their sister laughing aloud as Joe made motions with his hands.

'It's nice ter know she's given Regan the elbow,' Frank remarked.

'I'd like ter fink so, but 'e can be a persuasive bastard,' Jim replied.

'I don't fink even Regan would relish tanglin' wiv Big Joe,' Pat told them. 'Come on, let's join 'em.'

'Oh no yer don't,' Jennie said sternly. 'Give 'em a chance ter get ter know each ovver.'

A pretty young woman with blonde hair winked over at

Jim Flynn and got a response, and for a few minutes the two flirted with their eyes.

'I'll see you lads in a minute,' he said mysteriously.

Con slipped his arm round Jennie's waist. 'It's a good night,' he remarked with a twinkle in his eye.

'It is now,' she said, snuggling up to him.

Tucked away in the far corner, Sadie and Big Joe were chatting happily together.

'I really like what I do, Joe,' she told him. 'It gets a bit scary at times an' I don't like goin' on theatre duty, but I know that nursin's fer me.'

'I'm glad for you, Sadie,' he replied. 'That's the way I feel about the navy, but like you say, it ain't all bonzer.'

'No, I don't s'pose it is,' she said, giving him a knowing look. 'You try an' keep out o' trouble. I don't wanna see you in one o' those 'ospital beds.'

'They don't take matelots at your place, do they?' he asked.

'Look at those lot gettin' all lovey-dovey,' Alf Coates remarked from his usual vantage point.

'Yer only young once, Alf,' Danny said philosophically.

'Lookin' at them kids canoodlin' takes me back,' Alf chuckled. 'We're bloody past it now though, ole mate.'

'You speak fer yer bloody self,' Danny told him indignantly.

'You ain't on anuvver promise wiv Widder Winkless, are yer?'

'You mind yer business.'

'It's nuffink ter do wiv me, but once yer done the deed don't sit there complainin' that yer back's gorn again,' Alf replied.

330

Danny looked up to see Big Joe squeezing past on his way to the toilet. 'Wotcher, mate,' he remarked. 'You ain't off yet awhile, are yer? We ain't seen anyfing of yer yet.'

'No, I've just gotta drain the dragon,' Joe replied. 'I'm busier than a one-armed Sydney taxi driver with the crabs in here tonight. How are you keeping?'

'Well, can't complain,' Alf said, and a wicked grin appeared on his face. 'By the way, we ain't seen anyfing o' your mate.'

'My mate?' Joe queried, then he caught the old man's drift. 'Aw, let me guess. Ugly as a hatful of arseholes, and never shuts his bunghole long enough to think. Last seen kissing the road. Nah, we fell out. He never bought a round.'

'Talkin' o' which,' Danny said with a wink and a winning smile, glancing diplomatically at his glass.

The evening wore on, the damp and fogbound darkness outside providing a blessed relief, and in that wartime interlude, while the skies were quiet, a few long-lasting alliances were tightly bonded.

Chapter Twenty-Eight

Carter Lane was very quiet on that bitterly cold and gloomy Sunday morning. For most of the folk it was the first taste they had had for what seemed like ages of sleeping in their own beds without fear of being disturbed by an air raid, and on awakening they took the opportunity of a lie-in. Frank and Iris Ross were no exception, but their daughter Brenda was up early, and after lighting the fire and making herself some tea and toast she sat by the hearth wrapped in her thick corded dressing gown. In the breast pocket was the poem Pat had given her and she had read it over and over again before going to sleep last night. She took it out again, wanting to memorise the last two lines so that she could recite them to Pat, and make him aware that she understood it all now.

'To Lucasta, Going to the Wars'

Tell me not, Sweet, I am unkind
That from the nunnery
Of thy chaste breast, and quiet mind,
To war and arms I fly.

True; a new mistress now I chase,
The first foe in the field;
And with a stronger faith embrace
A sword, a horse, a shield.

Yet this inconstancy is such
As you too shall adore;
I could not love thee, Dear, so much,
Lov'd I not honour more.

Richard Lovelace.

The words had made her cry, and now her eyes began to mist again. The sad pride of the poem had served to purge her mind of all her doubts and selfish anger. The two of them had been inseparable once, and she remembered taking his sticky hand in hers and going to the corner shop for Golly bars and bags of hundreds and thousands. How clearly she remembered the times they sat at the kerbside rubbing shoulders as she taught him how to make a cat's cradle from a length of string she worked between her fingers.

Brenda stared into the flaring coals and saw the tall lean lad who had now begun to treat her with a new respect, and she smiled to herself as she recalled how she had thrown back her shoulders to let him see that she too was growing into a woman. The innocent kisses came later, stolen in the darkness of the wharf doorways and on the muddy foreshore as the tide ebbed and the summer sun dipped down in the sky to leave its orange and purple afterglow. Halcyon days, they seemed now, when the growing pains were hard to bear and the strange feelings in her loins made her shake and tremble with a desire that she did not fully understand. Her childhood fondness, natural and unaware, was now a full-blooded love for him, a yearning for him to come to her in the dead of night, to share her bed and enter her aching body. But how could she open her heart to him, how could she unlock the feelings and desires that beat inside her and let them take wing?

As she prepared to leave the house Brenda was under no illusions. They were grown-ups now, and grown-ups often had to make choices. She no longer cared to walk to the altar pure and chaste, to deny the temptations of love out of respect for the proper order of things. The war had made her see life in a different light. The world was not rose-coloured any more, just cold and grey, and life had to be lived to the full, while it was still there to be savoured. Marriage could wait, love could not, lest the war took him from her forever, as it had already taken so many others.

She saw him on the corner, his greatcoat pulled up around his ears and his face red with the wind. He smiled, the easy smile that she knew so well, and she felt a warm glow deep down inside. He took her arm and kissed her cheek before they set off along the quiet street.

'I cried last night when I read that poem,' she told him.

He smiled. 'I think it said it all, all that I wanted ter say but couldn't find the words for.'

'Will yer come back ter me soon, Pat?' she asked.

'Soon as ever I can.'

'In a few weeks?'

'The trainin' finishes in two weeks,' he replied. 'I should be able ter manage a forty-eight-hour pass.'

'I'll want you all ter meself, darlin',' she grinned.

335

'Every wakin' minute of every hour.'

The train was about to leave and Pat took her in his arms. He could feel her body pressed to his and he kissed her full lips with all the passion within him, then he climbed aboard, turning to look out of the door. 'I love you, Brenda.'

'I love you too, Pat.'

The guard raised his flag and the young woman reached out and touched him. 'The last two lines o' the poem. Say them ter me.'

'I can't remember 'em.'

'I can,' she said smiling. ' "I could not love thee, dear, so much, loved I not honour more." '

The train moved away from the platform and he blew her a kiss. She waved until the carriage disappeared round the bend out of sight, then she turned away, tears welling up in her eyes. 'Damn this war,' she cursed aloud, hurrying from the platform out into the winter gloom.

The fog was back with a vengeance that evening and the Luftwaffe would stay away for the second night running. At the Flynn household it was a quiet time, with Frank and Jim recovering from their lunchtime sortie to The Sun, undertaken solely for medicinal purposes according to Jim. Dolly and Mick relaxed in the fireside chairs, warmed by the coke fire as they listened to the wireless, and upstairs Sadie and Jennie chatted together while they waited for Con and Big Joe to call.

'If the picture's over in time we could call in The Sun fer a nightcap,' Jennie suggested.

'Good idea,' Sadie replied. 'I expect Frank an' Jim'll drag themselves up there.'

'Will they mind, you goin' back termorrer instead o' ternight?' Jennie asked.

'Nah, long as I'm there fer nine o'clock,' Sadie told her. 'That's when us trainees usually start.'

'You an' Joe looked a very nice twosome last night,' Jennie remarked.

'We talked an' talked,' Sadie replied. 'I told 'im there was no way back fer me an' Len Regan an' 'e asked me if I'd be 'is gel.'

'Ah, that's nice,' Jennie sighed. ''E is a sweetie, so old-fashioned.'

''E's not that old-fashioned,' Sadie said indignantly.

'You know what I mean,' Jennie replied. 'Big Joe reminds me o' those fellers in the ole films, all manly an' charmin'.'

'The perfect gentleman, 'cept fer some fruity sayin's 'e's got.'

'Yeah. 'Ere, I 'ope 'e wasn't too pissy ter kiss yer goodnight.'

'Course 'e wasn't,' Sadie said quickly.

'What was it like? Did it make yer toes curl up?'

'Jennie, don't be so nosy.'

'When Con kisses me I'm all of a tremble.'

Sadie shook her head slowly. 'Look, are you all ready?'

'All but me stockin's,' Jennie told her. 'I'm leavin' 'em till the last minute in case I ladder 'em.'

'Well, will yer go an' make a cuppa while I finish gettin' ready?'

'Yeah, okay,' Jenny said without attempting to move from the edge of the bed. 'I'm so glad Pat an' Brenda got back tergevver again.'

'We don't know fer sure, do we?' Sadie replied.

'I do,' Jennie said. 'You could see the look in Pat's eyes when 'e said Brenda was gonna see 'im off this mornin'.'

'It's a shame Pat 'ad so little time wiv Frank an' Jim,' Sadie remarked thoughtfully. 'Still it was a really good night, wasn't it?'

'Not 'alf,' Jennie said with passion. 'Con enjoyed 'imself too. I'm gonna see as much of 'im as I can while 'e's 'ere. God knows 'ow long it'll be before 'im an' the boys get 'ome again.'

There was a knock at the front door and Sadie jumped up quickly. 'Bloody 'ell, they're early. Quick, get yer stockin's on.'

As the night wore on the fog thickened, but by morning it had gone, giving way to a bright and bitterly cold day, and people went off to work knowing that the respite from the bombing was over. In the Lockwood household the discussion of the previous day continued, but try as she might Charity could not persuade her sister to change her mind. 'All right then, if you insist, but I'm coming with you,' she said adamantly.

'I'd like that,' Cynthia told her. 'It'll make it easier for me if you're there.'

They left the house, with Cynthia holding on to Charity's arm and walking upright and proud, the collars of their heavy coats turned up against the elements. They made their way into Munday Road and up the steps of the police station and Cynthia took a deep breath as they walked through the doors. 'I'd like to see Chief Inspector McConnell if you please,' she said.

The desk sergeant knew the sisters well enough not to ask

questions. 'If you'll just give me a minute I'll see if he's free.'

As they were escorted along the corridor Rubin McConnell came out of his office to greet them. 'Good mornin', ladies. What can I do for you?' he asked.

'I've come to report a murder,' Cynthia told him.

The inspector looked shocked. 'You'd better come in the office,' he said, pulling up two chairs in front of the desk.

While the sisters made themselves comfortable McConnell phoned for Detective Sergeant Johnson to join him and the detective sat at the back of the room with a notepad in his hand.

Cynthia cleared her throat. 'As I said I want to report a murder, namely the murder of Aaron Priestley.'

'But we already have that information,' the policeman said quickly.

'If I'm not mistaken you are assuming my husband was murdered, but you don't know for sure.'

'I think we can be sure, Miss Lockwood. The wound tells us as much.'

'Well, I can tell you for sure, because I know the identity of the person who killed him,' Cynthia went on.

'You know the person responsible?'

'Yes, I do.'

'You saw the murder?'

'I was there.'

'Good Lord! And you've only just thought of telling me. Who was it?'

'Me.'

'You!'

'Yes, me.'

McConnell swallowed hard. 'Are you trying to make a fool of me, Miss Lockwood?' he asked sternly.

'Heaven forbid,' Cynthia replied with equal seriousness.

'You're telling me that you killed your husband?'

'Yes. I killed him with a single blow to the head with a hammer, then I put him in the bassinet that I used for the bagwash and wheeled him round to the hole the workmen had dug in the factory yard in Munday Road and tipped him in it.'

The policeman reached into the desk drawer and took out a folder. 'This is what I call the Lockwood file,' he said in a long-suffering voice. 'Over the years you've both come in here with snippets of information to report to me. The last, let me remind you, was the case of the pillar-box. Now you turn up first thing on a Monday morning, expecting me to believe that you actually killed your husband and then tipped him in the hole.'

'Of course I expect you to believe me,' Cynthia said quickly. 'It's the truth.'

'And you're prepared to make a statement to that effect?'

'Yes.'

McConnell leaned back in his chair and wiped a shaky hand over his face. 'Why did you kill him?'

'Because I could not stand any more of his bullying, his physical and mental abuse, that's why.'

The policeman picked up a plain sheet of paper and laid it down on the blotting-pad in front of him. 'Right then, let's . . .'

'Just a moment,' Charity cut in. 'You'll be wasting your time taking a statement from Cynthia. She didn't kill Aaron. I did.'

'No, she didn't.'

'Oh yes, I did.'

McConnell held up his hands. 'Now just a minute. Both of you couldn't have killed him.'

'I did it,' Cynthia said calmly. 'I've lived with the secret for over ten years, and now the body's been found I feel bound to confess. I prayed for guidance and the Lord has answered me. I killed Aaron Priestley.'

'No, she didn't. I did it,' Charity declared. 'And you know full well, inspector, that you can't charge both of us, considering the evidence you have.'

'Oh I see,' McConnell replied with sarcasm. 'Well, in that case let me make you a little proposition. Perhaps Cynthia could give me her version first and then you can give me yours. On the basis of what you say I'll make the decision as to which one of you I formally charge. If that's to your liking.'

'That's fair of you, inspector,' Cynthia said. 'Well to begin with, Aaron had been beating me unmercifully that evening, and then he went out to the pub. Later he came home very drunk and started to hit me again. I grabbed a hammer that was lying on the sideboard and struck him with all the force I could muster. I knew he was dead because his eyes opened wide and then went all glassy. So I got the old bassinet and put it by the bed. It wasn't very difficult to roll him into it and then I took him to the hole. It was raining very hard and it was also very late. There wasn't a soul about. When I tipped him into the hole I saw him slither down to the bottom and there was a sort of muddy puddle there. He just disappeared.'

McConnell opened the folder and studied it for a few

moments. 'Tell me, Miss Lockwood, did you tamper with the body once you had done the deed?'

'In what way?' Cynthia asked with a puzzled look.

'Well, did you remove any of his clothing, take off any rings or a wristwatch maybe?'

'Certainly not.'

'And I suppose if I asked you to give me your version it would be similar to your sister's,' the policeman said, eyeing Charity closely.

'Exactly.'

'Now let me tell you both something,' he continued. 'When we removed the remains from that hole the pathologist did a thorough check and he found that there were two joints missing from the ring finger of the left hand. We know from the photograph you supplied us with that Aaron Priestley wore a large ruby ring on that finger. So it follows that whoever killed him tried to take the ring off and when they found it was too tight to remove they chopped the finger off. It wasn't either of you. You said that you didn't tamper with the body after death.'

'Someone could have seen the body in the hole and decided to help themselves to the ring,' Cynthia replied.

'The evidence we have doesn't support that theory,' McConnell told her. 'The remains were lying face up with the arms at the side. Besides, you said the body disappeared under the water and mud.'

The two women looked at each other in confusion. 'Well, if you're sure I suppose we'll have to go along with it,' Charity said. 'Come along, Cynthia, let's not waste any more of the nice policeman's time.'

As soon as the two had left the office McConnell reached

into his desk drawer for a bottle of whisky and two glasses. 'Can you imagine either of those two hammering anyone to death?' he sighed.

Johnson smiled as he accepted the tot of whisky. 'What possesses them?' he asked with a slow shake of his head.

McConnell tapped the folder with his forefinger. 'When you've time you should go through this,' he replied. 'They've been coming in here for years with all sorts of information and requests. I think they're just seeking attention, though I could be over-simplifying it. Whatever it is, those two women have plagued me for years.'

Johnson sipped his drink. 'Well, we know the Lockwoods couldn't have killed Priestley, but someone did, though I don't think we're ever going to find out who it was.' He emptied the glass and stood up, a smile suddenly lighting up his face.

'What is it?' the inspector asked.

'I was just picturing the old biddy pushing that pram through the streets with a pair of legs sticking out,' Johnson told him.

'I just had a thought too,' McConnell remarked. 'I've just had my first whisky and it's only ten thirty. Those two will be the death of me.'

Chapter Twenty-Nine

Time hung heavily on Con Williams while Jennie was working during the day and he spent the time sorting through his adopted grandmother's belongings at the flat in Dockhead. The rent was paid up until the end of the month but things had to be disposed of and arrangements made for the furniture to be cleared. Mrs Crosier was very helpful in getting everything moving and it was she who arranged for the Salvation Army to collect the bits of furniture and clothing that might still do someone a turn. The crockery was all cracked and chipped and the few pots and pans only fit for the dustbin.

'Ida didn't 'ave much, did she?' Con remarked to the elderly lady.

'A lifetime o' struggle, that's all she 'ad,' Mrs Crosier replied sadly. 'Never mind, Con, she did right by you an' I'm sure she'll be favoured up there.'

The papers and documents in the flat were of no importance, mainly receipts and old letters from relatives and friends, and Con could find no insurance policy that would serve to reimburse the local church for their kindness in arranging a dignified funeral for the old lady. 'I'm a bit surprised,' he remarked. 'She was always tellin' me that she'd put a few bob aside fer 'er funeral.'

'Yeah, she used ter put a few coppers in that jug every week,' Mrs Crosier told him, 'but then one day when I was doin' a bit o' cleanin' for 'er she asked me ter pass the jug down to 'er. She was sufferin' wiv that phlebitis at the time an' she couldn't move out o' the armchair. I watched 'er count the coppers an' then she gave me one o' those saucy smiles she was good at. "This wouldn't even bury our ole tomcat," she said, "an' I don't fink I'm gonna last enough ter fill the jug up. 'Ere, take it an' bring me back a nice little bottle o' tiddly." What could I do? It was 'er wish, so I fetched 'er a small bottle of gin. I was worried though, what wiv 'er complaint. I didn't fink the gin would 'elp 'er. Anyway I looked in on 'er that night an' there she was 'appy as Larry goin' frew all 'er ole photos. I left 'er sleepin' in the armchair and she told me later that was the best night's sleep she'd 'ad in ages.'

Con thanked Mrs Crosier for all her help and then closed up the flat, leaving her with the key for when the Salvation Army people called. It was as if the door had closed on a large part of himself and he felt alone and empty inside. His leave was up tomorrow and tonight he would stay at the working men's hostel in Dockhead, which he felt was preferable to staying another night in the grimy, lonely flat with all those childhood memories crowding in on him.

Following their visit to the police station the Lockwood sisters felt drained, but as always Charity was a rock. 'Now listen to me, Cynthia,' she said resolutely. 'I know it came as a shock to hear about the missing finger. It's a complete mystery, but we'll never know the rights of it, so it's not worth dwelling on it. It's all in the past now and I think we should agree never to talk about the matter again.'

'I think you're right,' Cynthia said.

'We must stop pestering that nice inspector too,' Charity added. 'He has enough to do without us troubling him.'

'Yes, you're right,' Cynthia replied. 'But it doesn't mean we should walk around with our eyes shut.'

'No, of course not,' Charity said. 'If we do see anything untoward happening it's our duty to report it and I'm sure that the inspector would be grateful, but let's not get carried away.'

'I couldn't agree more,' Cynthia replied.

This was to be the last family meal before the boys went back from leave and Dolly had asked Jennie to bring Con along. 'The poor sod's all on 'is own an' I can't let 'im go to a cafe or a bloody fish shop fer 'is tea,' she said. 'I've managed ter get a nice joint o' beef an' there'll be plenty ter go round. 'E might as well stay 'ere ternight too. 'E can sleep in our Sadie's bed.'

That evening Con arrived in uniform, carrying his kitbag and a small case ready for the journey back to camp the following morning, and Dolly spared no effort. She used her best white linen tablecloth with the green china dinner set, the meat was tender, the vegetables were done to perfection and her special meat stock gravy was relished hungrily by Frank and Jim in particular, who loved to soak their bread in it.

Watching them wipe their plates with thick slices and seeing Con follow suit, timidly at first, made her want to hug them all. She was reminded of peaceful times when her children were all growing up, when a grazed knee or a bump on the head was something she could deal with. Now the young men were going off to war, and what good could she be, standing by with the medicine chest?

When the meal was finally over Dolly had to get ready for her nightly spell on the mobile canteen and Mick left for his fire-watching duty at the nearby fire post on the roof of the Defoe Street bacon factory. Frank and Jim, sensing that they were going to be in the way, decided to go to The Sun for a game of darts. Jennie was grateful for the opportunity to be alone with Con but she made light of it. 'We'll pop in the pub later, once I've tidied up,' she remarked.

It was quiet in the house now and Con sat in the armchair staring thoughtfully into the fire while Jennie busied herself in the scullery, but she soon came into the parlour and immediately slipped onto his lap. 'We've 'ad so little time alone,' she said regretfully.

He smiled. 'Never mind, it's bin very nice, just ter be wiv yer.'

She put her arms around his neck and kissed him. 'We're alone now,' she sighed.

He pulled her across him and kissed her open lips, feeling the warmth of her slim shapely body. 'I would 'ave liked to 'ave taken yer ter the flat, but I couldn't, Jennie,' he said with a heavy breath. 'It's dingy an' depressin' an' I just couldn't ask yer. I couldn't 'ave relaxed there an' I don't fink you could 'ave neivver.'

'It's all right, Con, you don't 'ave ter feel guilty,' she said, and her face broke into a saucy smile. 'I know yer a little bit frightened o' me.'

He smiled as he held her close. 'So yer've sussed me out.'

'I was only joking,' she told him. 'I bet yer've bin wiv lots o' gels.'

'I've 'ad a few dates, but I've never bin serious wiv anyone before,' he replied quietly.

'Are we serious?' she asked.

'I thought so,' he grinned.

'Well then, stop talkin' so much an' kiss me,' she said huskily.

Their lips met and Jennie could no longer hold herself in check. Tonight was the last night they would spend together for a long time and she was determined to make him love her fully. She ran her fingers through his hair and then slowly undid the buttons of his shirt, slipping her hands onto his chest. He was aroused, cupping her small firm breasts in his hands and she encouraged him, undoing the buttons of her blouse and unclipping her bra. The feel of his large hand on her bare skin made her shudder with pleasure. 'I want you, Con,' she whispered. 'I've dreamed of this. Let's go upstairs.'

As she slipped from his lap she caught the uncertain look in his eyes. 'What's wrong?' she asked.

'I've . . . I've not got any . . .'

'Who needs 'em?' she said smiling at him. 'It's not the week fer me ter get pregnant anyway.'

They climbed the stairs and Jennie took his hand in hers as she led him into her bedroom. Her arms went round his neck and she arched her body into his, daringly and provocatively, moving sensuously against his rising ardour. They kissed hungrily and she undid the buttons of his trousers, making him gasp as she held his stiff erection. Manoeuvring

349

round she fell back on the bed, pulling him down on top of her. He had trouble getting out of his thick uniform trousers and she helped him urgently, panting with the passion swelling inside her. Their naked bodies touched, pressed together and he gritted his teeth as she guided him into her, unable to wait any longer, and Con's inexperience was matched by Jennie's almost bursting desire for him. She groaned as she felt his first thrust deep inside her and his movements became frantic as they hastened to a frenzied and delicious climax.

Big Joe stepped down from the bus outside the Woolwich Military Hospital and made his way into the gravel forecourt. He was wearing his uniform and greatcoat, with his naval cap at a saucy tilt. Sadie had told him that she was confined to the nurses' quarters during the week but some of the women trainees engaged in clandestine meetings with their boyfriends. She had said it in a matter-of-fact way while they were chatting at the pub and he knew that Sadie was not hinting for him to come and see her, but here he was, and he felt almost as nervous as he had when he slipped into the dinghy that night in the Mediterranean.

The night sky was clear, lit by the waning moon, and the large main building loomed up in front of Joe as he assessed the strategy of his self-appointed mission. He guessed that the nurses' quarters would be to the rear of the building but he did not want to be mistaken for some voyeur or pervert, so he decided to tackle the problem with a frontal assault and use diplomacy, falling back on high explosive as a last resort. Walking boldly through the main doors he sauntered up to the reception area and smiled. 'Good evening, sister,' he said to the young nurse on duty. 'I phoned earlier about an appointment with . . .'

'Yes, we have the message,' the nurse told him, smiling at being called sister. 'If you'll just take a seat I'll get someone to attend to you.'

Big Joe nearly fell over with surprise, and before he could respond the nurse picked up the phone and said simply, 'The seaman's arrived.'

Joe was still wondering if Sadie had somehow anticipated his visit when a large stern-looking sister approached and whispered a few words in the nurse's ear. She nodded and hurried off, following the martinet and leaving Joe scratching his head. Someone was coming towards him, a male nurse walking quickly. 'If you'll follow me,' he said.

Joe shrugged his shoulders and did as he was bid.

'In there,' the nurse told him. 'Slip your bottoms off and put the gown on. You'll find it on the bed.'

Once again Joe made to protest but the man was already hurrying off.

'Is this a military hospital or a bloody loony bin?' the Australian mumbled to himself.

'Haven't you made yourself ready yet?' a voice said, and Joe spun round to see a Medical Corps captain glaring at him.

'I think there's been a few wires crossed, sir,' Joe remarked.

'A few wires crossed? Is that how you describe catching the pox?' the medic said sharply. 'You phoned the hospital for an emergency check for VD, didn't you?'

'No, I bloody didn't,' Joe said quickly. 'I've been too busy to catch me breath, apart from anything else. I'm here with a message for one of the nurses and it's all gone a bit arse-up.'

The officer sat down heavily in the chair and laughed. 'My God. You almost got the umbrella up your pride and joy.'

'I'm very sorry, sir, but I didn't get a chance to give 'em the drum,' Joe explained.

The captain narrowed his eyes for effect. 'That's an Aussie accent if I'm not mistaken?' he said.

'Sydney, to be precise.'

'Well now, you're a long way from home.'

'Bermondsey's been my home for a couple of years now,' Joe told him.

The captain looked at him closely. 'You say you have a message for one of the nurses?'

'Trainee nurses, to be exact,' Joe replied.

'Name?'

'Miss Sadie Flynn.'

'I know her. Good prospects. Very good prospects in fact,' the captain remarked. 'The message. Nothing bad I hope?'

'No, sir. Her two brothers have lobbed, sorry, come home unexpectedly on embarkation leave and they wanted to let her know. They tried to phone but all the lines are down in Bermondsey.'

'Right then,' the medic said officiously. 'Proceed in an orderly fashion to the nurses' quarters and if that barbarian matron there gives you any problems tell her I gave you permission.'

'That's very kind of you, sir,' Joe said saluting smartly.

The barbarian matron turned out to be a sweetie in Joe's estimation, and when a very surprised Sadie appeared in the reception area the elderly woman allowed the two to use her office and even sent a nurse for some tea.

'I had to see you, Sadie,' Joe told her. 'I'm going back off leave tomorrow.'

'I know,' Sadie replied, stroking the back of his hand. 'Everyone seems ter be goin' back termorrer. The boys, Con, and now you too. I'm gonna miss yer, Joe.'

'I'm gonna miss you too, Sadie,' he replied. 'I know we've already said our goodbyes but I couldn't get the picture of you out of me head. I needed to see you once more, just to look at you so I can keep it fresh in me mind.'

'You took a chance o' gettin' court-martialled just ter take anuvver look at me?' Sadie said shaking her head slowly. 'I should feel gratified, but I'm not, I'm angry. You're incorrigible.'

'Is that contagious?' he asked, smiling easily.

Her composure slipped and she gave him a big grin and leapt into his arms. 'Take this back off leave with yer,' she said, kissing him passionately on the lips.

The matron peered into the room and Sadie quickly straightened her dress. 'He's just leaving, matron,' she announced.

Joe strolled out of the hospital whistling happily, smiling at the nurses and a nervous-looking sailor in reception. With a bit of luck his next tour of duty would be in the North Atlantic, which meant he would be home again before too many months, providing his ship steered clear of the marauding U-boats.

Chapter Thirty

It was a very quiet Christmas for the Carter Lane folk. The Luftwaffe stayed away but with the shadow still hanging over their lives the Yuletide was celebrated in a reserved and thoughtful way. For many families it was a time to drink to their absent sons and reflect hopefully on what the new year would bring. Con Williams and the Flynn boys had now reached the Middle East, as had Chris Wickstead with his battalion of Royal Fusiliers. Ivy Jones' son Jerry had been posted to Scotland with his Royal Marine squadron and throughout the festive season they were engaged in training for a special mission behind enemy lines. Freddie Bromilow the Grenadier joined his battalion just before Christmas to learn that they were bound for India and Dennis Wilson was serving on a destroyer somewhere in the North Atlantic. As for Big Joe Buckley, he was surprised to learn that he and Petty Officer Stone had been awarded the Distinguished Service Medal, also awarded posthumously to Petty Officer Chivers and Leading Seaman Preston. He also learned that he was being sent to Plymouth for further underwater training.

With Christmas over the raids began again, but after the

severe bombardment of December the twenty-ninth, when the Thames was at its lowest ebb and the City of London burned all night, the raids became more spasmodic. It was during this time that the work done by the Royal Engineer bomb-disposal squad was properly assessed, and for his part in saving the children's hospital Sapper Alec Conroy was awarded the Military Medal. People now began to sleep more in their own beds, though they were often roused by the wailing of the air-raid siren in the dead of night, and it was time too for the ARP personnel in the command post in Carter Lane to wind down their operations. Both Karen Watson and Nigel Bayley immersed themselves in their daily jobs, and any pleasure in getting back to normality was overshadowed by their sadness at seeing less of each other.

As the bitterly cold winter gave way to a mild spring, people felt as if they were slowly emerging from a long dark tunnel. Light nights were ahead and sunny days, but the menace was still there, and it was brutally brought home by a sudden and savage air attack in early May. The Luftwaffe flew over in strength, once again picking the night when the Thames was at its lowest for the year. The raid started at six thirty in the evening and wave after wave of bombers flew over the capital leaving devastation in their wake. Their prime targets were the docks and the East End and during the eight-hour raid seven hundred tons of high explosive and one hundred thousand incendiary bombs were dropped. Almost fifteen hundred people died that night and eighteen hundred more were injured.

Dolly Flynn and Liz Kenny worked around the clock with their canteen van and Mick Flynn, Bill Harris and Bert Kenny felt utterly exhausted as they fought ceaselessly with the rest of the fire watchers to put out the incendiaries. Jennie and Peggy Freen pedalled to and fro carrying messages and during one sortie Irene Copley was knocked off her bicycle by blast and badly shaken up.

The morning came as a blessed relief and people went to work still in shock, dreading what the coming nights had in store for them, but they were not to know at the time that the terrible night they had just experienced was indeed the end of the Blitz. The Germans had now turned their attention eastwards and Russia was suddenly invaded. More bombs were to fall on the capital at various times but in comparison the damage and casualties were light.

Summer days were arriving and operations to repair the battered capital were quickly getting under way. Dolly and Liz were now made redundant and the firemen at the Old Kent Road station presented them both with signed illuminated certificates of merit. Jennie Flynn took her leave of the command post, and Karen and Nigel spent some time together tidying up the converted house that held so many memories of warm caresses in stolen moments and secret kisses. Now it was time to move on, and Karen felt particularly sad as she made her weekly trip to the nursing home tucked away in the pretty countryside of Buckinghamshire.

Life had been sweet and kind to her in the years before the war. She had met Douglas Price, a fellow student, at a college dance and they immediately fell in love. Two years later they were married and Douglas followed his father into the family's engineering business. The young couple lived in a nice house in Buckinghamshire and enjoyed all the trappings of wealth, travelling abroad and partying on a lavish scale. Then tragedy struck. Douglas was riding his powerful motorcycle through a country lane one dark night when he was hit head-on by a speeding car. For almost a month the young man lay in a coma with massive head injuries, and when he finally regained consciousness the doctors realised that he had suffered irreversible brain damage. Douglas was now imprisoned in a broken body, dependent on others for his every need.

As she sat in the train, watching the colours of summer flash past the window, Karen relived those terrible early days after the accident. The trauma of the constant vigil at his bedside and the horror and devastation she felt when the doctors spoke with her and Douglas's father had never fully left her, and only the compassion and unselfish love shown by Nigel Bayley had helped to comfort her and give her some relief, albeit brief and occasional.

The room was sunlit and quiet, tastefully decorated, and they were left alone, with a call button at hand should Karen need assistance. Douglas sat slumped in the wheelchair, his body at an awkward angle, his head tilted unnaturally as he mumbled unintelligible words, his tongue hanging out of his mouth and dribbling onto a pad fixed to his front. He was frail and his condition was getting worse, but Karen smiled bravely as she tried to communicate with him. She spoke of mundane things, of flowers in bloom, of the pink roses that Douglas had once cultivated to arch over their front door and along the wall of the house. She persevered, but it was like trying to draw water from a dry well. He had left her for ever, that bright spirit of his trapped in a limbo, his eyes rolling and his hands twisting in spidery gestures.

He closed his eyes in sleep and Karen sat staring at him, angry at the arbitrary, meaningless blow fate had dealt them.

A young man with everything to live for, now lost to the world in a wheelchair, his life irrevocably snapped. And every time she thought it would be better for him to die she felt horribly guilty for wishing his life away. He still breathed and moved, and inside that damaged brain his feelings and intelligence might still somehow be intact, like a prisoner in dead flesh. She could sense a presence in his manner, in his rolling eyes. Was he trying to tell her of his suffering, or remembering the time they had together? She would never know, but she must never desert him or forsake him, not while the tiniest spark of life remained. God would never forgive her. Forsaking all others, in sickness and in health, till death us do part. Thank goodness for Nigel. He understood fully, and made her existence bearable.

Karen sat deep in thought as she travelled back to war-scarred London. The doctors had told her that Douglas was losing his fight and at most he would only survive for a few more months. She almost shut her ears and her mind to the news, lest she wish the time away. Better too that she did not tell Nigel the news. Better to carry on as though nothing had changed, enjoy the brief, incomplete moments with him and remain at some kind of peace with herself.

Through the long summer months of 1941 the women of Carter Lane stuck together in a common bond of support and encouragement. They still knitted woollens for the forces and met together on Friday evenings in the saloon bar of The Sun to chat and exchange news. A letter received from a serving son was proudly brought along and read out to the rest without any inhibitions. Maps of the war situation published in the newspapers were studied and particular attention was paid to the war in the Libyan desert where the Eighth Army were fighting.

The younger women were drawing closer too and Brenda Ross made a point of calling round to the Flynn home whenever she got a letter from Pat. He was now based in East Anglia and flying on bombing missions to the heart of Germany. Jennie had never really got to know Brenda very well, but now with both their boyfriends on active service the two women grew closer.

'D'you know what, Brenda, I fink you an' me should 'ave a night out,' Jennie said to her one evening.

'We could go ter the pictures,' Brenda suggested.

'I was finkin' more of goin' dancin',' Jennie told her.

'I used ter like dancin' but I dunno,' Brenda said hesitantly. 'It could get a bit tricky.'

''Ow d'yer mean?'

'Well, when it gets ter the last dance.'

'Yeah, there's always some flash feller fancyin' 'is chances,' Jennie agreed, 'but we don't 'ave ter wait till the last dance.'

'I dunno, it could be awkward tryin' ter get away, especially if some feller's got 'is eye on yer.'

'You're prob'ly right,' Jennie conceded. 'We'll go ter the flicks instead then.'

'When?'

'This Saturday night?'

'Okay, you're on.'

Pat Flynn was now a flight sergeant and tail gunner on a Wellington bomber, and he shared his billet with another flight sergeant by the name of Tom Darcy with whom he had become very friendly. Tom loved poetry and spent a lot of his free time reading the works of the greats, Chaucer, Spenser and Dryden, as well as Tennyson and the earthy verse of Kipling. 'All life is there in the works of those poets,' Tom remarked to Pat as they lounged on the grass outside their billet one hot September day.

'Well, I 'ave ter say that one about goin' off ter the wars certainly touched Brenda,' Pat replied. 'It said all I wanted ter say.'

'I suppose in fifty years' time there'll be poems taught in schools about this war and the effect it had on people's lives,' Tom said thoughtfully.

''Ow come you got interested in poetry?' Pat asked him.

'I dunno really,' Tom reflected. 'Maybe it was escapism, trying to find beauty where it didn't exist.'

'In the land of dark satanic mills,' Pat said smiling.

'Yeah, sort of,' Tom said, shifting his position on the grass. 'I was born in the Midlands and we moved around a lot as a family, but my lasting memories of that time are belching chimneys and damp foggy days spent in the sloping cobblestoned streets of little industrial towns. I was very young when we lived there, then when I was about ten or eleven we settled in Derbyshire. Christ, what a difference. There on our doorstep were the peaks, and I used to spend hours just tramping up those slopes to the top. The views were like nothing I could describe, with shades of colours and shifting textures stretching as far as the eye could see. Poetry can describe such a landscape though. Tennyson can.'

'It's far removed from the business we're in though,' Pat replied soberly. 'When we're goin' out I look down over the countryside an' marvel at the sheer beauty of it, an' then we cross the Channel wiv our load o' bombs, our bomb-aimer presses the button an' whoosh.'

'That's war,' Tom sighed. 'They come over and try to turn our cities into burning ruins and we do the same to them, only the difference is, they'll get it tenfold, twentyfold. The rumour is we'll be getting four-engined bombers next year. The Lancaster, I believe it's called. The bombload will be greater and the destruction more widely spread. But we have to remember that the London Blitz didn't bomb the people into submission and I don't honestly think that we can bomb the German people into submission either.'

'I s'pose not,' Pat agreed, 'but if we succeed in destroyin' their war industry it'll certainly shorten the war.'

Tom Darcy nodded. 'Keep that conviction at the front of your mind, Pat, and you'll stay sane,' he said smiling.

'And you keep readin' that poetry book of yours,' Pat replied.

Tom got up and brushed the loose grass cuttings from his uniform. 'We'd better get ready for the briefing,' he remarked, then when Pat had straightened his jacket he said, 'By the way. If I cop it before you I want you to have this book. I've already said so inside the cover, look.'

Pat read the words. ' "To Patrick Flynn, my good pal, with best wishes for a safe and successful tour of ops." Fanks, Tom. I dunno what ter say.'

'There's nothing to say,' Tom said with a carefree smile. 'Come on, let's go.'

Inside the briefing hut a hubbub of voices was suddenly stilled as the station commander and his executive officer stepped onto the rostrum. 'Our target for tonight is Essen,' he announced. 'Visibility status is expected to be light cloud and a full moon.'

The subsequent murmur of voices stopped when the commander held up his hand. 'We have information that a squadron of German night fighters has moved into the Utrecht area of Holland, so be on your guard. That's all. Will pilots and navigators please remain.'

Once outside the hut Tom put his arm round Pat's shoulders. 'I hope I didn't get to you,' he said, 'talking about bequests.'

'Of course not,' Pat told him. 'This time termorrer we'll be sunnin' ourselves as usual.'

As they strolled over to the mess hut Tom suddenly smiled. 'I'm writing a piece of poetry.'

'Is that a fact,' Pat said grinning back. 'Can I take a look?'

'I'd prefer it if you waited till it's finished,' Tom confessed.

'I'll look forward to it, Tom.'

The evening grew dark and the roar of engines shattered the countryside quiet and bent the long grass. Laden Wellingtons taxied out to the runway, roaring off into the night sky one after the other, moving into formation as they climbed to operational height. Soon they were passing over the moonlit North Sea towards the coast of Holland and Pat heard his pilot give the order to test the guns. The short burst was repeated by other planes, and then there was only the steady drone of the engines as the formation flew on towards their allotted target in the heart of the Ruhr.

Chapter Thirty-One

With the Nazi war machine directed towards Russia and the threat of invasion diminishing, people began to change their way of thinking. There was a difference of tone in the papers and in broadcasts on the wireless, an apparently concerted effort to get the populace to change from their siege mentality to a more positive outlook. Metal collections were redoubled and people were encouraged to hand in all their old pots and pans and any scrap metal they had to aid the war effort. Competitions were held throughout the country for slogans urging folk to buy savings certificates, producing such gems as 'Lend your money to defend, freedom is the dividend', and in Carter Lane the knitting circle was encouraged by the Lockwood sisters to keep up their efforts.

More and more young men were being called up and single women were now required to register for war-work. Incoming convoys were suffering terrible losses at the hands of the U-boats and certain foods became scarce in the shops. Life at home continued to wear a wartime cloak, but cinemas and dance halls were still open for business and football matches and greyhound racing meetings took place as usual. Another year was drawing to its end and maps took up more space in the newspapers as the fighting in the Middle East intensified. Every day there were accounts in the papers and on the wireless of the RAF bombing missions into the heart of Germany, and the inevitable postscript: 'Some of our planes failed to return.'

At an RAF bomber base somewhere in Lincolnshire there was a general feeling of relief when news came through that bombing raids were to be suspended for three weeks after that coming night's operation, allowing the air crews to train on the new type of aircraft coming off the production lines. There was talk too that maybe some leave would be available. The squadron had taken a terrible pounding during the last few months and the number of crew replacements had now overtaken the original number of personnel present when the base first became operational.

'There's going to be a change of tactics when we get the Lancaster,' Tom Darcy remarked to Pat. 'With four-engined bombers we'll be going right into Eastern Germany and the Balkans.'

'Don't remind me,' Pat replied. 'Essen's far enough.'

Tom ran a hand over his face and leaned back on his bed. 'Terry Tomlinson and his crew have just completed their tour of ops,' he said.

Pat shook his head. 'They're well due fer their rest. God, I've only done seven.'

'I've got nine,' Tom told him. 'To be honest I thought the Essen raid was going to be my last. Fensome did a marvellous job coaxing the old crate back home.'

Pat studied his friend. The strain was telling on him and he wondered if Tom got the same impression about him. 'If we get any leave I'm gonna spend mine sleepin' an' gettin' drunk, in that order.'

Tom grinned. 'No, you won't. You'll be awake early, tossing and turning and trying to get back to sleep again, and then you'll be kicking your heels for most of the day. In the evenings you'll take that girlfriend of yours to the flicks or dancing, then when it all gets too much you'll be glad to get back here.'

'You've gotta be jossin' me,' Pat laughed. 'There's no way I'll be lookin' forward ter comin' back ter this camp, ter this God-forsaken part o' the country.'

Tom grinned. 'All right, you just wait and see,' he replied. 'When I got that shell splinter in my shoulder on my second trip and they patched me up I got a seven-day pass. It was lovely for the first couple of days, but then I got restless. My girlfriend got me looking at engagement rings at every opportunity and she was constantly making plans for us after the war was over. How could I tell her that every time we go on a bombing mission the odds shorten and we'll be bloody lucky to live to see the end of the year, let alone the war.'

'We'll see it out,' Pat said encouragingly. 'You an' me both.'

'I like your style,' Tom Darcy replied. 'Ever the optimist.'

'What else is there?'

'Acceptance.'

'Of what? Not reaching the magical twenty ops?'

Tom leaned forward on the bed, clasping his hands. 'Yeah, that's about it,' he said quietly. 'I've accepted that sooner or later I'm going to cop it, and I've told myself that it doesn't matter whether it's on the next trip or the nineteenth. That way I don't worry so much. All right, I say a silent prayer every time we lift off, but then after that I try not to think about it. I think about the poetry I've read that day, and I look around at the planes flying in formation and wonder what torments the crews are suffering as we approach the target. It makes me feel detached, complacent in a way, though not about my job on that mission. I realise that I'm there in that tail bubble to help protect the aircraft and crew, but I tell myself that everyone on the flight's tempting fate, the hunter with a giant hand that can reach out and pluck any of us out of the sky in a moment. Sometimes when we turn for home and my spirits surge I start to think about a piece of poetry that's impressed me and try to add my own verses to it. That's my acceptance, Pat my friend.'

Pat Flynn was quiet for a while, absorbing what Tom had said, then he swung his legs over the edge of the bed and sat facing him. 'It's said that we should all be aware of our mortality, Tom, but I couldn't function if I 'ad ter dwell on that advice,' he replied. 'I look forward to a bright future in a peaceful world, wiv a wife an' kids, a nice 'ome ter live in an' a good job ter go to. I dream about my kids growin' up wivout the fear of war, an' eventually bringin' their kids round ter see us. That's what I cling to. That's what keeps me from crackin' up.'

'You hang on to that, Pat,' his friend said smiling. 'Dream hard enough and it'll see you through.'

On Saturday night Brenda and Jennie walked arm in arm to the Trocadero cinema at the Elephant and Castle and sat through a dreary pre-war melodrama, in which the heroine finally died of consumption and the hero sought comfort in the arms of the heroine's younger sister. Jennie wiped the

occasional tear away while Brenda was still trying unsuc-
cessfully to get involved in the story. Her thoughts were
elsewhere, prompted by the letter from Pat that she carried in
her handbag, and as the film drew to its close she had
finalised her own script. She would be the heroine and Pat
the hero, but their story would have a happy ending. Daring,
shocking, and one to keep the people talking.

'Stupid film,' Jennie said sniffing, as they walked out into
the moonlit night.

'Yeah, it was a bit morbid, wasn't it?' Brenda agreed as
they set off home along the New Kent Road.

'Never mind, it'll be great ter see Pat next weekend,'
Jennie reminded her.

'I can't wait,' Brenda sighed. 'I'm takin' the followin'
week off. I wanna spend as much time as I can wiv 'im. I've
only seen 'im twice this year an' I'm missin' 'im terrible.'

Jennie smiled sympathetically. 'Those forty-eight-hour
passes don't give yer much time tergevver, do they?'

Brenda shook her head. 'When I got the letter this mornin'
I answered it straight away,' she said. 'Pat should get it early
next week. I told 'im I was takin' the week off an' I said . . .'

'It's all right, luv, yer don't need ter tell me,' Jennie said,
sensing her friend's sudden embarrassment.

'Jennie, would yer mind me askin' you a very personal
question?' Brenda ventured.

'Nah, course not,' Jennie replied with a smile. 'We are
good friends.'

''Ave you . . . I mean, are you an' Con . . .'

'Lovers?'

'Yeah, that's what I was tryin' ter say.'

'We made love the night before 'e went back off leave,'

Jennie said matter-of-factly. 'It was the first time fer us an' I wanted ter give Con somefing ter remember while 'e's away. I'm pretty certain 'e'd never made love wiv a gel before an' it made what we did seem right an' good. What must it be like fer a young man ter go off an' fight a war wivout ever experiencin' love.'

'Me an' Pat 'ave never done it,' Brenda said bravely, encouraged by Jennie's forthrightness.

'No, I didn't fink you 'ad,' Jennie remarked.

'Does it show wiv us?'

'No, it's just circumstances that make me say that,' Jennie replied. 'You an' Pat were like two little peas in a pod when you were kids. Love didn't come along an' kick you right where it 'urts, it was always there, an' I imagine it grew wiv yer both. I've always thought that you two would find it difficult ter suddenly become lovers in the full sense o' the word. You know what they say, chaste down the aisle an' chased into bed.'

'You're very perceptive,' Brenda told her, 'an' you're dead right. We agreed ter wait till after we were married, but fings 'ave changed now. Like you just said, 'ow terrible fer a young man ter die wivout knowin' what love was all about. 'Ow terrible fer the gel that's left wiv nuffink for 'er to 'ang on to.'

They held arms tightly as they turned into the Old Kent Road, sensing a new closeness between them.

'I'm scared, Jennie,' Brenda said suddenly. 'I'm scared that one day Pat won't return from a bombin' mission an' I'll be left alone. I can't let that 'appen.'

'It won't, luv,' Jennie said kindly. 'You an' Pat were made fer each ovver an' you'll get married one day when all this is

370

over. I'm sure God's lookin' out fer the two of yer.'

'I was gonna tell yer about that letter I sent to 'im,' Brenda remarked. 'I told 'im just 'ow I felt an' I said I wanted us ter become lovers. Does that sound awful?'

Jennie laughed aloud. 'I fink it sounds wonderful.'

'I want us ter go away fer a week, somewhere nice an' quiet in the country,' Brenda went on.

They turned into the backstreets, walking through Defoe Street into Carter Lane, and Brenda turned to face her confidante as they reached her front door. 'Fanks fer lettin' me bend yer ear,' she said smiling.

'An' fank you fer lettin' me in on yer plans,' Jennie replied, returning her friend's smile. 'Yer secret's safe wiv me. You two should grab every bit of 'appiness yer can. Me an' Con did, an' it'll sustain us both while we're apart.'

Brenda smiled shyly as she reached into her handbag for her front-door key. 'It won't be much of a secret when both our families find out we intend ter spend a week away tergevver,' she remarked.

'Don't let it worry yer, Brenda. You can 'andle it, I'm sure,' Jennie replied with a saucy wink.

Pat Flynn's mind dwelt on the coming leave as he fitted himself into the cramped gun turret. 'Please God get me through this night,' he mouthed aloud as the engines roared into life.

The Wellington bomber lifted up into the night sky, banking to join the gathering air armada that was bound for Cologne. The planes flew in tactical formation out towards Holland, above a sea that looked calm and empty. Ahead there were gauntlets of gunfire to run, and maybe night fighters to contend with, but for the moment there was just the noise of the calibrated engines. As they neared the target, flak began to burst around them and they could see fires raging from incendiaries dropped by the pathfinders. Over the target the calm voice of the bomb-aimer could be heard on the intercom. 'Left, left, steady now. Bombs away!'

Bursting cannon shells splintered fuselages and peppered wings, and Pat saw a Wellington going down in flames. 'Did anyone get out?' the pilot shouted into the intercom.

'No one.'

Another Wellington lost a wing and it spiralled down, and yet another spurted flame from one of its engines.

'All right, chaps, let's get this kite back to Blighty. Christ! We're losing oil from the port engine.'

Another bomber lost its tail section and turned over before dropping down in a large arc. Pat saw three parachutes billowing out below and gritted his teeth. If the three were lucky they'd spend the rest of the war in a prison camp, but stories were emerging of flyers being killed summarily by Gestapo units. Gunfire increased and the pilot made a quick manoeuvre to dodge the searchlights, then came the race for the coast. The port engine was faltering but they managed to maintain their height and Pat experienced a glorious feeling of release as the enemy coast slipped away below them.

The remainder of the journey home was accomplished with crossed fingers as the port engine threatened to pack up altogether and it spluttered and faded as the airfield came into view. The pilot made a perfect touchdown, and as the plane taxied to the side apron the jeeps were ready. The tired, shaky crew were transported to the debriefing hut where other crews were already giving their accounts of the mission.

'I saw number seven go down in flames.'

'I can confirm that.'

'Did anyone get out?'

'No one.'

'There was no time.'

Tom and his crew had not returned and Pat sat on the step of the billet waiting for any stragglers to fly in, but as the dawn light filtered into the sky he realised with sickness in his stomach that the names of Tom Darcy and his crew would join the ever-growing list of flyers killed in action.

The lonely billet was hard to face now. All that remained were a few possessions in the locker, and the book of poems lying there on the bottom of Tom's crumpled bed. 'What does it matter,' he had said. 'The ninth or the nineteenth.' He was gone now, for ever, his spirit lost to earth among the heavens.

The book was dog-eared from constant use, the cover grubby and stained, but Pat clutched it to his chest with delicate reverence, the most valuable book he would ever hold. The days ahead would never be the same now and he slumped down on Tom's unmade bed, his tears falling as he cried in the painful solitude of the quiet billet.

Chapter Thirty-Two

Brenda Ross was employed as a secretary in an old-established firm of solicitors in the City and her elderly boss was very sympathetic to her request for a week off outside the holiday season. She had been truthful in explaining that her future husband was coming home on leave and she wished to spend some time with him. Simon Whatley was aware that Brenda's young man was a flyer, and with a son of his own flying Spitfires he knew just how she felt.

'Yes, of course we'll manage, Brenda,' he said kindly. 'Miss Fredericks can stand in for you and it'll give her some good experience. You just enjoy your time together.'

Frank and Iris Ross were not so accommodating however, and they reacted with alarm and dismay that their daughter could be so brazen as to go away for a whole week with Pat Flynn before they were married.

'It's not right,' Iris told her. 'Me an' yer farvver 'ave always tried ter bring yer up right an' you end up lettin' us both down. I'm really shocked.'

Brenda shrugged her shoulders. 'I'm sorry, Mum, but you 'ave to understand the way fings are,' she replied. 'Me an' Pat are gonna get married anyway when the war's over an' if we could we'd get married sooner.'

'That's not the point,' Iris went on. 'A young gel should go ter the altar pure. The ovver business should wait.'

Brenda looked at her mother with disgust. 'Ovver business? Is that what you call it?' she stormed. 'I'd prefer ter call it love.'

'Well, I'd call it lust,' Iris said sharply. 'You young gels don't seem to 'ave any morals at all. I tell you somefing, I wouldn't 'ave dared go ter my muvver wiv the news that I was gonna spend a week away wiv a young man. Me an' yer farvver did fings right an' we expect you ter do the same.'

'Yeah, but you've gotta remember it was peacetime when you an' Dad got married,' Brenda puffed. 'The war's changed fings, changed people's way of lookin' at fings.'

'Oh yeah, blame the war,' Iris growled. 'I s'pose yer'll blame the war if yer go an' get yerself pregnant.'

Brenda felt tears of anger rising and she swallowed hard. 'Turn that wireless on any mornin' an' listen ter the news,' she said furiously. 'Yer'll 'ear about last night's bombin' raid over Germany. Listen ter the end of it, the bit about the number o' planes that failed ter return. I listen to it, an' every time I 'ear those words I go ice cold. I fink of Pat an' I wonder if the Flynns are gonna be one o' the families who get a telegram ter say their son's amongst the crews shot down. The way I see it, Pat's livin' on borrered time an' me an' 'im are gonna grab what 'appiness we can while we can, an' if God willin' 'e survives the war I'll be quite 'appy ter walk down the aisle wivout wearin' white.'

Iris realised that she was never going to make her daughter see reason and she sighed in resignation. 'I can't stop yer doin' what yer've planned but fer goodness' sake be careful,' she warned. 'I couldn't 'old me 'ead up round 'ere if yer got yerself pregnant.'

On the cold autumn weekend that Brenda and Pat were reunited, Sadie came home to hear that Joe had managed to get a forty-eight-hour pass.

'Joe called in an' we've 'ad a nice chat,' Dolly told her. 'I said to 'im yer'd give 'im a knock soon as yer got 'ome.'

'I must look a right mess,' Sadie fussed as she studied herself in the parlour wall mirror.

'Yer look just fine, luv,' Dolly remarked, 'but before yer go there's somefing in terday's paper I wanna show yer. It's about that Macaulay bloke. 'E's bin shot dead.'

'Shot dead? I can't believe it!' Sadie gasped as she grabbed the newspaper.

'Bermondsey Businessman Murdered.

The body of Johnnie Macaulay was discovered late last night on the steps of a Brighton hotel. He had been shot twice in the chest and was pronounced dead on arrival at the hospital.

Macaulay was a successful Bermondsey businessman and entrepreneur whose interests included boxing and greyhound racing. He was recently involved in a business deal with a South Coast consortium and the Brighton police have declined to make any comment other than that they are treating his death as murder.'

'You did the right fing givin' Len Regan the elbow,' Dolly told her. 'Whoever killed Macaulay could be after Regan too.'

'I've gone all cold,' Sadie said in a shocked voice. 'I met some o' those people once an' they scared me ter death.'

'Well, it's not your worry now,' Dolly said positively.

Sadie hurried along to the Kennys' home and Big Joe met her at the front door with a big hug. 'You look very nice,' he said smiling broadly.

'I've just got 'ome,' Sadie replied. 'My 'air looks a real mess.'

'How about me taking you out for something to eat,' Joe suggested.

'Now?'

'Why not?'

'Where can we go?'

'What about your old Saturday usual?'

'Pie an' mash?'

'If you like.'

'I'd love it,' Sadie said enthusiastically.

'I'll just go and get me cap,' Joe said. 'I don't wanna get caught improperly dressed, though there's not much chance of running into a shore patrol in the Old Kent Road.'

They strolled out of Carter Lane chatting busily, with Sadie holding his arm and leaning close against him. 'This is a lovely surprise,' she remarked as they walked out into the Old Kent Road.

'I'm being posted abroad very soon,' he told her. 'I don't know where yet but the old bush telegraph has it as Gibraltar.'

'Will you get embarkation leave, Joe?' she asked.

He shook his head and sighed. 'It's all very hush-hush. We could be off like a bucket o' prawns in the sun.'

They walked into the pie shop and joined the queue,

watching as the shop assistant served up steaming-hot meat pies and large scoops of mashed potato, topped with a liberal amount of parsley liquor, as well as stewed or jellied eels in thick china bowls.

'Do you know something,' Joe said. 'When I first arrived in London I couldn't abide this sort of food, but now I love it. Just watching it being served up makes me mouth water.'

'Yeah, me too,' Sadie replied. 'When we were kids I used ter take our tribe down ter Manzies' pie shop in Tower Bridge Road fer our Saturday dinner. I was in charge o' the money.'

'Do you wanna double up?' Joe asked her.

'Double up?'

'Yeah, have a double portion.'

'No, I couldn't manage that much, but you double up,' she told him smiling.

They were finally served and they found a bench seat at the back of the crowded establishment, chatting together between mouthfuls of food, and later as they strolled along the wide thoroughfare looking at the shops Joe slipped his arm around her waist and steered her to a vacant wooden bench beneath a tall spreading plane tree. 'Let's sit down for a second, I've got something to show you,' he said mysteriously.

Sadie waited intrigued as Joe took a tiny cloth-covered box from his greatcoat pocket. 'I want you to have this,' he said, opening the box with care.

Sadie saw the ring with its single diamond and gasped. 'You mean this is fer me?'

Joe nodded. 'It's been sewn into the side of a grubby old bag o' mine for years, an' even when I was living on the bones of me arse without a brass razoo I never dreamt of selling it. It was left in trust for me when I was a kid and I could never find out who it was from. It's been like a big silent mystery in me life, and it made me think that sometimes something happens to you that's too mysterious and too big for you to understand. I felt like I wanted to give it to you.'

Sadie stared down at it and blinked hard before she looked up into his deep blue eyes. 'What a lovely thought,' she said with feeling.

Joe looked embarrassed as he took the ring from the box. 'Let me see if it fits your finger,' he said.

'It's perfect,' she sighed.

Joe smiled, and was taken by surprise as Sadie kissed him on the lips. 'I'm glad you like it,' he said.

'Like it? I love it,' she whispered. 'It's so beautiful.'

They set off back to Carter Lane with Sadie chatting eagerly about her nursing job, trying to calm the excitement fluttering inside her, and as they turned into Defoe Street a large car pulled up beside them. Sadie turned and saw Nosher beckoning to her and she leant down to the open window.

'I was just comin' round ter see yer, Sadie,' he told her urgently. 'It's all gone boss-eyed. Macaulay's bin done in an' Len Regan's 'idin' out.'

'I read about Macaulay,' Sadie replied. 'It was in terday's paper.'

'Len wants ter see yer,' Nosher said. 'There ain't much time.'

Sadie looked at Big Joe anxiously and he nodded. 'It's all right, I'll come with you,' he said.

'I dunno about that,' Nosher replied quickly.

Big Joe fixed the older man with a hard look. 'She goes nowhere without me, mate,' he growled.

'All right then, I ain't got time to argue wiv yer,' Nosher said impatiently. 'Get in.'

They climbed into the back of the large saloon car and Nosher put his foot down, swinging it back into the Old Kent Road. 'Regan's 'idin' out in Lambeth,' he said. ''E's wiv Donna Walsh. You remember 'er?'

'Yeah, I remember 'er,' Sadie replied.

Joe looked bemused by the situation and he glanced at Sadie. 'This Macaulay joker. Wasn't he the gang boss you were telling me about?'

'Yeah,' Nosher piped in. 'I run Macaulay down ter Brighton two days ago an' then yesterday Len Regan told me ter stand by ter take 'im down there too. The next fing I know is the Walsh gel's bangin' on me front door last night. Two geezers came in The George pub askin' fer Len, an' when 'e fronted 'em one o' the bastards knifed 'im.'

'Oh my God!' Sadie gasped. ''Ow terrible. Is 'e 'urt bad?'

''E got it in the stomach but they fetched a doctor ter patch 'im up. 'E'll be all right so the quack said but 'e's very weak from loss o' blood. It's that bastard Brighton mob what done it, excuse me language.'

'What does 'e want wiv me?' Sadie asked him.

Nosher shrugged his shoulders. 'Donna Walsh 'as cracked up an' Len's fast run out o' friends. We're all 'e's got left.'

They reached the Elephant and Castle and crossed the wide thoroughfare into Lambeth Road. 'I'll need ter drop yer off short,' Nosher told them. 'There may be someone on the lookout an' they'll recognise the car. I'll wait where I drop you off till I 'ear from yer. It's number nineteen Fensome Lane, 'alfway down Lambeth Walk. Be careful 'ow yer go.'

Sadie and Joe walked along the main road and turned into the little backstreet trying to look as unobtrusive as possible, but they were observed by two bulky men wearing dark overcoats who were standing across the street. As they reached the front door of number 19 the two men had come up behind them. 'Visitin' Mr Regan, are we?' one asked.

Joe turned round casually. 'I don't know about you two, but we've come to see Mrs Brown,' he said calmly.

'On yer way, sailor boy, an' take yer bit o' skirt wiv yer,' the man growled. 'This 'ouse is out o' bounds.'

'Shut your bunghole and choof off, drongo,' Joe growled back at him as he raised his hand to the doorknocker.

One of the men grabbed Joe by the lapels of his coat while the other one quickly pulled out a switchblade but the big Australian butted the first one across the bridge of his nose and swung him round towards the knifeman. Sadie had moved away out of reach and she watched in awe as Joe threw the bloodied villain at his compatriot and smartly planted a size eleven shoe in a tender spot. The man screamed out as he doubled up and Joe punched the knife-man in the throat and grabbed his wrist. The switchblade went spinning into the gutter and the few onlookers who had stopped to watch stood wide-eyed as the assailant did a cartwheel onto the pavement. A broken nose, a dislocated shoulder and a painful groin were enough to send the two villains scampering off in panic and Joe smiled. 'That navy training is the bloody business,' he remarked. 'Are you okay?'

Sadie nodded, still trying to control her shaking. 'I've never bin so frightened in all me life,' she gasped.

Donna Walsh looked pale and gaunt as she led the two into the dark passage and up the bare staircase to the first floor. ''E's in 'ere,' she said, pushing open the door and standing to one side.

Sadie and Joe walked into the dingy room and saw Len Regan sitting back in an armchair with his hand pressed to his side. He was unshaven and dressed in bloodstained trousers and a heavy sweater. 'I'm sorry, Sadie, but I 'ad ter try an' contact yer,' he said in a tired voice. 'Yer've 'eard about Johnnie?'

'Yeah, it was in the papers.'

The villain looked up at Joe. 'Are you . . .?'

'My boyfriend,' Sadie cut in. 'An yer've got 'im ter fank fer sortin' out those two 'orrible gits outside.'

'You sorted 'em out?' Len replied with a surprised look.

'Yeah, they weren't very friendly,' Joe said sarcastically.

'I'm sorry, Sadie, but I thought yer'd come alone an' I was 'opin' they'd fink you was visitin' the people upstairs.'

'Well, it's a good job I didn't come alone,' she countered.

Len winced at the pain in his side. 'I really didn't want you dragged inter this,' he puffed, 'but Donna's crackin' up an' she can't 'andle it. Those two goons outside were just watchin' in case I tried ter get away. The big man 'imself's due any time now an' I'm trapped 'ere.'

'Who's the big man?' Sadie asked.

'It doesn't matter, you wouldn't know 'im anyway, but 'e's out ter get me the same way 'e got Johnnie.'

'But why?' Sadie asked in confusion.

'It's too long a story an' too complicated,' Len replied,

'but if I tell yer Johnnie Macaulay was rippin' the consortium off yer'll understand.'

'Skimming the profits?' Joe remarked.

Len nodded. 'That an' more. I warned Johnnie but 'e wouldn't listen. 'E underestimated 'em. Country bumpkins 'e called 'em. Some bumpkins.'

'We gotta get you out of 'ere before those two get some 'elp,' Sadie said anxiously. 'Joe, 'elp 'im up an' I'll get Donna.'

They stepped out into the afternoon sunlight with Sadie holding on to the distraught Donna's arm and Joe following, holding up Regan. Two streets away they saw the car and it quickly drove across to them. Len Regan was manoeuvred into the front seat of the saloon then Sadie, Donna and Joe climbed into the back, and Nosher breathed a huge sigh of relief as he accelerated away from the kerb. 'I wasn't sure if you was gonna make it,' he said, glancing quickly round at Sadie.

'Fanks a lot,' she replied with some humour, then she leaned forward and touched Len on the shoulder. ''Ave you got somewhere ter go?' she asked him.

'Yeah, I got a pal up North,' he told her. ''E'll let me an' Nosher stay there till fings quieten down.'

'An' then?'

'I've got some money stashed away,' Len replied. 'I'll start again. Me an' Nosher tergevver.'

Sadie looked at the woman sitting beside her, her bloated face wet with tears. 'An' Donna?'

'Yeah, Donna too,' Len said. 'She needs the country air more than I do.'

Joe and Sadie stepped out of the saloon on the corner of

Lynton Road and set off to walk the short distance to Carter Lane.

'Joe, I'm sorry. I wouldn't 'ave wished this on yer for the world,' she said humbly.

He grinned a little lopsidedly, the grin that Sadie had come to love. 'No sweat, kid,' he replied.

'You were wonderful the way you 'andled those two men,' she told him.

'It was no trouble,' he said grinning even wider. 'That character Popeye does it on spinach; Big Joe does it on pie an' mash. I just hope it's not all been in vain.'

''E'll make it,' Sadie remarked. 'I've learnt the 'ard way that Len Regan's a no-good, liberty-takin' git, but 'e's one o' those who'll fall over in shit an' come up smellin' o' roses. Besides 'e's got Nosher, an' Donna, God 'elp 'im.'

Chapter Thirty-Three

Brenda had found the Gloucestershire country hotel in a *Tatler* magazine that was lying around in the waiting room at her office and it seemed perfect. There were nice colour photographs of the grounds, and the prices did not seem too expensive. It was advertised as being open all year round and ideal for a quiet retreat from wartime city life. With fingers crossed she phoned the hotel from the office during her lunchtime and was able to make a reservation for a week in a double room under the name of Mr and Mrs Parkes, her mother's maiden name. She then slipped out of the office and did something which she prayed she would be forgiven for. She went into a jeweller's shop and bought a cheap imitation gold band, the sort women wore when they had secretly pawned their wedding ring.

Brenda had always considered herself to be a Christian, although she was not a regular churchgoer, and what she had done troubled her that afternoon. Maybe it would be taking the Lord's name in vain slipping on the ring without the blessing and vows, but in her heart she felt that God understood. She was doing this out of love, and if her plan worked out fully she would know that God had really colluded.

On Monday morning Brenda and Pat set off from Paddington Station, relaxing in a comfortable carriage along with two elderly ladies dressed in tweeds with hats pulled down over their coiffured grey hair. When the train pulled in at Swindon two soldiers got into the carriage and sat chatting quietly together. The ladies talked occasionally, mainly in monosyllables and nods, but everyone seemed to keep to themselves and Brenda was content. One slip of the tongue, one unthinking word might serve to ruin the pretence, and for a whole week they wanted to masquerade as Mr and Mrs Parkes.

It was mid-afternoon when the train pulled into Cirencester and soon the two young people were speeding through the country lanes in an ancient taxi. Pat was wearing his uniform with a brevet over the left breast pocket, a single wing and the letters AG enclosed. Brenda wore a heavy fawn winter coat and high-heeled shoes, with a silver scarf wrapped loosely around her neck. Her fair hair was cropped short and waved around her ears and she carried a brown leather handbag.

'There we are, sir,' the driver said as he steered the car into the gravel drive of the Firscroft Hotel. 'I hope you'll enjoy your stay.'

Pat tipped the driver and Brenda suppressed a giggle as the man touched his forehead in a salute before driving off.

'Come on, Mrs Parkes,' Pat said with a grin as he picked up the large suitcase.

The proprietress smiled as she pushed the register towards Pat. 'We're usually pretty quiet at this time of year but we do have a few guests who stay here regularly,' she remarked. 'If you'll bear with me I'll see if I can find Norman. I'm Mrs

Withers by the way. Actually I'm holding the fort for my husband. He's in the navy.'

Brenda took Pat's hand in hers and gave it an encouraging squeeze as the woman went out. She soon returned followed by an elderly man who shuffled along behind her with stooped shoulders.

'Show our guests to room sixteen, Norman,' Mrs Withers told him. 'Oh by the way, dinner's served from seven thirty till ten and breakfast is at seven till nine thirty. If there's anything you need, do come and see me.'

Norman led the way along a corridor grunting with the weight of the case and Pat wished he had offered to carry it. The florin brought a warm smile to the old man's face though and he shuffled off to make himself scarce.

Once they were alone Pat took Brenda in his arms and kissed her. 'Just fink of it,' he said sighing contentedly. 'One 'ole glorious week wiv just you an' me.'

She hugged him tightly. 'This'll be our unofficial 'oneymoon an' I want it ter be perfect, Pat,' she said with feeling.

'It will be, darlin',' he told her. 'Let's unpack an' take a look round before dinner.'

The Firscroft was set amid rolling hills and was fairly isolated, with just a hamlet called Oakley about half a mile westwards. The two young people walked hand in hand along the winding lane towards the small village through a crisp carpet of fallen leaves. Overhead the sky was leaden, a winter dusk that brought a chill and Brenda shivered.

'You're cold, let's get back,' Pat said quickly.

'It's all right, I just 'ad a bad moment,' Brenda replied.

'A bad moment?'

'Yeah, I was just finkin' of us tergevver an' 'ow fragile it all is.'

'Not us. Not our feelin's,' Pat remarked with a supportive squeeze of her hand.

'No, not us, the situation we're in,' Brenda said sighing. 'I couldn't 'elp finkin' 'ow the war could so easily take it all away from us. All our plans, all the love we share. If anyfing 'appened ter you I could never share a love wiv anybody else.'

Pat was about to reply but the drone of an aircraft in the evening sky grew very loud as it passed overhead above the sodden clouds. Brenda was right, how fragile it all was. Fate was the hunter and life itself was made of fleeting moments, of happiness taken greedily and unashamedly, of filling one's cup to the full, and an acceptance of it all. 'Believe me, darlin', we'll grow old tergevver,' he said with conviction. 'You'll come ter feel it too, as time goes by.'

They had their evening meal in the tastefully decorated dining room and took the opportunity of discreetly studying the other guests. There was an elderly couple who hardly spoke, the heavy-set woman idly glancing around while her husband read a folded evening paper as he ate. Another couple were sitting nearby, younger and obviously in love. The man was paying a lot of attention to his vivacious partner and she responded with demure smiles. Another guest sat alone at a table, a bulky middle-aged man in a tweed suit and brown bow tie over a cream shirt. He ate the meal with relish and beckoned with a mouthful of dessert to the frail-looking waitress for some coffee. The one other diner was an old lady who picked at her food, her eyes darting around like a bird wary of capture.

The vegetable soup and the main dish of plaice were delicious and the sweet of raspberry trifle and coffee served in tiny cups rounded the meal off to perfection. Later, as the cold winter night cloaked the countryside, Pat sat trying to read the evening paper while he waited for Brenda to finish in the bathroom. After a while he folded the paper up and leaned back in the settee, staring up at the ceiling and its ornate cornices lit by the bedlamp, and he began to feel increasingly nervous. Both he and Brenda were inexperienced in the art of love and he desperately wanted to please her. She was a virgin and his total knowledge of physical love amounted to a youthful fumbling with a more worldly wise girl which had been little short of a disaster, at a time before he and Brenda had started going out together seriously. He would have to be careful too not to get her pregnant. She obviously trusted him and he dared not betray that trust.

'It's all yours,' she said as she emerged from the bathroom and Pat swallowed hard. She was wearing a long black diaphanous nightdress which clung to her shapely figure and complemented her fair hair, which she had fluffed up around her ears and over her forehead. She looked lovely and he struggled for words as she swayed towards him.

'Do yer like it?' she said with a shy smile.

'God, you look . . . you look gorgeous,' he fumbled.

She went over to the bed and pulled the covers back and Pat turned away from her to go into the bathroom, hardly daring to dally. He showered, shaved with care and dabbed on a sprinkling of lotion, then combed his short sandy hair back from his forehead. Last of all he cleaned his teeth, brushing furiously and hoping that the meal had not made his breath smell. He was feeling as nervous as a kitten as he donned his pyjama bottoms and stood looking at himself in the mirror. This was stupid, he told himself after another splash of spirit to his flushed face. This was supposed to be what men bragged about.

'Pat? Are you all right?' Brenda called out.

'Yeah, just finished.'

'Pat?'

'Yeah?'

'What are these fings under the piller?'

'Oh Christ!' he hissed under his breath. 'She wasn't s'posed ter find them.'

He walked into the bedroom looking at her sheepishly and saw the amused smile on her face. 'I gotta be careful, Brenda. We've both gotta be careful,' he said quickly. 'What 'appens if you get pregnant? I'd be well out of it, but you'd 'ave ter face the neighbours every day. Then there's yer muvver. God, she'd go mad. Yer dad too. What would 'e say?'

'Who ses I'm gonna get pregnant anyway?' Brenda replied. ''Ow d'yer know it's the week? Gels can't get pregnant any time. It's all ter do wiv the monthly cycle.'

'Yeah, I've read about that,' Pat said, 'but I 'appen ter know it's not certain. I read that some women fall fer kids any time.'

'Oh, so you're an expert on such matters, are yer?' she replied smiling.

'Don't wind me up, Brenda,' he pleaded. 'I'm scared.'

'Come 'ere, you big daft sod,' she said kindly, and then she pulled him to her and hugged him. 'Listen ter me an' get this inter that fick skull of yours. I'm not gonna let you use anyfing. I want this week ter be somefing I'll never ferget. I also want ter make a baby, our baby.'

'You can't be serious, Brenda,' he replied in a shocked voice. 'I've just spelled out the problems.'

'They won't be our problems,' she told him firmly. 'If my muvver an' dad are shocked then it's their problem. I want our baby an' if God ferbid somefing 'appens ter you there'd still be a part of you wiv me fer ever. Can't you see?'

'I can see what yer mean, but I don't fink you've thought it frew,' Pat said anxiously. ''Ow could you support the child? You'd 'ave ter pack up work. And fink of the stigma.'

'Sod the stigma an' sod the consequences,' she growled. 'Pat, I want your child an' I've never bin so sure of anyfing in my 'ole life. Now will you reach over an' turn that bleedin' lamp out, or shall we leave it on?'

He sighed in resignation, switching off the light and lying down in her arms, suddenly realising that he was calm, deeply calm, and he could sense that she was too. She caressed him as he stroked her soft skin through the satin nightdress, feeling the delicious roundness of her young body. 'God, you're beautiful,' he gasped.

She eased herself up, allowing him to slip her nightdress off her, and as she slipped it over her head he kicked his pyjama bottoms off. They lay side by side, their warm skin touching, and his hands gently moved down from her stomach, feeling the small bulge and the softness of her pubic mound. She was wet and ready and he let her take control, easing him into her. He arched his body and pressed, and she stiffened as he broke her maidenhead, then she found his lips and he responded, kissing her with all the passion he could no longer contain while he hardly moved inside her. He was on the verge and so was she, and with a cry of excitement she moved quickly on him and he suddenly exploded.

They lay locked together, he recovering his breath and she purring with satisfaction. 'It was very quick, but it was complete, darlin',' she told him.

'I couldn't wait any longer,' he said as he moved and raised himself up on one arm. 'I was so scared of spoilin' it for yer.'

'Let me 'old yer,' she sighed. 'Sleep, darlin'. Sleep sweetly.'

Outside the barren trees moved like dervishes in the rising wind and the heavy cloud began to scud across the dark sky, revealing brief glimpses of a waxing moon. A night creature screamed and the window frames rattled, but nothing troubled the young lovers. Pat breathed shallowly in Brenda's arms as she lay awake beneath the warm blankets, utterly contented and feeling more than a little wicked. Poor Pat. He had looked so shocked. He moved and mumbled her name and she squeezed him to her. What the future held for them both was in the lap of the gods, she knew, but nothing and no one could take away the memories they would both carry away with them when the week was over.

Snow fell and settled, and the countryside was a pure white blanket as the train rattled on towards London. Two young people sat in the corner of the crowded compartment, their bodies touching, their hands clasped. Neither spoke for a long time, each wrapped up in dreams and the warmth of a fulfilled love. Soon he would be flying again, and she would wait, every morning dreading the words 'Some of our aircraft are missing.' Waiting and hoping, praying and wondering, and at the same time, please God, eager for the first signs to let her know that the Almighty had smiled down sympathetically on their liaison, that she was carrying Pat's child.

Chapter Thirty-Four

The Carter Lane folk celebrated the Christmas of '41 with a new-found optimism. America had now come into the war and there had been some military successes in the Middle East, while in Europe Russian troops had managed to hold up the German advances and were now counter-attacking on a wide front. At home the weather was very cold and the food shortages were becoming more severe, but the general feeling was that in the coming year things were going to get much better.

Early in January Brenda Ross went to the hospital, where it was confirmed that she was pregnant. Now she faced the task of breaking the news to her parents and she was determined to make them see that it was what she had hoped and prayed for. She knew how much they both loved her and was sure that after the initial shock they would be sure to rally round her. What she was not prepared for, however, was her mother's first reaction.

'I knew it,' Iris said calmly. 'Muvvers can sense these fings an' I could see it in yer face.'

'In me face?'

'Yeah, yer look like yer face 'as filled out a bit an' yer eyes are bright.'

Brenda took a deep breath. 'Look, Mum, this wasn't an accident,' she began. 'I wanted Pat's child an' I 'ad ter talk 'im into it. It wasn't easy.'

'No, an' I'd 'ope not,' Iris said indignantly. 'As a rule men don't seem ter realise that it's the woman who 'as ter bear the brunt of 'avin' children, not them.'

'I expected a different reaction, ter tell yer the trufe,' Brenda said. 'I thought yer'd go off alarmin'.'

'Don't you worry, yer dad will when 'e finds out,' Iris replied. 'I knew what you was up to though, but what could I say ter dissuade yer? You're not stupid, you know the implications. There's the neighbours fer a start. They'll be givin' you a right name. Then there's the money ter fink of. Yer'll lose yer job an' babies 'ave ter be fed.'

'Don't worry, I've got some money put away,' Brenda said. 'It's not a lot but it'll tide me over fer a while. Pat'll make me an allowance as well. I'll get by.'

'We'll get by,' Iris told her in a firm voice.

Brenda hugged her tightly. 'I'm very lucky to 'ave a mum like you,' she said affectionately. 'Some gels would 'ave bin turned out onter the street.'

'I can understand why yer've done this,' Iris remarked, 'but it's a big step, a big decision, an' yer gotta be sure that yer can face up to it. If anyfing 'appens ter Pat, God ferbid, it's gonna be very 'ard for yer, an' me an' yer dad won't always be around to 'elp yer out.'

'Don't worry, Mum, I've thought all this frew very carefully,' Brenda said quietly. 'I want Pat's child more than I've ever wanted anyfing in me 'ole life. We do love each ovver.'

'I should bloody well 'ope so,' Iris replied with passion. 'Yer'll 'ave ter get married as soon as yer can now.'

Brenda nodded. 'I'm gonna write ter Pat ternight,' she said. 'Wiv a bit o' luck they'll give 'im some leave. In the meantime I'll go an' see the vicar at St James's Church an' get the banns put up.'

'Yer'll need Pat wiv yer, I would 'ave thought,' Iris told her.

'I dunno, but I'll see the vicar anyway,' Brenda replied, then she smiled. 'I just 'ope Dad's as understandin' as you about it.'

'Yer'd better let me break it to 'im,' Iris suggested. 'When 'e comes in you make yerself scarce, till the dust settles.'

'Promise me somefing, Mum,' Brenda said. 'If anyfing 'appens ter stop me an' Pat gettin' married quickly don't let the neighbours get ter yer. There'll be a lot o' talk once I start ter show, it's only ter be expected, but decent people will understand. They won't all be callin' me a loose woman.'

'Well, at least we'll 'ave one family on our side,' Iris remarked.

Early in January '42 a secret high-level meeting was held at the War Office in Whitehall, and gathered together with the chiefs of staff of the armed forces and top Government ministers was a tall, studious-looking individual who went by the code name 'Moonbeam'. He held the floor for fifteen minutes, and when he finished speaking anxiety and concern was etched on everyone's face.

'We sent out two agents,' Moonbeam began. 'They were successful in making contact with the appropriate French resistance workers and able to confirm that highly skilled aeronautical engineers have been dispatched to Germany along with Albert Deschard, the French scientist, who's known to be top in his field, the development of rocket fuel. What's more, Deschard was reportedly seen recently at Peenemünde on the Baltic. Reconnaissance photos of the area tell us that there's a large building programme going on there. It's early days yet, but all the signs point to the site being made ready for the construction and deployment of revolutionary weapons that would have a far-reaching and devastating effect on long-range targets. We have no choice but to destroy the works before they become operational. Any delay could well change the whole course of the war.'

Air Chief Marshal James stroked his chin thoughtfully. 'It would be a long-distance mission, the losses could be catastrophic,' he pointed out.

Moonbeam nodded. 'Unfortunately I don't see that we have any alternative,' he replied. 'Our information tells us that the buildings under construction are very well guarded, as well as being isolated. Sabotage would not achieve the necessary results, even if our agents could penetrate the complex. The building programme is far too extensive.'

Air Chief Marshal James met later with the war minister and top ranking officers of Bomber Command, and the decision was taken to send a heavy force of Lancasters to Peenemünde on the night of the next full moon.

Mick Flynn found himself outnumbered on Saturday evening, and without much encouragement from Dolly he decided to go to The Sun for a few drinks with Bert Kenny, whose wife Liz had been invited to the get-together at the Flynns' home.

'Yer can't talk wiv men around,' Dolly said. 'They're

eivver puttin' their spoke in or tryin' ter organise everyfing.'

'You're jokin', ain't yer?' Liz grinned. 'My Bert couldn't organise a piss-up in a brewery.'

Dolly smiled as she poured the tea into her best china cups. 'The reason I asked yer ter call in this evenin', Liz, is ter do wiv Brenda an' our Pat,' she remarked. 'I wanted you ter be the first ter know. They've decided ter get married.'

'Well, it's about time,' Liz replied. 'If any two kids are made fer each ovver it's those two. When's it ter be?'

'The first Saturday in March,' Dolly told her. 'It was touch an' go but they've allowed Pat a forty-eight-hour pass.'

'It's a bloody shame,' Liz remarked. 'They won't 'ave much time tergevver, will they?'

Jennie and Sadie had been sitting listening and they smiled at each other.

'They'll make it count,' Jennie said with a saucy smile.

Dolly ignored her. 'Brenda an' 'er muvver are comin' round soon, but I want you ter stay, Liz,' she said. 'We're gonna get fings organised in plenty o' time an' you can put yer two penn'orth in.'

'Are yer sure?' Liz asked.

'Course,' Dolly said quickly. 'You've always got on well wiv Iris Ross, an' after all, we're all neighbours tergevver. I'm gonna suggest we talk ter the vicar about 'irin' that big room be'ind the vestry, the one the scouts an' cubs use.'

'That'll be nice,' Liz replied. 'There's a joanna there an' my Bert's fick wiv the pianist at The Sun. 'E might be able ter persuade 'im ter play at the reception, unless yer know anybody else.'

Dolly shook her head. 'No, I'll leave that ter you, luv, soon as we can sort the room out.'

'I reckon the Jackmans'll chip in wiv an extra few rations,' Sadie said between sips of her tea. 'They're pretty good like that.'

'Will Brenda be in white, d'yer know?' Liz asked.

'I dunno, I expect so,' Dolly replied.

Jennie and Sadie exchanged quick glances. Both had been taken into Brenda's confidence and from what they had gathered from their friend, her mother was vehemently against her going down the aisle in white.

'It doesn't 'ave ter be white, does it?' Jennie queried. 'I'd be quite 'appy ter get married in blue or pink.'

'You would,' Dolly said, giving her a quick glance. 'Anyfing ter be different.'

Sadie smiled at her sister's comic expression. 'As long as yer take the vows an' it's all done wiv decorum what difference does it make what colour yer wear on the day?'

'It's all about purity, that's what,' Dolly told her. 'It's tradition.'

'Sod tradition,' Jennie growled under her breath.

At that point Brenda and her mother arrived, and after they had been given a cup of tea and made comfortable the conversation continued.

'Yer don't mind Liz bein' 'ere while we talk, do yer?' Dolly asked.

Iris Ross smiled. 'Of course not. The more the merrier. I'm 'opin' it'll be a big turn-out at the church too.'

Brenda sat by Jennie and Sadie at the table and Jennie secretly squeezed her hand in support as Iris began to lay out the plans for the day. 'I've bin lookin' at some rose-pink taffeta at that shop in Tower Bridge Road,' she remarked. 'You know the one, that does all the weddin' dresses.'

'So yer 'avin' pink then?' Dolly said.

Iris nodded as casually as she could. 'Yeah, it'll make up lovely, an' we've decided to 'ave my sister's two daughters as bridesmaids. Louisa's seven an' Betsy's goin' on nine. They're both beautiful kids wiv fair curly 'air. They're a right couple o' Shirley Temples.'

'I dunno who Pat's gonna 'ave as best man,' Dolly said, pinching her chin thoughtfully.

''E's tryin' ter get one of 'is mates at the camp ter do it,' Brenda cut in, 'but it all depends if they'll give 'im leave or not. It's very dicey at the moment, what wiv all the nightly raids goin' on.'

Dolly refilled the empty teacups and then made herself comfortable in the armchair. 'Now this is what I 'ad in mind . . .'

Pat Flynn reclined on the hard bed and stared up at the dusty rafters of the billet. The letter resting in his breast pocket had confirmed what he already knew in his heart, but try as he would he could not dispel the nagging fear deep down inside him that he might well never live long enough to see his son. It would be a son, he felt sure; fair-haired and bonny, and with his mother's looks. Seventeen missions under his belt and ten more still to go before his tour of ops was completed was not something he wanted to dwell on, but it was impossible to put it out of his mind in the way Tom Darcy had. Tom had been resigned to the fact that he would not survive his allotted missions but Pat now prayed harder than ever to be spared.

'Briefing in ten minutes,' the orderly sergeant called into the billet and Pat sat up quickly. There had been a lot of activity at the base lately, he recalled, with a couple of visits from the bomber group commander, and everyone seemed to sense that the next bombing mission was to be an important one involving the whole six-hundred-strong force of number five bomber group.

'The target for tonight is Peenemünde,' the camp commander said bluntly. 'We'll have a full moon and we'll be attacking in full strength.'

'Christ almighty!' a navigator sitting next to Pat exclaimed in the sudden hubbub of voices. 'That's in the Baltic, if I'm not mistaken.'

'You don't need me to remind you that you'll be flying over enemy territory for more than nine hours in all,' the commander continued, stabbing the large wall map with his pointer stick, 'so operational procedures and tactics will have to be strictly adhered to. This target is by far the most important one we've attacked yet and it's imperative that it's taken out. The full moon will assist you in precision bombing and I'm confident that you'll all give an excellent account of yourselves and the mission will be a totally successful one.'

While the pilots and navigators stayed behind for further briefing the rest of the crews left the hut looking very serious. The Berlin bombing raid had been bad enough but this was something else, and Pat went back to the quietness of his billet to write a letter to Brenda. When he had finished it he took out a folded slip of paper from inside the back cover of the poetry book Tom Darcy had given him and put it in with the letter. There was one more letter to write, to his family, and then he did something he had never done before. He went to the camp chapel.

Chapter Thirty-Five

The people of Carter Lane were proud of the contribution they had made to the war effort. Their sons and brothers had gone off to fight and they themselves had done their bit. Most of the men had been fire watchers or ARP wardens during the Blitz and Sadie Flynn was an army nurse. Her sister Jennie had been an ARP runner and Dolly Flynn, along with her old friend Liz Kenny, had been in the front line serving refreshments from a mobile canteen. The Wilsons' girl Claire was serving in the Land Army and the Lockwood sisters were running a very efficient scheme knitting comforts for the armed forces, and as if that was not enough, Big Joe Buckley the Aussie and Alec Conroy had both been decorated for gallantry.

'It makes yer proud,' Danny Crossley remarked to his old pal Alf Coates. 'A little backstreet like this, wiv people just out ter mind their own business an' get on wiv their lives, an' then the war comes an' it brings out fings in people yer'd never 'a' guessed. Take that Conroy boy fer a start. 'E wasn't gonna wear a uniform, d'yer remember?'

'Too right I do,' Alf replied. 'I remember that nasty git

Cafferty goadin' 'im, till Big Joe sorted 'im out.'

'No one can say this little street ain't done its bit,' Danny said sticking his chest out as he picked up his pint.

The old men's assessment of Carter Lane's war effort was true but premature, for the full story had not yet been written. On Monday morning a major in the Royal Engineers called on Mr and Mrs Conroy to tell them that their son Alec had been killed while seeking to defuse an unexploded bomb which had been found in the Surrey Docks. Londoners read the account in the evening papers of how Sergeant Fletcher and Sapper Conroy had been working on what was thought to be a routine job when the bomb exploded, but everyone in Carter Lane already knew and they were quick to rally round the distraught Ted and Rene Conroy.

Death in the line of duty was the terrible consequence of armed conflict and it had been borne by the older generation, who were still haunted by the Great War and the terrible losses it had engendered. Now the younger generation were experiencing it as well, and Carter Lane went into mourning, not only for Sapper Conroy, but for Freddie Bromilow too.

'It's 'ere in the Star,' a tearful Dolly Flynn pointed out to Mick.

'Bermondsey Guardsman Wins Posthumous V.C.

Corporal Frederick Bromilow of the Grenadier Guards rallied the survivors of his squad and led a charge against a Japanese machine-gun post in Malaya. Though wounded he charged a second post single-handed and succeeded in silencing it before he fell. Corporal Bromilow died of his injuries, and for his bravery he was awarded the Victoria Cross.'

Once again the neighbours rallied to comfort Amy Bromilow, who held her head high and walked proud, despite the desolation in her heart.

'It makes yer wonder what's next,' Mrs Wilson remarked sadly to Ivy Jones. 'This street's more than paid its dues.'

The women were soon to find out. On Tuesday morning they heard over the wireless that a large bomber force had successfully attacked strategic targets in Eastern Germany, but that some of the bombers had failed to return.

Brenda Ross heard the news too, and as always she prayed that Pat had returned safely. That evening Mick Flynn opened his front door to a telegram boy and with shaking hands and his heart thumping he tore open the small fawn envelope and read that Flight Sergeant Patrick Flynn's aircraft had been shot down over Germany and he was missing, presumed killed.

The sudden and tragic loss of three brave sons out of one small Bermondsey backwater was chronicled in the local newspaper, but other streets too had suffered losses and everyone knew only too well that the toll would rise as long as the war lasted. In many homes now little mementoes of childhood were jealously guarded and photos of smiling young men shrouded in black velvet stood on mantelshelves, sideboards and in bedrooms, and a dark depression descended upon everyone.

Brenda Ross learned about Pat from Jennie, who had bravely volunteered to go to her, and for a long time the two sat together in the dimly lit parlour, sharing their grief over a lost brother and lover. Words of comfort and a shoulder to cry on were all Jennie could offer initially, but she realised she had to find something to say, even though her own heart was breaking, some few words of hope that her friend could cling on to. 'Look, I know it's only a slight chance, Brenda, but Pat could 'ave baled out,' she said. ''E could be a prisoner o' war, please God.'

'I 'ope an' pray ter God 'e is,' Brenda replied tearfully, 'but I gotta face it. There's bin bits in the papers about our airmen bein' killed by the Germans when they bale out over there. Even if 'e is alive 'e could be badly injured, burnt even. Oh God, Jennie, what am I gonna do?'

'Do as I'm gonna do, Brenda. Pray fer 'is survival,' Jennie told her with passion. 'That's all any of us can do.'

It was dark when Jennie returned to her grieving family and tried to comfort her distraught parents. Eventually she went to her room, wanting to be alone with her thoughts. Pat had to be alive, she told herself. They would hear soon that he had been taken prisoner. He had to live, for Brenda and the baby she was carrying inside her. What else was there to do but cling on to the tiniest hope that somehow he was still alive. Yes, he was alive and one day soon he would be reunited with them all. Con and the boys, Frank and Jim would come home safely too and people would learn how to smile again. Life would be good once more.

The short days and the long lonely nights of winter seemed never-ending, but very slowly the weather became less severe and gentle April showers burst the buds and drew forth leaves on the bare branches. Plane trees were now full of chattering starlings and a warm sun shone down from a less threatening sky.

In the High Church of St James's the vicar preached a sermon about loss, in which he described the passing of a loved one as merely a passage to another room, a room which awaited us all and where we would all be together again one day. Brenda tried to believe as she sat between her mother and father in the lofty church and gently felt the growing life move inside her. She had to be grateful, she told herself. Pat would live on in their child, and the glorious memories of that last week they had spent together would never fade.

Alf Coates was a very perceptive old man, a thinker who drew on his life experiences and deployed them effectively in his arguments and discussions with Danny Crossley, an old friend of many a long year, and on Sunday morning he wore a serious expression on his face as he sat with Danny in the public bar of The Sun. 'I saw Amy Bromilow yesterday when I was standin' at me front door,' he began. 'I watched 'er dab at 'er eyes as she came out o' the 'ouse an' then she frew 'er shoulders back an' walked up the turnin' as if ter say, I'm copin' all right. She knocked at the Conroy 'ouse an' Rene came out, then the two of 'em walked over ter Dolly Flynn's front door arm in arm. Dolly comes out an' I saw the three of 'em march off out the turnin'. They didn't 'ave any shoppin'-bags wiv 'em so they wasn't goin' down the market.'

'Just off fer a stroll, I expect,' Danny replied.

'Well, it was a nice bright day yesterday,' Alf went on, 'so I decided ter take a stroll meself down Lynton Road an' over the bridge ter the church gardens. They're well tended, an' the place 'as got that lovely quiet an' peaceful feel about it. The sort o' place yer can sit an' ponder. Anyway, as I walked in the gate I saw the three of 'em sittin' on a bench. They never saw me 'cos I dodged round the ovver pathway. It wouldn't 'ave bin right to intrude on 'em. I realised then that that's where they go ter share their grief. I felt very emotional ter tell yer the trufe.'

'It's bloody sad,' Danny sighed as he picked up his pint. 'Still, they most likely get some sort o' comfort there.'

'I s'pose so,' Alf agreed. 'Who was it said, yer nearer ter God in a garden than anywhere else on earth.'

On Sunday afternoon Karen Watson laid a sprig of flowers against the marble headstone, and after a few moments alone with her thoughts she hurried out of the cemetery. The sun was shining and a few feathery clouds rode high in the azure sky. Nigel was waiting by the gates and she slipped her arm through his.

'Are you all right, Miss Watson?' he asked.

'Yes, Mr Bayley,' she replied with a faint smile.

They set off along the quiet tree-lined avenue to the main thoroughfare and caught a bus back to Bermondsey. Neither said anything for some time, then Karen turned to him. 'Thank you for being so understanding,' she said. 'I needed to do it alone. The last goodbye.'

He smiled. 'You've been very brave, darling,' he told her.

'Life has to move on,' she said, 'and I take great comfort in knowing that Douglas is at peace now. He doesn't have to suffer any more.'

Nigel nodded, then he studied his clasped hands for a few

moments. 'Are you still sure about Canada?' he asked.

'Yes, I've no doubts whatever, dearest,' she replied. 'My father was Canadian and it'll almost be like going home, for me at least.'

'It'll be a wonderful experience for me too,' he said with enthusiasm. 'I could apply to join the Mounties, or maybe I could become a lumberjack.'

'Oh no you won't,' Karen told him firmly. 'There'll be plenty of openings for someone with your qualifications.'

'By the way, Miss Watson, if you look out of the window you'll observe that we're now approaching the Elephant and Castle.'

'So?'

'Well, I thought it might be as nice a place as any to do my duty.'

'You're not intending to kiss me on this bus, are you?' Karen replied in mock horror.

'No, certainly not,' Nigel said grinning, 'but I would like to take this opportunity to formally propose to you. Would you do me the honour of becoming my wife, Miss Watson?'

'I'd be delighted, Mr Bayley.'

He sighed contentedly, and then as the bus slowed down at the Bricklayers Arms he nudged her. 'We'll get off here,' he said. 'There's a jeweller's shop in Tower Bridge Road and I've seen an engagement ring in the window that we should be able to acquire with a stout housebrick, if you feel up to a quick dash afterwards.'

On Monday morning Bernard Shanks busied himself rewiring a new transformer into a battered old wireless set, and when he had finished he went into the front of the shop.

'Er excuse me, Mr Levy, could I slip out fer a while?' he asked.

'Yes, of course.'

'I won't be long.'

'Take your time.'

Bernard hurried from the shop and made his way to the Labour Exchange in Peckham Road. 'I'm lookin' fer a post as wireless mechanic,' he said to the elderly bespectacled clerk.

'Are you unemployed at the moment?' the official asked.

'No, I'm in employment but I wanna leave.'

The clerk looked at him over his glasses. 'Any special reason?'

'Yes, as a matter o' fact there is,' Bernard told him. 'I've good reason ter believe my employer's goin' off 'is 'ead.'

'Goodness me,' the clerk replied. 'Who is your current employer?'

'Mr Albert Levy. Levy's Wireless Shop, Old Kent Road,' Bernard said quickly.

The clerk took his glasses off and proceeded to polish them on a large handkerchief. 'As you know, your job comes under the reserved occupation category,' he remarked, 'and you'll need our authority to change jobs. We can fix you up in another post under the circumstances, I feel sure, but you'll need a green card and on it you have to state your reasons for leaving your present job, so I suggest you let me have the details.'

''E talks ter cupboards, well one cupboard in particular,' Bernard replied. ''E finks there's somebody in there called Abel.'

'Abel?'

'Yeah, Abel.'

'And where exactly is this cupboard?'

'In the workroom where I do the repairs.'

'Have you confronted him about this?'

'No fear,' Bernard said quickly. ''E gives me the creeps.'

'And he talks to this Abel while you're present?'

'No, 'e waits till I go ter lunch, then 'e talks to 'im.'

'So how do you know this?'

''Cos I came back unexpectedly one day an' 'eard 'im.'

'What exactly was he saying?'

'It was somefing about payin' 'is dues,' Bernard went on. 'Mr Levy was tellin' Abel that when the new synagogue went up there was a place reserved for 'im on the wall.'

'Good Lord!'

'It was scary,' Bernard said with a shiver. 'I went in the workroom expectin' someone ter be there but Mr Levy was on 'is own an' 'e was lookin' right at this cupboard while 'e was talkin'.'

'And what was his response when he saw you standing there?'

''E didn't see me. I crept out again an' made a noise as though I'd just come in the shop,' Bernard explained.

'Umm, this is very strange,' the clerk replied.

'I'll say it is,' Bernard declared smartly. 'It's put the fear up me. I even looked inside the cupboard a few times. I can't stay there much longer.'

'All right, we'll see what we can do, but you must work your notice,' the clerk impressed on him. 'Come and see me again once you've left Mr Levy's employment.'

Bernard Shanks walked out of the Labour Exchange feeling a lot better, but back in the workroom he could not help glancing up at the cupboard occasionally, half expecting a Yiddish ghost to jump out on him.

On Monday evening Jennie came home from work to find her mother sitting in the armchair sobbing into a handkerchief with Mick standing over her, his arm round her shoulders. 'Oh my God no!' she cried. 'Con? The boys?'

Mick shook his head quickly and smiled at her. 'No, luv, it's our Pat,' he said, his voice breaking. 'The Red Cross 'ave been in touch. They've confirmed that Pat's alive. 'E's a prisoner o' war.'

Chapter Thirty-Six

1944

On Tuesday morning the 6th of June listeners to the wireless were told to stand by for an important announcement, and a few minutes later the newsreader came on the air to say that Allied armies had landed on the coast of France. The invasion had begun and the streets suddenly filled with excited people who listened to every newscast with bated breath. This was the beginning of the end, everyone felt. The war would be over by Christmas and serving sons, husbands and brothers would all be coming home.

A few days later the truth began to dawn. Fighting was heavy and the Allied armies were making slow progress against a fanatical enemy. There was still a long way to go, and with that realisation came another sobering development. Six days after the invasion a new weapon was aimed at London, and once again the dreaded air-raid siren rang out at all times of the day and night as the flying bombs made their appearance.

The rocket-propelled weapon flew low in the sky and looked like a cigar-shaped firework as it came over spurting flames and roaring like a badly tuned motorcycle, then abruptly it spluttered and there was silence. The bomb suddenly dived and reduced another street to rubble, another factory or tenement block to a heap of smouldering ruins. It could often be seen during the day, and people tended to watch the flying bomb's progress and then throw themselves to the ground as it fell, getting up again to dust themselves down and gaze at the large pall of black smoke appearing from somewhere beyond the rooftops. The bombs soon became known as 'doodle-bugs' or 'buzz bombs' and once again London was in the front line. The invading Allied forces were now hell-bent on overrunning the launching sites in Northern France before the Nazis could use the more nightmarish weapons they were rumoured to be readying.

Cynthia Lockwood was a rather efficient person who kept a list of special dates and memos in her little notebook, and every now and then she consulted it to keep check. 'Goodness me, how time flies,' she said aloud to herself as she saw that in a few days' time it would be Charity's seventieth birthday. 'I must get her something really nice.'

A few months earlier, during a stroll through the East Street market and out into the busy Walworth Road, Charity had chanced to remark on a silver pendant in a jeweller's window. It was priced at four pounds seventeen and sixpence, and Cynthia had tried to persuade her sister to buy it. Charity would not hear of it however. 'Much as I'd love it, it would be sinful to be so extravagant at a time like this,' she said firmly. 'Those sort of things are for birthdays and special occasions.'

Cynthia had made up her mind that she would buy the

pendant, but therein lay the problem. Charity always insisted that they went out together. On this occasion Cynthia was unwontedly adamant. 'Look, Charity, I'm only going to get you a birthday card,' she sighed. 'I don't want you looking over my shoulder to see which one I pick. Goodness gracious me, I am capable of going to the Old Kent Road on my own.'

'But supposing one of those doodle-bugs comes over?'

'Then I'll do what everyone does in the circumstances, I'll throw myself down on the pavement.'

'How undignified,' Charity snorted.

'It's better than catching the full blast,' Cynthia reminded her.

'Well, for goodness' sake be careful and try not to be gone too long,' Charity bade her sister.

Cynthia set off feeling quite excited. The East Street market was bustling and the sun felt warm on her face. She made her way to the end of East Street, and just as she waited to cross Walworth Road she heard the dreaded roar. The flying bomb came over from the direction of New Cross and started to splutter. Cynthia had turned back from the kerbside and was seeking the shelter of a brick wall when someone crashed into her, sending her spinning. There was a blinding light and an explosion in her head as it cracked against a kerbstone, and a trickle of blood began to drip down into the gutter.

Back in Carter Lane Charity got on with the chores and then she made herself a refreshing cup of tea. Two hours later Cynthia had still not returned and she felt that something must have happened to her. The air-raid siren had sounded about an hour after she had left the house but it hadn't lasted long and no flying bombs had landed locally. 'That sister of mine'll be the death of me,' she said aloud as she slipped on her coat and hat.

The landlord of The Sun shook his head. 'No, luv, she 'asn't been in 'ere terday,' he said sympathetically.

Charity was not surprised, though she had had to make sure. Cynthia had her faults but she wasn't a secret drinker. The Jackmans had not seen her either and as Charity walked round the block then back up to the Old Kent Road she was beside herself. There was only one thing to do, and she turned on her heel and went to see Chief Inspector Rubin McConnell.

'You say your sister's gone missing?' the policeman said as he pulled up a chair for her. 'When?'

'She's been gone for over three hours,' Charity told him.

McConnell stifled a sigh. 'Look, I think maybe you're being a bit hasty,' he remarked. 'She could have gone to see a friend and stayed for a while.'

Charity shook her head. 'We never go out separately,' she informed him. 'The only reason she's gone out alone this time is because she wanted to buy me a birthday present. I'm seventy on Friday.'

'Well, you certainly don't look it,' the policeman said smiling.

'Right now I feel every bit my age,' Charity grumbled. 'Something must have happened to her.'

The inspector picked up the phone and rang the two local hospitals. 'There's no report of a Miss Lockwood being admitted to either,' he said finally.

Charity dabbed at her eyes with a lace handkerchief she took from her sleeve. 'I'm so worried,' she said tearfully.

'Look, I'll put someone on the case,' McConnell told her. 'In the meantime you go home and try not to worry. I'll be in touch soon as ever I find out anything.'

While Cynthia was being checked over at St Giles' Hospital in Peckham she regained consciousness but was not able to give the attending police constable any details about herself.

'This does happen occasionally when a person has suffered a severe knock on the head,' the casualty doctor told the officer. 'Her memory should return within a day or two. At least there's no fracture to the skull, but she needs rest.'

The policeman nodded. 'I'll need to find out who she is for my report,' he replied. 'Her next of kin will have to be informed.'

'Nurse, will you show the officer where the lady's things are?' the doctor asked.

The nurse led the way to a side room. 'Apart from her clothes she was only carrying this purse,' she said.

The policeman opened it and counted five one-pound notes, one half-crown and a few coppers. In the side pocket he found a folded slip of paper with a few words on it and he frowned. 'Any idea what this might be?' he asked the nurse.

She glanced at the piece of paper and smiled. 'They're brand names of wool,' she told him.

'Ah, this looks promising,' the policeman said as he took out a receipt. 'It's a pawn ticket. King's Jewellers and Pawnbrokers, Old Kent Road.'

Peckham police station was hard-pressed that afternoon dealing with the aftermath of the flying bomb attack, which had left a small backstreet in ruins and caused a lot of disruption to local services, and the desk sergeant shook his head when the police constable filed his report. 'We can't spare anyone to follow this up,' he said irritably, then as an afterthought added, 'Maybe we can pass it on. The Old Kent Road comes under C division.'

At six o'clock that evening Inspector McConnell knocked on the Lockwoods' front door after making a detour to speak with the pawnbroker. 'We may have a lead,' he told Charity as she showed him into her parlour. 'A woman answering to your sister's description was admitted to St Giles' hospital in Peckham early this afternoon with head injuries.'

'Oh my God!' Charity gasped.

'It's all right, the injuries were only superficial,' McConnell was quick to explain. 'The woman has a loss of memory, which is not uncommon in such cases, but the doctor feels sure that it's only temporary. As a matter of fact a police constable accompanied her to the hospital, and although he could find no identification there were two clues, a pawn ticket issued from a pawnbroker's by the name of King in Old Kent Road, and a slip of paper with some brand names of wool written on it.'

Charity looked a little puzzled. 'Cynthia would have no reason to use a pawnbroker's,' she said with emphasis, 'but she might have jotted down some brands of wool for reference. As you know we run a forces' comforts scheme. I just wish Cynthia had had her identity card on her. I always carry mine with me wherever I go.'

'Yes, it would have expedited matters, and it is supposed to be carried at all times,' McConnell replied. 'I'll take you to St Giles now if you like.'

Charity found her sister propped up in bed with her head

swathed in bandages, looking very pale and drawn, but she now had full recollection of the accident.

'The doctor told me it wasn't loss of memory, more like confusion,' Cynthia explained.

'Inspector McConnell brought me here,' Charity told her. 'Wasn't that nice of him.'

'Yes, he's a very nice man.'

'He's waiting outside and he'd like a few words with you for the report he has to write,' Charity said.

Cynthia looked suddenly sad. 'I never got that present for you,' she said regretfully.

'I'm not worried about the present, as long as you're all right, dearest,' Charity replied with a sweet smile. 'I'm going now so that the inspector can have a chat with you, then you must get some rest.'

McConnell took Charity's place at the bedside and leaned forward with one hand resting on the spotless quilt. 'How are you feeling?' he asked.

'A little shaky,' Cynthia told him. 'It was very nice of you to bring Charity in your car.'

The policeman smiled. 'I wanted to have a word or two,' he replied.

'Charity said you would,' Cynthia remarked, patting his hand.

'When you were brought in you were unable to give the doctor any information about yourself,' McConnell told her, 'and the policeman who came in the ambulance with you had to search through your purse to see if there was any name or address inside. He found a pawn ticket.'

Cynthia closed her eyes tightly and the inspector looked at her with concern. 'Are you all right?' he asked anxiously.

She opened her eyes and bit on her lip. 'Yes, I'm all right,' she sighed. 'I take it you went to see the pawnbroker.'

He nodded. 'The ticket number indicated that it was issued back in 1929. As a matter of fact, the pawnbroker had to go down to the cellar and search through some old receipt books.'

'Did he tell you what it was issued for?'

'Yes, he did.'

'So you know enough now to bring charges?'

'Not really, but I would like you to tell me everything,' the inspector said with an arched eyebrow. 'If you feel up to it, of course.'

'I'm ready,' Cynthia sighed. 'This has become a burden that I sometimes found hard to bear, but I did manage to bear it, not for my sake but for Charity's. She never knew the full truth, and when I explain everything you'll understand.'

'I'm listening,' he said quietly.

Cynthia took a deep breath. 'The night before Aaron died I was subjected to the most vile form of brutality from him, which I won't dwell on, but suffice it to say that I felt I was going to die by his hand. When he came home the next night and started to hit me again, I grabbed the hammer from the sideboard and killed him with a single blow to his head. Charity was staying with me that night in the spare room, and I woke her up after I realised I had killed Aaron. We talked for some time and came to the conclusion that Aaron was too wicked a man for me to swing for, and decided we should get the body out of the house.'

'And the ring?' the inspector queried.

'His hand was resting on the top of the blanket and I saw

422

the ruby ring shining in the light,' Cynthia continued. 'Why leave it on him, I thought. It was a very valuable ring and I remember thinking it would be the only nice thing I ever got from him. All right it might sound calculating, but you never knew the man, and that night I was capable of anything, God forgive me. Anyway, I took up his hand and I remember how cold and clammy it felt. I tried to remove it but I couldn't get it over the knuckle. Then Charity told me to leave it. "It'll only bring you bad luck to remove it," she told me. I said I would, but when she went out in the yard to fetch the old bassinet I took the hammer and used the back part to chop off Aaron's finger. I hid the ring and Charity never knew.'

'Was that why you never mentioned the finger when we spoke at the station?' the inspector asked.

Cynthia nodded. 'For a while after I killed Aaron I experienced a lot of misfortune. Small things that all seemed to add up and I began to feel that Charity was right. The ring was bringing me bad luck, so I pawned it. Strangely enough my luck seemed to improve within a very short time and Charity and I started to enjoy life once more. Aaron's body was not discovered and it seemed that the Almighty had forgiven me, so we lived the lie. As far as anyone knew my husband had deserted me.'

'Then after all those years the mystery of Aaron's disappearance was resolved by that bomb in the factory yard,' McConnell remarked.

'You'll probably laugh at this,' Cynthia replied, 'but I felt I had angered God in some way and he was punishing me by letting Aaron's remains be found. I felt that the only way I could atone was to make a clean breast of it, but then when the time came to confess I found I couldn't bear to let Charity know I'd deceived her and lied to her about the ring, so I kept quiet. I told you about my bad luck, but Charity had her share too. She fell in love with a very nice widower and he died suddenly of pneumonia. Nineteen thirty-two it was. They were engaged to be married, as a matter of fact.'

'That's very sad,' the inspector frowned.

'Will Charity have to know about me deceiving her?' Cynthia asked anxiously.

'I can't say what the outcome will be,' McConnell told her. 'Look, I need a cigarette. I'll send your sister in and then I'll come back and we'll continue our chat.'

Fifteen minutes later he came into the ward again and smiled at Charity as she got up to leave. 'I promise I won't be more than a few minutes,' he said.

'When I come out of here will I be taken to the cells and have my fingerprints taken?' Cynthia asked fearfully.

The policeman smiled and shook his head. 'You were telling me earlier that maybe God was punishing you for something you'd done,' he reminded her. 'Well, I believe in God, although I have to say I'm not a churchgoer. Nevertheless I'm convinced that the Lord does work in mysterious ways. Just now I walked out into the hospital grounds and I took a cigarette out to light it, but lo and behold I'd no matches. Then I spotted some men pulling down the ruined building across the street and they had a fire going. I walked over and took a piece of paper out of my pocket, reached into the fire for a light and started to smoke my cigarette. I'd been puffing away merrily when it suddenly dawned on me. I'd lit the cigarette with that pawn ticket, the only piece of evidence I had to connect you with the crime. No evidence, no case to answer. If I was you, Cynthia, I'd try to get some rest. No one need ever know our little secret, not even Charity.'

'Certainly not Charity,' Cynthia replied with a smile. 'Take care, inspector, you really are a very nice man.'

'You take care too, Cynthia.'

Chapter Thirty-Seven

Albert Levy opened up his shop on Monday morning and went into the workroom to make himself a cup of tea. Bernard Shanks had terminated his employment the previous Friday evening and had left everything neat and tidy. There were no outstanding jobs of work and it was now a question of getting someone in quickly, he thought. Until then it did not make sense to accept repairs but he could manage to do the accumulator-charging himself for the time being.

'Where did I go wrong, Abel?' he asked his old friend as he sat sipping his first mug of tea for the day. 'The lad seemed quite happy here, and I never pushed him, even though there were some times when I felt he was slacking. It seemed a weak excuse he made for leaving, if you ask me. Most of us have to travel to work and this new job he's got in Peckham isn't all that much nearer where he lives. He still needs to catch a bus.'

The sound of the air-raid siren startled Albert and he sighed in resignation as he put his steaming mug down on the workbench. 'It's a bit early this morning, Abel,' he remarked. 'Never mind, I can make another cup of tea before I open up. I don't expect any customers before the all-clear sounds.'

Just then there was a loud report from the direction of the shed out back and Albert jumped again. 'I bet that lad forgot to press the carboy stopper right in and the gases have made it pop,' he said as he got up from the stool. 'It wouldn't have happened in your time, old friend.'

Everything seemed in order when Albert walked out to the shed. The two carboys of acid were fully sealed and the electricity control panel was switched off. What could it have been? he wondered, scratching his head. Suddenly he became aware of a throaty roar that grew louder and louder, and he crouched down in the shed as he heard the engine splutter. There was a loud swishing noise and then an explosion that sent him reeling backwards against the wall. Dust and smoke filled the air and Albert staggered out to find that the front of his shop had been blown out. More frightening was the sight of the fallen girder that had crushed the workbench and splintered the stool he had been sitting on only a couple of minutes ago. The wall cupboard was still in place but its door was lying on the floor. He had always kept that cupboard locked. Inside were a few mementoes of Abel, and a photograph of him in a cheap iron frame. It was facing Albert now, and Abel's smile seemed to be wider than usual.

'That bang was your doing, wasn't it?' the shopkeeper said, shaking his head slowly. 'You wanted me out of the room, you sly old fox.'

The flying bomb had landed on a furniture shop a few doors away and when Albert saw the carnage he was physically sick. Casualties were being moved and attended to, and there were people sitting at the kerbside in shock. Two policemen were carrying a body out from the butcher's shop and a pair of young women with their heads covered in blood were being comforted by some shopworkers from down the road.

'Bloody 'ell, Albert, we've bin searchin' frew the debris fer you.'

The shopkeeper turned to see Bill Walker the greengrocer staring at him in disbelief. 'I was out the back checking the accumulators when the bomb landed,' he told him.

'Fink yerself lucky,' Bill remarked. 'You'd 'ave bin killed stone dead otherwise. All I can say is there must be someone up there lookin' after yer.'

'You could be right, Bill,' Albert said reverently.

Jennie Flynn arrived home that evening feeling very fortunate to have survived the bomb. The baker's was less than fifty yards away from the furniture shop and it was only the protective paper stripping which had saved the front window from shattering. As it was the ceiling plaster had showered down and the morning batch of bread and rolls had been ruined.

'I managed ter save these fer the baby,' Jennie said, taking two jam tarts from a paper bag. 'I'm gonna go over an' see Brenda ternight.'

'She 'ad the baby out in the pram this mornin',' Dolly told her. 'We sat in the church gardens chattin' fer a while. That little mite's gettin' on fine. Jabberin' away 'e was, good as good. 'E's really got our Pat's looks.'

'Poor little sod,' Jennie joked.

'There was more on the wireless this mornin' about some prisoner o' war camps bein' overrun,' Dolly said. 'I 'ope an' pray one of 'em's where our Pat is.'

'Wouldn't it be lovely,' Jennie replied excitedly. ''E'd be 'ome fer Christmas.'

'I s'pose they'd let us know by telegram,' Dolly said. 'Trouble is, every time the telegram boy cycles in the turnin' yer fear the worst.'

'Don't you worry, Mum,' Jennie told her with an encouraging smile. 'We're survivors. It'll all be good from now on, you'll see.'

Brenda reached out and extracted Patrick from the high chair. 'Come on, you little monster,' she said smiling. 'Let's get you ready fer bed. I want you lookin' all pink an' shiny when Aunt Jennie arrives.'

Frank Ross chuckled as the baby protested at having the remains of his evening meal wiped away from his cheeks with a wet flannel and Iris pulled a face. 'What's that naughty mummy doin' ter my little chubby-chops then?' she cooed.

Frank watched with pleasure as Iris followed her daughter and the baby into the scullery. When Patrick was born his wife had seemed to take on a new lease of life, he thought. She had bathed, changed and fed the baby whenever she could, as well as taking up her knitting once more. It felt as though the house had really come to life again and Frank was happy. It hadn't been too bad really, he considered. There had been a bit of talk, which was only to be expected, but on the whole the street folk had been very supportive and understanding. Pat would be released soon, please God, and then there would be a wedding to look forward to, and a reception where he would most likely get completely plastered. And he wouldn't be at all surprised if Iris did too.

The Christmas of '44, the coldest for more than fifty years, was celebrated quietly, but the new year was seen in with much enthusiasm. This would surely be the year when peace returned once more, when families were reunited and life could begin anew.

On the twenty-second of January a Russian patrol came upon a country road and saw the barbed-wire fencing up ahead. When they peered through the wire they saw scenes which turned even their battle-hardened stomachs. A pile of frozen bodies lay in the snow and people moved amongst them, living, breathing skeletons. The Russian troops would soon discover that the huts they saw were full of starving inmates, many dying of typhus and diphtheria, and beyond the camp was a deep trench full of bodies shot by the SS before they left. The patrol realised they needed to summon help at all speed, and very soon the whole world was to know the name of Auschwitz.

That same day the advancing Soviet forces overran Stalag 27, a prison camp for airforce personnel.

The long and roundabout journey home from the camp in Poland had taken its toll, but Pat Flynn now felt excitement pulsing through him as the train drew into Waterloo Station. Flags decorated the platform and a military band was playing as the train squealed to a halt and the carriage doors swung open. He could see her now. Yes, it was her, holding a baby, his baby. His legs felt like jelly and he swallowed hard as he shouldered his kitbag and hurried along to her. She shouted his name almost hysterically and they hugged, gently for fear of harming the baby between them, then she handed him his son Patrick.

Back home in Carter Lane there would have been a more public homecoming but too much tragedy had touched the street for flags and bunting, Dolly reasoned, though the Conroys and Amy Bromilow were there to welcome Pat home. Mick brushed away a tear and blew hard into his handkerchief, while Dolly, Sadie and Jennie fussed and pandered to Pat's every need.

'Look, Mum, I might look tired but I'm okay, really,' Pat protested. 'I can move ter get the paper, an' I can undo me shoelaces. Just sit an' relax, an' let me catch me breath.'

Brenda sat on the hearth rug at his feet, with her head resting against him as he stroked her hair. Patrick was sleeping on the settee covered with a blanket and the house was quiet. Dolly, Mick and their daughters had gone to The Sun, along with Frank and Iris Ross, and Jennie had promised to come home to mind the baby later so that Pat and Brenda could join the families for a celebration drink.

'You don't need ter talk about it now, Pat,' Brenda said quietly.

'It's all right, it was a long while ago an' it doesn't bovver me any more,' he replied. 'I saw a few of our planes go down in flames an' I knew we'd got some flak damage ter the port wing but the pilot told us we'd manage it back okay, wiv a bit o' luck. It wasn't ter be though. Our luck 'ad just run out. We were caught in the belly an' the starboard engine an' we tipped over. The plane was goin' down an' the pilot gave the order ter bale out. We all managed ter clear, except the bomb-aimer. 'E'd took the full force o' the blast. We landed

432

in a field near a large wood an' after we buried our chutes we set off. God knows what we were tryin' ter do, apart from evadin' the Germans. We were 'undreds o' miles inside Germany at the time we baled out. Anyway, as we got near the wood we were suddenly confronted by a German patrol. They must 'ave bin out lookin' for us. There was nuffink we could do. They roughed us up a bit an' dragged us into a lorry. As it 'appened the German officer who grilled us wasn't too bad. 'E spoke good English an' gave us cigarettes. 'E told us that we were lucky 'is men found us before the SS unit operatin' in the area got there, or we'd 'ave bin shot out of 'and.'

'Don't tell me any more, darlin',' Brenda said quickly.

'That's about it anyway,' Pat replied. 'They stuck us on a train an' we ended up in Poland.'

Brenda reached out and took up the handbag that was lying at her feet. 'I've kept your letter wiv me all the time,' she told him, taking it out of the zip pocket. 'The poem made me cry.'

Pat smiled wistfully. 'As I said in the letter Tom never got round ter finishin' it, so I did it for 'im. I fink 'e would 'ave wanted me to.'

Brenda opened the letter and read the poem aloud while Pat stared distantly into the glowing fire.

'The Mission

The engines roar, we lift and climb,
Aiming for the moon.
Down below the fields, the Downs,
Behind us all too soon.

Now it's a calm and silver sea below,
But we must sail the sky.
Though full of hopes and aspirations,
Some of us must die.

The bombs away, we'll bank for home,
The fires burn below.
We remember it was London burning,
Not that long ago.

With the starboard engine feathered,
We set out for the coast.
Beyond, the sea, our sceptred isle,
And there we'll drink our toast.

We'll raise our glasses, spare a thought,
For those who had to die.
We know they've cast their earthly bodies,
And their spirits soar the sky.

Their names will be on monuments,
They will not feel aggrieved,
As long as we remember,
Once they walked, and talked, and breathed.

Tom Darcy'

She saw that his eyes were misty and she reached out to him.
'I love you, Pat Flynn,' she whispered.

'I love you too, Brenda Ross,' he said intensely. 'More than honour. More than life itself.'

Epilogue

Pat Flynn and Brenda Ross were married during the spring of 1945, and later that year, soon after the Rifle Brigade returned from the Middle East, Con Williams and Jennie Flynn got wed.

Frank and Jim Flynn returned to work at the brewery looking lean and tanned, and they soon found themselves being pursued by the Gordon twins, Denise and Diana, who worked in the accounts office. The Flynn boys were adamant though: marriage was not for them, not yet awhile, there was too much catching up to do.

Big Joe Buckley had been sent to the Far East and when he returned after the Japanese surrender he had a chat with Sadie about the future. 'I've always considered meself a rover,' he remarked, 'but now I'm a petty officer in the King's navy I kinda like it, Sadie. It fits me like a bum in a bucket, so I've decided to sign on for another five years.'

'If that's what yer wanna do, Joe,' she replied. 'It's that way wiv me an' nursin'. It's what I really wanna do.'

'We can make it work though, kid, the two of us together.'

'Are you talkin' about marriage, Joe?'

'Too bloody true.'

'Is that a firm proposal?'

'You bet.'

'Then there's only one fing I can say ter you.'

'Go on, kid, I can take it.'

'The answer's yes, you great oaf.'

Rabbi Friedman was pleased with the way his restoration fund for the synagogue was coming on and he was looking forward to work starting that year. 'Don't misunderstand me,' he said to Albert Levy one afternoon over coffee. 'It's laudable that you should want to remember Abel Finkelstein with a large bronze plaque in the entrance hall, and it's very generous of you to make that donation to the fund, but you're a businessman and I'm sure you'll appreciate what I'm going to say.'

'Which is?'

'A slightly smaller bronze plaque and a slightly larger donation might make better sense,' the rabbi replied. 'Have a word with Abel if you're not sure.'

Albert Levy arched his eyebrow as he took out his cheque book. 'What's the use of discussing it with Abel,' he growled. 'He's on your side anyway.'

Karen Watson and Nigel Bayley sailed for Canada early in 1946, and after due consideration Nigel decided against joining the Royal Canadian Mounted Police. Instead they prospered in the retail business, selling electrical appliances.

Carter Lane survived until well into the sixties, when the area came under a redevelopment programme. Smart houses now stand where once there were two-up, two-down homes, but interested visitors might still chance to wander into Carter Walk and maybe catch a glimpse of what has passed, and what was lost.

Postscript

Very few areas of Britain escaped the German bombing and all the major cities suffered heavy damage and loss of life. The cathedral cities of Bath, Exeter, York and Canterbury were badly damaged in what were known as the Baedeker Raids, and the terrible daylight raid on Coventry led to the word 'Coventration' entering the English language.

In London alone there were seventy-one major air raids between 7th September 1940 and 16th May 1941, during which nearly 19,000 tons of bombs were dropped. A total of 43,000 civilians lost their lives during that period, more than half of them in London. 86,000 were severely injured, and a further 150,000 were slightly injured. Over 2,000,000 homes were destroyed or damaged, sixty per cent of them in London.

At the end of the Blitz the Heavy Rescue Services in Bermondsey were asked by the Government to nominate a few of their men for bravery awards. Their reply went as follows: 'Medals? We don't want no f— medals. Everybody in Bermondsey should get a f— medal.'

Lest we forget . . . as time goes by.

Maggie's Market

Dee Williams

It's 1935 and Maggie Ross loves her life in Kelvin Market, where her husband Tony has a bric-a-brac stall and where she lives, with her young family, above Mr Goldman's bespoke tailors. But one fine spring day, her husband vanishes into thin air and her world collapses.

The last anyone saw of Tony is at Rotherhithe station, where Mr Goldman glimpsed him boarding a train, though Maggie can only guess at her husband's destination. And she has no way of telling what prompted him to leave so suddenly – especially when she's got a new baby on the way. What she can tell is who her real friends are as she struggles to bring up her children alone. There's outspoken, gold-hearted Winnie, whose cheerful chatter hides a sad past, and cheeky Eve, whom she's known since they were girls. And there's also Inspector Matthews, the policeman sent to investigate her husband's disappearance. A man who, to the Kelvin Market stallholders, is on the wrong side of the law, but a man to whom Maggie is increasingly drawn . . .

'A brilliant story, full of surprises' *Woman's Realm*

'A moving story, full of intrigue and suspense . . . a wam and appealing cast of characters . . . an excellent treat' *Bolton Evening News*

0 7472 5536 9

HEADLINE

The Glory and the Shame

Harry Bowling

On the night of Saturday 10th May 1941, amidst the carnage and devastation caused by enemy bombers, Joe Carey and Charlie Duggan risked their lives to save those trapped in an air-raid shelter. Yet six men and women perished, including the popular George Merry – a man whom the Totterdown folk believe was the hero of the hour.

By 1947 the inhabitants of the street are rebuilding their lives – but the legacy of war is a powerful one and for the families of Joe and Charlie, the future seems to be inextricably bound to the past. And then young Sue Carey meets Sam Culkin, an ambitious journalist, determined to further his career through a series of articles on the heroism of the people in wartime London. Already faced with both a violent factory strike and the frequent street fracas between the Barlows and the Sloans, the inhabitants of Totterdown Street must now cope with news which exposes not just the glory of the past but the shame as well.

'The king of Cockney sagas' *Publishing News*

0 7472 5544 X

HEADLINE